# The Hollow

January 2004 —

Donna —
  Best wishes. I hope that you enjoy Rob and Katie and the folks at Steven's Hollow.
  Nancy M. Hyde

# The Hollow

Nancy M. Hyde

iUniverse, Inc.
New York Lincoln Shanghai

# The Hollow

All Rights Reserved © 2003 by Nancy M. Hyde

No part of this book may be reproduced or transmitted in any form or by any means, graphic, electronic, or mechanical, including photocopying, recording, taping, or by any information storage retrieval system, without the written permission of the publisher.

iUniverse, Inc.

For information address:
iUniverse, Inc.
2021 Pine Lake Road, Suite 100
Lincoln, NE 68512
www.iuniverse.com

The small town of Logan, West Virginia, does exist, and in my memory it is every bit as beautiful as it's depicted in this novel. The Cincinnati Reds baseball team is real, too. However, this is a work of fiction; Rob McKenzie never played for them. Rob, Katie, Steven's Hollow, and all the people who inhabit Logan County on the pages of this book are products of my imagination. In this story, any resemblance seen, or imagined, to any person, living or dead, or to any place or event the reader is familiar with, is entirely unintended and coincidental.

ISBN: 0-595-29457-X

Printed in the United States of America

**To Dick Hyde, with love:**

I couldn't have written this story without your unwavering love and optimism, Dick. From the time *The Hollow* was only a glimmer of a plot that would not go away, up until it reached its final draft, you listened to each and every plot change, read countless revisions, made fabulous suggestions, and gave me an extra nudge each time I needed one most. I thank God every day that you're the one He chose to walk beside me on this journey.

# Acknowledgments

I've been blessed with wonderful friends…true friends who are priceless. More than a few shared in this effort and are due special recognition for their assistance with *The Hollow*:

Audrey Fischette: Your knack for finding plot inconsistencies got me out of a hole early. Mere thanks aren't nearly enough.

Helen and Desi Desarmeaux, Jane Dowling, Bob Jones, Betty Herron, and my sister Nona Southers, who read preliminary drafts: Your constructive comments were very helpful, much appreciated.

Carolyn Stapleton: Thanks for explaining how divorces are handled in the State of West Virginia.

Susan E. Wolford: How many drafts did you eventually read, Sue? You're a writer's perfect reader. What would I have done without your enthusiasm and long-distance help?

Cork and Martha Grandy…an exceptional couple! Martha, you were the one who lit the spark and encouraged me way back in the beginning. As Rob and Katie came alive for you, they came alive again for me. People like the two of you are rare, and I value above jewels our friendship.

Pastor Tom Schafer: Thanks for some very helpful suggestions, and for permitting me to paraphrase some of your inspiring words from the pulpit. Pastor Matt

Harlow, who's only a figment of my imagination, will never be as kind and caring and knowledgeable a pastor as you.

Beverly Zabka: You're such a cheerful person, Bev, it's a delight working with you. Shall we do it again?

Amy Hyde, Ricky Hyde, and Jennifer Hyde: What can I say? You must have grown weary of hearing about imaginary West Virginians who live up a fictional hollow, but you never let it show. Thanks for never saying out loud that you thought Mom was crazy.

Brennan Calder Hyde: What a wonderful gift you've been to our family this year! Gram'ma Nancy and Gram'pa Dick never understood the amazing joy that grandparents bragged about until you came along. May God always hold you in the palm of His hand and keep you safe.

Joe and Suzie Takacs: As neighbors, you're the best. I'll never forget those afternoon meetings on our patio, where we solved all the problems of the world.

Last, but not least, my brother C. D. Mullins, Jr: You never push, Buddy, but you don't need to. You encourage with love and lead by example. Nothing's more effective than that.

# Prologue

▼

The moisture-laden mist that engulfed Kathleen Mitchell's Ford Explorer as she approached the West Virginia border floated like tufts of light gray cotton candy from the rugged cliffs that bracket the interstate highway coming in from Virginia. It didn't bother Kathleen at first. She thought it was just a low-lying cloud hovering on top of the mountain, one she'd be able to pass through fairly quickly. But that turned out not to be the case. Within minutes, it was so thick she could barely see the blue and yellow "Welcome to the State of West Virginia" sign that stretched over the road.

Strange...very strange, she thought, turning on her low-beam lights so she could see. It was also kind of spooky, reminding her of ghost stories her brothers, Brian and David, used to tell on their front porch after dark when they were kids. The origin of those hair-raising tales, handed down from generation to generation in the mountains as gospel, was murky to say the least. But whether or not the stories were true, they always seemed scarier...more gruesome...when the weather was eerie like today's.

*I should have picked another day for this trip. Almost any other day would've been better than this!*

Visibility continued to be poor in the higher elevations around White Sulphur Springs and Lewisburg, where wispy tendrils of that pea-soup mixture still clung to the road, and for miles Kathleen kept running in and out of patchy fog.

An hour later, as she exited I–64 outside Beckley to merge with the heavier traffic of the West Virginia Turnpike, she ran into a fierce electrical storm. "Oh, man, what next?" she muttered under her breath, not wanting to wake her teenage son sleeping peacefully beside her in the passenger seat.

Suddenly, a strange feeling of helplessness and dread came over Kathleen...almost a sense of foreboding...like someone walked over her grave. She started to shiver, but her cold chills and goose bumps weren't related to the weather. No, fourteen years ago Kathleen had vowed she'd never return to Steven's Hollow where she grew up, yet here she was again, within shouting distance once more of her hometown.

And she was not returning home again by choice. She had been summoned there by a lawyer from Logan who'd discovered a problem with her long-ago divorce.

"This matter's too complicated to straighten out over the phone," Dan Hoffman had warned, "but I assure you it can be easily remedied." He urged Kathleen to meet with him at his law office in Logan as soon as she could, and he promised to explain the entire situation in detail then.

Kathleen knew she could have—and, in retrospect, *should* have—insisted on a complete explanation at that time, but she'd been too afraid of what the lawyer might say to insist that he clarify everything over the phone. Knowing the meeting between them would be awkward at best, she had procrastinated for days, delaying her trip home for as long as she could. The truth was, she didn't want to deal with her divorce again, not at this late date. It had been one of the lowest points in her life until she'd finally been able to put it behind her, thinking it was over once and for all. She wasn't looking forward to picking it up again now.

Kathleen frowned, then released a shuddering sigh. The lawyer had not summoned her to a face-to-face meeting just to give her good news, not after all the time that had passed.

*What if Rob discovers what I've done?* That sobering thought, more than any other, filled a quivering Kathleen with dismay. She pressed a hand against her queasy stomach and warned herself not to dwell on that now. She'd be a basket case soon if she did.

The heavy rain continued unabated, and if traffic continued to move at a snail's pace, she'd be hitting Charleston in the middle of rush hour. She hadn't planned to stop for the night, but she'd had about all she could take of bad weather, poor visibility, heavy traffic—and her runaway thoughts—for one day.

"Hey, Mom. Looks like we've run into quite a storm. When did that happen?"

Drawing a deep breath to steady herself, Kathleen glanced over at her son who was just waking up, his eyes still soft from sleeping. Just looking at Bobby brought a smile to her face. It embarrassed him when she said he was handsome, but there was no other word for it—he was a good-looking kid. People sometimes said he looked like her, but that wasn't true. With those uniquely colored eyes—sea-green with gold flecks—and brown hair that would soon be streaked and lightened by the sun, he was an almost perfect clone of his father. Very few people, however, knew about *him*, and Kathleen intended to keep it that way.

Bobby was usually a good traveler, unless a trip took too long. And Kathleen was beginning to suspect this trip would. She had hoped he'd sleep until they arrived in Logan County, but that wouldn't happen now. From the timbre of his voice, he would soon be wide awake to stay.

"Yeah, sleepyhead," she said, just loud enough to be heard over the now-dwindling storm, "it's been raining pretty heavy for almost an hour. While I struggled through a torrential downpour…and Noah built himself another ark…you were snoring away like a lumberjack sawing logs."

Still drowsy, Bobby snorted softly in disbelief. "C'mon, Mom. Quit your teasing."

"Well, maybe it wasn't actually an adult-sized snore," Kathleen said, smiling a little as she continued to kid her good-natured son. "It might have been more like a discreet little snuffle—" she shot another glance at him before looking back at the road "—you know, sort of like a mini-snore?"

She thought she detected the beginning of a smile on Bobby's lips, but he wasn't about to give her the satisfaction of a full-fledged grin, not after she'd teased him about snoring.

Waking up fully, Bobby flexed the muscles in his shoulders and stretched out legs that had outgrown two sets of jeans already this year. When he twisted to toss his pillow into the back seat of the car, a brief glance assured Kathleen that his seatbelt was still fastened. As a single parent, she'd been solely responsible for Bobby's well-being from the day he was born, and although he felt he was old enough and mature enough at thirteen to be in charge of himself, that responsibility still rested heavily on her shoulders. She just didn't make an issue of it in front of him anymore.

As Bobby settled back down in his seat, Kathleen heard him muttering to himself. "Snoring, my foot," he said, barely above a whisper. "I'll get out my tape recorder when we get back home, and I'll show you who snores." Delighted laughter bubbled up in Kathleen's throat. She ruffled Bobby's sleep-tangled hair when he looked over and grinned.

Bobby, who'd officially become a teenager last month, was, in Kathleen's slightly biased opinion, a normal, well-adjusted young man who had kept most of his little-boy niceness. He had a strong will of his own, though, and was no one's follower, which pleased his doting mom. The task of raising a child alone had been somewhat less daunting because he was such a great kid.

Although she didn't consider it a negative trait, Bobby *was* highly curious, just as she had been at his age according to her mother. Kathleen knew he'd ask a million questions once he realized they were now in West Virginia. It would be impossible to concentrate on her driving and on his questions. "The weather's getting worse, I have the beginning of a tension headache, and I'm feeling a little keyed-up on top of all that," she told Bobby. "Want to stay in a motel tonight and get an early start for Logan tomorrow? We can stop outside Charleston if you'd like. What do you think?"

Before those words were even out of her mouth, Kathleen knew what Bobby's answer would be: if the motel had cable-TV, if he could stay up half the night watching *Nick at Nite* re-runs, and if there was a McDonald's nearby, his answer would be yes. And it would divert his questions for a while.

Bobby knew she'd be seeing a lawyer in Logan, but he didn't know why. And she didn't want to tell him yet.

In truth, Kathleen Mitchell was coming home for the first time in fourteen years to divorce Bobby's father.

Again.

# CHAPTER 1
▼

After picking up dinner at a McDonald's drive-thru last night and eating in their room, Kathleen should not have given in to Bobby's plea to eat there again for breakfast. She kept telling herself it wasn't that important, that he was active enough to work off any excess fat grams he might consume this morning. But the truth was, she felt guilty about making this trip to Logan without explaining fully why they had to come. In her defense, she had alluded to her legal problems a time or two in general terms; it wasn't her fault those few tidbits of information had zoomed right over his head. Bobby hadn't questioned her about it since their last discussion, which was days ago, and he could have brought it up again at any time. At least that's what Kathleen had told herself more than once.

Setting aside her vague feelings of disquiet, Kathleen nibbled at a plain biscuit and drank a cup of black coffee while Bobby downed a breakfast that would make a construction worker smile: two Egg McMuffins, orange juice, a large milk, and an order of pancakes with syrup.

Kathleen chuckled, watching Bobby eat with such gusto. But then she thought about the day ahead of her and quickly sobered. She jutted out her chin, stiffened her spine, and braced herself for whatever might come of her talk with Dan Hoffman.

Thoughts of that meeting were never far from Kathleen's mind, but she had decided overnight that her life was too full of positive things for her to succumb to that strange sense of impending doom that had descended on her yesterday. As she waited for Bobby to finish his gargantuan breakfast, she caught herself making a mental list of them: a mother, two brothers, and two nieces she loved dearly; a strong personal faith in Jesus Christ that sustained her day-to-day; the small, spirit-filled church in Woodbridge, Virginia—her anchor since she'd discovered its friendly congregation; and most of all, her son.

While she had to admit that her personal life—the dating part, anyway—wasn't absolutely perfect and thrilling right now, it was...well, fair to middling. Her writing career continued on track, and that was something that always boosted her spirits. Another of her children's books had been nominated for a literary medal this year.

Convinced anew that, in her life, the positives far outweighed the negatives, Kathleen pulled out of McDonald's feeling more optimistic than she had during yesterday's storm.

The road from Charleston through the mountains into Logan, notorious in the past for its up-and-down switchback curves, was now a calm and easy one-hour drive since Corridor G, the improvement to Rt. 119, had straightened out those dangerous turns and flattened the hills. Kathleen couldn't begin to imagine the amount of dynamite and man-hours required to bring about that phenomenal feat, but she sure did appreciate the end result of someone's hard labor.

As Kathleen drove along, she looked around, the corners of her mouth turning up in a smile. Even the sun seemed more brilliant without yesterday's worries weighting her down. The trees, greening out, were bright with fresh spring colors, clean and still dewy after being washed of dust by the rain that ended in the middle of the night. The beauty of West Virginia on an early June morning—and taking a moment to thank God for His bountiful blessings—was enough to cheer anyone up. Kathleen found herself relaxing, truly relaxing, for the first time in over a week.

Excited about visiting West Virginia and seeing his grandmother at her home instead of Myrtle Beach where they usually met, Bobby carried the sporadic conversation, commenting every now and then on the small towns they passed. "West Virginia sure is a far cry from Woodbridge," he said, taking his eyes off the passing landscape to peer around at his mother.

"Yeah, this area is different from what we're used to in the city," Kathleen agreed. "But it's very nice, too, in its way."

Miles of comfortable silence fell between them as they listened to country music on the radio and watched the scenery roll by. After a while, Bobby turned the volume down and angled around in his seat. "Mom, can I ask you something about my dad?"

Kathleen sighed, praying for patience. Before embarking on this trip, she had sensed that coming to West Virginia would stimulate Bobby's interest in his father again. While she never volunteered information herself, she did always answer the questions he asked. Recently, knowing Bobby wanted to learn more about his other biological parent—which was the way Kathleen often thought of her ex—she had sometimes hovered on the brink of telling him everything he wanted to know. But then she'd remember what his father had done and be more convinced than ever that keeping his identity a secret from Bobby was still the right way to go.

But it was getting harder, keeping that secret from him.

"Come on, Bobby," she finally said, tilting her head, "give me an estimate here. In your thirteen years *plus*, how many times would you say I've told you about your father?"

"Come on, Mom," he said, imitating her tone of voice exactly, "you and I both know it's been a lot of times. But Grammy says I inherited my inquiring mind from you, so what's your point? I refuse to play that stupid 'Find the State License Plate' game again on this trip, so what else is there to do till we get to Grammy's? You might as well tell me about my father one more time."

Kathleen tried unsuccessfully to suppress a sigh. She supposed it was only natural that Bobby would want to fill in the blanks about the father he'd never seen, a person whose existence he must doubt once in a while like he had the tooth fairy and the Easter bunny when he was younger. But during each of his interrogations, especially his more recent ones, she'd felt as if she were on a swaying tight-rope, balanced precariously between giving Bobby enough information to appease him but not enough to upset the status quo.

She did not want to tell him there might be a problem now with her divorce from his father. That would only open up another can of worms.

"Do you still have that picture of my dad around somewhere?" Bobby asked. "I saw it when I was little, but not recently. I can't even remember what he looks like."

"I'll check when we get home," Kathleen said in an offhanded manner, knowing she'd put it off for as long as she could.

But Bobby had already filed her answer away. He'd make sure she didn't forget. Because he didn't want to only see a picture of his dad; he wanted to know exactly who his father was. And he would hound his mother until she'd told him everything he wanted to know, starting today. Once he'd ferreted out a little more information from her, he figured everything else would fall right into place, like ducklings in a row behind their mother.

When he spoke again, Bobby's voice sounded strange to Kathleen. There seemed to be a different kind of hitch in it somehow. "You know all my friends have dads, don't you, Mom? I'm the only one who doesn't."

"Yes, that's true, but you do have two wonderful uncles," Kathleen responded. The smile she attempted wavered briefly before settling into a firm, straight line. "Brian and David love doing things with you."

"You know something, Mom?" Bobby challenged, his voice beginning to rise. "As nice as they are and as much as I love them, I'm not interested in my uncles right now. I know everything there is to know about them. Tell me about my dad."

A look of confusion clouded Kathleen's features at Bobby's belligerent words. He had never been this aggressive in his questioning before, and she wasn't quite sure how to handle this new and bolder Bobby Mitchell. Her memories of Bobby's father were colored by the unhappy past they had shared, and by her disillusionment with him as a man, but up to this point she'd walked a fine line between being fair and being brutally honest. Undoubtedly, Bobby hoped for an unblemished picture of his father to carry into adulthood as his role model, but that wasn't what he would get if she told him the truth about Rob and what had happened between them in the past.

But once more, for Bobby's sake, Kathleen decided to walk that fine line again.

"Okay, kiddo, here goes," she said, pausing for a moment to clear away the large lump of negativity that seemed to be lodged in her throat. "Your father lived in Logan as a kid, and I grew up in the coal camp at Steven's Hollow. We went to the same schools during junior high and high school, and then we both attended West Virginia University in Morgantown. He played several sports in high school, but only baseball in college. I was a cheerleader for a couple of years, but most of the time my nose was stuck in a book."

Mentioning college brought something else of importance to Kathleen's mind. "I'm not real proud of this, Bobby, but the very day your father finished college, we sneaked off and got married. Looking back, I realize we shouldn't have done it that way. Please promise you'll learn from my mistake and never do that yourself!"

"I won't, Mom, Scout's honor," Bobby said, raising his right hand. He smiled his lopsided grin, a grin that was almost identical to the ones that had graced his father's face in the past. "And you know what else?" he added, still grinning. "I'll probably tell you everything I do—in minute detail!—till I'm at least twenty-one."

Tearing her eyes away from her son and back to the road, Kathleen scoffed. "Sure you will. Just like Brian, David, and I told Mom and Dad everything we did!" Bobby laughed and allowed that his mother was probably right.

Kathleen threw a half-smile Bobby's way in return. "So, as I've told you the other seventy-five times you asked—or has it now been a hundred?—your father left West Virginia to work shortly after we were married. I stayed home to help Mom take care of my dad, who'd been hurt in the mines. When we found out we couldn't be together the way we had planned, your father and I got a divorce. I went back to Morgantown, finished college, and then I had you."

"Have you seen my father since then?"

"No, not in person."

Bobby didn't notice the ambiguity of that reply.

Kathleen's concise responses to Bobby's questions sounded flat and lifeless, like a pre-recorded message that'd been stuck in a tape recorder and played back so many times the quality was compromised. And why not? The words and nuances were precisely the same each time they talked about his father, the same as she'd rehearsed them long before Bobby even thought of asking questions. But the words "your father and I got a divorce" stuck in her throat this time around.

"Where was he when you heard from him last?"

"Denver."

Kathleen knew she'd moved into dangerous territory with that answer. It required her to pass on another clue, and she hated adding anything new to the facts she'd already given Bobby. Admittedly, she hadn't told him everything she knew about his father through the years, but she'd never resorted to out-and-out fabrications either. It simply wasn't a part of Kathleen's makeup to lie.

"Then he went to Ohio," she added, knowing Bobby's father had moved to Cincinnati the year after they broke up. And she presumed he lived there still.

For years she'd worried that Bobby might add up all the odd bits and pieces of information she'd given him and figure out who his father was for himself, but that hadn't happened yet. And truthfully, if she could be sure it would be the end of it, Kathleen wouldn't mind giving Bobby the name of his father now. But for reasons that seemed valid at the time, she'd decided years ago to not tell Bobby's father about Bobby, and that was the rub. She couldn't abandon the course of action she'd chosen back then, not without having to face a host of repercussions.

"Be honest, Mom. Do you think I'll ever meet my dad?"

"I just don't know, Bobby, and that's the honest truth. I don't even know exactly where he lives now. The last time I saw him was shortly after he left West Virginia, and as I said, we haven't met again since we broke up."

Not a little boy anymore, Bobby's interest, and his questions, were changing and maturing as his body grew. "Why'd you get a divorce, anyhow? Did you and my dad just stop loving each other?"

A plethora of memories assailed Kathleen as she pondered that question, and again she sighed deeply. "No, not exactly. We loved each other a lot at first," she admitted, "but obviously not enough as things turned out."

This time Bobby was the one to sigh deeply. "You know what I've always hated most? Never hearing from him. All I know are the things you've told me when I asked. I'm sure he knows more about me than I do about him."

Words failed Kathleen, and when she faltered, Bobby noticed. "Mom?" he asked, arching his brow. "What did you tell my father about me?"

Kathleen sucked in her breath, exhaled choppily...then confessed. "Nothing."

At first, Bobby felt and looked as if he'd been struck by lightning. But after weighing Kathleen's words and working it out for himself, he became incensed. His father didn't know anything about him? Nothing at all? He straightened in his seat and glared at his mother. "Are you saying my dad didn't know anything about me before he left West Virginia?" He spoke precisely. "And you didn't call him up when I was born and tell him about me?"

"Well, first of all, Bobby, I didn't know I was pregnant with you when he left West Virginia, so how could I have told him then?" Kathleen's voice started out at little more than a whisper, but became stronger, more defensive, as she spoke. "You've known from the beginning that your father and I were divorced before you were born, that he wasn't around when I had you. Why are you acting so surprised by it now?"

"Well, yeah, I knew you were divorced. But I assumed he knew about me...that I was the reason he never came around us."

Kathleen could not allow her son to believe something that was so blatantly untrue, so she rushed to reassure him. "Oh no, honey, that isn't true. The divorce didn't have anything at all to do with you, please believe me. The divorce was just between your father and myself. He never rejected you, Bobby, never! He rejected only me."

Bobby's voice cracked, and it dawned on Kathleen that it wouldn't be too many years before her son became a man. "Then I want to meet my father now," he demanded. "You have to help me get in touch with him."

Kathleen exhaled loudly, then fell silent. What she had just told Bobby was absolutely true...as far as it went. She didn't know exactly where his father lived...but she could get a message to him anytime she wished. How could she explain that to her son? How could she tell Bobby she'd kept such vital information regarding his father away from him for years? Her mind went totally blank. *I do not want Rob to learn about Bobby. Not now. Not ever.* The very thought caused an ache to form in the middle of Kathleen's chest, like an ice pick had pierced her heart and made it bleed.

Kathleen appeared composed and in control on the outside, but inside she was a mess. She made herself calm down, refocus. Before Bobby's desire to find his father caused her to soften her stance toward her former husband, she'd force herself to remember it all: the acrimonious words Rob had used so skillfully as weapons when they were last together—words that had hit their target with cruel, painful precision…his hateful actions…and his ultimate betrayal.

# Chapter 2

▼

Memories from the past flowed over Kathleen, weaving their way through her mind like a sepia-tinted movie—a movie that starred Rob McKenzie.

Rob McKenzie...veteran first baseman for the Cincinnati Reds.

Rob McKenzie...once the love of her life.

What an awesome athlete Rob had been! Few previously-held college baseball records remained intact by the time he ended his playing days at Morgantown; he had broken most of them. And Kathleen had attended every game, cheering him on from her favorite seat near first base, where Rob could look over and smile at her between plays.

West Virginians have always loved baseball with a passion, and long before Rob McKenzie ever played his first game of catch with his father, baseball was already the most popular participatory sport in the state. Because the Cincinnati Reds were the closest team geographically to the coal mining area in the southern part of the state, most Logan County fans rooted for them. So when Rob received an offer in January of his senior year to play baseball for the Reds, it ranked right up there with hitting a jackpot or winning the lottery, even though everyone knew he'd have to start at the bottom of the heap with Cincinnati's farm team in Tampa.

No one expected Rob to stay in Tampa long. They figured he'd move up through the ranks fairly quickly.

The Reds wanted Rob to report for duty in time for spring training that year, but he refused. He didn't want to leave WVU before earning his bachelor's degree. Rob was convinced he would make it in professional sports, but he agreed with his father that it might be wise to have a degree to fall back on if things didn't work out. After scouting Rob for four years, the Reds balked at that logic, but Rob dug in his heels, creating just a minor snag in a win-win situation worth some give and take by both sides. Other clubs had contacted his agent, too, hoping to sway Rob in their direction, but he wanted to play for the Reds. Cincinnati's general manager didn't want to lose out on signing the most sought after college athlete of the decade, so a compromise was struck: Rob could complete his undergraduate work at WVU, then report to the Tampa Tarpons, ready to play ball, on the first Monday following his final scholastic exam.

Rob and Kathleen, close friends from the moment they met, had realized in college that their love for each other was more than just friendship. It was a once-in-a-lifetime romantic experience. The thought of being separated from each other was so intolerable, they decided to get married at the end of that semester and go to Florida together.

Running away to get married seemed mysterious and exciting, like living out a fairy tale. But after they'd had their blood tests done and were standing in line to apply for their license, Kathleen's conscience began nudging her. "How do you feel about this?" she asked her husband-to-be. "I'm starting to get a little bit worried, myself. Should we tell our parents about our plans?"

"We can, I guess," Rob admitted. "But what if they ask us to wait? We don't know when I'll be home again. I don't want to go to Florida without marrying you. Is that what you want?"

"No, it's not," Kathleen said emphatically.

So, three days later, with their two closest friends as witnesses, Rob McKenzie and Kathleen Mitchell were married. They'd been best friends and closest confidantes for years, but on that day in May everything changed.

They became lovers.

\* \* \* \*

They had been so young then, so naive and inexperienced, that years later it still amazed Kathleen how they'd approached marriage with such exuberance and a total lack of inhibition. She could still close her eyes and hear Rob's voice in her mind as he laughingly explained it to her. "Come on, Katie-girl, use that brilliant brain I know you've got. After using the 'think' system for years, why wouldn't we know exactly how to love each other when we finally got the chance?"

Looking back now from a more mature viewpoint in a much more promiscuous age, Kathleen had no regrets for the way things had worked out for them. At least not as far as their marriage itself was concerned. She was still glad they had waited until they were married to make love with each other.

But she could have wept anew, reliving their innocence. They had believed, since they were married, nothing would ever come between them again.

They were wrong.

*   *   *   *

It was as if it happened yesterday, the memories were so clear.

Kathleen remembered how, on the Sunday afternoon following their impetuous marriage, she and Rob had reluctantly left the rustic cabin at Blackwater Falls State Park to begin the long trip home to Logan County. There was no way to know how their parents would react to news of their elopement, but they knew they had to bite the bullet and tell them they were married. The Mitchells would probably protest Kathleen's plan to go to Florida the next day with Rob, but so be it. She and Rob were over twenty-one—old enough to make their own decisions.

Their feelings of dread and anticipation over facing their parents at home cast a shadow over the entire afternoon, so much so that they were unable to enjoy the majestic mountains and picturesque landscapes as they drove through that unfamiliar but beautiful part of the state.

Instead of congratulations, the young couple was met at Steven's Hollow with catastrophic news: Kathleen's forty-eight year old father, David James Mitchell, a skilled and careful miner, had been crushed in a cave-in at the mine where he worked. He was alive, but barely. The doctors had told Kathleen's mother he might never recover.

The Mitchell family, like every other coal mining family in the area, knew that mining was a hazardous occupation. Danger lurked around every corner in a mine and there was no foolproof way to predict when or where disasters might strike.

Emphysema and black lung, insidious and deadly diseases caused by the inhalation of coal dust, were ever-present fears for the men who worked the mines. Those conditions ultimately led to slow and painful deaths, but because they occurred over time, they were easy to ignore until a deadly diagnosis was made.

Fatalities and major injuries involving cave-ins and slate falls were not as prevalent as emphysema, black lung, and some of the less serious coal mining injuries, but they were the most dreaded because they occurred without warning. And that's what happened to David Mitchell. Not having been injured before, he never expected something like that to happen to him.

So things at home did not go the way a stunned Kathleen and Rob had envisioned they would.

Lettie Mitchell and Rob's parents, Mike and Mary McKenzie, were not pleased with the news of their elopement. They were, in fact, dismayed that their children would marry without coordinating their wedding plans with them. They accepted the marriage as a *fait accompli*, but other than acknowledging it had happened, the stress they were under kept them from addressing it directly. Expressing neither opposition nor approval, they let the fact of their children's marriage lie untouched as they bemoaned the fate of David Mitchell.

Then something unexpected came up, something there was no getting around.

Kathleen's father required round-the-clock nursing care, which would quickly deplete the Mitchell family's financial resources if they couldn't augment his care on their own. Mrs. Mitchell took Kathleen aside to discuss the situation privately with her. "Katie, you'll have to give up this foolishness about going to Florida with Rob. Can't you see you're needed at home?"

"Well, I can see that someone's needed here, but Rob and I are married and my place is with him. I'm torn, Mom, I really am. I want to help you out, truly I do, but I also want to be with Rob. Can't you understand that?"

Beside herself with worry, Kathleen's mother didn't know what to do. "Brian can't stay and help me for long," she said. "He has a job to go to. Besides, Ellen needs his help with their new baby. And David—he wants to stay, but he just can't. I don't even want him to, truth be told. If he drops out of medical school now, he'll lose the grant that pays his tuition. He's working two jobs just to cover the rest of his expenses, Katie, and even with that he can barely keep his head above water. Why, I'd never forgive myself if David gave up his chance to become a doctor just so he could be at home to help me out. You're out of school for the summer, anyhow. You're the logical one to stay."

Near tears, Kathleen admitted she, too, didn't know what to do.

"Well, there aren't too many choices available, and we wouldn't have time to figure them out, even if there were. I'm sorry this happened now…you know that. Whatever you decide, I'll understand, but I do need your help in caring for your dad." Against all odds, Lettie Mitchell continued to feel optimistic that her husband would fully recover. "It'll only be temporary, Katie, just till he's well enough for me to do it on my own." Lettie glanced across the room to where her new son-in-law was talking to Brian. "Even though his dad's not a miner, Rob grew up here," she said. "Surely he can relate to what we're going through."

As the vigil wore on, Kathleen talked with Social Services and her father's doctor, seeking a better solution to the problem that haunted them all. But nothing that would work came to mind. They must have entertained a dozen healthcare scenarios, none of which fit their situation exactly.

Rob felt it was his job to support Kathleen in this time of trial, not offer unsolicited advice. But he suspected that the world as he knew it was coming to an end. Who else, other than Kathleen, could assist her mother during her father's stay in the hospital and his recuperation at home—if he survived his injuries? Selfishly, Rob continued to pray that, if pushed, Kathleen would choose to go to Florida with him.

The newlyweds sat side-by-side on a lumpy sofa in the waiting room across from Brian, Ellen, and David. Lettie Mitchell continued to pace the hall, unable to sit still for any amount of time. After what seemed like hours, but was really only minutes, Mike and Mary McKenzie left for the cafeteria, saying they would return soon with fresh coffee and sandwiches for everyone.

Conversation dragged as they waited for the latest update on David Mitchell's condition.

Kathleen and Rob were legally married and wanted to stay together, but that fact still had not sunk in with Kathleen's family, especially her mother. It became increasingly apparent to everyone that Lettie Mitchell could not cope alone with the blow she'd been dealt. Lettie wanted Kathleen to be the one to help her out for a while, but she'd made her pitch. She wouldn't mention it again.

Each time Kathleen looked at her mother, she saw a woman at the end of her rope, a woman trying desperately to hold things together while her husband of twenty-seven years lay motionless in a nearby hospital bed.

Kathleen could not resist the appeal she saw in her mother's tearful eyes, so she agreed to stay. It was only when a relieved Lettie Mitchell broke down completely and sobbed that Kathleen understood how much her decision to stay meant to her mother.

Rob had feared Kathleen would reach that conclusion, but for Kathleen there was no other choice. As she told him what she felt she must do, he became angry…hurt…then frustrated.

When the two of them were alone at her parents' home later, Kathleen wept. Totally distraught, she realized belatedly that she hadn't talked the situation over with her new husband before making her decision. She attempted to rectify that, but her tearful promise to join Rob later fell on deaf ears. "Why can't you leave your father in your mother's care? The women from our church will help out, you know that they will." He continued to plead until his voice sounded hoarse, hoping against hope that a miracle would suddenly occur and Kathleen and he could go on with their plans. "I need you desperately, Katie, I can't tell you how much I need you. And we're married. Isn't your place now with me?"

"Oh, Rob, I love you more than life itself and long to be with you, but this situation is only short-term, I promise. I'll join you in Florida as soon as I can. They're my parents. Please try to understand why I have to do this for them."

Usually a caring individual, easy to get along with, Rob dug in his heels this time. No matter what Kathleen said, or how much she pleaded and cajoled, she could not convince him to agree to alter their plans.

It rankled Rob that she'd made such a critical decision without asking for input from him. But Kathleen reminded him that he'd sat beside her like a knot on a log for hours, never speaking up one way or the other until the die had been cast.

When Rob left the Mitchell home that Sunday night, his final words, spoken in anger, seemed to echo from the oft-papered walls. "If you don't come with me now, Katie, don't bother to come later." He slept at his parents' house that night, and his father drove him to the airport early the next morning. Three days into their marriage, it seemed the honeymoon was over. They would see each other in person only one more time.

\* \* \* \*

As soon as he stepped off the plane in Tampa, Rob called from a pay phone to apologize for his selfish, thoughtless words, but things were not the same between the two of them. For their marriage to flourish as they wanted it to, the young couple needed to be together. And being together was impossible then.

The highlights of Kathleen's long and draining weeks that summer were the anxiously-awaited calls she received from Rob each Sunday night. It didn't matter where his team was playing, he found a phone and called to say he loved her more than ever and wanted her with him.

But as time passed and her father's condition failed to improve, their dream of being together started to fade. With each telephone call they grew further apart, even though, week after week, Rob came up with one reason after another why Kathleen should leave her parents and join him on the road. Frustrated that she couldn't, and unable to make Rob see why, Kathleen cried herself to sleep each Sunday night after hanging up the phone. She could not forsake her mother and father, and her inability to do what he wanted her to do was causing her to lose Rob.

During her family's terrible ordeal, there were times when David Mitchell, in a drug-induced, pain-lessened state, knew Kathleen was there, caring for him. When he was lucid, they talked about her marriage to Rob.

"Don't stay here, Katie," her father choked out. "Rob's a fine young man who's going places...you go with him. It doesn't matter who takes care of me...I'm dying, baby. Think about yourself for a change."

Kathleen's marriage was teetering on a shaky foundation, and there was nothing she could do to make it right. But she would never tell her father that. With their hands loosely linked atop his crushed and broken body, Kathleen and her father wept openly together. She knew she'd never leave him now, not in the mortally-injured shape he was in, not even for Rob—the man she loved above everything else. "Things will work out in time for Rob and me," she whispered near her father's ear, forcing a smile into her voice. "You just concentrate on getting stronger."

\* \* \* \*

A few happy memories could be found among the painful experiences of that long-ago summer, but only Kathleen knew where they were hidden and how agonizing it would be to unearth them. She also knew she'd have to face them again—head on—before she could cast them off forever. Breathing in and out slowly for several shaky breaths, Kathleen made herself recall her last weekend with Rob.

Those few days were, at the same time, the happiest...and the saddest...days of her life.

\* \* \* \*

Near the end of July, Rob was sent to Denver to play with Cincinnati's Triple A team there, the Zephyrs. No other rookie minor leaguer that season had moved from Single A to Triple A ball in so short a time. An elated Rob sent Kathleen tickets to fly to Denver for a long weekend when the Zephyrs were playing at home. He had even arranged for her brother David to stay with her parents for a few days so she wouldn't worry about them.

Since their blissful honeymoon weekend at Blackwater Falls, the two young lovers had not been together, but Kathleen didn't worry that Rob might stray.

She knew women hung around the stadiums all the time, available to any player who wanted one, but Rob assured her that they held no appeal for him. He loved her, he vowed, and only her. If they couldn't be together all the time—which *was* the present reality of their situation—then he promised to settle for whatever time he *could* be with her.

* * * *

Driving along in her Explorer so many years later, her son at her side, Kathleen remembered that last weekend with Rob as if it, too, were being played out in front of her again. Her heart raced with the same apprehension she'd felt back then over seeing him again. Still reeling from the emotional trauma of their previous parting, she had hoped their time together in Denver would heal their failing marriage.

* * * *

He was the first thing she saw when she walked off the plane. Leaning against the wall outside the arrival gate, one foot braced against its rough-textured surface, he scanned the incoming passengers, looking for her. Several yards away, her steps faltered. She stopped to adjust the strap of her carry-on bag and slowly ran her eyes over the breathtakingly handsome man in front of her. From the top of his sun-streaked brown hair…down over the Zephyrs t-shirt that emphasized his baseball tan…over his well-worn jeans…down to the bottom of his white, Nike-shod toes, she checked him out.

And he returned her quiet, thorough appraisal.

When Rob turned the full force of his expressive, gold-flecked eyes on her and grinned, Kathleen's nervousness departed. Unmindful of the crowd around them, Rob opened his arms and she rushed into them, giving herself to him completely. He threw back his head and laughed as he danced her around in a circle. "Oh, how I love you, Katie-girl," he repeated over and over, holding her close and kissing her. "God knows I'll always love you."

"I've missed you so much," she responded, nuzzling his neck. Nothing could erase the smile that was stuck on her face. "It's like heaven being with you."

Their time together that weekend could only be described as idyllic. Ignoring the difficulties they'd been experiencing in their personal relationship, they immersed themselves in each other, spending as much time together as they could.

Rob introduced Kathleen to his teammates and their families, and she sat in the stands with the other wives and their children during the game. The raucous group of women and kids rooted loudly for the Zephyrs as the team soundly defeated their opponents five-to-two.

Loving each other at night, and waking up in each other's arms each morning was a dream come true for both Rob and Kathleen. On Sunday morning, they even found a small church with a friendly, outgoing congregation where they could worship together again. They refused to let anything unpleasant enter the peaceful haven they'd created, and things could not have been better between them…until Sunday night.

The minor league season was winding down, and Rob finally confessed that he was slated to leave in September to play fall and winter ball in Puerto Rico. He wasn't coming back to West Virginia at the end of the season. Kathleen cried as she packed to leave Denver, not knowing when they'd be together again. Obviously forgetting he had resolved to be satisfied with whatever time he could get with his wife, Rob again urged Kathleen to leave Logan and come follow him.

"I can't do that yet," Kathleen said, fighting back tears. "Dad's doctors aren't sure he'll recover, and truthfully, he probably won't. His chest was crushed so severely that all they're doing now is keeping him comfortable while we pray for a miracle."

Staying at home and facing her father's injuries and imminent death on a daily basis had, of necessity, matured Kathleen quickly. Reveling in his unprecedented athletic achievements that summer, Rob had been able to hold true maturity at bay. He tried to explain how exhilarating it felt playing professional baseball, something he loved more than anything else in the world except Kathleen, but she couldn't seem to get it. She'd always been an avid baseball fan, but stacked up against what her father was going through, baseball now seemed like a trivial, childish game to Kathleen. She and Rob, best friends for most of their lives, barely knew each other now. He wasn't the man she thought she'd married, and she had become a woman, not a girl.

"If you don't come to be with me now, Katie, don't come at all," Rob said at the door of their room, repeating almost word-for-word his previous ultimatum.

"You know I want to be with you more than almost anything, Rob. Haven't I told you over and over again that I love only you?" Kathleen's eyes reflected the lights from the parking lot in front of the motel. "But I can't desert my parents."

She reached out to wrap her arms around Rob, needing reassurance that he'd still want her when everything settled, but he jerked away. He scooped up her luggage and stormed to his car. They drove to the airport in silence.

As Kathleen started up the ramp to the door of her plane, Rob caught her arm and spun her around. "Go ahead and get a divorce when you get home. The way it is now, I'm here in Denver, neither married nor single, and you're still your mother's little girl, living at home. This weekend, I gave you another chance to decide what you wanted, and guess what, Katie? You didn't choose me. I can't take it anymore, seeing you only every now and then as a part-time wife. That's not what marriage is about. I'd rather not see you at all! I want you to divorce me, Katie. Just do it quickly, and let me know when it's over so I can get on with my life."

Kathleen reached out for him with hot tears spilling over her cheeks, but Rob walked away. He never looked back and further words between them seemed pointless.

What Kathleen didn't know was that other passengers, too, watched the tall, good-looking young man walk away from the gate, his head held high as silent tears fell down his face.

The long flight from Denver to Charleston was without turbulence, uneventful even for most of the passengers filling the seats of the 747. But it was a sad trip home for Kathleen Mitchell McKenzie, who sobbed quietly all the way back to West Virginia.

When she disembarked in Charleston, a message awaited Kathleen. Her father was in intensive care again.

After retrieving her car from satellite parking, Kathleen drove in a mental haze to the hospital in Logan. When she saw the look of fatigue and utter despair on her mother's face, she knew the end was nigh. The two of them sobbed as they fortified each other for what they knew would come soon.

David James Mitchell, who'd just turned forty-nine the week before, died early the next day.

# Chapter 3

Rob could not…or perhaps, as Kathleen feared, *would* not…return to West Virginia for her father's funeral, but she wasn't surprised. They'd said their good-byes at the airport in Denver.

When she called to advise him that her father had passed away, the conversation was brief, and he seemed almost glad for obligations that kept him away. The pain of their final encounter was so fresh and so deep that Kathleen figured the last thing Rob needed was to play the role of loving husband, a role he no longer claimed as his. She didn't even ask him to come home.

When Kathleen's brothers and her sister-in-law, Ellen, took in her gaunt face and the dark circles under her eyes, they decided they'd take care of her themselves. She never mentioned Rob again, and they never asked what had happened between them in Denver. He was not there for the burial of her father, which spoke for itself as far as her family was concerned, but Kathleen never told anyone why.

The day after her father's funeral, Kathleen hired former Logan County Circuit Court Judge Benjamin Johnston, who'd gone back into private practice after retiring from the bench, to start divorce proceedings.

"This is a simple divorce," the Judge told Kathleen, "the best kind of all from a lawyer's point of view. With no children, and no jointly-owned property to divide, it shouldn't take any time at all to complete."

Because she'd been married for such a short time, Kathleen stipulated that she'd revert to her maiden name once the divorce became final. She was adamant, too, about one other thing, although the Judge counseled against it: she would not accept alimony or any other monetary support from Rob.

Judge Johnston took Kathleen's sworn deposition in Logan shortly after the paperwork was filed. He advised her then that the final divorce decree would be entered as soon as Rob's deposition, supporting her allegations that the marriage was irrevocably broken, was taken at a law office in Colorado.

Kathleen wanted nothing at all from Rob. She paid for the divorce with money she'd earned the previous summer working at the *Logan County Sentinel*, then made plans to return to WVU to complete her senior year.

\* \* \* \*

By the time she arrived back at college feeling weak and losing weight, Kathleen's nerves were shot. She forced herself to eat but couldn't keep much of anything down. When her feelings of queasiness continued, she suspected that a persistent case of stomach flu was causing her symptoms. In October, when her illness began affecting her studies, she finally gave in and visited the free medical clinic on campus.

*Pregnant.* She couldn't believe the clinic's physician when he said she was two months along. Where can I turn for help? she wondered. What will I do? Should I contact Rob to tell him what's happened?

In a daze, Kathleen began the long walk back to her apartment, passing along the way the newsstand in front of the college bookstore where the current tabloids were displayed. On the front of one was a large photo of a heavily-made-up young woman wearing a rumpled, skimpy negligee. If Kathleen had harbored any expectation before then that Rob might shoulder this responsibility with her, the headline above that picture wiped it out: Baseball Groupie Found in Bed of Former WVU Baseball Star in Puerto Rico.

That baseball star was Rob McKenzie.

Kathleen couldn't bear to read the rest of the article. Frozen in place, she began to sob. The part-time cashier, a student who had seen Kathleen around campus, noticed her distress and helped her over to a bench near the sidewalk where she could sit for a while. Handing her a small paper cup filled with cold water, the kind clerk insisted on waiting there with Kathleen until she felt like walking home.

At that defining moment, when she glanced once more at the headline that had broken her heart again, something inside Kathleen died. She made a decision then that would alter her life forever. She would not tell Rob...or anyone in his family...about the baby. It would be *her* baby, hers alone, and she would love him—or her—forever.

Throwing herself into her studies, Kathleen graduated early in December with an English degree. And, thank goodness, her morning sickness appeared to be over. After moving from her rented apartment in Morgantown to Brian and Ellen's spacious new home in Woodbridge, Virginia, she helped Ellen care for Janie while searching for a position in her field. In late-January she found a job writing children's Bible stories at home, which enabled her to support herself and put aside the money she needed for prenatal and delivery care.

On May 4th, almost one year to the day after their ill-advised elopement, Rob McKenzie hit a game-winning, grand-slam home run against the Detroit Tigers in his first official game as the starting first baseman for the Cincinnati Reds. And Kathleen was totally unaware that history was being made in Cincinnati that day.

Because, unbeknownst to Rob, on that same day one of life's strange coincidences occurred. Early that morning, long before his major league career took off with that phenomenal hit from his bat, Kathleen Mitchell gave birth to their son. She named her baby Robert Michael Mitchell. When the hospital's birth registration clerk asked for data on the baby's father, Kathleen's conscience wouldn't let her deny her son his father's name, at least not officially. She listed "Robert Michael McKenzie, address unknown, Cincinnati, Ohio."

Looking at her newborn son, soft and sweet and hers alone, Kathleen vowed again that she would never tell Rob about her baby or return to Steven's Hollow. Smiling down at her beautiful son, Kathleen sighed and fell asleep again beside her child.

She slept all the way through Rob's dramatic major league debut. And no one in her family even mentioned it to her.

\*   \*   \*   \*

Sitting in the car beside that same precious son, now thirteen, Kathleen felt overwhelmed by images from the past that she'd tried her best to leave behind long ago. Tears pooled in her eyes, scalding her lids. As much as she hated disappointing Bobby, she knew deep down in her soul that she never wanted to meet Rob McKenzie in person again.

"This is how it has to be," she said. "Your father made it perfectly clear years ago that he never wanted to see me again. And I don't want to see him. I'm sorry, I simply cannot help you with your search."

"Then tell me this. Did my father say the same thing about me?"

Kathleen was near the end of her rope. "Don't try to start something, Bobby. I already told you he didn't."

It was a mistake, bringing that up again, and Kathleen knew it. This defiant teenager seemed like a stranger to her. "Yeah, you said that before, didn't you? This is all your fault!" Bobby's face began to crumple, and he struggled not to cry. "You want to know something? Keeping that from me was more than just unfair, Mom. It was mean. I thought I'd done something when I was a baby that kept him from coming around, but now I know that's not true. He doesn't even know I exist. And never did!"

"Bobby, please listen—"

"No, Mom, *you* listen. I was sort of teasing when I said I'd always tell you everything. But let me tell you one thing right now that's for sure: someday I won't need your help to find my father. I'll find him by myself."

Kathleen couldn't deal with a rebellious Bobby while speeding along at fifty-five miles an hour. Pulling off the road at a deserted gas station, she turned the engine off and covered her face with her hands. She didn't like having Bobby witness her loss of control. Although she had cried many private tears during the years she'd raised her son alone, this was the first time she'd cried in his presence like this.

A moment later Bobby's arms snaked around Kathleen to hand her a tissue. "I'm sorry I made you cry," he said, hugging her awkwardly. "But can't you see? I need to find out who I am…not just who my father is."

Kathleen turned to rest her cheek against the top of his head. "I can't face any more right now, sweetie. It's my fault you're hurting, and that breaks my heart. I don't want to talk about this when it sounds like we're fighting—you know how much I hate that. I promise I'll discuss it with you later. Can't you just be patient for a while?"

"Yeah, I guess. But maybe I'd better tell you the rest." Bobby confessed, "When Uncle David and Uncle Brian were at our house for Easter, I asked Uncle Brian if he could use the FBI's database to look for my father. He said I'd have to talk it over with you first. If you say it's okay, he'll do it. I'd rather hear about my dad from you, Mom, but I am going to find him one way or the other, whether you help me or not."

Remembering the secrets she'd been harboring in her heart for years nearly tore Kathleen apart. Soon, because she had promised, she'd have to tell Bobby everything he wanted to know about his father. His name…where he could be found…and that there might be a problem now with their divorce.

As she gazed blindly out the side window of the Explorer, Kathleen mulled over the choices she'd made on her own when she was just twenty-two. Her decision to keep Rob's true identity a secret from Bobby, and Bobby's birth a secret from Rob, had seemed absolutely justifiable to her at the time. But now, in the space of mere seconds, those reasons raced amok through her mind and caused only confusion. As they began stacking up once more in logical order, one right on top of the other, Kathleen started to waver. Perhaps she *had* made a mistake. Perhaps she hadn't handled things as well as she'd thought she had back then.

Kathleen shuddered, her self-confidence shaken to the core. She had lived most of her life presuming that her divorce from Rob was final years ago. Rob had undoubtedly believed the same thing. He had no inkling there might be complications now.

Nothing Dan Hoffman had said on the phone caused Kathleen to feel optimistic about her meeting with him. She'd pondered her dilemma for days, wondering what she could do, and the only answer she'd come up with so far was, not much. She didn't know exactly what the problem was as yet, but her main goal was to get rid of the stumbling block—whatever it was—before Rob found out it existed.

Something struck Kathleen with such force that she clenched her fists into a tight ball in her lap. Her entire conversation with Bobby about finding his father might soon become moot. If she had to meet Rob face-to-face about the problem with their divorce, how could she continue to keep Bobby's birth a secret from him? She hadn't seen Rob in years, but she still knew this much about him: if he discovered he had a son, a son whose birth she'd kept a secret from him for over thirteen years, she'd be facing more than just Rob's anger. He'd want to see his child, and he'd demand every legal and emotional right available to him as a father. Kathleen could not let that happen, she just couldn't. She had to see Dan Hoffman right away. She'd be a nervous wreck till she did.

Resuming her trip on Rt. 119, Kathleen arrived in Logan all too soon. She felt emotionally drained, totally wiped out, and no closer to a solution to her problem than she had been the day before.

*   *   *   *

Finding a vacant parking place anywhere around the courthouse on Stratton Street was a miracle that people in Logan often hoped for—and rarely attained. Someone backed out of a space directly across from Aracoma Drug, however, and Kathleen eased into the spot. Once parked, she dug out her cell phone to call Dan Hoffman. Those legal tangles she'd procrastinated over and fretted about could not be straightened out too quickly for her now. Informed that the lawyer was in court and not expected back until the end of the day, she asked the secretary to put her down for his next available appointment, which was two o'clock the following day.

Well, Kathleen thought, the sooner this is over, the better off I'll be. She quietly groaned and closed her eyes. Knowing how she loathed both written and spoken clichés, her family and friends always teased her unmercifully when one of those slippery little devils slid into her mind or her writing to shock her.

The sound of Kathleen's quiet moan alerted Bobby. No longer sulking, he'd been looking around while she talked on the phone. "What's wrong?" he asked, twisting his head in her direction.

"Nothing, really. Just a wayward thought. Believe me, you don't want to know."

"Sure, I do. You moaned, which you don't usually do when you're thinking. Are you sick or hurting or something?"

"No, nothing like that," she declared, her lips curving into a smile. "A mental cliché just slithered by and bit me on the ankle."

Bobby knew his mother well. They looked quickly at each other and chuckled. "All right, it's confession time." Although he never wrote them down, Bobby did keep a mental list of Kathleen's errant clichés. "Is it one I've heard before?"

"I respectfully plead the fifth, your Honor," Kathleen said with a smile. "I'm not giving you anything to hold over my head."

"If I catch you at a weak moment, you will."

"Maybe so, but not now." Kathleen was still smiling when she started the engine again.

Feeling revitalized now that she'd finally set things in motion with the lawyer, Kathleen felt no real pressure to rush to Steven's Hollow. When she had called her mother the night before to say they'd be spending the night on the road, Lettie Mitchell had mentioned that she'd already stocked the cabin where Kathleen and Bobby would be staying with enough groceries for a month. Well, her mother was prone to hyperbole upon occasion, but Kathleen believed her this time. So unpacking seemed to be the only real chore awaiting them at the cabin.

Though anxious to see her mother, Kathleen knew that half an hour one way or another wouldn't matter to her mom. But Bobby had been poised on the edge of his seat since entering Logan, avidly absorbing the ambience of downtown where historic brick buildings seemed to have risen like a phoenix from the coal dust that had clogged every crack and crevice of the town during its heyday. An extra half hour together might help her and Bobby regain their previous feelings of closeness with each other.

Kathleen followed Bobby's gaze to the lush, green mountains surrounding the town whose history was so rich and so varied. There was so much she wanted to share with Bobby, she debated what to show or tell him first. Indians had once hunted game in Logan County's fertile valleys, and the number of places bearing Indian names was indicative of the area's Native American history. She'd start there, Kathleen decided.

"When it was formed in 1823, Logan County and the town that is now the county seat were named in honor of Chief Logan, an Indian chieftain," she said. Like most children his age, Bobby loved learning about Native Americans. Kathleen threw out that interesting tidbit of historical information first to further whet his interest in her hometown.

Instead of rushing through Logan, she drove slowly along its main business area, pointing out some of her old hang-outs, including the building that housed Logan's daily newspaper, the *Logan County Sentinel.*

Logan's population and economy had tripled at least, maybe even quadrupled, since Kathleen moved away from Steven's Hollow. She exclaimed over all the new stores and restaurants that had sprung up like toadstools around town. "You must have lived here in the Dark Ages," Bobby teased. "What year did you say you were born?"

"Never mind that," Kathleen sputtered. "Just pay attention to *old ladies* like me. You might learn something from us."

Even with the influx of new businesses, the pace of small town traffic seemed tame compared to the seemingly endless gridlock on I–95 in Northern Virginia that they were used to. There were only a few traffic lights in Logan, but that didn't mean the town had no traffic problems at all. Kathleen avoided side streets, where vehicles were lined up waiting to merge into through traffic on Stratton and Main, so she and Bobby were able to zip in and out of town easily.

After a leisurely side trip to Midelburg Island where she'd gone to school, Kathleen glanced down at her watch. It was a little early for lunch, but she took the by-pass around Logan and followed the curve of the Guyandotte River toward the familiar square shape of Mabel's Drive-In Restaurant. Parking out in front, she and Bobby strained to read the faded menu painted on the wooden fence behind the building. A waitress wearing a black and white uniform, identical to the one Kathleen had worn while working there in high school, walked over to the driver's side of the car to take their order.

"Carrie?" a surprised Kathleen asked, recognizing the waitress.

"Katie? Katie Mitchell?" was the happy reply. Carrie and Kathleen laughed as they checked each other out. Neither one of them had changed a bit, they declared.

"I can't believe this, Carrie. Running into my best friend from high school as soon as we drive into town is a miracle. What are you doing here at Mabel's?"

"Not working for much of a salary, that's for sure!" Carrie said, pretending to grumble. "I don't know whether your mom mentioned it, but Billy Joe bought this place from Mabel last year. It'd been closed for almost six months, while Mabel tried to decide whether or not she wanted to keep it going by herself. It had gotten a little run down as Mabel aged, but it wasn't too bad, according to Billy Joe. People have been really supportive since we opened up again." She pointed out the number of cars in the lot. "I guess you can tell we're doing well. But just listen to me. You asked why I'm here today, and instead of just answering your question, I'm bringing you up to date on everything that's happened since the last time I saw you!" Kathleen looked at Bobby and smiled. Carrie had always been a talker. Carrie continued, getting to the point, "As part of our deal to buy the drive-in, I promised Billy Joe to help out whenever he needs me—gratis, of course—until he gets the drive-in up and running again. He rarely needs me to come in, but today one of his regular waitresses had a doctor's appointment in Charleston at noon. She won't be in until the evening shift."

"Well, I'm glad Billy Joe needed you today. And that you've kept up your carhopping skills. We sure racked up a lot of experience working here together in high school, but I'm too rusty now to even try to keep up with a bunch of orders. I'd be screaming for help within minutes!"

Kathleen drew Carrie's attention to Bobby. "Carrie, this is my son, Bobby Mitchell. Bobby, this is my very best friend from when we were teenagers. She used to be Carrie Snodgrass, and I'm sure you've heard me mention her that way, but she's now Carrie Taylor."

Bobby shifted his Oakley sunglasses to the top of his head before leaning across his mother to shake Carrie's hand. Seeing him, Carrie was clearly perplexed. She raised her brows and looked at Kathleen. Kathleen recognized Carrie's look of confusion, but she didn't want to discuss Bobby with anyone yet, not even Carrie. "We'll talk later," she promised her friend.

Though early, the drive-in was busy, and a couple of cars had honked their horns for service. "Sounds like you're being summoned," Kathleen told her friend, "so how about a double order of your delicious fries with extra ketchup, a diet Coke, and a regular Coke for my friend here and me?"

"Sure. I'll be back in a jiff," Carrie said, walking away. Half turning, she looked back at Kathleen's car, puzzled by what she'd observed.

Kathleen knew she'd be seeing that same look of perplexity on other faces around town as people noticed Bobby. Carrie was only the first of many who'd be intrigued by his appearance. Bobby closely resembled his father at thirteen, and his father was extremely well-known in Logan County. She had not expected to run into any of Rob's friends this soon, though, and hadn't quite figured out how to handle their curiosity about her son.

When Carrie delivered their food, Kathleen rolled the window up a few inches so Carrie could slip the edge of the tray over the glass to secure it. Grinning, Bobby began singing the theme song from *Happy Days* under his breath.

"Hey!" Carrie said, acting insulted. "We aren't that old, Bobby. We worked together in the 80s, not the 50s!" She settled the tray firmly over the window, testing to make sure it was braced against the door. "You've got a good little singer there, Katie," she said. "Is he—?"

Kathleen cut Carrie off in mid-sentence, smiling to soften somewhat her firm retort. "Like I said, let's save it till later. Okay?"

"Sure thing," Carrie responded, walking away. She wondered why Kathleen was so stingy with information about her son. She couldn't remember right off where she had seen them, but she recognized Bobby Mitchell's green eyes from somewhere. It would drive her crazy till she figured it out.

While they ate their fries, Kathleen entertained Bobby with tales of the customers she used to get while waiting cars at Mabel's. "We knew who everyone dated, who cheated on their steadies, and who cruised the parking lot on Friday and Saturday nights looking for pick-ups," she said. "I will tell you, though, Mabel was a tough old bird. She'd fire any employee who blabbed at school about what they saw while working here. But it was still fun to be in the know, even if we did have to honor Mabel's strict rules and keep our secrets to ourselves."

"Come on now, Mom, tell the truth. I'll bet you and Carrie talked to each other about everything and everyone you saw here, didn't you?" Kathleen laughingly admitted that they had kept the phone lines between their houses hot, talking over what happened during their shifts.

Through the walk-up window, Kathleen could see Carrie's husband, Billy Joe Taylor, flipping hamburgers on the grill. After she and Bobby had finished their snack, she left him in the car while she carefully removed the tray from the car door and carried it over to that window. Billy Joe was filling multiple orders with so much rhythm and grace he had to've been humming some 1980s Dan Fogelberg tune under his breath. And he wore a clean but well-worn apron with "Mabel" stitched on the bib that Kathleen could have sworn she'd seen the real Mabel wear a hundred times or more.

"Hey, in there," she yelled to Billy Joe, "long time, no see." She switched to an exaggerated drawl. "My, Mabel, how you've changed. Didn't you use to be a woman?"

Turning to see who was attempting to catch his attention, Billie Joe flipped the hamburger he was cooking onto a bun, wrapped it up, and threw it and a large order of fries onto a tray. He deftly handed it off to the waitress working the other side of the lot, then rushed outside to hug Kathleen.

"The cook's taking a break," he yelled loudly to anyone who might be listening, employees and customers alike, then walked arm-in-arm with Kathleen to her car. Kathleen introduced Bobby to Billy Joe, who still resembled the high school athlete he'd been eighteen years before. She sputtered and protested as Billy Joe began telling Bobby wild, distorted stories about how disrespectfully she and Carrie had treated him in school.

"We worshiped the ground you walked on, Billy Joe! You know we did. How can you say such awful things about us?"

Billy Joe placed his hand over his heart. "Katie...sweet Katie...why didn't you say you adored me back then?"

"Because she knew you were mine and didn't poach," Carrie answered for Kathleen. She walked up and wrapped her arms around Billy Joe's waist from behind. "Why do you think Katie and I are still speaking to each other?"

Billy Joe twisted around to place a quick kiss on top of Carrie's head, smiling at Kathleen as he did. "I think Katie had her eyes on someone else back then, Carrie. Someone who was pretty special in his own right."

"Wow, will you just look at the time?" Kathleen said before Billy Joe could add anything more. "It's been marvelous running into you guys," She needed to get Bobby away from there. Now. "We haven't seen Mom yet, so we'd better hit the road," she added.

"Please call me while you're here, Katie. Let's get together and catch up on old times," Carrie said, smiling her good-bye.

Waving an acknowledgment, Kathleen backed carefully onto the road and turned west, heading back toward Steven's Hollow.

"Wow," Bobby said, "thanks for stopping there. I didn't know they had drive-ins like that anymore. It sure is neat. But why were you in such a hurry to leave? I had some things I wanted to ask Mr. Taylor."

"I know you weren't quite ready to leave, Bobby, but I was," Kathleen said kindly but emphatically. "I promised to tell you everything you need to know once we get settled at the cabin, and I will. But don't question anyone else about your father. This is just between you and me."

Kathleen's eyes flew open when Bobby said, "And my father."

# Chapter 4

It had been nearly a decade and a half since Kathleen last set foot in Logan County. As she signaled to make the lefthand turn up Steven's Hollow, it felt as if she'd never been away. Mountain laurel and wild azaleas bloomed profusely on the steep slopes she and her brothers had explored so thoroughly as kids, and she could have sworn that nothing at all had changed during the time she'd been gone. Glancing at Bobby, a pleased chuckle escaped her lips. His eyes were opened wide in wonder, and a huge grin split his face.

"Welcome to Steven's Hollow, Bobby Mitchell," she said. "Think you'll miss Northern Virginia while visiting here?"

"Are you kidding? Wow! Steven's Hollow is exactly the way you described it. I love Woodbridge, but I can't wait to climb these hills." Bobby's smile turned sheepish. "Thanks for suggesting that I bring hiking boots." Kathleen sputtered and almost choked on a laugh before shaking her head. When she'd first made that suggestion, Bobby had protested vigorously, insisting he could get by on this trip with just athletic shoes. She'd finally had to order him to pack those boots!

She cuffed him on the shoulder, still smiling. Despite the problem that had brought her back home so reluctantly, and her quandary over how to explain it to Bobby, she delighted in having this time in West Virginia with her son. "Those hiking boots you so wisely decided to pack will keep you safe from snakes while you're roaming the hills," she promised. "But you'll still need to be careful where you step."

Kathleen looked around, almost as enthralled by the beauty of the mountains as Bobby. "Steven's Hollow is more than ten miles long," she explained. "Did I say that before? It's one of the longest hollows in the state." Bobby nodded, mesmerized by the towering hills that loomed over the hollow.

Some things in the hollow had changed, Kathleen noted, and not all of them for the better. Scattered among the new houses that had sprung up like weeds were some dilapidated, rusty, run-down double-wide trailers. In her opinion, which she shared quite freely with Bobby, they were a blight on the landscape. Kathleen hated seeing them there.

Nearing an Amoco station, she slowed the Explorer to a crawl and directed Bobby's attention to three red, white, and blue tow trucks with "Snodgrass Amoco" stenciled on their sides. "Carrie's father, Jason Snodgrass, owns that station," she said. "He's Logan County's most gifted mechanic and also one of its most successful entrepreneurs."

The parking lot in front of Robin's Hair and Beauty Boutique, attached to the left side of the Amoco station, was filled with Cadillacs, Buicks, and large SUV's. A couple of other cars were parked haphazardly on the edge of the road in front of the shop.

Kathleen checked her rearview mirror, and seeing no traffic behind her, stopped in front of the station. "See Robin's shop over there?" she asked, pointing to the beauty salon. "That's where I got my first professional haircut when I was about ten. Up until then, Mom just cut my bangs and let the rest of my hair grow. Robin must have thought I was crazy that day. I kept my eyes squeezed tight the entire time she was cutting. Sure that I'd be bald without my curls, I wouldn't even look in the mirror to watch what she was doing!"

As she related that embarrassing experience, Kathleen felt herself blushing. She still didn't like beauty salons all that much, but for her they were a necessary evil. Her thick, curly, dark brown hair, cut to shoulder length, was short enough to care for herself between haircuts but long enough to twist into a ponytail and tuck into a baseball cap when she attended Bobby's baseball and soccer games.

Scanning the hodgepodge of signs obliterating most of Robin's half of the station, Bobby cocked a brow in disbelief. "Who is Robin, anyhow? And what in the world does she do inside there? There must be eight or ten cars out in front of her shop, not counting the ones almost blocking the road. Why are they all bunched up together like that around her place?"

"Well, Robin is Carrie's mother," Kathleen said. "When Mr. Snodgrass bought this land to build a gas station, Robin told him to build it big. She planned to close her shop in town and start a new business here, using half of his space. That wasn't part of Mr. Snodgrass's original plan, so the two of them had a knock-down, drag-out argument about it. Naturally, it wasn't long before everyone in Steven's Hollow had picked up the details from either one or the other of them. Robin didn't speak to Mr. Snodgrass—or cook or clean or go to work in town—until he caved in. Which he only did ungraciously, I might add.

"But to answer your question, Robin calls it a full-service beauty salon. She does a land-office business in perms, dyes, shampoos, blow-drys, styling, and local gossip."

"Well, she seems to have added nails and tanning to that list, too," Bobby said. He rolled down his window to better see the front of the building. "Isn't that a yellow line down the middle of the lot? Most of the cars seem to be clustered on Robin's side of the line."

Remembering when that yellow line first appeared was a trip down memory lane for Kathleen. "Oh, my goodness, I'm glad you asked about that. It's such a funny story it still makes me laugh. I told you that everybody knew about the fight they'd had about Robin coming there to work, right? Well, after Mr. Snodgrass finally gave in and said she could set up her shop in the other side of his station, he scrambled around looking for a way to save face. He endured a lot of kidding from the men who stopped by each day to check on the progress of his building project, and I feel confident that each one of those guys put his own two cents' worth in about what Mr. Snodgrass should do. Because finally, no doubt egged on by his friends, Mr. Snodgrass told Robin she'd have to promise to keep all those biddy hens, as he called them, in line. He even threatened to tow away any of her customers' cars that trespassed on his side of the parking lot and got in the way of the men who hung out—or as he said, *transacted business*—at the station."

Bobby had a twinkle in his eyes. "So was that a declaration of war between the biddies and the buddies?"

"No, not exactly." Kathleen smiled, too. "It was quite an event, though, the day Robin's Hair and Beauty Boutique opened. Almost everyone in Steven's Hollow, and a lot of people Robin knew in Logan, came out for the event, including, as you said, the biddies and the buddies." She gave Bobby a high-five and a grin to acknowledge that skillful turn of phrase.

"Robin bought hundreds of multi-colored balloons and, early on the day of her big celebration, let Carrie and me tie them everywhere. As the crowd started to gather, Mr. Snodgrass brought out a bucket of paint and a big wide brush. As he meticulously measured the parking lot and marked the pavement with chalk, everyone wondered what he was planning to do. People started to snicker when he began painting a bright yellow six-inch-wide stripe right down the middle of the lot."

Bobby grinned, feeling as if he had witnessed it himself. His mother was quite a storyteller, he acknowledged silently...and not just on paper.

"Robin's rather spunky and has a heck of a temper, so nobody knew how she'd react to what he had done. But it soon became plain that Robin was taking it well. Instead of being angry, she started to laugh. And so did all those people who'd been holding their breath. Everyone started to cheer when Robin jumped over the wet stripe and gave Mr. Snodgrass a big kiss that left a cherry-red lip print on his face. He didn't wash it off for the rest of the day, and everyone smiled each time they saw it."

Still chuckling, Bobby asked, "How do they get along now?"

"Fine, I assume. All I know for sure is that Robin has kept that promise she made. Mom says Robin still warns new customers not to park across the yellow line. Mr. Snodgrass still re-paints it every couple of years, but not because it's a big problem between the Snodgrasses anymore. He does it more as a reminder to Robin's customers that they need to stay on her side of the line."

Bobby's eyes twinkled again. "If we stop by the station while we're here, should I ask Mr. Snodgrass about the faded yellow line?"

"Please don't!" Kathleen said, pleased that he had liked her story.

\*     \*     \*     \*

Steven's Hollow was still home to Kathleen in a way, but she detected so many changes she knew it wasn't exactly the same home she remembered from her youth. Most of the houses in the small mining community had started out as four-room bungalows with detached outhouses. They'd been built by McCormick Coal Company's carpenters and rented to the men who worked the mine. Kathleen could still close her eyes and conjure up the unique smell of the paint the company had used to spruce up the houses every other year. When the coal vein at Steven's Hollow petered out and the mine was abandoned, the coal company had sold the houses at a fair price to current renters.

"Look there," Kathleen said, pointing to a house across the road. "That's where my friend JoEllen Curry lived."

Kathleen would not have recognized the Curry's place had she not remembered its location. Someone had added two small wings onto the original square, changing it into a modified ranch-style home that bore no resemblance to the small bungalow she'd visited with JoEllen. Several other homeowners in that same row had added porches, balconies, and patios for external facelifts and a touch of modern-day class.

"What are those bright orange bushes?" Bobby gestured toward a house two doors down from the Curry's.

"That's a wild azalea people here transplant from the hills," she answered. "It's called a torch azalea. See its fiery color?" She puckered her brow. "They seem to be especially lush this year, but maybe it just seems that way because I haven't seen torch azaleas in a while."

Pointing out the differences between the free-flowing wild azaleas and the globular-shaped domestic ones, Kathleen gave Bobby an informal botany lesson. The bright domestic azaleas, colorful when viewed individually, were stunning when massed so closely together that a bird could hardly nest in their branches.

Rose gardens were abundant along the roadway, too, especially near fences. "You should have seen the way my mom rooted roses," Kathleen told Bobby. "In the fall she would stick cuttings in the ground and cover them with an upside-down Mason jar, making a cheap mini-greenhouse for herself. Over the winter, a miracle would occur. The 'stick' would root and, by spring, turn into a tiny rosebush. I never got tired of watching that amazing process."

Kathleen's lecture could have gone on longer, she was enjoying herself so much. But Bobby's eyes had glazed over. When he agreed so quickly that some of the homeowners along that road were indisputably green-thumbed gardeners, she knew she'd rambled on too long and he was bored.

Kathleen giggled, thinking about that unasked-for and plainly unappreciated botany lesson she'd just conducted for Bobby. Her enthusiasm for her subject had apparently underwhelmed her son.

With a remnant of that smile on her face, Kathleen rounded a curve in the road and saw a house under construction just off to their right.

"Look!" Bobby said, pointing in the general direction of the new construction. "Isn't that a Habitat house over there?"

After a quick look to her right, Kathleen nodded, feeling the same kinship Bobby did with Habitat. The two of them had worked on a Habitat project in Dale City, Virginia, just last summer, but only after she'd researched Habitat for Humanity herself. She'd learned online that volunteers from all walks of life, with widely diverse experiences and degrees of skill, worked on Habitat houses under the guidance of a master carpenter. That the individuals a house was intended for worked alongside the volunteers for a set number of hours during the project, paying for part of their house with sweat equity, was another plus for Habitat as far as Kathleen was concerned.

She and Bobby had been impressed by Habitat's philosophy, and the weeks they spent working on that house, getting to know the new owners and the other volunteers, were the most memorable weeks of that summer. Glancing again at the house under construction, Kathleen regretted that they would not be in Steven's Hollow long enough this trip to help with that particular project.

Then, without warning, Kathleen's stomach dropped to her toes like a half-full bucket of coal. Her breath caught in her throat, and for a moment she couldn't inhale or exhale. A McKenzie Construction Company truck was parked in front of the house. She hadn't seen one of Rob's father's work trucks in years, and seeing one now almost caused her to panic. She inhaled deeply, filling her lungs to capacity, then exhaled slowly. She had to calm down. Otherwise, she'd have to explain her sudden discomposure to Bobby.

Her calm demeanor lasted only until she recognized the laughing man who was leaning against the hood of the truck, poring over house plans with the other volunteers. As she neared the front of the site, he glanced up, a leftover grin on his face. Kathleen gasped, positive that Bobby could hear the irregular thumping of her heart. That smiling man was Rob McKenzie. Even in her oxygen deprived state, her initial, brief impressions were painfully thorough and astute. Every bit as handsome as ever, Rob's hard-hat-covered light brown hair was streaked with blond, and his smile hadn't changed one iota. That smile should be licensed as a lethal weapon by the State of West Virginia.

A lump the size of a golf ball stuck in her throat.

Rob looked up, and a look of shock appeared on his face. His mouth snapped shut, erasing his cheerful grin. The men and women around him turned to see what had caused his astonished change of expression.

Without taking his eyes off Kathleen, Rob thrust the blueprints over to another hard-hatted individual dressed in the same manner as he—jeans, Habitat for Humanity t-shirts, and what looked like steel-toed work boots—then jogged toward the road.

Kathleen's heart had never beaten this fast before.

She had to avoid Rob at all costs; she couldn't stand seeing him now.

Rob jumped into his truck and bolted out of the driveway, headed in her direction.

With only a few seconds to decide what to do, Kathleen stomped on the gas pedal. She was soon driving far too fast for that narrow, curvy road.

"What's going on?" Bobby had never seen his mother act like this. She was normally a more-than-competent driver, but he didn't like the sudden burst of speed as she gunned the car up the road.

"Don't worry," Kathleen said, "everything's under control." She couldn't explain why she'd sped away so quickly. Trying to outrace Rob on this road was hopeless. By now his truck was almost touching their bumper. With Bobby in the Explorer, too, Kathleen began to feel afraid for them both. Her heart raced, her pulse pounded, yet she didn't want to stop. She might have to talk to Rob sometime…but, please God, not today. She had to clear her head of the residual damage from the past before facing him again.

When the next straight stretch of highway loomed in front of them, and the road ahead was clear, Rob pulled to the left, easily passing Kathleen's SUV. Once in front of her vehicle, he slowed down, turned on his emergency blinkers, and motioned for her to pull over. Kathleen ignored his gestures, but Rob wasn't about to take no for an answer. He slowed to a crawl and turned his truck diagonally across the road, forcing her to stop.

Rob jumped out of the truck like a cowboy on his way to a showdown. Kathleen lowered her head to the steering wheel, emotionally spent. The muscles in her neck tightened, and she could feel the throbbing of the pulse in the back of her head.

"Mom? You okay?" Bobby asked, a concerned look on his face. Without raising her head, Kathleen nodded.

Rob limped back to the Explorer with his eyes on Kathleen. He signaled for her to roll down her window. "Katie," he asked, a tremor in his voice. "Is it really you?"

When she heard him speak, Kathleen looked up. His voice sounded hesitant…a little unsteady…to her. Reaching past the open window to lightly touch the side of her face, Rob seemed to be in shock. "I can't believe it's really you, Katie-girl…after all this time, it's you."

Kathleen jerked away as if Rob had touched her with a laser, not his calloused hand.

She was sorry for once that Bobby had such impeccable manners, that he'd never met a stranger. Bobby gave Rob a questioning look through the dark designer sunglasses he wore most of the time. "That was sure a wild and scary ride," he said, leaning across Kathleen. "Hi, I'm Bobby Mitchell. Did you know Mom when she lived here?"

Relying instinctively on his own faultless manners, Rob acknowledged Bobby's introduction. "You might say that. I'm Rob McKenzie."

After shaking Bobby's hand, Rob didn't consciously look at the teenager again; he had eyes for only Kathleen. But his mind did register what he'd heard, and it devastated him. *Bobby Mitchell? Katie has a child?* Unless the information he'd gleaned from his friends through the years was in error, Kathleen had never married again. During the first few years after their divorce, imagining her married to someone else had been such agony for Rob, he couldn't bring himself to ask the people he knew about her. But a year or so back, when he'd stopped at Billy Joe and Carrie's place to catch up with them, Carrie had volunteered that Kathleen was still single and a published author of children's books. And that was all Carrie knew.

"Honestly, Rob," Carrie had said at the time, "getting information out of Mrs. Mitchell is like digging meat from a fresh black walnut—almost impossible! That woman thinks everything is classified."

That conversation flashed through Rob's mind as he stared at Kathleen. "We need to talk," he said. His voice was stronger, but his mind reeled with long-suppressed emotions: sorrow, regret, and shame—mostly shame. Now that they were this close to each other again, he wouldn't let her get away without granting him a few moments of her time. He didn't want to have a serious discussion with Kathleen on this well-traveled road, and he certainly wouldn't talk with her about anything in front of her son. He noticed suitcases in the back of the Explorer. "Are you staying at the cabin?" he demanded. "Or your mom's?"

Kathleen's voice finally returned. "Where I'm staying is none of your business."

Rob became more and more resolute. "That's where you're wrong, Katie. I said we need to talk, and we will. If I have to, I'll just camp out on your mother's doorstep. You'll show up there sooner or later."

Kathleen's anger grew at his audacity, but at least she'd stopped shaking.

"Bobby, I won't be a minute," she said, jerking open her door and exiting the Explorer.

Rob followed her to the back of her vehicle, where she looked at him and hissed, "What on earth do you think you're doing? Are you crazy? You're scaring my son." Kathleen placed her hands on her hips, her expression grim. "Listen up and listen good, because this is the last time I'm telling you this. I will not see you, and I will not talk to you either. Not now. Not ever. This is a public road, McKenzie. If you don't want me calling the police, move that stupid redneck truck of yours and let us pass."

Bobby tried to see what was going on, but the windows of the Explorer were obscured by mud that had splattered on them during yesterday's storm. He could hear mumbling from outside the SUV, most of which seemed to be coming from his mom, but he couldn't really tell what they were saying.

Why was his mom being so rude to that guy? He was just an old friend of hers who wanted to talk, wasn't he? Was there something else between his mom and the stranger that he didn't know about? And why did that guy look so familiar?

Behind the truck, a flush of anger suffused Rob's face, and he slapped the palm of his hand against the tailgate of the Explorer. "Don't give me that stuff! I'm not in the mood for it. You ignored me before, but you can't ignore me now. We're both finally here in Steven's Hollow, Katie, and we are going to talk." Sweeping his hand in the general direction she was heading, he leaned closer. "I'm guessing you'll be at the cabin. You can bank on seeing me there at seven o'clock."

When Kathleen refused to look at him again or respond in any way, Rob reached out and forcibly turned her face so he could peer into her eyes. "Look at me, Katie!" he demanded. As she glared into eyes that were identical to Bobby's, he said, "Seven o'clock. Be ready to talk. And don't try to avoid me. I'll find you wherever you are."

Kathleen shouldered her way past Rob and jumped into her vehicle. She glanced out the side window and, for the third time since their impetuous marriage, watched Rob stride away.

With a vicious twist of the key, she tried to restart the Explorer, which was already running. The gears ground loudly before she even knew what she'd done. "I'm sorry, Bobby," she said. "Just give me a minute, okay?"

Kathleen's head spun, and she found the entire situation to be totally exasperating. Why was Rob here now? She hadn't done a thing in the world to deserve this. She'd been a good wife, the small amount of time she was married. She'd done everything by the book when she filed for divorce. She'd hadn't even sought Rob out through the years for moral *or* monetary support. Yet here he was, in Logan again, sure to make a bad predicament worse.

There had to be a way to avoid the confrontation Rob seemed to be hankering for. But what? Try as she might, she couldn't think of a thing that might actually work.

Still silent, she looked over at Bobby. He had to be full of questions, but what could she say? That the man he'd just seen was his mysterious, absentee father? She didn't think so! This was the worst possible time and place for her to disclose that piece of information to him.

Kathleen didn't want Rob within a hundred miles of Logan County, not while she and Bobby were here. Okay, she'd concede that it wasn't Rob's fault she hadn't told Bobby about him before, and she'd admit that her objections to Rob's presence at Steven's Hollow might seem illogical to some. But she couldn't help it. She wanted Rob gone!

Disturbed by his mother's agitation, and knowing intuitively that he couldn't say or do anything to make things better right now, Bobby opted to say nothing.

He was curious about the vibes he'd intercepted between Rob McKenzie and his mom, but he'd bide his time until his mother was willing to explain those crosscurrents to him. "Hey, Mom," he said, hoping to lighten her mood, "I sort of like 'Katie-girl.' Can I call you that, too?"

Unaware of Bobby's deeper thoughts and concerns over what had just happened, his easygoing acceptance of the situation came as a surprise to Kathleen. She would've expected him to be puzzled, and maybe even scared. He wouldn't have heard her discussion with Rob outside the Explorer, but he would've heard Rob assaulting their vehicle in anger. Almost against her will, Kathleen smiled, picturing that. She hoped Rob's hand was still smarting!

Appreciating Bobby's serendipitous sense of timing, Kathleen reached over to give him a hug. "Not Katie-girl, please!" she protested. "Mom is just fine."

Kathleen's smile was still shaky, but she had recovered slightly from that unfortunate encounter. "Bobby, if I die tonight, please tell everyone I observed a miracle today. Bobby Mitchell, alias Mr. Curious—the most inquisitive person alive—just gave his mom an unexpected break. I owe you big time, kiddo." Kathleen paused dramatically. "But wait a minute…just a minute…you're being awfully nice. You weren't possessed by an alien today when I wasn't looking, were you?"

"You're funny, Mom, but not very, so don't give up writing. You'll never make it as a comic."

Still a little on edge, Kathleen put the Explorer in gear. Driving at a slower pace up Steven's Hollow, she tried to recall exactly what it was Rob had said. *You ignored me before…you can't ignore me now?*

What was that all about? She had *never* ignored him.

# Chapter 5

At his parents' house later, Rob sat on the side of his bed with his elbows on his knees. He marveled at the way his day had unfolded. Running into Kathleen again, years after he'd given up hope it might happen, was an answer to his prayers.

When he had seen Kathleen drive by the Habitat House, it had hit him with a vengeance: he'd been making do with only dreams of her for way too long. But once the floodgates opened, so many memories and emotions spewed out and assailed Rob, he feared his head might explode, just processing them.

And not all of those memories were good ones.

The heartless way he'd dealt with Kathleen in Denver had haunted him for years, and he'd had a difficult time accepting the finality of their estrangement, although he had initiated it himself. He kept hoping he'd wake up one morning and discover it had all been a nightmarish dream, that his angry words and actions had been supernaturally erased from both of their minds in the middle of the night. But after being served with divorce papers and having his deposition taken, he'd had to face the fact that his marriage was over.

All he could say about that period in his life is, he coped. Memories of that last week-end with Kathleen were permanently embedded in Rob's thoughts—a constant reminder of his irreparable loss. In that mental tape, which he played over and over again in his mind, he saw a happy, fun-loving, totally devoted Kathleen sharing everything she was and everything she had with him...until that fateful Sunday night when he tossed his wife and his marriage away. After their final good-bye, things were never the same for Rob. Loneliness, shame, and despair had torn him up for years.

Old friends who still lived in Logan reported that Kathleen never visited there, that she hadn't been back there at all since their divorce.

Rob's mind still reeled from seeing her that afternoon, and for a man reputed to always be cool under fire, he felt unbelievably nervous about seeing her again. Yes, he had vowed to hunt her down that afternoon, no matter where she was. But why set himself up for another rejection? Kathleen had made it plain before that she wanted nothing to do with him. Why not just forget about meeting with her? God had forgiven him already for all of his sins, including the way he'd treated Kathleen. Shouldn't that be enough?

No. Because it was Kathleen's pardon he needed so desperately now.

It was his fault their marriage broke up. When he told Kathleen to get a divorce, he had intended to rid himself of the frustrations their part-time marriage brought him. He'd even convinced himself that, without her, his personal and emotional life would soon be on the upswing again.

So after saying good-bye to Kathleen in Denver, Rob began training in earnest. By sheer physical determination he turned himself into a stronger, more focused player. He ate right, worked hard. He practiced on the field longer than any of his teammates, spent more time with the pitching machines, and worked rigorously in the weight room at the gym. And that grueling training schedule finally paid off. His efforts hardened his body and sharpened his mind.

But Rob soon found out that he missed Kathleen much more than he'd expected. An advocate of the "nothing ventured, nothing gained" philosophy, he decided to get in touch with her again. So he wrote a note to Kathleen, discarding a trash can full of rejects along the way. But it was all to no avail. Kathleen never replied.

Rob's stats that first season in Denver were incredible, but it was while playing fall ball in Puerto Rico that he became a leading, must-have candidate for the major league. Obsessed with advancement by then, he hungered for a chance to play in the majors. What wasn't clear, even to Rob, was whether he wanted that success for himself...or to show Kathleen he could make it alone.

Rob returned to West Virginia in December to celebrate the holidays with his parents, but he spent so much of his time on a fruitless search for Kathleen, he began to feel like a stalker. After a rainy, miserable Christmas, ruined for his parents by his nasty, dismal mood, Rob returned to Puerto Rico.

And it was there he hit rock bottom.

Arriving back at his motel after practice one day, exhausted and wanting nothing more than a hot shower and bed, an envelope postmarked "Steven's Hollow" was waiting for him. That letter came from Lettie Mitchell, not Kathleen. "Katie never wants to see you again," Mrs. Mitchell wrote. "She wants you to leave her alone."

Kathleen had not even bothered to write him herself. She'd had her mother do it for her. Rob tried to convince himself it was Kathleen's loss, not his, but his efforts were unsuccessful.

When the Reds approached his agent about a multi-year contract, it seemed anticlimactic. Rob had no one important in his life to share the good news with except his parents. He had never felt more alone than he did then.

There he was, on the verge of achieving his lifelong dream of playing in the majors, and the only person he wanted to share that milestone with was his wife. But she wasn't his wife anymore. That one-paragraph letter Kathleen had sent via her mother couldn't have been more explicit: she had cut him out of her life completely, just as he'd asked her to do. Rob couldn't even blame Kathleen for his low spirits, though he tried. She had only done to him what he'd done first to her.

Rejection was hard to take, Rob found, when he was the one doing the taking instead of Kathleen. He understood the full depth of her pain only when he experienced it for himself.

But early in February that year, an encounter in a Cincinnati bar transformed Rob's life forever.

Rob had flown from Puerto Rico to Cincinnati that day to sign his first contract with the Reds. After the signing ceremony, he accepted his agent's invitation to stop off at a local bar to celebrate the occasion with some of Cincinnati's front office people and, hopefully, some members of the squad who were in town.

When the current members on the team heard that Rob would be in Cincinnati that day to sign his contract, word passed quickly through the grapevine about the post-signing party. Though a non-drinker himself, Pete Sanders, the team's shortstop, had decided to drop by to meet the rookie he'd been asked to keep an eye out for. Rob's agent and the Reds' general manager were at the bar replenishing their drinks when Pete walked through the door.

Pete recognized Rob McKenzie right away—he was the only person in the bar who looked like he needed a friend. The celebration was gathering steam around him, but Rob sat at his table nursing a soft drink and looking ill-at-ease while he waited for his agent to return. His new teammates had all said hello and had welcomed him warmly to the team, but then they'd wandered off to sit with their own special friends.

Rob had just begun twirling his glass and making wet circles on the surface of the table when Pete came over to introduce himself. "Hi, Rob, I'm Pete Sanders.

We have a mutual friend in Denver, Bill Bell, who wanted us to meet. Remember Bill? He and I are both members of the CCA, a group you might not be familiar with."

Rob smiled and stood to shake Pete's hand. "Nice to meet you, Pete, I'm looking forward to being on the team with you." He grinned. "Isn't Bill a great guy? When he was my batting coach in Denver, he helped me get rid of more than a few nasty habits." He added, "And I've heard of the CCA, too."

Rob had overheard his teammates in Denver mention Pete Sanders, a founding member of the Coalition of Christian Athletes—a name its charter members had chosen for their group because it spoke for itself. The CCA, established by just a handful of professional players, had grown by leaps and bounds since its inception two years before. Their charter was simple, consisting of only two precepts, but it worked. First, the members of the group looked out for each other and their fellow players without pushing their religious beliefs on anyone who disagreed with them. And secondly, they were there to help any player who asked for help, whether that individual's distress was physical, emotional, or psychological.

"When Bill heard about your contract yesterday, he called me, all excited," Pete said. "Knowing I live here year-round, he asked if I'd look you up when you got to town. He's hoping I'll keep an eye on you while you're here." Looking around, Pete concluded that Rob's agent wouldn't be returning to the table anytime soon. "Mind if I sit down and share a Coke with you?"

"Sure, have a seat. I'll even treat you to a Coca Cola or Pepsi. You and I are probably the only soda drinkers in here tonight." Rob pointed at the empty beer bottles on nearby tables and to the men drinking with their elbows on the bar.

Rob signaled the waitress for two more soft drinks.

"I'm pretty plain speaking, Rob," Pete said, settling into the chair next to Rob's. "When you get to know me better, you'll learn that for yourself. So if you think I'm off base here or nosing into something that's none of my business, tell me to butt out." Pete smiled, which softened his inquisitive words. "When I saw you sitting here drinking a soft drink instead of a beer or a whiskey and water, I had to wonder why. Do you dislike the taste of alcohol? Or are you a Christian, too?"

"I am a Christian," Rob admitted, "but I confess I haven't been a very faithful one this past year. I used to go to church every Sunday, first with my parents and then with my wife, even before we were married."

"Oh, yeah? Bill never mentioned you were married."

Rob frowned and sat with his eyes downcast. By focusing his attention on the bubbles in his glass, he avoided looking at Pete. "Well, it'd be more accurate to say I was married. My wife divorced me last fall."

At twenty-three, Rob seemed awfully young to have been married and divorced. Although Pete wondered what had happened, he didn't want to ask. "Hey, this is a big day for you," he said instead. "Signing a contract like yours is the culmination of a lifelong dream. I remember signing my first one. Man, was I excited!" Rob didn't look very excited, so Pete lowered his voice. "Is your divorce the reason you're sitting by yourself and looking glum while everybody else celebrates your good fortune?"

"I guess so. I do feel sort of blue. It's just that nothing seems important without Katie, not even this. And you're right, Pete. I've looked forward to this day since I was about twelve."

"You want to talk?"

Rob had not had anyone to talk with except his parents, at least no one he could trust, since losing Kathleen, who'd been both his wife and best friend. "Yeah, I think I do, if you don't mind listening."

Pete had clear, friendly blue eyes and an open, honest smile. Rob knew instinctively he could place his trust in this guy. "I listen well, Rob," Pete said. "Lay it on me, buddy!"

Seeing the two guys with their heads together, talking so seriously, the other celebrants avoided their table.

Pete listened closely as Rob explained his situation. "Katie and I loved each other so much, I can't describe it," he said, his voice sounding tormented. "What is wrong with me?" he asked, not really expecting Pete to answer. "I threw my wife and my happiness away as if they meant nothing to me."

Rob's voice shook as he described David Mitchell's accident and the terrible things he had done, the awful things he had said to his new wife at the time. He told Pete about writing to Kathleen, seeking her forgiveness. He described his trip back to West Virginia for Christmas and, finally, the note Kathleen had sent him by way of her mother.

"Katie never wants to hear from me again," Rob stammered. "The last thing I said to her was, divorce me. I even told her to let me know when it was over so I could get on with my life. But you know what? My life since then has been no life at all. I messed up the best thing that ever happened to me."

"Well, that part of your life may well be over," Pete acknowledged after a pause. "But only God determines the future. From what you've said, you did eventually attempt to make things right, even though those conciliatory steps weren't successful. Knowing Katie doesn't want to see you anymore has to hurt real bad, and I sympathize with you about that, but I know one thing for sure from personal experience, Rob. You can't handle this by yourself. You need to quit beating yourself up about it and turn your past *and* your future over to God."

"You're right," Rob admitted, "but that's hard to do."

"I know it's not easy, not when you're used to doing things on your own, but it is what you have to do." Pete paused to take a deep breath. "You know something, Rob? Just think about it. You're not dealing with this by yourself anymore. I'm here to help, if you want. I've got six or seven years on you age-wise, and I hope we'll be playing on the same team together for a lot of years to come. I sort of feel like we're going to be good friends." Pete looked around the bar, where small scattered groups of men were clustered together here and there, talking, telling jokes, and just having a good time. No one was paying attention to them, but even if they had been, Pete wouldn't have cared. "I don't want to embarrass you," he said, "but as your new teammate and friend, would you like me to pray with you about this?"

Rob nodded.

"Our Father God," Pete prayed quietly but boldly in the middle of the barroom, "your child, Rob McKenzie, is hurting some kind of bad. He still loves his ex-wife, and she once loved him, too. Only you know what's best for them now. Help Rob embrace the fact that you work in all things for the good of those who love you…and I truly believe that Rob does. Bless his life abundantly…and Kathleen's. If it's your will that they be together again, work it out for them. But if that's not your will, then help Rob accept that, too. Make him a conduit of your love, God, filling him so full of your spirit that it spills over onto everyone he comes in contact with. Show him how to serve and honor you again in everything he does."

When Pete finished, Rob surprised him by picking up the prayer in a soft, shaky voice. "Lord, I give myself to you again. Forgive me for neglecting you this past year and thank you for blessing me, even when I ignored you. Forgive me for the sins I committed in my life and in my marriage." Rob prayed in a conversational tone of voice. "You know what, God? I know Katie doesn't want me in her life anymore, but that's okay. I can accept that. I realize now that what I want and need most in my life is you. From this day on, help me be the kind of man you want me to be."

Tears glistened in both Rob's and Pete's eyes when they looked up at the end of their prayer. When the two men stood, Pete threw an arm across Rob's shoulder and grinned. "You know where to find me, Rob, if you ever need a brother. I'll keep in touch with you and so will the other members of the CCA. In the meantime, look around and see if there isn't someone out there who needs *your* help, okay?"

As Rob nodded, Pete smiled again. "Come on, buddy, let's get out of this bar. Neither one of us belongs in here. I'll give you a ride to your hotel."

*   *   *   *

Running into Kathleen so unexpectedly that afternoon had been nerve-racking for Rob, but that didn't excuse his boorish behavior. Slamming his fist into the back of her car…now that was a juvenile stunt if ever there was one. He wasn't proud of the way he had acted.

Nothing bound the two of them together anymore, but Rob still felt an unexpected tingling of pride when he recalled how well Kathleen had held her own in that encounter. Good for her, he thought—and enjoyed a bittersweet, solitary chuckle. Apparently, she'd learned through the years how to handle herself. She didn't need him or anyone else running interference for her or giving her assistance.

Then why did he still want to be Kathleen's knight in shining armor?

Rob sighed. He had to make her listen to him tonight. He couldn't put the past behind him once and for all without her forgiveness. After today's fiasco— his fault, he admitted—he wasn't sure he could discuss things calmly with Kathleen on his own.

"Heavenly Father," he prayed quietly, "please give me wisdom and patience and love enough to see me through tonight." Rob covered his face with trembling hands and remembered the rest of that afternoon's awful encounter. "Oh, God, please help me," he begged. "Katie's not my wife anymore, but knowing she has a son by someone else just tears me apart."

# Chapter 6

"Mom, is everything okay?"

Kathleen realized she'd been gripping the steering wheel so hard that her fingers had started to ache. Her knuckles were white, and she hadn't even noticed. No wonder Bobby sounded so worried. Deep in thought, she'd been reliving her encounter with Rob. "I guess I am a little tense," she admitted, flexing her fingers and forcing herself to smile. "But other than that, everything's fine."

Three miles from the Habitat house, where they'd had first encountered Rob, she turned into the long driveway of the place where she grew up. Rounding a curve, she saw again her childhood home.

Kathleen slowed her SUV to look around. Two years before her father's death, McCormick Coal Company began liquidating some of their assets in the area, and rumors started floating around that the mine at Steven's Hollow would ultimately close. Kathleen's father, an astute businessman, had worked out a deal with McCormick to buy the two-story mine superintendent's house where his family lived and most of the mountain at the back of their home. It was on the far side of that mountain that David Mitchell, a gifted but amateur carpenter, had constructed a get-away lodge that he and his friends had planned to use as a base camp for hunting and fishing. While visiting her mother this time, Kathleen and Bobby would stay at that cabin.

Lettie Mitchell had made extensive renovations to both the inside and outside of her home through the years. She had shared pictures of her efforts each time with her daughter and grandson, so Kathleen and Bobby knew what to expect. Even so, the house looked better to them in person than in photos.

One thing had been conspicuous by its absence in the photographs her mother had taken, and Kathleen hastened to point it out to Bobby. The coal bin, where a dump truck used to deliver their coal by the ton, was gone. Bobby had laughed at the pictures of Kathleen and her brothers standing in that bin, covered from head to toe with coal dust. She wanted him to see where the bin used to be located, just behind the house.

"You ought to be glad we don't burn coal for fuel in Virginia," she said. "It's dirty and an awful lot of work. When we were kids, my brothers and I had to use a hatchet to break large chunks of coal into pieces small enough for Mom to burn in the stove. The only good thing about that nasty chore was that we could work off our anger and frustrations with each other while hacking away at those large lumps of coal!"

They were half way up the brick walk on their way to the house when the front door opened. Lettie Mitchell rushed out, followed more slowly by Kathleen's brother Brian. Brian's daughters Janie and Sally were last, but impossible to overlook. They were jumping up and down, shouting, "Welcome to Steven's Hollow, Aunt Katie and Bobby."

The familiar warmth of home enveloped Kathleen once she was within reach of her mother's nurturing presence again. They hadn't seen each other for several months, so she ran to her mother, hugging her first. Failing in her attempt to return Kathleen's embrace and hug Bobby at the same time, Lettie Mitchell laughed out loud. "It's great to see both of you," she said, hugging them individually. "I can't believe you're really here!"

As Brian jogged the rest of the way to greet her, Kathleen's smile turned into a full-fledged grin. How she loved her crazy, fun-loving brother! He was a dashing figure of a man, good-looking with short blond hair. Women adored his piercing blue eyes, and the bolder ones had even told him that a time or two. But Brian had more going for him than good looks. His mischievous sense of humor and genius IQ drew people in general to him, not just women.

Kathleen hid a smile, thinking about the single women at church who'd had their eyes on Brian through the years. Oh, the stories Brian could tell, if he had a mind to. It never ceased to amaze Kathleen how far some women would go to attract her brother's attention.

Although Brian refused to divulge information about the women he met, and would never admit to being aggressively pursued by any of them, he did tell Kathleen a story one time about a woman like that. A hypothetical woman, he insisted. An imaginary situation, he maintained. Yeah, right, Kathleen thought.

The woman Brian called her Suzie—which Kathleen didn't believe for one minute was really her name—had, for some reason, decided she'd deliver a hot casserole to Brian's house each night around dinner time. He tried every excuse in the book to get her to stop, but nothing worked. Night after night passed, and casseroles began piling up in his refrigerator and freezer.

Eventually, in a last ditch effort to put an end to the casserole blitz, Brian waylaid Suzie at his front door one night when she was making a delivery. Holding up a hand to halt her entry into his house, he threatened to switch his membership to some other church, or quit his job at the FBI and move out of state, if he ever laid eyes on another casserole—delicious though they were.

The surprised Suzie had blushed when she finally understood how far Brian would go to escape her clutches. She hadn't meant to come across as so brazen, she swore. Things just got a little out of hand.

But Suzie wasn't as hardheaded as she'd previously appeared to Brian. "Don't do anything drastic," she implored, still blushing. "Pastor McGuire would kick me out of church if I caused you to leave." She sighed, suddenly self-conscious. "But let's stay friends, all right? And forget that I embarrassed you? I'll see you in our singles class on Sunday."

And then, Brian later told Kathleen with a grin on his face, the kicker came. As Suzie turned to walk down the steps with her latest undelivered offering in hand, she'd smiled at him over her shoulder with a twinkle in her eye. "Using the money I'll save on casserole ingredients," she said, "I can buy myself an expensive, slinky new dress. I'm warning you now, Brian—it'll probably be red, and I'll wear it on Sunday. Be on the lookout."

Sure enough, the dress *had* been red. And it had looked expensive. But Suzie wore it to church. It only verged on being slinky.

Brian, who had been watching Kathleen in silence while their mother and the girls talked with Bobby, raised an eyebrow, mutely questioning her look of amusement. "Just thinking about casseroles, Brian, honestly. They are just *so* fascinating!" Kathleen confessed, cluing him in.

"You're fresh, Katie," he said, reaching out to slap her lightly on the bottom. "Mom and Dad should've spanked you more when you were little."

Kathleen laughed. Two years older than she, Brian had been the foundation of her support system for years. He, too, was a single parent, his young wife Ellen having passed away eight years ago after a short bout with cancer.

"Hey, Uncle Brian," Bobby said. "I didn't know you were coming to Logan. Cool!"

"Good. I'm glad to finally be able to surprise my favorite nephew."

"Yeah, sure," Bobby scoffed. "That statement's really lame. I'm your only nephew. I hate to tell you this, U. B., but I've heard that one from you so often, I stopped listening years ago!"

"Your mom is sure to agree with that statement. She must have said a thousand times you never listen."

Brian winked at Bobby before throwing his arm around Kathleen and heading back toward the house. "I would've called you before you and Bobby left Woodbridge if I'd known we were coming home, too. But I wasn't sure I could make it till yesterday afternoon. You know the girls, once they found out Bobby was coming to Logan, they just had to be here to show him around. I had just put the finishing touches on a fairly complicated project, so I gave in to the girls' nagging and took time off to be here with you. We left early this morning and only got here a few minutes ago ourselves."

"At least you missed the rain," Kathleen said. "It was some kind of fierce yesterday evening. It was so bad on the Turnpike, Bobby and I decided to spend the night in Charleston instead of coming on home. I lost several hours, and more than several dollars, stopping for the night with him."

"Katie, Katie," Brian teased, "let me tell you how things are supposed to be done. Listen up now, you hear? *Most people plan before they act.* You get it? Plan. Then act. Tell the truth, did you check the weather forecast before you left home?"

"Well...no," she said, confessing her lapse of common sense. Brian and her mother chuckled.

The youngsters had moved aside to talk privately. Janie and Sally had recently begun noticing boys, and that was always a favorite subject for discussion. Bobby, being naturally friendly and involved in a slew of extracurricular activities, knew a bunch of teenage boys who were the kind of guys his young cousins liked most: already interested in girls.

Almost overnight the two girls, especially Janie, had turned into harmless flirts who liked to practice their latest techniques on Bobby. But Bobby was smart enough to know he held the upper hand with the pretty cousins he'd grown up with. He could refuse to introduce them to his friends if the kidding got out of hand. With that always in the back of his mind, Bobby usually dished out as much as he took.

Kathleen and Brian rarely interfered in their children's verbal skirmishes—unless they got out of hand. When the kids started teasing back and forth, they tried to ignore them.

"Bobbb...y?" Janie had finally perfected a fake southern drawl. "Come hug your cousins hello, sweet thing!"

"Sure thing," Bobby said, advancing on her. "I need something new to tell my friends."

"You talk to your friends about me?" Fourteen-year-old Janie immediately abandoned her drawl. "Bobby Mitchell, what have you said?"

"Just that I thought you practiced kissing on lemons." Unimaginative, yes. But on the spur of the moment, the best Bobby could do. He couldn't think of anything original to say, so he fell back on something a friend once said about a girl at school he didn't like. He suspected Janie knew that he was only teasing, anyhow.

"Hug me, Janie. Let me tell them how you hug," he said. "And you, Sally. Come give me one, too." Bobby held both arms out to his side and did his Frankenstein walk toward the girls.

"Grammy, Grammy...make him stop. I'm so embarrassed!" Unlike her usual happy-go-lucky self, Janie whined. "I'll never be able to face his friends!"

Twelve-year-old Sally looked on with disbelief. "Stop it, Janie," she said emphatically, sounding exactly like her father. "Bobby's just trying to get you riled up."

"Oh, go on with you," their grandmother interjected. "Teenagers! I'm not sure I can survive the three of you if you can't get along." Amused, Brian and Kathleen smiled at each other. Their mother liked nothing more than being with her grandchildren.

"Dad, can we show Bobby around now?" Janie asked, already recovered from her snit. "Or do we have to wait till they get settled at the cabin?"

Brian looked at Kathleen. "What do you think, Katie? You call it."

"Go ahead, show him around for a while," Kathleen said. "We'll visit here for half an hour, Bobby, but then we'd better drive on around to the cabin. Don't wander too far."

Lettie Mitchell had shown Kathleen photographs of the alterations she'd made to her house since David Mitchell's death, but Kathleen had never seen the changes in person. She asked for a tour.

Being partial to well-lit, cheerful houses, Lettie had asked her contractor to incorporate lots of glass into the renovation plans, so panoramic views of the ever-changing mountains and wildlife were showcased in every room. Lettie drew Kathleen and Brian's attention to two tail-twitching gray squirrels who were scampering up and down an oak tree just outside the living room window. They could hear the squirrels chattering back and forth to each other as the skeptical pair kept a watchful eye on the three youngsters down by the garage.

No wonder her mother had such difficulty leaving home for the few weeks she spent with her children and grandchildren in Myrtle Beach every summer, Kathleen reflected. She adored the changes her mother's contractor had wrought in the home she'd known so well as a child.

Finishing their tour in the kitchen, Kathleen poured a cup of fresh-brewed coffee for herself, then sat down at the table across from her mother. Once seated, she gave out a deep sigh.

Standing with his back to the counter, Brian sipped from his own cup of coffee. After a moment, he tilted his head to the side and looked hard at his sister. She seemed a little tired to his trained eyes. "Unlike David, I'm not a psychologist," he said, "but from the looks of you, I'd say you've recently had a dose of bad news. You didn't hear anything more from Dan Hoffman, did you?" He knew about the cryptic call Kathleen had received from that lawyer, and how much she'd dreaded coming back to Steven's Hollow.

"No, but I did call his office as soon as we got into town. He was in court and not expected back until tomorrow. I made an appointment for then."

"Well, if it's not something Dan Hoffman said, did you just find out something about a mutual friend of ours that I suspected but was afraid to mention before? Could that be what caused that loud sigh and the dark shadows under your eyes?" Brian lifted one of his ash blond brows as he waited for her answer.

Sensing precisely what he meant, Kathleen bristled. "You mean to tell me that you knew Rob was back in Logan and that I might perchance run into him? You knew I had to come home to straighten out this mess, and you didn't even mention he'd be here. That's low, Brian."

Brian was unaffected by Kathleen's rebuke. "There was nothing to tell, because I didn't know anything concrete. You'd better never play poker, Katie, because it was the look on your face that gave it away. I only *suspected* Rob might be here and that's all I said. But even if I had known for sure, why tell you? Since your all's divorce, you haven't shown even a passing interest in what he's been doing. I didn't see any reason to share what I heard *or* suspected."

That hurt, because Kathleen knew it was true. Wanting Rob to avoid coming to Logan simply because she had decided to stay away herself was absurd. His family was here, for Pete's sake! What he chose to do with his life was none of her business.

She hated having to ask Brian about Rob, but knowing her brother, he wouldn't tell her anything unless she did. "Well, you suspected right. I did see him today, but only briefly. Do you know why he's here?"

Lettie Mitchell, who'd been silent since pointing out the changes to her home, suddenly turned hostile. "There's no reason for you to have anything at all to do with Rob McKenzie, Katie. As torn up as you were by the way he treated you when your dad was dying, you ought to just look the other way if you see him on the street. He didn't care enough for you to come home for the funeral, so what do you owe him? Just finally get the divorce right this time and forget about him."

Finally get the divorce right this time? Had she heard her mother correctly? *Finally get the divorce right?* Kathleen was deeply wounded by her mother's words. Lettie Mitchell seemed to assume that any problem now with the divorce was Kathleen's fault. But Kathleen held her tongue, having learned long ago that confronting her mother about anything rarely brought about a change of heart in the opinionated woman who'd given her birth.

"You said years ago you'd never have anything else to do with him," her mother continued, uninterrupted. "Why change that now? It's as plain as the country white paint on these walls that there wasn't much going on between the two of you, else he'd have been more attentive than he was."

Lettie Mitchell let out an unladylike snort. Clearly she'd said more than she'd planned and was feeling disgusted with herself. She glared at Kathleen. "Well, now, I've had my say. That's all there is to it as far as I'm concerned."

Her mother's anger astounded Kathleen. After she and Rob had legally parted ways, she and her mother hadn't mentioned his name to each other. Through the years, Kathleen had depended on her mom for emotional support, especially when pregnant with Bobby. But in all that time, she had not intercepted one single clue that her mother felt that bitterly toward Rob.

"Rob's not the only one to blame for what happened," Kathleen admitted, hoping her mother might listen to reason. "You asked me to stay home after Dad's accident, knowing Rob didn't want me to, and I stayed. But Rob was my husband then, Mom. I guess he could claim I wasn't very attuned to his needs either."

Brian and Kathleen looked at each other, alarmed by their mother's flushed countenance, which only got worse as Lettie Mitchell became more and more agitated.

"How could he think that about you? That is stupid and ridiculous, and you know it. I don't want you speaking to him while you're here, Katie, you hear me? And that's the end of it. I don't want to hear Rob's name mentioned again."

"Mom," Kathleen began, "you're being unfair. Checking on my divorce is the only reason I came back to Logan. Since Rob is here and the divorce involves him as much as me, at some time or other we'll probably have to sit down and talk about it, whether I want to or not." She carefully sidestepped telling her mother about Rob's threat to track her down that evening. Why make matters worse?

Lettie Mitchell jumped up from the table and left the house without another word, rushing down the steps to where her grandchildren stood talking to each other outside the garage.

Kathleen turned to Brian. "Did I miss something here? I thought Mom supported me. What happened to make her attack me the way she just did?"

"I don't have any idea. Her outburst surprised me as much as you. But let's let that go for a bit. I think now, more than ever, you need to hear what I know about Rob."

Brian took Kathleen's silence as a sign she was ready to listen. "Haven't I always told you that throwing out the sports section of the paper unread the way you do is really crazy? Well, through the years I've read every one of mine from cover to cover. I've kept up with Rob, Katie, and not just because he's my former brother-in-law and hails from my hometown. Rob's one of the most dynamic baseball players of our generation."

Kathleen braced her elbows on the table and rested her chin in her hands.

Brian twisted to set his empty cup in the sink. "After he moved up to the majors the year Bobby was born, Rob's career with Cincinnati mushroomed. He has the highest fielding percentage of any first baseman in the Reds' organization, Katie, and I'm talking the highest *ever* fielding percentage. His runs batted in have been the highest in the league for four years in a row."

"I do know some of that, Brian. I haven't been totally ignorant about where Rob's been or what he's done through the years," Kathleen said, defending herself. "Only someone blind and deaf could miss all the references made to him on TV and in the papers. Not everything's on the sports pages, contrary to what you, David, and Bobby seem to think. I may not have searched specifically for news of him, but I'm not totally oblivious to what's going on in the world!"

"Rob was injured in a play at home plate on Sunday. Did you know that?"

Kathleen's skin paled as blood drained from her face. "He's going to be okay," Brian quickly added. "The injury occurred as Rob raced toward home plate during a rundown. He twisted wrong and strained a thigh muscle, they think, which will require some rest and physical therapy to heal. He's been placed on the disabled list for three weeks, but the team's spokesperson assured the press that they expect him to recover quickly and soon be as good as ever."

As Brian watched, the color slowly returned to Kathleen's face.

"I haven't talked to him myself—you know I wouldn't do that unless you wanted me to—but Rob is thirty-six years old, Katie. I figure if I were in his shoes, I'd come back to Logan, where the media and fans wouldn't hound me all the time, and recuperate at home. He could even receive physical therapy at the hospital here if he chose to. I understand they're pretty good at what they do.

"So, Katie," he said, finishing his report, "that's really all I know. And I know that because, unlike you, I read the sports pages and watch the news on ESPN. I really didn't know for sure Rob was here; that was just a lucky guess based on what I thought he might do when he got hurt *and* the stricken way you looked when you arrived."

Kathleen had never thought of Rob being injured playing ball; baseball was more about talent, physical conditioning, and skill than danger. Yet hearing about his recent injury had affected her more than she would have expected. If anyone had asked before today, she'd have said it didn't matter to her one way or the other what happened to Rob McKenzie.

But Rob's injury added even more stress to an already stressful dilemma. With Dan Hoffman's summons hanging over her head, she had enough to worry about without fretting over Rob. She'd long since severed her marital ties to Rob McKenzie—physically, emotionally, and psychologically—so that wasn't what worried Kathleen. If Rob stayed in Logan while recovering, how could she keep him from finding out about Bobby?

Sensing Kathleen's inner thoughts, Brian reached across the table to squeeze her hand. "Katie, you know how much Ellen and I loved you. We enjoyed having you with us when you were pregnant and after Bobby was born, and both of us cried a little when you moved." Brian smiled, remembering those days. "I remember praying for you and helping you breathe when you were in labor, then sitting up at night with you when Bobby was fretful as a baby. I know I've told you this before, but we missed you both like crazy when you found a place of your own."

He stopped to swallow. This conversation was not an easy one for Brian, but he knew it was time for a discussion like this to take place. "Because I do love you, sis, I'm butting into your business. Please keep an open mind and listen carefully to what I have to say, okay?"

Kathleen nodded. She knew what was coming.

"Rob McKenzie's a superstar, Katie, not just your average, everyday baseball player. He's one of a kind, a megastar. Someday Bobby's going to see his father's name in the Baseball Hall of Fame. Doesn't he deserve to hear about Rob from you before that happens?"

With a knot of guilt clogging her throat, Kathleen spoke in a whisper. "You're right. I should have told Bobby the truth about his father from the beginning, and I promise to tell him everything soon. But right now I need to ask you something else. Please, Brian, just answer my question without teasing. Did Rob ever marry again?"

"No."

# Chapter 7

▼

Kathleen and Brian stared at each other in silence, each consumed by their own flyaway thoughts. They were visibly startled when the back door flew open with a bang, ending their long overdue discussion. Their children rushed into the house, sounding like the Tower of Babel as they talked over each other.

"Mom, you'll never believe this; it's just so cool. You know the Coalfield Jamboree, that theater in town we noticed today? Janie says they're having a string of concerts there this summer featuring West Virginia entertainers who've made it. Brad Paisley will be there tomorrow night!" Kathleen smiled in spite of herself. She couldn't remember the last time she'd seen her son this excited. "Janie told me Uncle Brian stopped to buy tickets as they came through town today. And he's planning to give you a night off while he takes the rest of us to see Brad. How about it, Mom? Can I go? Please?"

Glancing sideways, Brian winked at Kathleen. "If Bobby can't go or isn't interested, I'll find someone else to use his ticket. Maybe a friend of Mom's."

The three kids were appalled. They looked from one parent to the other.

Tossing a glance at Brian, Kathleen pursed her lips. "Gee, Brian, I'd really love a night off—I need to get some work done while I'm here—but I hate forcing Bobby to do things he doesn't want to do. I just don't know. Maybe I should say yes. What do you think?"

A twinkle appeared in Brian's eyes. "I think saying yes would be wise. And if you don't want a three-person insurrection on your hands, you'd better say it quick!"

"Oh, all right. I guess he can go."

"Thanks, Mom," Bobby said, hugging her quickly. "You were gonna say yes all along, so stop teasing." He placed both hands on her shoulders, tall enough now that their eyes were on a level with each other. "Here's a flash for you and Uncle Brian: adults are supposed to at least try to act mature! Ganging up on me's not nice."

Brian smiled. He had known the kids would love attending that concert. They had responded to country-rock music with a passion after taking line dancing classes as an elective at their school in Woodbridge last fall. And they were already fans of Brad Paisley, a talented young West Virginian who'd become quite a country music star in Nashville. Brad's more rambunctious songs, with a beat the kids could dance to, appealed to teenagers as well as older adults like Lettie Mitchell and her friends.

Kathleen was unfamiliar with the venue, even though she and Bobby had noticed the theater in passing. Brian explained that the Coalfield Jamboree concerts, always well attended, usually sold out early for acts like Brad Paisley's.

"The seats I got are actually pretty good," he said. "I figured we'd be lucky at this late date to get even marginal ones. Instructors from a local dance studio will demonstrate the latest line dance steps from the stage an hour before the concert begins, then give everyone diagrams of the steps to take home. And let me tell you, Katie, Janie and Sally are as excited as can be about that!"

Brian seemed pretty excited himself. "Heck," he admitted, "I'm looking forward to the dance demo myself. I'll teach you the most recent dance routines later, Katie, so we can stay a step or two ahead of the kids. You up to learning something new on this trip?"

Laughing out loud at *his* lapse of attention, Kathleen responded, "Just listen to yourself. You think they'll be handing out blindfolds tomorrow night for everyone under sixteen? Pay attention to me, Brian. Bobby, Janie, and Sally will see the same dance demonstration *and* learn the same steps *at the same time you do*. How far ahead of them will we be then?"

Brian sputtered, then laughed. He had spoken without thinking, a rarity for him. "You having a senior moment, older brother?" Kathleen teased. "Just think, you kidded me about not checking the weather forecast before I left home! Well, we have a saying about that in West Virginia. You know the one I mean, don't you? The one about the pot calling the kettle black."

Everyone laughed when Brian grabbed Kathleen around the neck and started messing up her hair. "Say 'uncle,'" he demanded, and didn't let go till she did.

Finger combing her hair back into some semblance of order, Kathleen started to giggle. "Honestly, Brian, you set an awful example for our children. Try for some dignity next time someone gets the best of you, all right?"

The kids looked at each other, shaking their heads. They were used to seeing Kathleen and Brian clown around with each other.

Once they knew Bobby would be going to the concert with them, the girls began begging Kathleen to eat supper at her mother's house that night. Knowing her mother had been out of sorts earlier, Kathleen didn't want to impose. "Mom, are you sure you have enough food for this army?" she asked.

Bobby wanted to stay so badly, he crossed his fingers behind his back. He turned and wiggled them so Kathleen could see how much he wanted his grandmother to say yes.

"Yes, I'm more than sure," Lettie said, pleasing everyone. "We've got enough hot dogs here to feed two armies. I was kinda counting on you staying, to tell the truth."

"Okay, Bobby, you win again," Kathleen said, "but we'll have to go to the cabin first to put our things away. I'll show you the way through the woods when we come over for dinner. We won't be able to stay out late, though, so I'm warning you now about that. I don't want to be walking back that way after dark."

Kathleen attempted to ease her mother's strange mood. "Since you're cooking tonight, Mom, why don't you all have an early dinner with us tomorrow night? I'll fry chicken. That way you won't have to cook before you leave for the concert."

"Sounds good. Eating somebody else's fried chicken is a real treat for me," her mother replied.

"Mom's fried chicken is the very best, Grammy," Bobby said, "and I should know. I'm the world's Number One Fried Chicken Fan!"

His grandmother finally smiled about something. "I guess your mom's fried chicken ought to be great; I'm the one who taught her how to cook, you know."

Brian's family was very familiar with the quality of Kathleen's meals. They'd downed the culinary successes from her kitchen as well as some of her more embarrassing culinary failures. Brian could cook, and often did, but his specialty was carry-out pizza. Kathleen feared the girls would live on fast food forever if she didn't have them over for healthier, home-cooked meals every once in a while.

The two teenagers and their pre-adolescent follower conferred again in the corner. "Aunt Katie, please, please, please let Bobby spend the night here tonight. Grammy's already said it's okay with her, and so did Dad. Since you'll be showing him the shortcut over the mountain this evening, he can come home that way tomorrow after breakfast. Please?"

Bobby, too, seemed eager to stay at his grandmother's that night. "It's summer and we don't have to get up early for school," he said, showing Kathleen that this time he'd crossed all of his fingers, plus his legs. "It'll be a co-ed slumber party. Say yes."

"All right, yes. I know when I'm outnumbered. Let's go now, Bobby. We can come back after unpacking."

Kathleen retrieved the cabin key from a nail inside her mother's back door, the same place her mother had kept her keys for years.

The unexpectedness of being in Steven's Hollow together had transformed the giddy kids into a loud, rambunctious threesome. As Kathleen drove away, Bobby dangled out of the SUV's window, yelling back and forth with the girls till they lost sight of each other.

Within minutes, the two of them arrived at the cabin.

While working with Habitat the previous summer, Kathleen had been exposed to basic building and carpentry skills, learning by observation that digging footers, pouring foundations, and framing and roofing houses were mighty hard work. But thanks to the helpful people she'd worked with on that project, terms like drywall, spackling, laying brick, spreading mortar, and installing insulation no longer sounded foreign to her. The skilled painters on that job had even taught her the best, and neatest, way to paint a room: clean and sand all surfaces thoroughly before starting, and invest in a paint roller with a hard core that doesn't yield. Kathleen had used that valuable information and her newly-acquired skill in redecorating her home office last fall.

So with that small smattering of knowledge in hand, she stepped out of the Explorer to gaze at the well-constructed, attractive cabin her father had built. She was awestruck anew by his carpentry skills. Although the side hollow where it sat was fairly wide compared to other hollows in the county, the cabin was beautifully situated on the lot. To conserve space and make heating and cooling the cabin more cost-efficient, her father had nestled it so close to the mountain that it was hard to tell where the back of the cabin left off and the mountainous slope behind it began.

Flourishing lilac bushes and hydrangeas flanked the front steps. Lush grass grew in the yard, but no further effort had been made to landscape the area. The yard, which blended into the mountain behind the cabin and led to the winding stream across the road in front, delighted the eye in its natural state.

Unfortunately, due to his untimely death, David Mitchell had not enjoyed hunting and fishing and visiting with his cronies at the cabin for nearly long enough. And he had died too young to know his only grandson. Suddenly filled with memories of the closeness she and her father had shared while he fought so valiantly for his life, Kathleen swallowed hard and wiped a tear from her eye. Even if she lived to be a hundred…no, a thousand…she would never regret a minute of the time she'd stayed at home to help care for him.

Unaware that this was an emotional moment for his mother, Bobby walked around the car with a smile of appreciation on his face. "Wow, I sure do like this place. Being here for a while should be fun." He pointed to the far side of a winding lane that meandered through the front yard and crossed the road. "What's that? It looks like a pool of some kind."

"That's a swimming hole your grandfather made by damming up the stream that comes out of the hills."

"How'd he do that?" Bobby asked, more interested in the logistics of the project than the final results.

"Well, as near as I can remember, since it was a long time ago, he first diverted the stream and then dredged out a hole the approximate size of the swimming pool he wanted. I know he brought in loads and loads of sand to cushion the bottom before he lined the pool with heavy industrial-grade rubber. Then I think he anchored the liner around the edges with some special kind of paving stones. The dimensions are about twenty by thirty, and it slants sharply down from the sides so it's about eight feet deep in the middle, which is a nice sized pool. Because the water's constantly moving, it doesn't really need to be filtered, but Mom does have someone come by to clean it out on a regular basis. She's a bear about making sure the water stays fresh and is safe to swim in."

That swimming hole and the water flowing over the dam had been a favorite summertime diversion for the Mitchell children and their friends. Though all of them knew better, they usually succumbed to its allure long before the high temperatures of July had warmed the water to pleasurable levels. Kathleen remembered shivering in the chilly water as they taunted each other. "It's only cold when you first jump in," they'd said. "The longer you're in, the warmer it gets."

Bobby rocked back and forth on his heels, anxious to explore. He wondered why his mother's mouth had widened into a grin, but she didn't explain. Kathleen couldn't wait to see Bobby's reaction the first time he jumped into water that cold! Lips still twitching, she pointed past the cabin and up the hollow to where the pathway disappeared between two oaks. "That's the path we'll take to go back to Mom's for dinner. It takes about twenty-five minutes to get there from here."

Looking back at the cabin, Kathleen admired the way the A-frame with its wrap-around porch and side patio blended into the woods. The front of the house was mostly glass with vertical blinds that could be closed for privacy, but she couldn't imagine shutting out the moon and stars at night. With no city lights to mute their glow, those natural night lights would appear larger and brighter up this hollow than anyplace else she had been. Bobby was an avid stargazer, having learned basic astronomy while working on a Boy Scout badge. One evening she'd ask him to point out the different constellations to her.

She could smell the faint odor of chlorine from the hot tub at the far end of the porch. If Bobby and the girls weren't tough enough to brave the swimming hole this early in June, they could lounge in warmer water there.

"You see that wooden swing and those two rockers on the porch?" she asked. "We're standing here like two petrified trees while they're waiting for us to unpack. Let's unload the car and settle in, then we can sit out here for a while with a couple of soft drinks. You think we'll have time for settling in *and* drinking sodas in the swing before dinner?"

Bobby concentrated intensely for all of three seconds before coming up with an alternate plan. "Let's treat ourselves first. We deserve it. Can't we have sodas in the swing and then settle in?" He waited wide-eyed for her answer.

But Kathleen recognized that look. It was the one Bobby always wore to project innocence, and she saw straight through it again. "Huh-uh. No way," she said, giving him a push toward the cabin.

Later, unpacked and with sodas in hand, they sat in the swing, sipping their drinks and pushing off with their toes just often enough to keep the swing in motion.

Everything seems so quiet and serene, Kathleen thought. She looked up at the mountain soaring into the sky. Soothed by the feelings of peace and contentment flowing out of the hills, she pushed her troubles to the back of her mind. She leaned back against a pillow, where she sat and talked with Bobby while she felt herself unwind. When she finally looked down at her watch, it was time for them to snap out of their lethargy and head over the mountain for dinner.

She still hadn't mentioned Rob or their divorce.

\* \* \* \*

The West Virginia mountains are renowned for their legendary beauty, for incomparable sights and sounds and smells not found in any other place. Hiking there is a delightful experience during any season of the year, but most West Virginians like Kathleen agree that late spring is the perfect time to enjoy their own personal Garden of Eden. The temperature is usually in the upper 70s or low 80s then, humidity is low, and there's an abundance of fragrant wildflowers in bloom.

As they entered the woods, Kathleen pointed to a pile of leaves left over from last fall. "Be quiet, and don't move," she whispered. "Describe what you see."

Bobby saw only a jumble of brown and tan leaves at first, but after standing still for a moment, he detected a slight rustling of the leaves. Then a tiny body emerged. Not wanting to spook the small animal whose back sported such brilliant stripes, he whispered, "It's a chipmunk!"

When the lively animal darted a short distance away, Bobby's nervous start caused his mom to laugh softly. "He's as fast as a gazelle!" Bobby said. "But look, there's another one over there." The pair of chipmunks stood on their back legs and looked around for a minute or two before disappearing into an almost invisible hole in the ground. "Aren't they about the neatest things you've seen?"

At home, Bobby collected and cared for injured animals of all kinds. So he was well aware that even cute chipmunks were wild and not to be tampered with. Seeing the pleasure he derived from that short encounter, Kathleen was delighted anew that Bobby finally had a chance to roam the same hills she'd enjoyed exploring as a child.

With enthusiasm, she told him how, in the fall of the year, she and her brothers had utilized cardboard boxes as sleds. After the vibrant autumn-colored leaves had dropped from the trees to cover every inch of the hillside, they would race their cardboard sleds from the top of the mountain all the way to the bottom, over the same paths they would later use as toboggan runs when it snowed. After two or three runs, the dry leaves crumbled and became so compacted that the hills were slick as ice. Kathleen grinned as she spoke, remembering how much fun that had been.

"Then I'm coming back in the fall," Bobby vowed.

"We might be able to arrange that," Kathleen said, hoping she could bring him back then.

The walk to Lettie Mitchell's took longer than the usual twenty-five minutes because they moseyed along, stopping often to watch squirrels scamper up and down the trees and rabbits hop away from the path. A deer and fawn, realizing they weren't alone in the woods anymore, stood as still as statues, apparently believing their lack of movement would render them invisible. But Kathleen and Bobby saw them and stopped to watch.

They marveled at the twittering of birds overhead, and once they stopped just to hear the wind blowing through the oak and walnut trees that were so thick in some places they blocked out the sun.

As they walked side-by-side, Bobby returned to their earlier conversation in the car. "Did you really love my dad?"

"Yes. Very much."

"Then I don't understand how two people who love each other enough to get married can end up divorced. Since you loved him, the divorce must have been my dad's fault, right?"

He'd asked an important question, which Kathleen answered honestly. "That's what I thought at the time, but now I'm not so sure about that. It was easy to blame everything on him at the time, but the truth is, I made a lot of mistakes, too. When I look back on the short time I was married to your father, I see a lot of things I should have done, but didn't, to make things better between us. So, no, it wasn't just his fault. It was partly my fault, too."

Bobby stopped and laid his hand on her arm. "I'm sorry for being so nosy. I know you don't like to talk about my father, but lately he's been on my mind a lot. I want to learn everything I can about him, but at the same time I feel sorta strange asking my questions of you—you know? Asking about him doesn't mean I'm not happy with you. I'm really glad you're my mom, and I'm sorry I made you cry in the car. I just need to know what kind of person my dad is and what he looks like," he said. "Can't you at least tell me that?"

Clearly, Bobby felt a connection with the father he had never known, even though at this point it was only a nebulous one. He was trying to work through his feelings in the only way he could...by seeking information about his father from his mother. Kathleen gave his shoulder a quick squeeze. "I do understand," she said. "I'll tell you as much as I can."

She began with a quivery smile. "As they say here in West Virginia, you're the 'spittin' image' of your father. In fact, he was about the same age you are now the first time I saw him, and you look a lot like he did then. He had the same thick brown hair as you, and eyes that were such an unusual color of green that people tended to remember them. His eyes have the same gold flecks in them as yours—remember when you used to look in my magnifying mirror and insist that those gold flecks looked funny?" Without a word, Bobby nodded.

"People often say you resemble me, but you really look like him. He was handsome—a word I'm not supposed to use in connection with you, right?—and smart. You get your athletic ability from him, not me, in case you haven't figured that out."

"Yeah, I could've guessed that," Bobby smiled. "You aren't exactly a jock. Tell me something else about him."

"Well, he was one of the nicest guys in our school, popular with all the kids. And like you, he was active in everything. His family lived in town, where his dad owned a big construction company, but your father wasn't a snob. A lot of the kids from Logan looked down their noses at those of us whose dads worked in the mines, but not your father."

"Was he serious, or fun, or moody, or what?"

"Well, he had a keen sense of humor, and I can tell you one thing: he was a terrible tease. Now, who do we know who's like that?" Kathleen said, forcing Bobby to grin. "He never smoked, drank alcohol, or used drugs, and neither did I. You come by your aversion to those things honestly. If you had known your father back then, Bobby, you might have chosen him for a friend. And he'd have liked you, too."

It hurt, digging up old memories to share with her son. But Kathleen reminded herself that Bobby was also Rob's son. In a way, those memories belonged to him, too. She sensed that there would never be a better time to tell Bobby everything…who his father was and about the problem with their divorce. But Bobby sidetracked her with a question she needed to concentrate on, and the moment slipped by. "Mom, if you had to do it all over again, would you do anything different?"

"Sure. I'd do a lot of things differently. But we can't change what's already done. You know that, don't you, Bobby?"

Kathleen ached to give Bobby everything he yearned for—a happy-family kind of future with both a mother and a father at home to do things with—but that was never going to happen. No matter what transpired now about the divorce, there would always be just the two of them: a single mother and her precious son.

"I'm trying to paint an honest picture of your father for you, honey," she went on, "and yet I must also be fair to myself. While I did hire the lawyer and file for divorce, it was only after your father assured me he didn't want to be married. A quick divorce was what he said he wanted."

"Well, he must have been crazy and blind if that's how he felt. You're prettier than all my friends' moms put together." Bobby grinned again. "And once in a while you're even kind of nice…like when you let me get my way."

Like a tenacious terrier with a small, juicy bone, Bobby persisted. "Why don't you date any of those guys who ask you out now? I answer the phone when they call, so I know they're calling for a date, but you never go out with anybody more than once or twice. What's up with that?"

"Well, some of them are all right—even sort of nice—but I've never fallen head over heels in love with any of them. It just seems a waste of time to date some guy I'm not all that fond of just to say that I'm dating."

Bobby was quiet for a moment. "You think you might still love my dad?"

Kathleen measured her next words carefully, not wanting to give him false hope. "I loved what we used to have together and how it felt being with him. Maybe someday I'll meet someone I can care about like that again. But whether I do or not, you need to understand that your father's a part of the past and we have to live in the present. I'm not pining away for romance, you know that, don't you, kid?"

"Well, I can't say I've noticed you wasting away," Bobby said with a smile, widening the distance between them by running backwards ahead of her into the clearing behind her mother's house. "I'll be watching closely for signs of that, though!" Yelling that, he raced off to join Brian and the girls who were firing up the barbecue pit in the yard.

*Kathleen...Kathleen,* her conscience scolded, *you have to tell him who is father is...and about the divorce. You just had the perfect chance, but let me tell you, girl...you blew it!*

"Yeah, yeah, yeah!" Kathleen muttered under her breath, ignoring the still, small voice that she actually agreed with for a change.

# Chapter 8

▼

Kathleen hadn't been to an old-fashioned West Virginia wiener roast in years, but she loved hot dogs skewered on stripped twigs and cooked out of doors. "Hey, Mom," she called, peeking through the screen door into the kitchen, where her mother was slicing onions at the sink. "Are we having s'mores for dessert?" She could almost smell and taste that delicious graham cracker, Hershey bar, melted marshmallow concoction she'd first sampled at the age of six in Brownie Scouts. She couldn't remember the last time she'd fixed one, but ever since her mother had mentioned cooking out, she'd been looking forward to having one again.

"Of course, you know we are. What's got into you, girl? You can't have a wiener roast without s'mores, can you?"

As she helped her mother carry the fixings for dinner outdoors, Kathleen wondered about the nutritional content of a dinner that included hot dogs with chili, mustard, and cole slaw; her mother's baked beans; s'mores; and lots of iced tea. Sweetened. The number of calories and fat grams in that menu boggled the mind. Kathleen figured she could substitute artificial sweetener for sugar in her tea without any problem, but she didn't plan to compromise at all on the rest.

Later, after helping her mother with post-dinner cleanup, Kathleen hugged all of them good night. When she got to Bobby, she grabbed him playfully by the ears and said he'd better behave himself if he ever wanted to sleep over at his grandmother's again. "Ab-so-lute-ly!" Bobby said with a wicked laugh as he ran back into the house with his cousins.

"Two hot dogs, I can't believe it. Why didn't you stop me at one?" Kathleen moaned to her mother. "I can barely waddle, much less walk, and I don't have time for a nap. I need to leave for the cabin before the sun goes down. I don't want to get caught on top of the mountain in the dark."

"Wait up, Katie," Brian said, dousing the remains of their fire. "Give me a minute to wash my hands, and I'll walk you home." Kathleen smiled at Brian's thoughtfulness. She had not been looking forward to crossing the mountain alone.

As they left the yard, the sun was beginning to set, and the mountains were beautiful at dusk. Kathleen inhaled the nighttime aroma of the woods. The smells had changed since she'd walked over for dinner. They'd gone from fragrant, floral perfumes to the muskier scent of fresh green growth and rich dirt.

Sticking to the middle of the path, Kathleen and Brian talked about things they remembered from previous jaunts through the woods.

"Look, don't bother trying to scare me with stories about ghosts," Kathleen warned. "I'm a grown-up now and sometimes write ghost stories myself. Plus, I'm not as gullible as I was as a kid. Man, you and David had vicious, gruesome imaginations. Loose Kamuda, my foot!" she said, bringing back memories of the headless creature Brian once swore lived in the woods behind their house. He and David had convinced her that the Loose Kamuda rose after dark from old, gnarly oak tree roots and searched for little girls to devour...little girls who, strangely enough, they said, looked exactly like Kathleen. That story had kept her glued to the house, too terrified to go out after dark, for several weeks one summer.

"Loose Kamuda?" Brian chuckled. "I haven't thought about that one in years!" With a straight face and tongue in cheek, he added, "The Loose Kamuda still lives behind Mom's house, you know. Way back in the woods, under the oaks."

"Yeah, right!"

They came out of the woods and started walking across the field to the cabin, still reminiscing about the fun they'd had as kids catching fireflies and keeping them in jars for as long as they could before letting them loose. "Katie, don't be alarmed," Brian said, putting out an arm to bar her forward momentum. "There's a truck in front of the cabin, and someone's sitting on the porch."

"Uh...Brian...you might as well walk over with me and say hello. It's Rob."

Ever the protective big brother, Brian scowled. "Rob McKenzie? What's he doing here? I don't feel right, leaving you alone with him. You want me to stay?"

Kathleen knew Brian would gladly oversee her reunion with her former husband if she needed him to, but she didn't. "No, I'm not afraid of Rob. When we ran into him today, he said he'd track me down later. Come on over and say hello."

Rob had been sitting in the rocking chair on the porch for a while, waiting for Kathleen to come back from wherever it was she had gone. Her SUV was parked in front of the cabin, so he knew she was nearby. Hearing voices and muted laughter, he glanced over at the path just in time to see Kathleen and a man he didn't recognize walk out of the woods, their heads close together. Now, for some reason, that didn't sit well with him. Who was that man? Was it the father of Kathleen's son? A strange sensation came over Rob, and after a moment, it hit him: he felt awkward, out of place, jealous. He prayed that those feelings weren't written all over his face for them to see.

Caught in Rob's unyielding, unsmiling gaze, Kathleen approached the porch.

"Katie," Rob said, fixing his look on the man who stood beside her. "Brian?" A smile split Rob's face as his old friend and former brother-in-law strode forward. Rob rose awkwardly, wincing from the pain in his leg. Kathleen hadn't noticed the effects of his injury earlier, but his pain and discomfort were quite evident now.

It took Rob a few seconds to stretch out his leg and stand up. By then Brian had climbed the steps and gripped Rob's hand as if to shake it. But Brian threw his arms around Rob instead, welcoming him to Steven's Hollow with a brotherly hug. Kathleen stood by, wondering what to make of the warm greeting between the two men.

"I'm glad to see you again face-to-face," Brian said, speaking first. "I've seen you several times from a distance, when the Reds played the Orioles at Camden Yard, but that just wasn't the same."

A look of relief passed over Rob's face. "Thanks, Brian. Those words make me feel like I've really come home. I just wish I'd seen you in Baltimore, too."

"Yeah, that would've been fun. But hey, I know you were injured last weekend. What are you doing in Logan?"

"Well, after that injury on Sunday, I was placed on the disabled list. When Dad heard that I'd be at loose ends for two or three weeks while in rehab, he suggested I come home and, if able, keep an eye on the Habitat house down the road for a few days. It's easy-duty work, supervising such enthusiastic volunteers, but my being here allows Dad to oversee a bigger job near the Capitol in Charleston."

"Like almost everyone else, I saw re-plays of that incident on the news," Brian said. "How serious an injury is it?"

Trying to concentrate on his conversation with Brian wasn't easy for Rob; his eyes kept bouncing back to Kathleen. She was more beautiful than ever. Her hair seemed shorter, and he saw no gray in the lustrous brown curls he remembered twining around his fingers when they dated in college. Her face was thinner now, more mature. With flushed cheeks and sparkling hazel eyes she was as stunning as ever.

"It only hurts when I overextend my leg or stand up too quickly," Rob said, forcing his attention back to Brian. "They prescribed muscle relaxers, rehabilitation, and rest, which I can get just as easily here as Cincinnati. I've had physical therapy at the hospital each day this week, and so far it's working out real well. It may not look like it when I'm struggling to stand up, but I am doing better."

"The big question is whether this injury will affect your career. Right?"

"Yeah, but the team's physician and trainer feel certain I'll be able to rejoin the team in three weeks. They just felt it would be better to take care of this now, while it's fairly minor, instead of letting it linger off and on all season. But, knock on wood, they do expect me to completely recover."

Brian sensed he was infringing on the time Rob had planned to spend with Kathleen. He didn't know why Rob was here, or why his sister hadn't mentioned his intended visit before, but they were both mature adults. It was their business, not his. He got ready to leave.

"Stop by Mom's one evening, Rob. I'll be there for a while with my two little angels, Janie and Sally. Bear in mind I'm using the term 'angels' pretty loosely here, although I would love to introduce them to you."

Rob's path had crossed Lettie Mitchell's when he'd visited Logan before. Kathleen's mother was still friends with his parents, but she never returned his greetings when he met her on the street or at church. He reckoned she was still upset about the way he'd treated Kathleen, and in truth, he didn't blame her a bit. He was thinking of that when he responded to Brian's request. "That sounds good, I'd like to meet your girls. But don't you think you ought to clear it with your mother first? See how she feels about it?"

"Why would Mom mind?" Brian asked. His eyes clashed with Kathleen's. They both remembered their mother's strange behavior that afternoon and what she had said about Rob.

Unmindful of the silent communication flowing between brother and sister, Rob measured his response. "I just think it would be wise to check with her first, that's all. I get the impression your mother might not welcome me as warmly as you."

Brian chose to not say any more. He had stayed longer than planned, and darkness would fall before he made his way back over the hill to his mother's. Borrowing a flashlight from Kathleen, he told Rob that he and the girls would probably be in town for a couple of weeks. "It sounds like we have some catching up to do. Give me a call when you're free. If you don't want to visit at Mom's, the girls and I can meet you in town."

"That sounds better," Rob said, watching him leave.

* * * *

Kathleen stood at the porch railing in silence as Brian crossed the field. At the edge of the woods, he glanced back and waved before veering in the direction of their mother's house. When Rob once again claimed Kathleen's attention, he raised both hands in a gesture of surrender. "Let me say right off, Katie, I didn't come here to argue. And I'm not interested in rehashing things I used to think were your fault." He lowered his hands to his sides. "So, with that said, will you sit down and talk with me awhile?"

Kathleen nodded. "Fighting about something that's over and done with is fruitless," she said. "I'll abide by your ground rules, too: no arguing, no assigning blame."

The past few days had been stressful, full of strain, and Kathleen's emotions hovered close to the surface, ready to erupt at the slightest provocation. She wasn't in the mood to debate the past, or anything else, with Rob.

Feeling calmer and less edgy than she'd felt that afternoon, Kathleen mentally patted herself on the back. *I can handle this fine! No problem. This isn't the same hothead I married fourteen years ago. This new, improved Rob McKenzie seems wiser, more mature, easygoing.* Then, as she watched, a slow, lazy, unexpected smile transformed Rob's features, morphing him back into the smiling young man she'd once married. And Rob McKenzie was temptation personified when he smiled at her like that. Kathleen looked away quickly. "Can I fix you something to drink before we talk? I have soft drinks and iced tea, but I can make coffee if you'd rather have that."

"Let's stay outside for a few minutes, then I'll take coffee."

Rob reached for her hand and his voice softened. "Let me touch you for a minute, Katie, while we talk. Okay? I'm well aware that we're divorced and I don't have the rights of a husband anymore, but there's something I've needed to say to you in person for a long, long time. My emotions were in a turmoil for months after I talked to you the way I did in Denver. I'm sorry for the things I said and did that summer that hurt you so much. If I could go back and undo them, I would. I was a real jerk, and I acknowledge that. We had something special together that was a gift from God, and it was foolish of me to throw it away like I did."

Kathleen slowly removed her hand, but Rob never took his eyes off hers. "Please don't push me away or think harshly of me because I brought that up right away. I'm not trying to come on to you, and I sure don't want to start any trouble between you and your son and his father. I just want you to know how I feel. I've prayed for years about what to say if I saw you again, and the message God kept sending me was to be totally honest, to not ignore any opportunity to talk with you that might someday come my way. I won't be trying to control you like I did before, Katie, or play any mind games with you."

The feelings of righteous indignation Kathleen had harbored against Rob for years lessened in importance beneath his honest, atoning demeanor.

The one mammoth, deceitful deed that she had perpetrated herself seemed to tower like a sequoia, casting deep, dark shadows over everything else.

Rob would never forgive her for the underhanded things she had done, Kathleen just knew it. He'd mentioned Bobby's father, yes. But he apparently had no clue who that was. Although there were a hundred questions zooming around in her head, vying for individual attention, one stood out in front of the rest: *How do I confess what I did?*

As they stood facing each other, they discovered that old habits die hard. Without any conscious effort on his part, Rob's hand drifted to Kathleen's shoulder, and she reached up to cover it lightly with one of her own. Not even close to a hug, which Kathleen might have found threatening, it was barely a butterfly touch.

"Before we say anything else, Katie, let me add this. You were my first love, and if the past fourteen years are any indication, I'll probably never have another love like you. I haven't forgotten what we once meant to each other, and I plan to treat you tonight with the respect I know you deserve. What happened between us years ago hurt you, and I regret that. But I'm not the same person I was back then. I won't be doing anything to hurt you again."

"Oh, Rob," Kathleen said, dropping her hand. As her head sagged toward her chest, she shut her eyes. "This is such an awful mess."

Rob placed a quick kiss on the top of her head. "Then let's go make that coffee. When we talk about it later, maybe we'll discover it's not as bad as you think."

No, it's worse than that, Kathleen thought. But with a nod she opened the door. Rob followed her through the living room and into the cozy kitchen.

Sitting at the kitchen table, waiting in silence for the fragrant coffee to perk, Rob's gaze swept over the interior of the cabin. He'd been there many times with Kathleen and her brothers to swim in the pool, but he had never been alone with

Kathleen inside the cabin before tonight. Though young, they'd known even then that that type of intimacy would've been playing with fire.

Although born and raised in the mountains, Rob didn't own a single gun and had never gone hunting. Even so, he knew this cabin wasn't the stereotypical hunting lodge he'd seen depicted in *Field and Stream* magazine. There wasn't a single stuffed deer head, stuffed largemouth bass, or stuffed wild turkey with tail and wings outspread on any of the walls. Instead, Mrs. Mitchell had used native crafts, braided rugs, and colorful hand-sewn quilts to create the quintessential, extremely comfortable, West Virginia mountain home. It looked like something out of *Better Homes and Gardens*.

Twilight eased softly into night outside the cabin. But in the living room, off to Rob's right, soft light from the lamps Kathleen had clicked on as they walked through that room cast a warm glow against knotty-pine walls. Through the front windows, Rob could still see part of the swimming hole and dam.

His chair slid smoothly along the hardwood floor as he moved closer to the table and turned his attention back to the kitchen. Apparently Lettie Mitchell had decorated that room, too, and it was beautiful. Khaki-brown counter tops were complemented by a cream-colored lace window valance with cutouts of bluebird houses running along the bottom edge. Profusely blooming African violets lined the window sill over the sink, adding splashes of color to the predominant wood tones inside David Mitchell's former retreat.

In the waning light of evening, the view down the hollow from the kitchen was breathtaking, serene.

"While I was waiting, I noticed that your mom has kept the dam in place. You think the water is as chilly now as it was the last time we swam there?"

Kathleen remembered that time, too. "Well, I won't be the one to find out, I promise you that. Let's leave that to Bobby and the girls. It was about this same time of the year, as I recall. And it was too cold *then* for me to take a chance on it *now*!"

"It was fun, though, wasn't it?" Rob smiled. "Do you remember how Brian heckled us that last day we were all here together, calling us cowards until we finally jumped in? He was wrong—it didn't get warmer after we were in for a while."

Kathleen added her own recollections to his. "I told Mom about that as soon as I got home that day. I complained that Brian hadn't learned much in his first year of college—he was still a world-class tease. She told me that a high school junior like me and a high school senior like you should have known better than to fall for a common trick like that." She smiled broadly as she related word for word that long-ago chat with her mother.

With only a little encouragement, Rob knew that he could very easily lose himself in that smile. He grinned back. "Your mom was right. We won't let him fool us again, will we?"

"Not about the swimming hole, we won't. But you know Brian—he always has a newer and slyer trick up his sleeve." Kathleen placed a sugar bowl and cream pitcher on the table before pouring two mugs of freshly brewed Starbuck's coffee. Sitting across the table from Rob, she sipped her drink cautiously and considered him over the rim of her mug.

If possible, Rob had gotten even better looking through the years, but his good looks weren't all Kathleen saw as she surveyed him. His face seemed more animated and open than ever, which only added to his allure, and the years had not diminished his manly appeal. The few strands of silver mixed in with the sun-kissed hair falling over his forehead added character, not age, to his likeness. Smile lines fanned out from the corners of his eyes, and those still-beautiful eyes held a calm, peaceful expression she'd never seen there before. Something good must have happened to change Rob McKenzie's outlook on life over time, and Kathleen would like to know exactly what it was.

As she silently absorbed his fascinating appearance, Rob was making an assessment of his own. Kathleen had been the nicest—and the prettiest—girl he had known growing up. But now she appeared to be even more breathtaking and charming than before. He decided on the spot that she was the most enticing and beautiful woman he'd ever seen—and he'd met a lot of pretty women since seeing her last. Kathleen was slim, not skinny. Skinny women had never appealed to him. Growing older and becoming a mother had matured the shape that only hinted at womanhood when she was a girl, leaving her more feminine, more alluring.

Deep in his bones, Rob knew that centering his attention on Kathleen's physical appearance was inappropriate. And more than that, it wasn't wise. He reluctantly tore his eyes away from the lush curves he knew were hidden beneath the t-shirt and slacks that she wore.

Kathleen remembered the tabloid headline she'd seen years ago, and her stomach ached again. Her lips began to quiver. She looked down, concealing her eyes behind tear-dampened lashes. Carefully setting her mug on the table, she stared down at her hands and struggled to regain her composure.

Dismayed by the trembling of Kathleen's lips, Rob reached out to lightly touch the back of her hand. "What happened just then, Katie? Are you okay?" His concern seemed so genuine that Kathleen started to cry.

Not wanting to fall apart in front of him, she blinked slowly and took a deep, cleansing breath. Even with that her voice sounded hesitant. "If we're going to really talk, Rob, and not just touch the surface of the past, there's one crucial question I have to ask. Then there's something vital I need to tell you. But first, who was that woman found in bed with you in Puerto Rico?"

What an insulting, off-the-wall, unexpected, and wild question that was, Rob thought, staring back at Kathleen. Where did she even get stuff like that? That was a dead issue as far as he was concerned, and had been for years. "I thought you understood about that, Katie," he said, since she was obviously waiting for an answer. "There was no woman in bed with me in Puerto Rico. Whatever you might think of me now, you can take my word on that."

"But what's to understand? I don't get what you're saying. It was splashed all over the paper at the time, printed there in black and white for everyone to see."

"Katie...Katie...just listen! The writers for those sleazy papers hound baseball players all the time, and they write things based on nothing. That's exactly what that was...nothing."

*Nothing? Well, maybe not to him!* Kathleen gritted her teeth.

Seeing the way she'd clamped her teeth together, and noticing the absence of expression on her face, Rob figured it might be prudent to explain the situation again. "Because I never went bar hopping with them, the guys I played ball with in Puerto Rico called me Preacher. It was all in fun, I thought, until one time when I was out of town, spending the night with another teammate and his family. That night the guys went too far. They hired a stripper who hung around the ball field to get into my bed to surprise me. They tipped off a photographer and one of the scroungy reporters who sometimes followed the team. In the middle of the night, when they hadn't heard me return to the motel, they all went to my room to check on the woman. When she opened the door, the photographer took a picture of her with the rumpled bed behind her, and the reporter wrote that story. I didn't know anything about it until I got to practice the next day and one of the guys, thinking it was a big joke, told me what happened.

"The story was cleverly written, Katie, but anyone reading it all the way through would have known I wasn't there. What the reporter wrote was true, to a point: there was a woman in my bed. The thing is, I wasn't in my bed with her. And he was careful not to say that I was."

"But if it wasn't true, why would he write something like that?"

Kathleen still doubted his word, and that was trying Rob's patience. It wasn't easy, having to defend himself on that same old matter again. "Since I signed my first contract to play in the minors, reporters have looked high and low for derogatory things to say about me. But I've never given them anything to write about that would hurt or embarrass me or you." Offended by her lack of faith, he said, "You've believed that crazy story for almost fourteen years, Katie? You should've known me better than that."

"Oh, Rob," Kathleen said in a voice that was barely distinguishable. "Let me tell you how I found out about that woman."

As Rob watched, a hot, wet tear slid from the corner of Kathleen's eye to drift slowly down the side of her cheek.

# Chapter 9

Kathleen's eyes appeared twice as large as normal when she raised them to Rob. Something was wrong, seriously wrong, he could tell. His first inclination was to insist that she tell him what was bothering her, but he didn't have the right to demand anything of Kathleen. Not anymore. He wasn't her husband. Not even her lover...the father of her son. "Look, Katie," he said, his voice gruff, "whatever's on your mind right now can wait. Nothing's worth making you cry."

"No, let me tell you," she insisted, reaching across the table for a paper napkin to blot the tears from her eyes. "Remember the last time we were together? Well, the beginning of that weekend in Denver was one of the high points of my life. Up until then I loved you so much I'd have given my life for you. When you said you wanted a divorce, at first I didn't believe you. But when I finally realized you meant what you said, I felt completely crushed...and worse, all alone."

Kathleen knew this time of sharing with Rob was a God-given opportunity to explain and accept, though never erase, their shared, painful past. But she must watch her words; she couldn't whitewash or slant her memories to make herself look better or Rob look worse. They'd been young, immature, and self-centered back then, and they had each made more than their own share of mistakes. But there was no going back and changing facts now. The two of them might never become friends again, at least not the same kind of close friends as before, but now that Bobby was searching so intently for this man—for his father—she had to forge a peaceful, personal relationship with Rob for Bobby's sake, if not for her own.

From what Rob had said, he'd already faced up to and conquered his own personal demons. It was past time for Kathleen to face hers. She had used her bitterness toward Rob to justify decisions she'd made entirely on her own for years. She had to put that animosity aside and tell Rob everything now.

And then…*please help me, God*…she'd have to explain it all to Bobby.

Telling Rob everything wouldn't come easy, but Kathleen just wanted to get it over with now. "For a moment, when I got on that plane in Denver," she began, "I was so distraught I actually considered abandoning Mom and Dad and doing what you'd asked me to do. But when I replayed the words you said at the door of the motel, I knew we'd never be able to work out an acceptable compromise together. With you it had to be all or nothing, now or never, and I just couldn't leave Mom and Dad on their own. They needed me too much, and that was my deal breaker. You and I had talked the subject to death, in person and on the phone, without either of us understanding the other's position. I felt nothing more would be gained by discussing it again. You said you wanted out of our marriage, and I said to myself, I'll give him what he wants. I took legal steps to let you go."

"I was a fool, and I knew it as soon as I walked out of the airport that day. We could have worked things out if we'd tried, Katie. I know we could have."

Kathleen brushed Rob's words aside with an impatient shake of her head. "Rob, I needed you desperately when my father died. Mom was encased in a shell of sorrow that was so thick I couldn't break through. She'd just lost the love of her life, too, only Dad was her lifelong companion, not just a two-weekend husband. Brian had Ellen. David, as Dad's oldest son, was immersed in his own misery. I was alone. Grief-stricken, too, I kept it bottled up inside because there was no one I could share it with. I needed you to help me through that terrible ordeal, but I understood why you couldn't come home at the time."

A look of remorse passed over Rob's face. "I'm truly sorry, Katie, but that excuse was just another sin I committed against you. I could have come home for your father's funeral, but I wasn't ready to face you again. The truth is, the team would have given me as much compassionate leave as I needed; all I had to do was request it. I'm ashamed to admit I didn't even ask. The bitterness I felt toward your father, your mother, your family, you—and yes, even God—overshadowed my reason at the time."

"Well, with the way we'd left things between us, I'm not surprised you reacted that way. But there's more. I wanted to write stories for children, which is how I make my living now, and that meant I had to finish school. So I went to Judge Johnston's office and initiated divorce proceedings as soon as we buried my father. I filled out the paperwork, and after the divorce complaint was typed that same day, I signed it in Judge Johnston's office in front of a notary public. He took my deposition before I returned to school in late August, and he said he'd made arrangements for yours to be taken by an attorney in Denver."

Rob acknowledged that his deposition had been taken at a law office in Colorado. "Why didn't they just take my deposition here when they took yours?"

"Well, for one thing, I believed you when you said you couldn't come home for my father's funeral. When I explained that to Judge Johnston, he said you probably couldn't come back for your deposition either, and that was fine with him. He didn't think having both marriage partners deposed together was a good idea anyhow. The expression he used was 'a divorce is entered into to dissolve a bad marriage, not to shed more blood.'"

"I wouldn't have characterized our marriage as bad," Rob muttered.

Kathleen began to tremble like a willow leaf ahead of a storm. "Well, you did ask for a divorce, Rob, so you must have felt our marriage was pretty loathsome at the time. But I'm not going to argue with you about that. What's done is done."

"Katie—"

"I really don't want to go into it now," Kathleen said firmly. "Please, while I can, just let me finish."

Rob gave a stiff nod of assent. Kathleen steadied her hands by clasping them together in her lap. "After I took care of all the legal requirements and had my statement taken under oath, I left for school." She looked up briefly, unshed tears in her eyes. "Rob, this is so hard for me to talk about. I hope you can forgive what I did."

Rob's expression was puzzled, but after that one quick glance, Kathleen continued. "When I signed up for classes, I doubled my course load so I could graduate early. During September my classes went great, but I was sick a lot of the time. I couldn't eat or keep down the small amount of food I was able to consume. I lost so much weight I thought the stress of my father's death and our separation had weakened my system, or that I had a persistent case of stomach flu. Finally, I went to the free clinic on campus to be checked out. The diagnosis was not the flu. It was more serious than that."

Rob blanched and covered his face with his hands. "I don't think I'm ready for this," he said. "I can't bear to think of you with a dreadful disease. What did they say?"

"They said I was pregnant."

Rob's head jerked back up. "Pregnant? You were pregnant?" His hands began to tremble, and he pierced Kathleen with angry eyes.

"Let me finish, Rob, before you say anything else. I want you to understand why I did what I did. As I left the clinic, I was in a state of shock, but still full of questions. What would I do? Where would I go to have my baby? How could I afford to pay for pre-natal care? I didn't even have a part-time job, so how could I support myself and a child? As I agonized over those things, I passed the college newsstand and saw a picture of a woman on the front page of a paper. I can still see the headline in my mind: BASEBALL GROUPIE FOUND IN BED OF FORMER WVU BASEBALL STAR IN PUERTO RICO. And it was *your* bed they were talking about. Seeing that headline, something died within me. I vowed I'd never tell you about my pregnancy and I'd never come back to Steven's Hollow. I didn't want to run into you, your family, or anyone else we knew. You didn't want me, and I didn't want your pity."

Kathleen's voice reeked of the same defiance she'd felt when she first made that vow. "You said you wanted to get on with your life as a single man. When I saw that headline that day, I accepted the fact that you had."

She dropped her head into her hands, then rubbed her eyes with her knuckles before looking up again. "I graduated in December and went to live with Brian and Ellen in Woodbridge. They'd just moved there to be closer to Brian's job at the FBI Academy in Quantico. Janie was still just a baby, and they had plenty of room for the four of us plus the baby I expected. I found a job in January and worked at home until months after Bobby was born. As soon as my finances allowed it, I moved into a small apartment of my own with him."

Rob's head throbbed, and his hands had started to shake. Thoughts of Kathleen becoming pregnant by another man sickened him. One thing—one question—kept running through his head as she spoke. Totally drained, feeling more than slightly queasy himself, Rob interrupted to ask the question that had gripped his mind so completely it wouldn't let go. "Katie, who is Bobby's father?"

Enraged, Kathleen jumped up from her chair. In a controlled, seething voice, she bit out, "That does it! You are so dense it's unbelievable! Get out of here." Rushing to the other room, she opened the door and thrust her finger in the direction of the porch. "You think I was with someone else while still married to you? How insulting can you get? I'm not even going to ask why you would entertain such an irrational idea, because I know why you would. You didn't stick around long enough to find out what kind of woman I was, did you? If you hadn't jumped ship the first time things didn't go your way, you wouldn't be asking that now."

She fought for control. Why let him know how deeply his words affected her, even now.

"But, Katie—" Rob began, jolted by her verbal assault. His thoughts continued to spin out of control. He'd never been attacked so scathingly by a woman before. "I only asked—"

"That's it! You've overstepped your bounds. Get out! You're just as pigheaded now as you were then." Kathleen's body and her voice were under only tenuous control. Before she reached her breaking point, she pushed Rob again.

Still confused, feeling utterly disoriented, and wondering what in the world he'd done or said that was so grievous, Rob tried again. "Katie—" he said as she forced him out the door.

Kathleen slammed the door in his face and locked it. She leaned against the door, almost in shock, not moving until she heard his truck start up and leave the hollow.

The truth hit Rob before he'd even reached the county road. How could he have been so dense? What had he been thinking? His question about Bobby's father had been mindless and obtuse. Rob pressed his fist against his lips, then shook his head as if to clear it. He hadn't really listened to everything Kathleen said as she'd tried to explain. Even without counting off the days between the time they were together in Denver and the time she'd gone to the clinic on campus, he knew who had fathered her child.

Why, oh why, had he asked who Bobby's father was? If he could hit a delete button and erase that stupid question, he would—the trash bin was the only place for it. Picturing Kathleen with another man must have scrambled his brain, but he couldn't imagine her accepting that as a legitimate excuse, even though it was true.

Clearly, Kathleen no longer yearned for him and what they'd once had together, at least not as passionately as he. But after seeing her tonight and touching her again, Rob wanted her with all of his being. He knew that an unrequited yearning for Kathleen would surely break his heart; he wasn't strong enough to endure such devastating pain as that again. He had to find a way to make things right again with her.

His mother and father were watching television in the den when Rob got home, but he passed them by with a hasty goodnight and went straight to his room.

He sat on his bed for hours, facing the past, and it hurt. As he thought of the years he'd missed with his son, of the experiences they could never go back and relive together, his distress was almost more than he could bear. He bowed his head and covered his face as tears of anger and bitterness and shame poured down his face.

Inwardly, Rob raged. How could Kathleen, who had once professed to love him more than life itself, bear his child and keep it a secret from him? Why would she do such a dastardly thing? Hadn't there been any time at all in Bobby's lifetime when she'd considered letting him—the father of her child—know about his son? She had to have realized that he'd want to participate in rearing his child.

*Kathleen never told me about Bobby...has she told Bobby about me?* That question came to Rob in the blink of an eye, merged in with all his other hurtful thoughts. He couldn't know the answer to that question, of course, but he suspected it was no. If Kathleen had shared the facts of his parentage with Bobby, Bobby would have shown some flicker of recognition when they met.

Rob had once been convinced that nothing could ever surpass the pain he felt after casting Kathleen aside. But what he felt then, as bad as it was, was nothing compared to the pain he was experiencing now. He could never recapture the thirteen years of fatherhood Kathleen had stolen from him.

And then the truth struck home. Part of the blame for Kathleen's actions must be laid at his door. He had set both their futures on a miserable course when he abandoned her in Denver. And there was no softer way to say it...he had abandoned Kathleen emotionally and physically. And not just that one time. Twice. Twice when she needed a friend...when she needed her husband...he had been neither a friend nor a husband to her. And that's what Rob regretted most. For a short while, all those many years ago, he hadn't cared a whit about what happened to Kathleen.

He'd tried molding her into the kind of wife he thought she should be, when all along he hadn't been much of a husband.

Inside, Rob ached. And seethed. But even as he raged over what had been snatched from him without his consent, he had to acknowledge his own culpability for what had happened, too.

There was no going back and changing the past. He hadn't known about Bobby before, but he knew about him now. He'd make that be sufficient. If Kathleen could forgive him for the transgressions he'd committed against her—and he surely planned to beg her to—then he would try to forgive her for keeping his son's existence a secret from him.

Once Rob calmed down and was thinking rationally again, he couldn't get over the miracle that dwelt just this side of his pain. He was a father. He, Rob McKenzie, was Bobby Mitchell's dad.

Rob knew he wouldn't rest until he'd seen Kathleen again. He felt too unsettled to sleep, and a heavy awareness of unfinished business hung over his head. But it was after midnight; he didn't dare go back to the cabin now.

He bowed his head. "Dear Lord, you know I'm hurting, and that a lot of it's my fault. I messed up big time, but please don't let things be so bad that they can't be straightened out. Neither Katie nor I can erase what we've done, but help us find some measure of peace about our situation…and let me be a father to my son."

Rob slept fitfully with his earlier words to Kathleen lying heavy on his mind. When he'd needed her to believe him about the stripper in his bed, he'd been so disappointed by her lack of confidence in him that he had said, "You should know me better than that." But what had he done when he could have shown his faith in Kathleen? He, too, had exhibited a total lack of trust. He could still hear Kathleen's angry words, chastising him again. "If you hadn't jumped ship the first time things didn't go your way, you wouldn't be asking that now."

*Oh, God…I am so sorry.*

\* \* \* \*

Lying in bed at the cabin, Kathleen, too, recalled the time she'd spent with Rob that day and couldn't sleep. She rolled from side to side, from her back to her stomach, and then tried all those positions again. But she couldn't fall sleep. She'd botched things up again with Rob, and that's what was keeping her awake. She'd only wanted to make things right, starting out. But anger overcame her common sense and she'd assaulted him with bitter words. No one deserved treatment like that.

It hurt, knowing Rob believed the worst of her. But she'd been just as bad. For years she believed that he had slept with another woman down in Puerto Rico, leaving her—pregnant and alone—in West Virginia. Which didn't make sense, now that she'd thought about it some more. With the facts being what they were back then, Rob owed her nothing. They weren't married to each other at the time, and she never told him she was pregnant with his child.

On top of that, she'd unfairly convicted Rob of being a thoughtless, insensitive clod. She hadn't even tried to confirm whether or not that tabloid story was true. She'd just accepted it blindly as gospel. And tonight, when he'd tried his best to explain, she hadn't really believed him at first.

Jumping to conclusions had been easy; regaining trust was harder than she thought. Would they ever have another opportunity to straighten things out? Sliding out of bed to kneel down on the floor, Kathleen prayed softly, "Lord Jesus, give me another chance to talk with Rob. He needs to know he's Bobby's father."

\* \* \* \*

At 5:30 a.m., the crowing of the roosters woke Bobby. He'd never been this close to them before, and their racket was enough to wake the dead. He'd been sleeping on the sofa in Grammy Mitchell's living room, so when he heard noises coming from the kitchen, he got out of bed and folded the mattress back into the sofa before dressing quickly and going in to have breakfast with her.

He was glad they were the only ones awake. It wasn't often they had quiet times like this together, especially when Janie and Sally were around. Lettie Mitchell wasn't just Bobby's grandmother. She'd always been his special friend, on the phone and in person.

Sitting at the table, staring into a cup of coffee, Lettie Mitchell didn't hear Bobby at first when he came in. "Grammy, did the roosters wake you, too?" he asked, wiping the sleep from his eyes. The night before, he and Janie and Sally had sat on the porch for hours listening to night sounds—frogs croaking, crickets chirping, and the next door neighbor's old dog snoring under the swing. Brian finally came downstairs at midnight and ordered them to bed. So Bobby was still a little groggy when he walked into the room.

"No, not the roosters," his grandmother answered, raising her head. "I was wrestling with my conscience after I went to bed. That's what kept me awake half the night." Getting up from the table, she fetched a box of cereal from the pantry and a carton of milk from the refrigerator. "You want more than that, my Bobby? How about some toast with strawberry jam from the freezer?" Bobby smiled. It had been awhile since Grammy called him her Bobby.

"Sounds great," he said. His grandmother's homemade bread, with or without freezer jam, was one of his favorite foods. She'd mailed it to him in Woodbridge several times, along with homemade chocolate chip cookies and store-bought candy bars, in what she called a care package.

Pouring milk over his cereal, Bobby said, "Grammy, can I ask you a couple of questions about my dad?"

Lettie Mitchell blew up. Red-faced, she turned away from the toaster. "I told your mother yesterday I didn't want to hear anything more about that Rob McKenzie." She was so agitated she didn't see the look of surprise and distress on Bobby's face. "I want her to straighten out that divorce thing, and this time if it's necessary I want her to make sure it's legal. She's got to get rid of him once and for all. He wouldn't even come to the funeral when your grandfather died. Did you know that? Now, I ask you, what kind of husband was he? I knew a long time ago she'd be better off without him. Why, of all times, did he have to come back here now?"

His grandmother dropped her head into her hands and started to weep, but Bobby didn't hear her sobbing. By that time, he was out of the kitchen, running for the path that led across the mountain through the woods. He needed to see his mother right away.

As Bobby ran, thoughts of what his Grammy said looped through his mind: *Rob McKenzie...my father's name is Rob McKenzie...the man from the construction site who chased us down in his truck...the man who looked sort of familiar.*

*Why didn't you tell me then, Mom...why?*

Propelled by an unaccustomed sense of urgency, Bobby sped through the woods, running faster than he'd ever run before. Fleeing from his troubled thoughts, he raced toward the cabin and his mother.

# CHAPTER 10

▼

The rising sun, in combination with the early morning fog that filtered through the trees, had turned the woods into an unearthly paradise, and everything seemed kind of scary to Bobby, quite different from the place he'd enjoyed so much with his mother the evening before. The forest surrounding him seemed to press closer this morning, and he wanted nothing more than to get to the cabin as quickly as he could to be with his mom.

Rushing wildly through the woods, he didn't notice the signs of another almost-perfect West Virginia day. The sun would soon burn off the wispy fog and warm the air, but for now the trunks of the trees were blurred, and Bobby's surroundings were as smeary as the finger paintings he used to hang with such pride on his mother's refrigerator door his first year in school. He couldn't tell if that was due to the fog or the moisture he kept wiping from his eyes, but whatever the cause, everything in front of him looked hazy, and several times he stumbled over broken limbs that had fallen from the trees.

As he hobbled off the path into the field near the cabin, Bobby stopped to suck air into his lungs. As he did he saw someone sitting on the porch: a man, swaying slowly back and forth in the swing. A gleaming red sports car, which Bobby thought might be a Mustang, sat in the driveway. He wasn't sure about the make of the car; the sun climbing over the mountain reflected off its sparkling surface so all he could tell from this distance was its color—red—and that it looked shiny and new. He liked cars, but too young to drive, he didn't know much about them yet. Some of his friends could identify vehicle makes and models from size, shape, and engine sound, but not Bobby. He was sure of just one thing: that red car did not belong in front of their cabin at six o'clock in the morning.

Gulping air into his lungs again, Bobby limped across the field. As he drew closer to the cabin, he noticed what the visitor wore—jeans, work boots, a dark t-shirt under an unbuttoned, long-sleeved, blue denim shirt, and a Cincinnati Reds baseball cap with #89 on it—but he couldn't tell who it was.

Rob was waiting there for Kathleen to get out of bed and come downstairs, knowing that the first thing she did in the morning, no matter where she was, was head for the kitchen to fix a pot of coffee. As soon as he heard signs of life inside the cabin, he intended to pound on the door until she let him in. He'd been sitting there for almost an hour, and he didn't care how much longer it took. He was determined to talk to Kathleen about what happened last night before checking on the construction site down the road. He'd wait as long as necessary in order to see her. He'd planned to meet the volunteers at the Habitat house at eight, but he figured she'd be up long before then.

Rob sensed movement to his left. When he glanced in that direction, he saw Bobby Mitchell coming off the path on the other side of the field. He watched as Bobby bent over, breathing hard like he'd been running. Rob stopped the swing with his toe, stood carefully to stretch out the kinks caused by his injury and sitting on the porch swing for so long, and started down the steps.

It was a beautiful sunrise, but neither Bobby nor Rob was interested in the beauties of nature that morning. They had more urgent things on their minds. Rob was looking for his son, and Bobby was looking for a fight.

As Rob walked toward Bobby, he felt his chest begin to swell. His heartbeat seemed disconnected to the rapid pulsing of blood in his veins and the frenetic racing of his mind. This boy, the one he was looking at fully for the first time ever, was his son.

Bobby walked toward Rob, recognizing him now as Rob McKenzie, the man his mother had tried to outrace the day before. This guy was supposed to be his father? Well, Bobby wasn't so sure about that. He had heard Rob slam his hand into their SUV yesterday; he didn't want a father with a nasty temper like that.

The whole morning was bewildering, but Bobby figured he had to believe his grandmother; she had no reason to lie about something as serious as this. He'd wondered and fantasized for years about having a real father, but now everything was happening too quickly for him to take it all in. He was breathless already from his frenzied flight through the woods. Seeing his father sitting on the porch—when he hadn't expected him to be there—caused his heart to beat even more wildly than before.

He hesitated, unsure what to do. Meeting his father was what he'd always wanted, but now he felt afraid.

Upstairs in the cabin, Kathleen awakened with a start. Her neck was stiff from sleeping in a strange bed, and she felt cranky from a lack of sleep. She needed to see Rob as soon as she could get dressed and track him down, but what she wanted most of all right now—what she had to have before she could properly function—was a strong, hot cup of coffee.

Despite her heaviness of heart, Kathleen noticed the beautiful dawn. She glanced out the open bedroom window just in time to see the sun creep over the mountain and color the sky a faded purple, muted red, and pale pink. Inhaling deeply, she closed her eyes and completely relaxed. What a gorgeous day this was turning out to be! She wished she could reproduce this brand-new, fresh-smelling morning on canvas with oils. She'd hang it on her wall to look at whenever she needed more peace in her life.

Glancing down from the glory of the sunrise, Kathleen cringed, and the beauty of the day began to fall apart around her. Bobby was stumbling down the path from her mother's house, and Rob was walking toward him from the cabin.

Rob has figured it out, she concluded, or he wouldn't be here now. Her eyes flew to Bobby. "Oh, no," she moaned. Her worst nightmare was coming to life, right before her eyes.

She grabbed a robe and pulled it over her cotton nightgown as she hurried down the stairs. She reached the porch just as Bobby rushed toward his father and thrust out his hands to push Rob in the chest. She heard him say, "I don't want you for my dad, you dumb jerk. You hurt my mother! You didn't want her, and I don't want you!"

Rob grabbed Bobby's hands so he couldn't thrash about or push him again. "Listen to me, Bobby Mitchell, listen! You may not want me to be your dad, but I am. You're stuck with that. And you're right, I did hurt your mother, but that was a long time ago. I'm never going to hurt her again."

Bobby lowered his head, wishing his arms were loose so he could cover his ears with his hands and block out the sound of Rob's voice. But they were immobilized by Rob's strong grip as Bobby tried without success to get away.

"Are you listening, Bobby? I will never harm your mother again, I promise. And I swear I'll never deliberately hurt you either."

Bobby was filled with a deep smoldering anger, but he knew that trying to fight someone taller and heavier—and in better physical shape—was pointless. Rob loosened his grip and stepped back so they could better see each other.

Kathleen heard everything from her vantage point on the porch. Sensing her presence, Rob yelled over his shoulder, "Why don't you put on some coffee? Bobby and I need to talk before we come in."

For a moment, Kathleen resented Rob's dictatorial manner, but her good judgment quickly returned. Rob only wanted her out of the way while he tried to reason with Bobby. Well, good luck, Mr. McKenzie, she thought with a smile, turning away. I'll bet you've never dealt with a stubborn teenager before, have you?

Bobby stiffened his legs and tried to dig in his heels, but Rob took him firmly by the shoulder and steered him to the rustic picnic table near the pool.

Back in the cabin, Kathleen measured out coffee and placed a Sara Lee coffee cake in the oven to warm. Once that was out of the way, she rushed upstairs to brush her teeth and change into jeans and a blouse. "I should be outside with them," she muttered. "This is just as much my business as theirs. They didn't even ask me to stay!"

Bobby, looking past Rob, refused to meet his father's eyes. He was furious with Rob for treating his mother so badly in the past, and for telling her to file for divorce. It was all Rob McKenzie's fault Bobby hadn't had a father of his own all these years. Why did he have to be his father anyhow? Why couldn't he have someone else for a dad, someone he picked out for himself?

Bobby sat at the picnic table, his bottom lip stuck out in a pout. He crossed his arms in defiance and stared over the pool. "Can't you see I don't want you for my dad?" he asked without turning his head. "You never came to visit me before, and I don't want you here now. Mom and I have gotten along fine without you. I don't need a dad, especially not you."

Rob ignored those hurtful, antagonistic words. "Bobby, I'm telling the truth. I didn't know I had a son till last night. I've already told your mother I acted like a jerk when we were married, just like you said. Telling her to get a divorce was the worst mistake I ever made."

Rob paused, and Bobby continued to stare out over the water. "Look, you've never had a father before, and I've never had a son," Rob said. "Can't we start out fresh together? I want you as my son, Bobby, even more than you can imagine. And no matter how happy you've been with just your mother, I think you need a father, too, whether you'll admit it or not. I'm not asking you to choose me as your bosom buddy, but we do have to get along with each other because your mother's a part of this, too. I'm not kidding, Bobby. If you don't cooperate now, you'll be harming Katie every bit as much as I did, and I doubt you want that to happen. Are you with me on this?"

Bobby kept his arms crossed, closing out Rob. Then he turned his head and looked straight at his father.

Rob's eyes never wavered. He knew what Bobby would see, looking at him. He had observed the same thing from the porch as Bobby had walked down the path to the cabin.

Bobby gasped. It was exactly the way his mother had said it would be. He saw his eyes and his ears, his nose and his hair, even teeth that never had needed braces, right there in front of him in someone else's slightly older body.

He wasn't old enough, or of the temperament, to hold onto anger that intense for long, but Bobby clearly was still upset. He tilted his head back and hoped to gain the upper hand. "All I've heard you say so far is that you're a jerk, that telling Mom to get a divorce was a mistake, and that you'll never hurt Mom or me again. But you haven't exactly apologized or asked forgiveness for any of those things...at least not in so many words." He turned a fierce, mulish expression on Rob. "I'm so mad right now I could spit, but Mom says we have to forgive people if they ask us to because that's what Jesus did. The way I understand it, if you don't beg for my forgiveness, I don't have to give it to you."

Rob's laughter didn't sit well with Bobby. It was too loud, and Bobby did not like it one bit. "Look, kid," Rob said, smiling, "your thinking is a little muddled on this forgiveness issue. Take my word for it, Jesus didn't say we had to beg for forgiveness. A person who's truly sorry has only to ask. I've repented to God for all the things you're holding against me, and He has already forgiven me. Since I am sorry for all those things you just mentioned, and I'm willing to say so, will you forgive me, too?"

Bobby said nothing at first, so Rob pushed. "Where's all that forgiveness you were spouting off about? You aren't one of those people who only pretends to follow the teachings of Jesus Christ when it suits some selfish purpose of their own, are you?"

"No, I'm not!" Bobby yelled, then quickly looked back at the cabin and lowered his voice. He didn't want his mother to see how he was acting. "All right," he continued, "you asked, so I'll forgive you. But I'm not forgetting. Don't you ever think that!"

Rob pinched his chin between a knuckle and his thumb, as if deep in thought. "How about you hurling yourself against me when I came out to meet you?" he asked. "I wasn't the one looking for a fight." Now that the worst appeared to be over, Rob didn't mind dragging out his time with Bobby. Even angry, the boy was an interesting kid. Rob's lips twitched; he could only guess at the amount of love and forbearance it had taken on Kathleen's part to raise a handful like Bobby alone. "Don't you think you owe me an apology for roughing me up?"

"All right! I'm sorry!"

Rob's response was more gracious than Bobby's had been. "I forgive you, too," he said mildly. "Are we even?"

"I guess so, but let me tell you something. I can't do anything about you being my father, but I'm not calling you Dad. Don't even think about asking me to. What do you want to be called?"

Rob didn't let his disappointment show. "You know what? It doesn't make any difference whether you call me Dad or not. You can call me Rob, or you can call me Mr. McKenzie, or you can even call me #89. I don't care how you address me, Bobby. The name you choose doesn't alter the fact that I'm your father. There's nothing you can do about that."

As Rob rose gingerly from the table to start back to the cabin, Bobby finally understood the significance of Rob's limp and the number on his cap. He stood there, staring at Rob, and suddenly felt light-headed. He could almost hear a clinking sound as the last piece of his DNA puzzle dropped into place. All the things his mother had said through the years—what his father did, the kind of person he was, and where he lived—fit together perfectly. The picture of his father was complete.

Bobby touched Rob on the arm. "What's your real name," he asked brokenly, "your whole name?"

"It's Robert Michael McKenzie. Why?"

"Are you Rob McKenzie, the baseball player for the Cincinnati Reds?"

"I sure am...your *dad* Rob McKenzie and Rob McKenzie the baseball player, to put things in order of importance." Rob cocked an eyebrow at Bobby. "I know what everybody calls you, you told me that yesterday. What's your full name?"

"It's Robert Michael Mitchell." Bobby either didn't hear or chose to ignore Rob's gasp. "My mom's last name is Mitchell. She's divorced, but I guess you know that. I thought my name—Robert Michael—was just a name Mom heard somewhere and liked. She never told me it was the same as my father's."

*Katie named our son after me*! Rob blinked as his eyes began to tear up and sting. He breathed deeply, then said, "Come on, let's go. The coffee's probably ready, and your mom's waiting for us."

As they walked side-by-side toward the cabin, Rob asked, "When's your birthday, Bobby?"

"May 4th. I was thirteen last month."

Rob smiled, delighted. "You were born on May 4th, thirteen years ago? Unbelievable! That's the day I hit my first major league, game-winning, grand-slam, home run. Well," he added, laughing at himself, "I have to be totally honest...that was my *only* major league, game-winning, grand-slam, home run, and I was lucky to even get that. I didn't realize it was the same day I became a father. May 4th was quite a momentous day for me already; now I know it was an even greater day than I knew at the time."

As they reached the top step, Kathleen came out the door and gently touched Bobby's shoulder. "You okay, sweetheart?"

"I guess so." Bobby hesitated a moment before looking at his mother. She preached and practiced—and even wrote about—patience and nonviolence. He wasn't sure how much of his reunion with his father she'd seen. She didn't look angry, so he assumed she hadn't witnessed much of their encounter. He felt relieved when she turned her attention away from him to Rob.

While Bobby watched, Rob beckoned Kathleen closer. They hadn't talked to each other yet that morning, and Bobby wasn't aware that his mother was the reason his father had arrived there so early. His mom had seemed sort of nervous earlier, when she first came out to the porch, but she didn't appear ill at ease anymore. When his father opened his arms, she walked into them for a brief hug before moving back.

"First things first, Katie," Rob begged, placing his hand over his heart. "Please tell me you're not married, that you don't belong to somebody else."

Puzzled..*and* surprised...Kathleen tilted her head. "No, I'm not. And I don't."

Reaching for her again, Rob held Kathleen close for a moment, breathing in the morning scent of her that he loved and remembered—that mixture of soap, shampoo, toothpaste, and the-woman-Kathleen he had missed for so long. They stood with their arms lightly wrapped around each other, saying nothing at first, as their son looked on with interest.

Rob kissed Kathleen on the cheek, then pulled back, looking down at her from his much greater height. "I couldn't sleep at all last night," he confessed. "I've been waiting on your porch for hours so I could apologize for being so stupid."

"I didn't sleep well either," Bobby heard his mother say. "I felt sick when I thought about the way I behaved. I should have explained everything calmly instead of getting mad. I'm really sorry. Will you forgive me for that?"

"You know I will, if you'll forgive me." Rob leaned forward, almost touching her forehead with his. "I do trust you, Katie-girl, despite how it sounded last night. It's clear I haven't handled this situation well at all, so will you accept another apology for what I was thinking, for that last terrible question I asked? I swear it was only a momentary lapse in sanity and not how I really feel deep inside. Even though I didn't know about Bobby before, I'm mighty proud now to know I'm his father."

"I do forgive you, Rob. I was no nicer than you."

Something seemed to tickle Rob, because he chuckled out loud. "Remind me not to take you on about anything else. For a small woman, you were pretty terrifying last night!"

When his mother laughed at Rob's strange statement, Bobby figured his parents had said about all they could to each other without getting mushy. "Can we have breakfast now, Mom? I have some questions for Rob."

"Oh, no!" Kathleen and Rob said in unison, entering the house. Rob uttered under his breath, "If he's an inquisitive kid, he must take after you." Kathleen grinned and ignored his remark. Rob didn't have any idea how very inquisitive Bobby could be. When it came to that specific trait, Bobby was in a league of his own.

Later, as the three of them sat in the sun-warmed kitchen having breakfast, Bobby questioned Rob incessantly, trying to work through his fluctuating feelings about their new, awkward situation. "Why did you tell Mom you didn't want to be married anymore?"

"I was pretty young then, only twenty-two, and I didn't handle our relationship well. I didn't have any experience, being a husband, and I know now that I was incredibly selfish. I only wanted three things, in this order: your mom, to play baseball, and to get my way in everything. It might not've been true, but I thought your mother loved her parents more than me."

He told Bobby the same things, more or less, that he'd told Pete Sanders when Pete and he first met. "The divorce was my fault," he said. "I told Katie I wanted her to file for divorce. But when she did, and I should have felt free, that wasn't how I felt at all. It was just awful, knowing there was no chance your mom and I would ever get together again."

Bobby glanced at his mom. "When I got up this morning, Grammy was drinking coffee in her kitchen. She didn't sleep much last night, she said, and some of the other things she told me sounded kind of weird. I just wanted to ask her some questions about my dad, but she said she didn't want to hear anything more about Rob McKenzie. Then she really got upset and said she hoped you'd get that divorce thing right this time. What did she mean by that?"

A stunned silence followed Bobby's words. Kathleen was appalled. She couldn't believe her mother had blurted out to Bobby what she had confided in her about the divorce. Kathleen was furious, too, that her mother had given Bobby the name of his father, even if it had been in a roundabout way. That secret was not Lettie Mitchell's to tell.

Rob was frowning when Kathleen glanced over at him. "What did that mean?" he asked.

Kathleen shrugged. "All I can say is, I don't know what it means. I guess that sounds strange, but I really don't know what's what right now. Dan Hoffman asked me to come see him in person about a problem with our divorce, but that's all. I don't know anything else. I'm supposed to see him at two o'clock this afternoon. I should know more after that."

Rob snapped his fingers, suddenly recalling something his neighbor in Cincinnati had told him earlier in the week, something that had sounded strange at the time. "Hey, I think he may have written me a letter, too. My next-door neighbor, who picks up my mail when I'm away, told me on Monday that I'd gotten a letter from a Daniel Hoffman, Esquire, in Logan. I didn't recognize the name, but I figured Daniel Hoffman must be someone running for political office down here who wanted something from me. I thought I'd just drop by his office one day to check it out while I'm here, so I didn't even ask my friend to forward the letter."

"Well, I'll let you know what I find out. Okay?"

Rob shook his head. "Huh-uh. If there's a problem with our divorce, it affects us both. I want to hear what he says for myself." When Kathleen didn't protest, he said, "I'm really pressed for time this morning. Would you mind calling the lawyer's office to ask if he'd like to see me today, too? I'm guessing that's why he wrote to me. If he needs to see us both, I'd rather hear what he says at the same time as you. If you don't mind, that is."

"I don't mind at all. I'll get in touch with Mr. Hoffman as soon as his office opens, then get back with you later."

Watching and listening, Bobby mulled over what he'd heard. *They might not be divorced?* He was on the verge of asking to go to the lawyer's office with them when Kathleen reminded him that he'd planned to go swimming with his cousins at Chief Logan State Park that afternoon.

Rob left, and Kathleen began to worry. What would happen, now that Rob knew about Bobby? She wouldn't mind granting Rob reasonable visitation rights, if that's what he desired, but only if it didn't adversely affect her own close relationship with Bobby.

True, Rob had helped create Bobby biologically. But for thirteen years she had raised Bobby without any other assistance from him.

Their family situation was sure to change to some degree now that Rob was in the picture. Bobby hadn't seemed overly thrilled earlier, when first meeting Rob. But now? Well, now Kathleen's eyes could see how things were going between the two of them. There was no way those two guys would ever let each other go.

# Chapter 11

Rob kept an eye on the road as he talked to the crew installing the front windows at the Habitat house. When he saw Kathleen's Explorer coming down the road, he stopped what he was doing to wave at Kathleen and Bobby. Seeing Rob, Bobby reached across his mom to press the horn, blasting out a loud and different kind of "good morning" to his father.

"Bobby!" Kathleen was mortified by what he had done.

"Sorry, Mom, I couldn't resist it. But he did wave first." Bobby grinned. "Besides, I doubt he'll mind. He'll just think it was you tooting at him."

Kathleen dearly loved her son most of the time, but there were times, like now, when she itched to wring his neck. "It's okay this time, but if you don't show more restraint in the future, I'm making you ride in the back seat when we drive into town." Bobby grinned again. It would take more than a stern warning like that to dampen his buoyant spirits. He'd finally found his father today.

After parking at Wal-Mart, where she planned to shop for groceries, Kathleen used her cell phone to call Dan Hoffman's office for Rob. "Mr. Hoffman is in, Ms. Mitchell," the receptionist informed her. "I'll put you right through."

The lawyer sounded anxious. "Ms. Mitchell, I see we have you down for two o'clock this afternoon. Is there a problem with that time?"

"No, the time's fine. I just happened to talk to Rob McKenzie this morning, and that's why I'm calling. Rob suspects you might want to see him about this problem, too. He missed the letter you sent to his home, but he's down here now and will be for a couple of weeks. Do you need to talk to him about this?"

That statement floored Dan Hoffman. A message from Rob McKenzie via Kathleen Mitchell? Maybe that old reprobate, Judge Johnston, hadn't been that far off the mark after all.

"Actually, Ms. Mitchell, I do need to speak with you both. Will Mr. McKenzie call later, or would you like to make an appointment now for him?"

"He really wants to come with me this afternoon. Would that be appropriate, or would you rather see us separately?"

"To tell the truth, it would suit me better if you did come together."

Dan buzzed his legal assistant, Betty Adams, after hanging up the phone. Betty had started working for the law firm at about the same time as Dan. An attractive, businesslike woman in her late-thirties, Betty took her position at the office seriously. A few years younger than Dan, she was one of the best dressed women in Logan, as befitted her position as legal assistant and office manager for the largest law firm in the county.

Dan looked up and smiled when Betty walked in. Both single, they'd worked in constant close proximity with each other for years. Neither dated much, both being committed to their jobs, but one of their colleagues swore he knew why Dan and Betty didn't date each other: they would be committing "extra-occupational infidelity" if they did. When Dan heard that, he slowly smiled. That could be true, he had acknowledged, winking at Betty behind their colleague's backs.

They did appear to be a perfect match. No one could understand why they never got together. Theirs was a unique and caring relationship. Dan depended on Betty completely at work, knowing if she ever quit her job he'd be lost without her help. She never held back or candy-coated her opinions, which was one of the things he liked so much about her. Unlike some lawyers who feel an advanced degree brings with it omnipotence, Dan appreciated Betty's advice and counsel—which he often heeded—and it showed in her monthly paycheck.

"Betty, something's happened that will surprise even you," he said, then proceeded to tell her what had transpired between Kathleen Mitchell and himself on the phone.

"You're not kidding, are you, Dan? I can't believe Rob McKenzie will be coming here today with Kathleen Mitchell. From the gossip I hear at the beauty shop and around town, they've avoided each other like hoot owls do daylight since Ms. Mitchell filed for divorce."

Dan swore up and down he was telling the truth.

They pulled Judge Johnston's file on the McKenzie divorce, which included the pleadings and correspondence sent by Rob McKenzie's Denver lawyer, and laid it on the corner of Dan's desk. Dan did everything but rub his hands together. He had avoided setting up this meeting for weeks. In fact, he had delayed contacting the parties for as long as he could, he'd dreaded it so much. Now both he and Betty found themselves looking forward to two o'clock.

* * * *

Kathleen finished grocery shopping at a little after eleven, but Bobby, being perpetually hungry, wanted to stop at the Dairy Delight to pick up an early lunch.

"What do you think," he asked, "should we take something by for Rob on our way home? You have to tell him about the appointment with the lawyer, right?"

Bobby's ambivalent feelings about his father had caused him a great deal of anxiety since meeting Rob that morning. He'd wobbled back and forth between two extremes. On one hand, he wanted to see more of Rob and get to know him better. But on the other, he didn't want Rob assuming he needed a relationship with him as his father. Rob hadn't been a part of his life up until now, and Bobby felt sure he'd never see Rob again once he and his mother left Logan to return home to Woodbridge. So he'd better learn everything he could about Rob McKenzie while they were in Logan together. Bobby wasn't exactly sure how to approach the ongoing situation with his father, but he did know one thing for sure. He was a teenager now. He didn't want Rob McKenzie treating him like a child, or even thinking he was one.

Unaware of Bobby's internal debate, Kathleen's first inclination had been to deny his request. But catching the expectant look on his face, she knew his question about lunch hadn't stemmed as much from hunger as from a desire to spend more time with his father. She decided to go along with Bobby this time, but she did issue a cautionary note. "If Rob doesn't mention eating with us, don't mention it yourself. We can drop off his lunch and take ours to the cabin."

Before actually placing an order, Bobby discussed the merits and faults of every item on the Dairy Delight menu, causing Kathleen to roll her eyes more than once at the young cashier who waited on them. They finally left town with five Dairy Delight double-sized hamburgers, two large orders of fries, two jumbo Cokes, one Diet Coke, and four ice cream sandwiches, double wrapped in an insulated bag. "This is what I'd call a man-sized lunch," Bobby said, grinning from ear-to-ear. "It's smokin'!" Kathleen leaned over to ruffle his hair. Her son was a delight...most of the time.

Rob hadn't done much at the Habitat site that morning before leaving for his physical therapy session, which had gone as well as could be expected for the current stage of his recovery, but his leg still ached. The therapist had assured Rob that he would ultimately reach one-hundred percent mobility, but not if they rushed things now. Rob was smart enough to know that three weeks of therapy couldn't be condensed into one, but he wanted to be well today.

He was standing by his truck—the volunteers having just gone to lunch—when Kathleen and Bobby pulled into the driveway behind him. He walked to the driver's side of the Explorer and leaned down to speak to Kathleen. "Hi there, Katie-girl," he said, wearing his most potent smile. "What did you find out from the lawyer?"

Kathleen relayed her conversation with Dan Hoffman to Rob, and made arrangements for him to pick her up at the cabin at one-thirty. "Can we drop Bobby off at Mom's on our way? I don't like having him walk over the mountain by himself, not without me being nearby. You won't even have to get out of the car at Mom's, I promise. We'll just dump him off and leave for town from there."

Fighting to hold back a grin, Rob agreed with that plan. His eyes had flickered over Kathleen's right shoulder a couple of times as she talked, and finally he couldn't hold back any longer. "Did you get lunch in town?"

Kathleen looked around. Behind her back, Bobby had been holding up the bags from Dairy Delight. "I don't guess it'll surprise you to hear that we did, will it?"

"Heck, no. Bobby's holding up three fingers. Does that mean what I hope it means, Bobby? That you picked up enough for me, too?"

Bobby nodded. "You want to eat in the car with Mom and me?"

"I don't think so," Rob said, and Bobby's smile faded. "Hold on, now," Rob continued, "don't get excited. Let me finish. I want to eat with you, just not in the car. I need to stretch out my leg. How about that table out back?"

As Bobby carried the bags of food to the table, Kathleen walked to the rear of her car for the freshly washed "lucky quilt" her friends often teased her about. That quilt had been used as a tablecloth for many an impromptu picnic and was great to bundle up in at some of Bobby's evening games when it got chilly. That's why the name "lucky quilt" had been coined. Kathleen was always *lucky* enough to have something to wrap up in while her friends sat on their cold hands, stomped their feet to keep warm, and complained because they hadn't had enough foresight to bring a warm blanket to the game for themselves.

With Rob holding one end and Kathleen the other, they flipped the quilt over the table. Once seated, Rob held hands with them and said grace.

"So, what're you doing in Logan?" Bobby asked Rob when they started to eat.

"I was injured in a play near home plate on Sunday and placed on the disabled list. Since I won't be able to keep up with the team for at least a couple of weeks, they let me come here for physical therapy and rest. I'm staying with my parents in town."

"What kind of injury is it?"

"A deep thigh strain I got running toward home."

"Does it hurt?"

"You bet. It hurts like the dickens. But it's not as bad as it was right at first. Now it hurts mostly when I stretch the muscles in that leg or get up from a sitting position."

"Where do you usually live?"

"Cincinnati."

"How long've you been playing in the majors?"

"Since the year you were born…thirteen years ago this past spring."

"Did you marry somebody else after Mom got a divorce?"

"No!"

"Why?"

Rob grinned. "You're only thirteen, and I don't want to embarrass you. You sure you want my answer to that?"

"No!" Kathleen said immediately.

"Yeah!" Bobby said, amused by his mother's response.

Rob bent his head toward Kathleen to check her reaction as he spoke to their son. "I haven't married anyone else because your mom's the only woman I've ever loved or wanted to marry."

Warmth spread from Kathleen's neck to her face as she felt herself blushing. Rob shouldn't gaze at her like that! She quickly looked down at her hamburger and took a bite, but the now-tasteless food just stuck in her throat. Rob smiled at her pink cheeks and discomposure, but she was disgusted with herself for baring her feelings that way. She might as well have taken out a full-page ad in the *Sentinel* saying: YES, I STILL CARE!

Bobby didn't notice any of that; he just continued asking questions. "How much longer do you think you'll be playing major league baseball?"

Rob took a long drink of his soda before replying. "You know something? I have absolutely no idea how much longer I'll play. That's one of the things I'll be thinking about while I'm here. When you're on the road as many days during the season as I am, and are as busy as I am in the off-season with endorsements and community service appearances, it's almost impossible to find enough quiet time to prayerfully consider something as serious as life-after-baseball. Ball players never want to think about that."

"But what will you do when you're too old to play ball?"

"Too old?" Rob arched his brows. "Excuse me? You haven't known me very long. Are you suggesting I'm old?"

Bobby knew Rob was teasing. "Well, you are older than Mom. That's almost pre-historic!" Rob smiled. "But you do know what I mean, don't you, Rob? What are some of the things you might like to do after you retire, whenever that is?"

"Well, I'm in good shape physically, other than this minor problem that's bothering me now. I'll probably play a few more years, but I don't want to do what some guys have done and play too long. I want to quit while I'm still at the top of my game, not when I'm sliding downhill. I earned a master's degree in history during the off-seasons, so I can teach if I want. I could even manage a major league team, or coach a minor league team, or go into broadcasting—although I'm not too sure about that. Though I like giving interviews on the radio and TV, and serving as a substitute color man for the networks when the Reds aren't playing, I seriously doubt I'd enjoy being on the air day after day after day.

"If I wanted to get out of baseball and do something else altogether, I could work with my father in building and construction. He has mentioned that to me a time or two when we've talked about the future. At this point, I just don't know what I'll do when I retire. Just thinking about it now freaks me out."

"How do you feel about having me as your son?"

"Bobby!" Kathleen interrupted. "That's impertinent! You know it's rude asking someone what they think about you. Withdraw that question, please."

"Will you just listen to her, Rob? Mom's watched so much Court TV she sounds like a lawyer. But I guess I really shouldn't have asked that, so I'll withdraw the question." Bobby looked back at his mother. "Did I do that right, Judge Mom?"

"You did fine. Just try not to be so nosy from now on."

"It's okay, Katie. He did put me on the spot to a degree, but I'm glad he asked that question. I'll ignore the Judge's ruling and answer it for him." Rob was teasing Kathleen now. "To tell the truth, Bobby, it's all so new that I feel confused, nervous, and almost frightened to death, knowing I'm a father. But without question, I feel lucky having you for my son. You're pretty remarkable."

Giving Bobby his full attention, Rob added, "Your mom has done a great job of raising you. You seem smart, have a good sense of humor, you're respectful most of the time, mannerly, and easy to get along with. I could tell how upset you were this morning, but you didn't hold on to that anger for long. You were reasonable about it, and I admire that in a person." Rob tacked on, "I just hope your mom will let me spend a lot of time with you so we can get to know each other better. Does that answer your question?"

"Yeah, thanks, Rob."

Feeling a little choked up, Rob glanced again at Kathleen. Other than to her, he couldn't remember ever making such a passionate speech before.

On one level, he felt sad. Nothing could make up for the thirteen years of Bobby's life he'd missed. He would see Bobby grow into a man—*please, God!*—but he would never see him as a baby, or a small child, or developing as a preteen. He'd missed out on T-ball, pushing his infant son around town in a stroller, seeing him master a tricycle on his own, teaching him how to ride his first bike. And coaching him in Little League.

On a deeper level, however, way down in his heart where only God could see, Rob was thrilled, awestruck even, knowing he had a son who was the kind of young man Bobby Mitchell seemed to be. It was almost as if a doctor had looked him in the eye early this morning and said, "Mr. McKenzie, congratulations. You've got a strong and healthy son."

With barely a pause to breathe, Bobby continued his interrogation. "So how did you feel when you saw how much I looked like you? You noticed that, didn't you?"

"Bobby!" Rob pretended to fall off the bench. "Give me a break. Your questions are making me dizzy! I feel like I'm watching a tennis match, looking back and forth between your mother and you. All this neck twisting is making me woozy! Have a heart and let me rest!"

Bobby sheepishly admitted, "Mom says I'm awfully curious. She has told me some things about you, but I guess I'm just anxious to ask you the things Mom didn't answer for me."

"Save some for another time," Rob begged. "I'm not leaving here anytime soon." All three of them laughed.

Bobby and Rob disposed of their trash, and Kathleen was folding her quilt when the volunteer crew came back after lunch. Several of them waved hello before returning to work. One of the workmen, obviously the crew chief and a personal friend of Rob's, walked over with a question. Rob answered the query, then said, "Before you get back to work, Harry, I'd like you and everyone else to meet Bobby Mitchell, my son, and Kathleen Mitchell, his mother. There's a remote possibility that Katie might still be my legal wife, but I won't know anything for sure until we talk to a lawyer in town this afternoon. Will you ask everyone to say a prayer and keep their fingers crossed for me?"

Everyone standing around them started to smile. On that note, Kathleen and Bobby left the crew to their work. Rob walked with them to the SUV. "Pick you up in a little while, Katie-girl. See you later." To Bobby, he said, "Goodbye, Mr. Curious."

"Hey, Mom calls me that, too."

Leaning down to see Bobby through the driver's window, Rob spoke across Kathleen. "You're just like Katie was at thirteen. Talk about curious! You should have seen her then. Everyone called her Miss Curious. Ever wonder where she got your nickname? There you have it."

* * * *

Kathleen reflected on Rob's conversation with Harry as she drove away from the Habitat house. What a disaster! She'd been living in a state of anxiety for days, wondering what Dan Hoffman had had in mind when he called her last week. Rob's quick assumption that their divorce might not be on the up and up could very well be right. The two of them might still be married. The fact that she'd filed for divorce wouldn't alter their legal situation.

Kathleen wanted to moan…or scream…she was so frustrated. But with Bobby sitting beside her taking everything in, she settled on clenching her teeth.

She hadn't expected to see Rob again, anywhere or anytime. Knowing he was here and would be seeing the lawyer with her this afternoon only added to Kathleen's frustrations. In the back of her mind, she had assumed—if her worst fears actually did come to pass—that she could quietly file for divorce again and let the court or the lawyers notify Rob when it was over. It would be harder, and messier, divorcing him, as it were, face-to-face.

"Oh, man!" she muttered, more anxious than ever about their meeting with Dan Hoffman.

# Chapter 12

▼

At twelve o'clock on the dot, Dan Hoffman's most pitiful client, Ellis Baisden, dropped by without an appointment, ready to chat with Dan for a few minutes about his case. Dan's plan for a leisurely meal flew out the window as he sat behind his desk, reassuring his client that his personal injury case was solid and that the insurance company should be settling on his injuries soon. By the time a more optimistic Ellis Baisden left happy, it was 12:45 p.m.

After Dan escorted Mr. Baisden to the door and had told him good-bye, he strolled through the empty reception area. Strangely enough, given the number of clients who came through there on a daily basis, and the intense, serious nature of the problems they brought into the office with them, it was a restful room. Its muted gray walls, slightly darker chair rails, and comfortable wing back chairs in shades of mauve and teal were easy on the eye, which was why Dan had chosen that color scheme last year when he'd forked over a bundle to redecorate that part of the office.

Nora Watson, his part-time receptionist, usually broke early for lunch. Dan assumed that was why Nora wasn't at her desk now. Changing directions abruptly, he headed down the hall to Betty's office. Her door was open, but she appeared to be so engrossed by a file on her desk that Dan tapped softly on the door frame to alert her to his presence.

When Betty looked up and saw Dan, she knew immediately what he wanted. He didn't even have to open his mouth. She didn't mind making coffee in the morning because she drank it herself, but she tried to avoid having to pick up Dan's lunch. He sometimes got distracted and forgot to pay her back, and she hated asking for the money.

"What would you like for lunch, Dan?" she asked, giving in gracefully with a smile. She had to pick up lunch for herself, so there was no extra work involved in picking Dan's up, too…this time.

Betty had felt sorry for the crippled man who'd just been in, even though he hadn't had an appointment. One of her unwritten rules for the office was to not sanction drop-ins. Allowing clients to stop by whenever they desired could soon get out of hand. Too many of them, unable to work, had nothing else to do except worry about their pending cases. They'd fill every seat in the reception area, checking with her or Dan at least once a day, if word spread that she condoned it.

But one look at Mr. Baisden's twisted legs and clumsy crutches had brought out the warrior in Betty, and she was ready to take on the insurance adjuster herself. Even though she knew Dan had a lot of thinking to do before the McKenzie and Mitchell appointment, she had buzzed him, knowing he'd take time to encourage Mr. Baisden even if it meant he'd miss out on lunch entirely. Dan Hoffman was a real softie when it came to his injured clients.

"You take advantage of me, Dan," she said, referring to lunch, "but you hit it lucky this time. I was just getting ready to call in an order to Mabel's. I'll pick your lunch up when I get mine."

"How about a fish sandwich and fries and a drink?" He surprised her by pulling a twenty-dollar bill out of his money clip. "Let me treat you." Betty felt like a dog, after having been so reluctant at first to help him out.

Not having to leave the office to buy lunch left Dan free to go over Kathleen Mitchell's divorce file again before the combatants were due to arrive. At that thought, he glanced up from the file for a moment, stared into space, and finally smiled. Perhaps, since they were coming in together, he should start referring to them as former clients rather than combatants.

Dan's law practice consisted mainly of personal injury cases involving automobile accidents, mining incidents, black lung cases, and social security appeals—nothing that was quite as interesting as the Mitchell/McKenzie matter he was refreshing his memory on now.

Judge Johnston had been as sly as one of Logan County's elusive red foxes, and his subterfuges usually worked. But in Kathleen Mitchell's divorce, his manipulative efforts had been thwarted by his unexpected death. Dan could feel himself starting to sweat. He'd pulled his old mentor's coals out of the fire before, but nothing so far would score as high on the Richter scale as this. Rob McKenzie was a baseball superstar and Kathleen Mitchell a renowned children's author. If not handled carefully, this could turn into an explosive situation. He hoped they both were calm and reasonable people, but given the fact that each of them was a celebrity in his or her own field, what were the odds of that being the case?

After Betty returned with their sandwiches, fries, and drinks, she and Dan moved into the conference room and ate their lunch together. As they waited for two o'clock, ever mindful that time was passing quickly, Dan discussed his thoughts and feelings about the Mitchell/McKenzie divorce with her. Not only was Betty his office manager and paralegal, she was his perfect sounding board.

* * * *

Rob's mother and father were at home when he pulled his Mustang into the garage beneath their house. Keeping a vehicle in Logan had been a good decision on Rob's part. It allowed him to have his own transportation there when he had an off-day in his schedule and flew home for a visit.

The plane had certainly been Rob's salvation this week. The Reds' team physician, Dr. Ted Brandt, had scheduled Rob's physical therapy sessions in Logan only after mapping out a treatment program with the local therapist and being assured that Rob could fly in and out of the Logan County Airport for the periodic check-ups he'd set up for him in Cincinnati.

His parents had just finished lunch when Rob walked in. His mother was tidying up the kitchen while his father drank a second cup of coffee before heading over to Charleston.

Delighted that Rob had come home while his father was still there, his mother asked if he'd had lunch. With Rob living in Cincinnati and they in Logan, his parents didn't feel they ever got to see enough of him. Though sorry he'd been injured, they were elated when he decided to recuperate at home.

Rob approached his mother, standing at the sink, and gave her a warm hug before responding to her question about lunch. "Yes, I ate, but maybe you'd better sit down with Dad before you hear where I ate and with whom I had lunch. It's sure to be a shocker." He led his mother to a chair at right angle to his dad. "Sit here, Mom," he said.

Mary Margaret McKenzie glanced quickly at her husband. Rob often joked with them because that was his nature, but he didn't seem to be joking now.

"Oh, my, Rob. I hope this isn't something serious."

"What's the problem, son?" Michael Joseph McKenzie had never had to help his only child out of a jam, but he'd do it in a heartbeat if needed. He squared his shoulders and waited.

"It's about as serious as it can be, Mom...Dad, but it isn't 'bad' serious—it's 'good' serious. I had lunch today with Katie Mitchell—"

Mary McKenzie interrupted, obviously excited. "Katie Mitchell is in Logan? She hasn't been here in years, and I hadn't heard a word about her visit this time." She looked over at her husband. "Mike, how long has it been since we talked to Lettie? I saw her in church on Sunday, but she didn't say a thing about Katie coming home. Did she mention it to you?"

"Not one word. Now, Mary, you know I would've told you something as important as that."

"—and her son, *my* son, Bobby Mitchell," Rob finished. He stared at his parents from under raised brows, trying to gauge their reactions to the bombshell he'd dropped into their laps.

"Katie has a son? Your son? How can that be? You and Katie have been divorced for years."

There was a characteristic bit of imp in Rob's grin when he spoke of his son. "There's no doubt about it, Mom, none at all. Bobby's thirteen, and he's definitely mine. He looks almost exactly like the pictures you have of me at that age."

It was awkward, painful even, telling them why Kathleen hadn't contacted him about the baby. Rob explained the circumstances exactly as Kathleen had related them to him, being careful not to lay all the blame for what'd happened on her.

Mary McKenzie started to cry. She was sixty years old, and for years her heart had filled with envy each time one of her friends had another grandchild. She and Mike had long given up hope on having one themselves. Perhaps she should be angry that Kathleen had delayed so long before telling Rob about his son, but all she could think of was having a grandson of her own.

His parents had never discussed it with Rob, since it wasn't any of their business, but they had worried about his continued lack of interest in romantic relationships since his divorce from Kathleen. They had often shared with each other their fear that he might never marry again. And it wasn't because Rob didn't date. He just didn't date much, and he rarely dated the same woman twice. For a while after his divorce, they knew he'd gone on blind dates arranged by fellow CCA members, and he'd even dated a woman or two he'd met through his church. But as the general public began to recognize Rob more when he went out, he'd become even more discriminating about social engagements. Rob had told them early on that many woman were interested in meeting Rob McKenzie, the famous baseball player. But very few of them were interested in meeting Rob McKenzie, just a man.

Stung by that unfortunate episode in Puerto Rico, Rob felt only contempt for women who hung around baseball stadiums and hotels looking for trophy dates with public figures. He avoided them like the plague that, in his eyes, they were.

To his parents' knowledge, Rob had not been in a serious relationship since his marriage with Kathleen Mitchell ended.

Seeing his mother's tears now worried Rob. He hadn't taken the time to consider how his parents might feel about this new turn of events. He'd been too consumed by his own rampaging emotions. As his mother wiped her eyes with the dish cloth she still held in her hand, he decided that no matter what his parents thought, he would cushion Kathleen and Bobby from any feelings of disbelief they might have about Bobby being his son. For what else could be causing his mother to cry?

Mike McKenzie slid his chair toward his wife and lightly squeezed her arm as he pulled her close and touched his forehead to hers. Mike was a man who didn't like tears, and it scared him to death each time Mary cried. Though shocked himself by Rob's good news, coming out of the blue as it had, he never doubted for a minute the truth of Rob's words. If Kathleen Mitchell had a thirteen-year-old son, then only Rob could be his father. *A grandson! Oh, the joy of it.* He kept his arms around Mary as she wept for the barren years they had been without their grandson…and the daughter-in-law who would have been like a daughter to them if they'd known. They couldn't change the past, Mike knew, but the future could be different if Kathleen would allow them some time with Rob's son.

Rob handed his mother a tissue from the box on the counter. Wiping her eyes, Mary said, "I didn't mean to scare you, son. You must think I'm the world's worst crybaby."

"He is my son, Mom," Rob said again.

"Of course he is," Mary said as a matter of fact, and Rob relaxed. He had feared disbelief for a moment, seeing her cry. But now there was a joyful glow on Mary's face. "Oh, Rob, if Katie would just let us get to know our grandson someday, it would be a dream come true for Mike and me."

Rob's parents arose from their chairs and moved to where he stood to wrap their arms around him. Mike McKenzie was not usually an emotional man; he was a man of profound courage who, next to God, was the backbone of his family, giving strength to everyone. Rob fought back tears when he heard his father whisper to his mother, "A grandson, Mary, our own grandson. What a blessing from God this is."

His father placed his large, gentle hand on Rob's head. "Oh, Rob, we do thank you for sharing that news with us today."

Not knowing what the outcome of the visit with Dan Hoffman might be, Rob kept quiet about his and Kathleen's appointment with the lawyer. He'd share that information with his parents later. Squeezing his father's hand and hugging his mother, he told them only that he had a business appointment in Logan that afternoon and would see both of them later.

*     *     *     *

Rob was not an indecisive man. He'd selected his own clothes and dressed himself alone from the day he started school. But while his mother and father talked quietly in the kitchen, no doubt discussing the news he'd just disclosed to them, he almost called them up to his room to help him choose something appropriate to wear. That afternoon's meeting was not just with Dan Hoffman. It was also with Kathleen.

He settled on a casual look: a pair of sharply pleated khaki slacks with a white short-sleeved dress shirt. He tried and rejected several ties, tossing them aside until his bed began to look like a den of multi-colored snakes. He finally chose a blue silk tie with khaki stripes that went well with his slacks. It was a hot day, but wanting to look his best for Kathleen, he pulled out a navy-blue summer-weight blazer and slipped it on.

Whew, he thought. The last time I took this much time to dress was when I took Katie to our Junior-Senior prom.

*     *     *     *

After putting her groceries away, Kathleen called Brian to bring him up to date on all that had happened since he left her at the cabin last night.

Brian was supportive, as always, but cautious. Bobby and Kathleen had been a tightly knit unit of two for thirteen years. He'd hate to see that closeness adversely affected by Kathleen's current legal problems, whatever they turned out to be. Anxiety over the outcome of her meeting with Dan Hoffman loomed largely over both of them.

So Kathleen was just as nervous as Rob when she finally got off the phone. She took the outfit she'd packed for the appointment out of the closet and held it up in front of her before rehanging it on the closet rod. It wasn't right, she decided, but couldn't pinpoint exactly what was wrong. A red skirt and black silk t-shirt met the same fate. Too casual. The navy blue sheath she usually wore with a thin gold necklace and gold earrings? Rejected. Too dressy.

Oh, no, she thought, closing her eyes. This is beginning to feel like a date.

She reached for the first thing she'd tried on—a kelly-green cotton-blend suit that looked marginally better now that she'd checked out the others. With shaky hands, she slipped on a pair of black patent-leather high heeled pumps and left the room without re-checking her appearance.

There was no time to change outfits again.

✳   ✳   ✳   ✳

As Dan Hoffman closed the manila file folder and set it aside, he glanced down at the inexpensive Timex he wore on his left wrist. It showed 1:55 p.m., and he'd just reviewed the last item in the Mitchell/McKenzie file with Betty. Standing, he flexed his shoulders and moved his head from side to side a time or two, working out the stiffness in his neck and back. He felt more at peace about the situation, now that he'd pored over it with Betty. He was not responsible for Judge Johnston's actions in the Mitchell/McKenzie matter. He'd do what he could to straighten it out, but nothing more was required of him than that.

"Thanks for listening and for your usual helpful input," he told Betty as she rose to leave his office. Then he sat back down behind his desk to wait.

# Chapter 13

Rob arrived at the cabin a few minutes early to find Bobby waiting for him on the porch. In swimming trunks and an oversized t-shirt, Bobby was loaded down with water toys, raring to go.

Rob raised a brow, silently questioning the origin of the strange looking object his son carried around his arm. "You'd better not make fun of this in front of Mom," Bobby warned. "She searched high and low to find one shaped exactly like this. It's one of a kind. Janie and Sally eat their hearts out every time they see it." That object was Bobby's favorite water toy—a grossly distorted inner tube. Sixty percent of its surface looked normal, but one side had a large bulbous protrusion, caused by a weakness in the rubber, that was perfect for sitting on or resting against in water.

Bobby also carried a bag of absolute necessities, things his mother insisted he take each time he went to the beach or the pool: sun block, a comb, an extra t-shirt, two towels—one to dry with and one to lie on, a small unisex change purse of Kathleen's filled with quarters for the vending machines, and a water pistol with a huge reservoir his mother didn't know he had.

By the time the two guys had sorted through Bobby's pool paraphernalia, Kathleen, too, was ready to go. She locked the door and joined them on the porch.

"Punctuality is a virtue I respect and admire," Rob said in lieu of hello. "How sweet it is that you're on time!"

"On time? Right!" Bobby snorted. "We both would've been ready early if Mom hadn't changed clothes so many times. Before you got here, Rob, I was pacing the porch, thinking she'd never be ready!"

Kathleen shrugged. She clearly needed a muzzle for her son.

Rob grinned. "Well, I applaud your final choice, Katie. You look great. If it's any consolation, I'm not wearing the first thing I pulled out of my closet either. For a while I was afraid I'd have to ask Mom or Dad to help me pick out a tie. Can't you just imagine that? Dad would've never let me live that down."

He recalled with appreciation how pretty Kathleen had looked early that morning, standing on the porch in her gown and robe with no makeup. But she was just as spectacular now in that green suit she was wearing. Its color enhanced the hazel specks in her eyes. The tips of her shiny brown curls, highlighted by the afternoon sun, swung loosely around her face as she helped Bobby settle his belongings in the trunk of the Mustang. Rob remembered exactly how her hair had smelled when he embraced her on the porch at the cabin, and he could imagine that scent again, even though she was a car's length removed from him now.

Opening the passenger door for Kathleen, Rob inhaled deeply as she passed. The light fragrance of her perfume tickled his nose, and he smiled. As he helped her find and fasten her seat belt, he looked down. Man alive, he thought, this woman sure looks good in heels. Alarm bells went off inside his head. He was beginning to like everything about Kathleen again. Maybe too much.

Kathleen had been inspecting Rob, too, out of the corner of her eye. He'd been a real looker when she married him, but he'd been little more than a college kid back then. He was dashing now, with the muscular body of a man. There were sought-after male models who'd relinquish years of their salaries to look exactly like Rob, she thought…and she should know. She'd dated one of them a time or two.

Once seated and buckled up, it occurred to Kathleen that her intense emotional reaction to Rob just didn't make sense. She hadn't seen him in years, yet last night and this morning…even now…a strong, sensual awareness seemed to hover between them, keeping her off balance. It was beginning to feel too much like the powerful emotions that overwhelmed them years ago and led them to elope.

Rob looked over just as Kathleen jutted out her chin. Uh-oh, he thought, lips twitching.

Kathleen fixed her unsmiling gaze on him for a moment, then narrowed her eyes. I will not have this, she decided, looking away. I will not allow my heart to overpower my mind again.

It was a short trip to Mrs. Mitchell's. Rob pulled into her driveway a scant few minutes later, wondering why Kathleen was so quiet. He hadn't spoken to Lettie Mitchell directly since Mr. Mitchell's accident—she had snubbed him each time he'd encountered her in town—so Rob felt on edge, knowing he'd be seeing her again. He hoped it wasn't the prospect of a meeting between the two of them that was bothering Kathleen. He planned to be *very* nice to her mother.

As his parents helped Bobby move his things to Brian's vehicle, Janie and Sally came rushing out to meet them. "Wow, Bobby, take a look at that car! A convertible with the top down! That's awesome!" Like Bobby, the girls didn't know much about cars, but they sure liked that shiny red convertible of Rob's.

At Kathleen's request, Brian had told the girls who Rob McKenzie was and why he and Bobby hadn't known about each other before. He had even given them an abbreviated version of Bobby's encounter with Rob that morning at the cabin, which Janie and Sally had seemed to accept at face value. The truth was, the girls could hardly wait to get to the park, out from under Brian's constant supervision, to pump Bobby for more details. They wanted every word, every fact, every nuance, every tone of voice reported to them—uncensored—by Bobby himself.

Bobby took charge, introducing Rob to Janie and Sally as if he'd been presenting his father to people for years, which pleased Kathleen. Janie blushed when Rob reminded her that the last time he'd seen her she was a newborn in diapers. He smiled at Sally, who was shy around him. "You'll have to show me a picture of you as an infant, Sally, so I can compare you two."

Bobby waited a moment while his cousins told Rob what they'd been doing since coming to town, then grabbed Rob's arm to lead him into the house. "Grammy, Grammy," he called, pushing open the door, "I have a surprise for you." Kathleen's hand curled around Rob's, lending support. She knew now how her mother felt about him. He lightly squeezed her hand in silent thanks.

Lettie Mitchell came out of the kitchen, wiping her wet hands on her apron and carrying the aroma of fresh-baked chocolate chip cookies with her. Brian had warned her earlier that Rob and Kathleen would be dropping Bobby off, and she had known from past experience that Rob would come in first to say hello. He always had before.

Lettie dreaded this encounter. But after grappling with the devil again last night, she was determined to make things right with Rob and Kathleen today. She'd known from the beginning that what she did to them was wrong; that, inevitably, she'd have to account for her despicable behavior.

Bobby was unaware of the tension filling the room. "Grammy," he said proudly, "this is my father."

Mrs. Mitchell's mouth moved slightly, but nothing came out. Seeing Rob in her home again, and thinking of all the years that had passed since he'd been there before, she felt the enormity of what she had done. Her face started to crumple, and she hesitated before speaking. "Rob," she finally said, "I know you have an appointment in town and can't stay long, but I have something to give you while you're here. Can I speak to you alone for a moment?"

Surprised, Rob glanced at Kathleen. She didn't seem to know what was going on either. After a slight shrug, he nodded to Mrs. Mitchell and followed her into the kitchen. Kathleen released his hand and walked into the living room with Brian and the children to give her mother and Rob some privacy.

Once they were alone, Mrs. Mitchell reached into her apron pocket, pulled out a packet of letters, and held it out to Rob. Rob reeled from the impact of what he saw. Unable to speak, he looked hard at Mrs. Mitchell. He recognized immediately what she clasped in her hand.

*Betrayed...betrayed...betrayed...betrayed.* The word reverberated in Rob's head, drowning out all other sights and sounds, making him feel dizzy. Every one of the unopened, unread letters he'd written fourteen years ago to Kathleen was there, held together with a rubber band that was as old, dried out, and brittle as the envelopes encasing his notes.

What Lettie Mitchell held in her hand required no explanation. Rob knew exactly what it was, and he knew what it meant. Kathleen had not seen any of the letters he'd written her. Mrs. Mitchell had apparently kept them from her daughter. And even though she'd given him the cold shoulder each time she'd seen him in town, he never suspected her duplicity.

Tears oozed slowly from the corners of Mrs. Mitchell's eyes. "I owe you and Katie an apology, Rob. I hope you won't hold it against me, what I did. But I won't blame you if you do. My only excuse is that Katie was hurting so much back then, I wanted to make things easier for her."

Rob closed his eyes and swayed. His skin paled, and his heart began to race.

"I'm not asking you to forgive me," Mrs. Mitchell continued. "To be honest, I don't see how you could. I've had a hard time myself, coming to grips with what I did. If it counts for anything, I haven't forgiven myself either." She thrust the letters out again to Rob, urging him to take them. "I couldn't make myself destroy your letters, even though I kept them from Katie. Every one of them is here. I need to give them back."

As Rob took the letters, all he could do was stare at Lettie Mitchell. Her emotional pain seemed to be genuine, and he believed her when she said she'd been truly repentant for a number of years. Even in the midst of his distress, he could empathize with that. In the split second it took to absorb her woeful appearance, Rob recalled the words Bobby had said to him that morning about forgiveness.

Then, almost as if he, too, were in the room with them, Pete Sanders' words came back to Rob, assuring him that God was in control. Finally, he remembered his own feelings of relief when Kathleen had absolved him for the way he'd treated her.

Rob was a man who knew how good forgiveness felt, especially to someone like himself who knew he hadn't earned it.

He took the packet of letters from Mrs. Mitchell and slipped them into a pocket inside his jacket. Wrapping his arms around his still-weeping ex-mother-in-law, Rob briefly closed his eyes. "I'm a forgiven man myself, Mrs. Mitchell, so how could I not extend that same pardon to you? I do forgive you, but I can't understand why this happened. I just wish we could go back fourteen years and make it all go away."

Rob knew offering Lettie Mitchell his forgiveness was one of the hardest thing he'd ever have to do, and right then it wasn't something he even wanted to do, truth be told. But as he spoke those cleansing words of pardon, a feeling of rightness flowed into his soul.

Rob's words and the caring look he turned on her melted the ice that had chilled Lettie Mitchell's spirit for so many years. It disappeared completely, too warmed by love and compassion to linger any longer.

There was nothing left for them to say.

With a quiet, "Thank you, Rob," Mrs. Mitchell turned and left the kitchen. In the living room, she embraced her daughter. "I'm truly sorry, Katie. You were a great daughter, staying home and helping me when your father was hurt. I should never have done what I did."

Kathleen felt utterly confused. "What's going on?" she asked her mother.

"I'd like Rob to tell you everything, but only when he thinks the time is right. It's up to him now."

Kathleen wanted to pursue the matter, but Rob placed his hand on her arm and squeezed it once in warning. "Come on, Katie, let's go. We don't want to keep Dan Hoffman waiting."

Kathleen and Rob returned to his car without mentioning the matter again, but Kathleen felt totally bewildered. "Rob? What happened in the kitchen between you and Mom?"

"I can't talk about it right now," he said, "so please trust me and don't ask any questions. What happened was a total shock. I need to think it through before I can share it."

Her calm acceptance of his words surprised even Kathleen, who usually questioned everything. "I do trust you...I think. But I'm really curious about what happened back there."

"Who wouldn't be?" Rob said, shaking his head. He ran a knuckle down the side of her face in a soft, assuring caress. "I'm not saying I won't tell you about it, Katie, I'm just asking you to hold off for a while, that's all."

Kathleen nodded. Rob placed his key in the ignition and started the car. They made the short trip to Logan in silence, and with every revolution of the Mustang's tires on the road, Rob agonized about the situation.

*Kathleen never saw his letters.*

During all those years, when he'd felt so rejected, she hadn't even known he'd written to her!

# Chapter 14

▼

Dan Hoffman rose from his chair to shake hands with Kathleen and Rob as Betty ushered them into his office. "Ask Nora to hold my calls, then come back," he said, as Betty turned to leave the room. "I'd like you to sit in on this meeting."

Betty nodded and left the room.

Kathleen remembered Dan, who was just out of law school and working as Judge Johnston's law clerk when she started divorce proceedings. He'd been very solicitous during her deposition with Judge Johnston, a time when she'd needed some kindly attention. He was just as impressive now as back then. Dan even looked like a successful attorney, with fashionably-styled short black hair that was just beginning to turn gray at the temple, stylish no-line bifocals, and a friendly manner that immediately put them at ease. He appeared dignified, seasoned by time. But beneath the surface of the man, Kathleen recognized the strong, fiery soul of a zealot. Slowly taking his measure, she decided that Dan Hoffman was the kind of lawyer who'd dig in his heels and fight to the end for the rights of a client. She would not want to face him in a courtroom—or across a negotiating table.

"May I get you something to drink?" Betty asked, returning to the office and closing the door behind her. "Soft drink? Juice? Coffee? Or water?"

"Just water for me, please," Kathleen requested.

"Water does it for me, too," Rob said, smiling at Betty. "Thanks."

Betty poured a glass of ice water for each of them—and one for Dan—from the cut glass pitcher that sat in a place of honor on the walnut credenza just inside the door. Kathleen recognized the pitcher, and the antique glasses, as well. Judge Johnston had pointed them out to her right before he took her deposition years ago. As she recalled, he'd found them at a local antique shop and had mentioned at the time how blessed he'd felt, being able to acquire a complete and undamaged set. Kathleen smiled, remembering that day. He had been a dapper, elegant man, Judge Johnston. Everything he did was first-class, from his engraved letterhead and envelopes down to the authentic oriental rugs that still graced Dan's polished hardwood floor.

When everyone was settled, Dan cleared his throat. "Mr. McKenzie and Ms. Mitchell, would either of you object if we record this conversation?" He pointed to a small cassette recorder on the corner of his desk.

"Not me," Rob said. "How about you, Katie?"

"No, that's fine."

Dan looked down to consult what appeared to be a list of questions he had previously prepared. It became apparent from that and the tape recorder, now running, that this would not be the informal meeting Kathleen had envisioned.

The lawyer's first question was for her. "Ms. Mitchell, did you have any contact—letter, telephone call, personal visit—from Judge Benjamin Johnston after the birth of your son?"

"No, the last time I heard from Judge Johnston was a few days before I went back to college. Shortly after I filed for divorce."

"How about you, Mr. McKenzie?"

"No, I never had any contact with Judge Johnston at all. My deposition was taken by another lawyer."

"Mr. McKenzie, have you remarried since your separation from Kathleen Mitchell?"

Wondering what that had to do with today's meeting, Rob answered no.

"Ms. Mitchell, have you remarried since your separation from Rob McKenzie?"

"No, I haven't."

"Then that's good. If either of you had married again, this situation would be even worse than it already is. I'll be blunt—the fact that neither of you has remarried makes this a bad news/good news situation. The bad news is, you are not legally divorced. The good news is that the matter can be expeditiously remedied."

Rob almost choked. "Not divorced? You mean, not divorced *at all?*" Shocked, he turned around and looked at Kathleen. Even though he'd mentioned the prospect of that at the Habitat house, he'd only considered it to be a remote possibility, not really likely at all. He could hardly believe what he'd heard. "Did you know about this, Katie?"

"No. I told you everything I knew this morning. Mr. Hoffman told me on the phone last week that there was a problem with the legality of the divorce, but that's all. Although I feared it could be something like this, I didn't know—and, strangely enough, didn't ask—exactly what the problem was."

"This is preposterous," Rob said. "I know for a fact that Katie filed for divorce; I gave my deposition in Denver. I can't believe we're still legally married and nobody mentioned it to us before now. How could something like this happen?"

"I've wondered that more than a time or two myself, Mr. McKenzie, I surely have. I'll go over everything with you, of course, but let me tell you something about Judge Johnston first. You still won't approve of his actions after hearing the kind of man he was, but it might give you some insight into why he acted as he did."

Dan leaned forward to rest his forearms on his desk. He re-stacked a few sheets of paper while he organized his thoughts. Only then did he look up. "Benjamin Johnston was a lawyer here in Logan County for twenty-five years before being appointed as a Circuit Court Judge. I'm sure you remember him, Mr. McKenzie, even though you didn't see him during the pendency of your divorce. Distinguished looking and debonair, he was right much of a fixture around town—well-respected, fair, and as tough as shoe leather in court. He was the kind of lawyer you wanted on your side if you were in serious trouble, because he fought tooth and nail for his clients. I learned a lot from him, including compassion for the good people in this county, when I served as his clerk."

Dan's inflection and the slight smile that flittered across his face from time to time as he talked about his former mentor led Rob and Kathleen to believe he had held the older gentleman in high esteem. "When Judge Johnston reached mandatory retirement age and left the bench, he couldn't seem to leave his judge's persona behind. His belief in fairness and justice was a strong and compelling motivator in everything he did. In fact, it became such an ingrained part of his personality that he kept making judgments after returning to this firm to practice law part-time. He was always, to himself and his older clients, still the Judge.

"Judge Johnston was selective; he worked only on cases that interested him. If he felt a slight nudge might help in reaching what he deemed to be the proper outcome of a case, he wasn't above shoving a little to bring about that appropriate—to him—conclusion."

The lawyer shifted his rueful glance to Kathleen. "I think that's what he planned to do in your case, Ms. Mitchell. But yours wasn't the only one he tried to give his magic touch. He would prod any of his clients into doing what he felt should be done."

He glanced between Rob and Kathleen. "I assure you both that I knew nothing about this particular matter until Betty was going through some old files to determine which ones we could destroy. When she got to your file, Ms. Mitchell, she had a strange feeling about it. Although Betty never worked directly for Judge Johnston, for some reason she remembered how upset you were when you came in to see him that first time. It struck her that she couldn't remember the outcome of your divorce. She pulled the folder and, astonished by what she found, immediately brought it to me. We then reviewed it together."

Dan slowly shook his head from side to side. "Judge Johnston should have handled your divorce the way we handle all our divorce cases, because divorces like yours are easy for a lawyer. There were no children or jointly-owned property, and Ms. Mitchell was adamant about not wanting alimony or monetary support of any kind. Your divorce was to be a legal and amicable parting of the ways. Why Judge Johnston took it upon himself to do what he did is beyond comprehension.

"So, to answer your original question, Mr. McKenzie, I can't tell you why Judge Johnston did what he did, but I can tell you what he did and how he did it. He left a paper trail for us to follow. Betty and I organized his notes, so you'll have no trouble following it yourself."

He cautioned them both. "Before you read the file, let me point out the three avenues of recourse available to you. First, you can make a big stink about this, but I would advise against it. Judge Johnston has been dead for years. I see no need to tarnish his reputation here in town. And reporting his actions to the West Virginia State Bar Association would serve no purpose. They can't reprimand someone who's deceased."

Dan lowered his chin and looked at them over his glasses. "I doubt any of us wants to see this bandied around by the press. I don't know about you, but having this unfortunate fiasco become the focus of a media frenzy is my worst nightmare.

"Secondly, you might be able to find a lawyer who'd try to make a case for legal malpractice against our firm. But such a case is almost totally without merit or appeal. Since neither of you has remarried, you haven't really suffered any provable damages. I was a law clerk in this firm fourteen years ago, not a partner. I doubt any court of law would find me responsible for something Judge Johnston did that I was neither a party to nor knew about, even if you chose to go that route.

"Lastly, Ms. Mitchell—or even you, Mr. McKenzie—can file again for divorce. Like Virginia, West Virginia is a no-fault divorce state. Once you state under oath that you've lived separate and apart for the past fourteen years, there will be no problem at all getting a divorce. Under the circumstances, I can expedite this matter for you. And you have my personal assurance that you'll be divorced properly and legally this time, even if I have to walk the papers through the court system step-by-step myself. The only hitch in all of this is that you now have a child to consider. The court almost always allows custody to go to the mother, unless there are compelling reasons otherwise, and I certainly believe that's what they'd do in this case. Hopefully, we can work out visitation and custody issues together. I suspect you'd both like to avoid a long, protracted—and costly—legal battle.

"But before you make any decision, I'd like you to see the file. I'll turn off the tape recorder, so feel free to discuss what you read with each other. Betty and I will wait in the outer office while you go over it thoroughly. Take your time, then when you're finished, we'll talk about what you want me to do. Is that acceptable to you both?"

Both Rob and Kathleen said it was.

Neither of them knew what to say as they began reading the file. At first glance, the original paperwork seemed authentic and in proper order. The Complaint for Divorce and the Notice of Deposition carrying Kathleen's signature were copies with the case number WV-LC-94 penciled on top of the pleading. The Certificate of Service at the bottom of the notice stated that a copy of the paperwork had been mailed to both Rob and the attorney Judge Johnston had recommended that Rob see in Denver.

The proper proof of service of the case papers on Rob was in the file, and his Answer to the Complaint, agreeing with Kathleen's allegations, seemed to have been timely and legally filed. Everything appeared to have been done correctly as far as they could tell. What could be the problem?

A copy of a handwritten letter to Rob's Denver attorney, Harold Smolenski, Esquire, was attached to the deposition notice:

"Harold:

"Per our telephone conversation, enclosed are copies of the paperwork in the matter entitled *Kathleen Mitchell McKenzie v. Robert Michael McKenzie*, Case No. WV-LC-94. I need you to depose the Respondent, Rob McKenzie, a young man who is playing baseball there in Denver. I would appreciate your scheduling his deposition as soon as you can.

"Attached please find a list of questions for the deposition that are required in divorce cases in West Virginia. In addition to the requisite questions, please ask Mr. McKenzie these:

"Are you a willing party to this divorce?

"Are you still in love with Kathleen Mitchell McKenzie?

"Do you have plans to remarry?

"Please follow the proper procedures for notarizing and sealing Mr. McKenzie's deposition. Have your law clerk mail both the original and a photocopy to me at your earliest convenience. I will deliver the sealed depositions to the Clerk of the Court when the time is proper.

"If I can be of assistance to you at any time, let me know.

"Sincerely yours, Judge Benjamin Johnston."

The original, sealed depositions of Kathleen Mitchell McKenzie and Robert Michael McKenzie, which never were filed with the court, were fastened to the front of the folder. Photocopies of both depositions, stapled together, were included with copies of the other legal papers in the file.

Setting aside Judge Johnston's letter to Harold Smolenski, Rob took the copy of Kathleen's deposition, she picked up a copy of his, and they began to read. They each knew how the other would've answered the usual questions. Kathleen had given most of that information to Judge Johnston at her initial interview: names of the parties, each party's date of birth, current domicile of each party, date of marriage, date and place of last co-habitation, a statement that they neither had children together nor owned property jointly, the reason for divorce, etc.

But neither knew how the other had responded to the extra questions Judge Johnston had suggested to Harold Smolenski.

Rob scanned Kathleen's sworn statement, holding his breath until he reached the part that most interested him:

"Q. Ms. Mitchell, you filed this action for divorce. Is this what you really want?

"A. Not really. Rob asked me to divorce him. He doesn't want to be married to me anymore. He says he wants to get on with his life, and this is my way of letting him go.

"Q. Ms. Mitchell, are you still in love with Rob McKenzie?

"A. I don't see why that's pertinent now, but yes.

"Q. Do you have any plans at this time to remarry?

"A. No. At this point, I don't think I'll ever get married again. Rob will probably marry again soon, since he wanted his freedom, but that's his decision to make."

For her part, Kathleen quickly scanned the pages of Rob's deposition until she found his answers to the questions she sought:

"Q. Mr. McKenzie, are you a willing party to this divorce?"

"A. Not really. I guess you could say I'm only willing if Katie has decided it's what she wants. She instigated this in the first place because I said I wanted to be free, but that's not true anymore. That was just another failed attempt to force her to leave her parents and stay with me. Since that hasn't happened, I have to assume she again chose her family over me and our marriage, and that a divorce is what she wants."

"Q. Mr. McKenzie, are you still in love with Kathleen Mitchell McKenzie?"

"A. Yes."

"Q. Then this may be redundant. Do you have plans to remarry?"

"A. No. I still feel married to Katie. She was my first and only girlfriend. I don't think I'll ever want to marry anyone but her."

"Oh, Rob," Kathleen said. "I didn't know they asked you those questions, too." When their eyes locked, they were unable to break the contact. What had they done to each other? What could they do now?

Rob glanced again at the papers in his hand before speaking. "Your answer to that last question sounds so sad," he said. "I feel ashamed all over again for putting you through so much. But I meant what I said at that deposition. It's been a long time, but I've never wanted to marry anyone else. What a mess this has turned out to be! You think we can ever straighten it out?"

"I'm overwhelmed by everything, Rob. I never expected this when Bobby and I drove into West Virginia yesterday. No wonder Dan didn't want to handle it over the phone! You and I do need to talk about this in depth, but not here. We've taken up enough of Dan and Betty's time as it is."

The words he'd read from Kathleen's deposition were a balm to Rob's spirit, and hope began to smolder inside him once more, hope that they might have a future together, after all.

They tore their eyes from each other and continued reading the file, wondering what other shocking things they'd uncover. The next item was a dated memorandum from Judge Johnston to the file:

"Several weeks ago, Kathleen Mitchell McKenzie completed the paperwork necessary to divorce Robert Michael McKenzie. After reading the answers Rob and Katie gave under oath to the last three questions posed at their depositions, it's obvious that neither of them truly wants this divorce. I have decided to hold the paperwork in the file until I can determine why these children—who are, of course, no longer children—made the life-altering decision to sever their matrimonial bonds. As a longtime friend of their parents, I owe it to the McKenzie and Mitchell families to allow their children a cooling-off period before filing the final legal papers dissolving their marriage.

"This matter is now tickled for further evaluation in one year. If the issues between them have not been resolved by reconciliation or mediation by that time, I will file the final divorce decree with the court."

In silence, Rob and Kathleen then read Judge Johnston's next—and final—memo.

"May 5th:

"I just learned that Kathleen Mitchell McKenzie gave birth yesterday to a son she named Robert Michael Mitchell. The child's father is officially listed as Robert Michael McKenzie, address unknown in Cincinnati.

"I will contact both parties to this action and advise them that the final paperwork in their divorce has not yet been filed, that their marriage is still valid.

"I will further ask if they have reconciled, if they wish to reconcile given their current circumstances, or if they desire that I file the final decree in this case.

"I will abide by their decision.

"Signed: Judge Benjamin Johnston."

Disbelieving, still in shock, Rob opened the door for Dan and Betty to re-enter the office.

Leaning against the edge of his desk, Dan explained. "Judge Johnston died in a car accident shortly after he wrote that final memorandum, obviously before he got in touch with either of you. In the transition from one lawyer to another, your file was placed among our closed cases. It seems that Judge Johnston did intend to follow up with you, even though it's apparent now he never did. His objectives may have been honorable, but his actions were unethical. Never before have I seen a case as botched up as yours.

"To be frank, public records in Logan County were not kept as efficiently back then as today. We were a bit late in joining the computer age, but we're there now. What happened then wouldn't happen today, I assure you of that."

Dan paused to take a sip of water. "In those days when a lawyer filed suit, there was little follow-up by the courts, but it was due to a lack of supporting technology and time, not to any lack of ability. I knew all the courthouse personnel back then, so I know for a fact that they were highly qualified individuals. They were just worked beyond their capacity with barely any technological support. Betty and I checked with the current Clerk's office, and while they're appalled that this case apparently fell through the cracks, they can't tell us why there was no follow-up. None of us knows for sure, but we all suspect—after tossing the facts around, back and forth—that Judge Johnston somehow took care of that himself.

"Ms. Mitchell," he continued, "since you've now read the file and heard me out, let me go over one of your options again. Ms. Adams is here to re-type the divorce papers today if that's your decision. There will be no charge for my services, the filing fees, or any other court costs. I'll take care of all that. Is that what you want me to do?"

"Don't," Rob choked out, with a pleading look at Kathleen. "Please don't."

Kathleen's body jerked in his direction. "What did you say? I'm not sure I understand."

"I said don't, and I mean it. Don't file again for divorce. We went that route before, and it was a mistake that I, for one, don't want to repeat. This time, let's go over our situation with a fine-toothed comb before making a decision."

Kathleen opened her mouth to speak, but Rob held up his hand to stop her. "I told you what to do before, Katie, but I'm not doing that now...well, at least, not exactly. Now I'm just laying the facts on the line. Please don't file any divorce papers yet. If you do, this time I'll fight you on it, tooth and nail. We're still committed to each other, and don't you try to deny it. We thought we were divorced, but as soon as we saw each other yesterday, we knew that the emotional connection between us was still alive and well."

"Rob—"

"I'm not arguing about this just for myself, Katie. As Dan said, we now have Bobby to consider. What seems to be a mixed-up mess at the moment might really be a priceless gift to us all."

"Rob—"

Rob reached out suddenly to clutch both of her hands. "Please, Katie, don't make me fight you on this, not until we've talked it through."

As soon as Rob paused to breathe, Kathleen spoke again, only this time she spoke louder. "Just calm down and listen to me for a minute, will you?"

Dan watched the two of them with interest, his lips twitching slightly. Rob McKenzie was doing an impressive job, fighting for his future. But from where Dan sat, Rob seemed to be preaching to the choir and didn't know it.

"I'm not signing anything today," Kathleen assured him. "You saw my reaction when I read your deposition, didn't you? I won't be doing anything irreversible this time."

Rob closed his eyes and exhaled a long, relieved breath of air. Kathleen squeezed his hands once and released them before turning back to Dan. "Thank you for being so compassionate about this, Mr. Hoffman, but I won't be taking you up on your offer. If we need help later on, can we call you for advice?"

"Sure," said Dan, his facial expression now under control. He didn't know why the by-play between Rob McKenzie and Kathleen Mitchell had struck him as being so amusing. But for a moment there at the end, Rob McKenzie had looked like a prisoner who'd been given a stay of execution. "There's no statute of limitations or any other restrictive considerations involved here, so you don't have to rush to a decision. What Mr. McKenzie said sounds wise to me, too. Take all the time you need to decide what's best for everyone. I'll be here if you need me, so give me a call." With that, Dan shook hands with Kathleen and Rob again, and the meeting was over.

After the two of them had walked out of his office, Dan looked at Betty. "That's one divorce I hope we never have to file."

"Yeah, that goes for me, too. I prayed for both of them while they were reading the file."

"I know," Dan said, grinning. "You move your lips when you pray for our clients."

Betty blushed. She didn't really mind that he'd noticed. Dan was known to have said a prayer or two for their clients himself.

\* \* \* \*

Kathleen's brain reeled. Trying to process too much information in too little time was exhausting. She could feel herself approach mental meltdown. First thing first, she needed to discuss everything with Rob. They needed to put what they'd heard that afternoon into some sort of logical order before telling anyone else. She didn't know what Rob had planned for the rest of the day, but she hoped—whatever it was—he'd set it aside to be with her.

In the hallway outside the law office, she touched Rob on the arm. "Let's find some place where we can be alone and talk. Even before we see Bobby, let's take some time just for ourselves to review what we heard. It's so complicated, it's giving me a headache. And I'm not even sure I understand everything that's involved." Frown lines puckered her forehead. "Am I selfish, wanting time alone with you before facing our families?"

"Not unless I'm selfish, too," Rob said. "That's exactly what I think we should do. And I know just the place where we can go and not be disturbed."

As they walked down the hall and out of the building, the light pressure of Rob's hand near the middle of her back felt comforting and reassuring to Kathleen...but only at first. When the sensitive skin beneath his touch began to tingle, what was meant to calm and soothe became, instead, something exciting and strangely disturbing.

# Chapter 15

▼

After a stop at Nu-Era Bakery, which everyone knows is the best place to go in Logan for sugar-laden, cream-oozing treats, Rob pointed his Mustang to a place where privacy was assured: the old, abandoned coal mine at the head of Steven's Hollow. Once a bustling enterprise, the mine hunkered now in lonely isolation, its once-bright steel tipple, wooden timbers, and glass windows rusted, decayed, and shattered. Twelve years of neglect had tamed the beast that once spewed ash and soot on Steven's Hollow.

They could still make out the narrow, gravel road that led past the mine and up Mine Hollow to the community's water supply—a concrete dam that blocked an unpolluted stream flowing out of the hills. Few of the No Trespassing signs that once peppered the area around the mine were still intact, and those that had survived were faded and broken, their painted metal pock-marked by target practice with .22 caliber rifles. The gravel road, once kept free of weeds by the frequent passage of teenagers and their vehicles, was overgrown now and messy.

Mine Hollow had been a popular place to hang out when they were in their teens. When there was no place else to go but home, and home was the very last place they wanted to be, kids gathered at the dam to swim and to talk. It wasn't the first time Rob and Kathleen had bought snacks at the bakery before driving up there, but everything seemed different today. Creepy. Snaky. Dirty. And quiet.

Rob moved the floor mats from his car to a pile of mining timbers stacked out in the open, an action that prompted Kathleen to smile. She'd seen him do exactly that a dozen times before. Sitting there this time, they reminisced about people they'd known in the past, ate the cream puffs they'd picked up at the bakery, and sipped steaming hot coffee out of insulated cups.

"Just think," Kathleen marveled, speaking softly, "the kids who once swam so recklessly here—braving snakes and turtles and what-have-you—are grown-ups now, many of them with children of their own, like us."

"Yeah, it is hard to believe how much things can change over time—places *and* people—until you witness it yourself." Rob, his mind still in the past, rubbed the top of his thigh, which had started to ache.

"That's true," Kathleen agreed, noticing his discomfort. "Just think how drastically our own lives have been altered in the last twenty-four hours. It's no wonder we went into a tailspin, trying to make sense of it all."

They licked every single, sugary crumb from their fingers, then stood to return to the more comfortable confines of the car. As Rob straightened and stepped forward, Kathleen pivoted. Only a few inches separated them. He could have moved back...if he'd wanted to. But so could she. Yesterday, maybe even last night, they would have. But after hearing what they had this afternoon, neither moved this time.

*They were still legally married.*

As their eyes met, each of them wondered what the other was thinking, how the other felt at this isolated moment in time. Their past experiences, and the love they once shared, drew them together, like magnets toward opposite poles. An electrical current of attraction arced between them, its intensity surprising them both. Shaking his head as if dazed, Rob was the first to move away, breaking the spell. "What should we do about this strange predicament we're in? How do you feel about what we heard today?"

"Well," Kathleen said, "Dan's initial telephone call, coming out of the blue as it did, upset me more than what we learned this afternoon. Maybe that's because we heard the news and read the file together today. Thanks for being so supportive, by the way. Having you there made all the difference in the world to me.

"I expected to hear bad news," she continued, "but I never envisioned anything like this. Dan seems to believe Judge Johnston acted out of good intentions, but he certainly left Dan, and us, with a mess to straighten out. I can't understand why they didn't discover the problem earlier, can you? That file was in limbo for at least thirteen years, and that's a long time. It's a wonder it didn't dry rot!"

Rob agreed that Judge Johnston had acted disgracefully. "Katie...uh...I've been wondering about something. Guess I might as well stop beating around the bush and just ask about it, right? Is there someone special in your life who'll be upset by the news we got today?"

Kathleen smiled slowly; he was so transparent. "No, not in a romantic sense, if that's what you mean. I work at home, and Bobby and I live a calm, orderly life, doing things mostly with each other. Except for the times when I meet with my agent or editor in New York, I'm pretty much a stay-at-home mom who runs an unpaid taxi service on the side for Bobby and his friends. You can't imagine the number of miles I rack up driving to and from school, soccer games, baseball games, church functions, and school activities with a carload of kids! The people I'm close to know that I'm divorced, but it won't matter to them one way or the other to find out that suddenly I'm not. How about you? Will your celebrity lifestyle survive this legal earthquake?"

All Rob could conjure up was a sad semblance of a smile. "Actually, my life's been sort of pathetic," he explained, "although up till this week I thought it was satisfying and full. I didn't realize how lonely I'd been until I saw you again and found out about Bobby. I'm acquainted with a lot of people, not close to many. I'm active in the men's ministry at my church when I'm there, but I'm on the road so much I haven't made many close friends in that group. Pete Sanders and the guys from the CCA have been my extended family since I moved to Cincinnati, so I'd like to share what we found out today with them—especially Pete, my best friend—but I won't tell even Pete if you don't want me to."

Kathleen assured Rob he could share anything he wanted with his friends.

"I haven't been seriously involved with anyone since the last time I saw you," Rob admitted. Kathleen arched her brows, her disbelief of that assertion easy for him to read. Rob chuckled. "You may find that hard to believe, Katie, but it is true. There's been so little romance in my life, I might as well have been a monk. Knowing now that we're still being married to each other, how could I be annoyed or disappointed that the file was lost and the legal outcome put on hold?"

Rob had been leery about telling Kathleen how he felt about her, but only at first. The truth was, he'd been lonely for what seemed like forever. He just hadn't known until now what was missing in his life.

"Pete thinks I've been carrying a torch for you for years. I always deny it when he brings it up, but I realized yesterday that he might just be right. When I looked up and saw that Explorer slowing down in front of the Habitat house, I thought at first that you were just another gorgeous woman checking out the guys. But when I noticed how much that woman looked like you, my stomach flipped. I tried to convince myself that it was just another one of my visions, that my eyes were playing tricks on me again, but that didn't work. I recognized you, Katie-girl. Deep down in my soul, I knew it was you. I couldn't have kept myself from coming after you if my life had depended on it."

He chuckled. "I was almost too scared to approach your car, for fear that I was wrong again. It wouldn't have been the first time I'd stopped a woman, thinking she was you when she wasn't. When I saw you close up, after all this time, my heart skipped a beat. It wasn't just *any* gorgeous girl in that SUV; it was *my* gorgeous girl. I asked myself the same old question I've asked a hundred times before: why did I drive you away?"

Baring his heart to Kathleen for the first time in years, Rob wasn't about to let the uncertainty of her response slow him down. "I need to make one thing crystal clear, Katie: I felt that way when I first saw you yesterday, long before I knew about Bobby. Those thoughts and feelings of attraction were just about you, and I want you to understand the time line here. I felt that connection with you *before* I knew you'd given birth to my son."

Kathleen's heart literally fluttered in her chest, like a happy host of angel wings railing against physical restraints. She had forgotten that a heart could react to another's heartfelt declaration that way. Rob wasn't interested only in Bobby, his son; he was still romantically interested in her.

"What Judge Johnston did about the divorce might seem to be a breach of ethics to Dan Hoffman," Rob stated, "but I see it as an answer to my prayers. I feel like getting down on my knees right now and thanking God for it."

It was now or never for Rob, and he knew it. Once Kathleen left Logan to return to Virginia, he might never get another chance to explain how he felt. He took a deep, steadying breath. "I've laid my emotions on the line here, Katie, but I need some feedback from you. You still attracted to me?"

Kathleen paused to consider her own feelings again before speaking. Seeing Rob leaning against his father's truck yesterday had evoked a classic approach-avoid response in her, to her dismay. Deep down inside, she had wanted to see Rob and talk with him again about the past, as he requested, but she'd also been afraid. She absolutely, positively could not face his rejection again.

Do I want to place myself in that position, even now? Kathleen asked herself that question as she pondered Rob's query. It wasn't easy, knowing what to do or what to say.

Even while presuming she was divorced, Kathleen had never felt incomplete as a person or less desirable as a woman because she'd been rejected by Rob. Her son Bobby, the love of her family, her writing career, and her faith in God, the four things that filled her days and nights to overflowing, had always kept her strong. She would've sworn she needed nothing, or anyone, more in her life…until yesterday. When Rob had stalked up to her car, the long-forgotten memory of their failed relationship had surfaced, expanding into a terrible ache and a hunger for what once existed between them. Get real, she'd told herself then, trying to be realistic. That's not going to happen.

With that in mind, Kathleen phrased her answer carefully. "Even when things were at their very worst, I cared for you." Although her feelings for Rob were growing stronger, she wouldn't admit to anything more than that. He maintained he had changed, and he probably had, but it would be foolish to give him the power to hurt her again.

Having Kathleen just care for him was not enough for Rob. Caring was a weak emotion, not at all what he wanted…not even close to what he had to have…from her. He yearned for all the things she had given him freely before: open, honest, mind-shattering, earth-shaking love and fiery passion. "Come on," he coaxed. "Let me make up for the hurtful things I said and did before, Katie. Take another chance on me."

Kathleen looked away from Rob for a moment before glancing back. "You aren't the only one to blame for what happened," she allowed. "I should have contacted you as soon as I found out I was pregnant. I'd like to go back and change that, along with a lot of other things, but that's impossible. I don't know what'll develop between us in the future, if anything, so I'm not making any promises I might not be able to keep. I am willing to take another cautious chance with you—sort of a 'let's play it by ear' approach for a while—if you can live with that."

Rob completely ignored the word "cautious," and the triumphant look on his face said it all: Rob McKenzie wasn't backing away from Kathleen Mitchell again. Suddenly he whooped so loud that anyone in Steven's Hollow—with windows raised—could've heard his joyous noise.

He'd told himself to take things slow this morning, but that was before he knew Kathleen still cared for him, too. Now the urge to touch her, really touch her, was so powerful he broke his unspoken promise by reaching for her. And Kathleen didn't seem to mind. She hesitated only slightly before moving into his arms. He dipped his head and grinned. "Does this mean we're going steady again, Katie-girl?" He could feel her muffled laughter against his chest.

It had been a strenuous day, and Rob could feel the dull ache in his leg getting worse. He held Kathleen close, tentatively at first, not taking anything for granted. They'd been separated for a long time, and it was only natural that he'd wonder whose lips she'd kissed, in whose arms she'd been held, since they'd last been together in Colorado. And she might be wondering the same thing about him. But why, even for a moment, give that thought the power to torment him? They'd never been in love with anyone except each other. Rob would stake his life, and his future, on that.

Kathleen's contented sigh eased his anxieties, and for the moment he was balanced on top of the world, hands raised high in thanksgiving. His heart whispered that this time they'd get everything right. He wanted to take things slow—really he did!—but there was no way he could resist kissing her the way he'd dreamed of since looking up from the Habitat house and seeing her drive by. He tangled his fingers in her curly hair and slowly molded his mouth to the softness and warmth and responsiveness of hers.

He tasted salty tears and leaned back. In a husky voice, he begged, "Please don't cry, Katie-girl." Lifting her left hand, he kissed her ringless finger and whispered, "I promise I won't hurt you again. You have my solemn word on that. All I want is a chance to prove how much I care for you. I know I caused a lot of tears before, but don't cry now. I never want to make you cry again."

Touching the corner of Kathleen's sweet, soft mouth again, Rob teased her lips with tiny, gentle kisses until he heard her broken sigh. "Oh, Rob," she whispered against his oh-so-tempting lips, "I do want things to work out well for you and me, but we've got to take things slow."

Rob closed his eyes as air rushed from his lungs. He didn't like hearing those sane, sensible words coming out of Kathleen's tantalizing mouth. Not when he wanted her *now*!

She reached up to wipe away the frown that creased his brow. "You know we can't just pick up where we left off before. That's unrealistic. We don't even know what kind of people we are now. I have no idea what your life is like or how you fill your days." She looked up at Rob, her brows furrowed in thought. "Let me give you an example," she said, after a pause. "How many days out of the year are you in Cincinnati? How much time do you spend on the road? I don't know your friends, where you shop, or where you go to church. And you don't know what I'm like either. How can we handle such strong emotions when we don't know each other anymore?"

Though she knew she must be firm on this, Kathleen wanted to reassure Rob she wasn't afraid their past would rise up again, repeating itself. "I'm not afraid you'll hurt me, that's not it. If God is giving us another chance for a future together, and it looks like He is, my head still says to take things slow."

A half-laugh, half-groan escaped Rob's lips as he rested his forehead against hers. "You know me too well, Katie. You knew I wouldn't like hearing we have to proceed cautiously, and I don't. I remember too well how it was when we were married. My hormones are acting like we're together again, so the last thing my body wants to hear is common sense saying, wait." He rubbed his nose against hers, his breathing unsteady. "I'm sorry, Katie. While my head may agree that you're right, the Neanderthal inside me says *she's yours—knock her in the head and drag her to your cave!*" He couldn't see Kathleen's smile, but he heard her soft chuckle.

Silent for a moment, Rob stared over Kathleen's head into nothing. "I want to do what's right, but I suspect we're poles apart on this. We are still legally married, which can be either a blessing or a curse. I don't feel real confident right now that I have the patience to wait very long for you. So before I mess things up by rushing you into something you don't want or aren't ready for, let me ask you this: will you go with me to see the new minister at Mom and Dad's church for advice on how to handle this situation? Ours certainly is an interesting problem. While we're not legally divorced, we're not quite emotionally married either. There has to be a proper way to work this out as the born-again Christians we are."

Rob exhaled, slowly tossing her a rueful grin. "God has to know the chemistry between us is every bit as strong as ever, that we still have this hunger for each other—" He looked at her intently, brows lifted "—I'm not alone here, am I, Katie?"

Resting her head against the buttons on his shirt, Kathleen slowly shook her head from side to side.

Rob smiled into her hair. "I'll bet the new minister—I think Mom said his name is Matthew Harlow—has never counseled anyone in circumstances like ours before. We ought to really make his day."

"Let's talk with him soon." Kathleen said.

Rob indulged himself for a moment, holding her close, their bodies touching from head to toes. The evidence of passion was there between them, sizzling like live wires touching metal. Her rapid breathing said she knew how much he wanted her. Rob knew he should give her more space, maybe even pull away a little, but he gave in to his feelings instead and moved closer. Then, with a low moan of regret, he stepped back and held Kathleen a few inches away. Cupping her face in his hands and gazing into her eyes, Rob came to a decision. "You're worth waiting for, Katie. Let me court you for a while. I'll want to, but I won't pressure you to cross the line you've drawn. I'll call Pastor Harlow tomorrow."

"Uh…you think you might be able to get him today?"

Rob grinned, flashing perfectly formed white teeth. He knew what she was thinking. "I'll try," he said, dropping a quick kiss on her cheek before they walked hand-in-hand to his car.

* * * *

"You have any plans for tonight?" Rob asked, opening the car door for Kathleen.

"Brian has tickets for the Brad Paisley concert, so I'm cooking a pre-concert dinner for everyone at the cabin."

"Sounds like you're following in your mother's footsteps. Man, I still remember some of the dinners that woman put together. Mmmm…mmmm…they were good! Delicious food. Tons of fun. I tell you, Katie, it doesn't get any better than that"

Intuition told Kathleen she'd just been tossed an impossible-to-resist hint-for-a-meal from the master hinter himself. But Rob artlessly avoided her gaze. She bit the inside of her bottom lip to keep from smiling. "Would you like to stay for dinner? I'm frying chicken."

Lifting his left eyebrow, and looking exactly like Bobby caught in mischief, Rob turned a crooked smile in her direction. "I'm glad you can still take a hint. For a minute there, I wondered! As you've probably guessed, there's nothing I'd rather do than join you all for dinner."

Kathleen closed her eyes. Two words, two words only, came to mind: alien possession. What else would explain what she'd done? Cooking for her family never stressed her out, but she hadn't cooked a meal for Rob since college. He'd probably been shocked when she said she'd fry chicken. At WVU, she'd cooked only three things—tuna casserole, hot dogs, and anything that could be made with Hamburger Helper.

"Well, I'm glad you'll stay," she finally said. "The concert starts at eight, but the kids will be antsy about getting there early. They're interested in seeing the dance demo before the show." She glanced down at her watch. "Yikes! We'd better get out of here; I need to start dinner. The kids will have my hide if I make them late tonight."

Rob assumed Kathleen would be going to the concert with the others, that his time with her was limited. He was reluctant to relinquish the privacy they were enjoying at the mine. He reached for her hand and described his earlier conversation with his parents. "I was prepared to duke it out with them if they'd questioned Bobby's paternity," he said, "but that didn't even enter their minds." He smiled when he told Kathleen how his mother and father had hugged him and cried when they learned about Bobby.

"That's really touching about the hugs," Kathleen said, "but go back a bit; I'm not sure I heard you right. Did you say you were prepared to 'duke it out' with them? You can barely get up after sitting for a while. You sure you're ready to take on your dad? He's a pretty big man, and I'll bet he's still strong from the construction work he does."

"Come on, Katie, show a little faith. Dad's twenty-five years older than I am!"

"Remind me to pass that comment on to your dad the next time I see him. If I try real hard, I can even get your tone of voice down pat."

"Do and die," Rob threatened, yanking gently at a lock of her hair. "You're right, though, about Dad. I get a lot of exercise playing ball, plus I work out at the gym to stay in shape, but he's naturally strong from the work he performs every day. And I tell you, Katie, nobody takes on Mike McKenzie, not even me."

Kathleen brightened, almost bouncing with excitement. "Hey, let's call your parents and ask them to eat with us tonight. And you ought to tell Bobby about your chat with them as soon as he gets home. We don't want him to be totally surprised when he meets them, whether it's tonight or some other time. I doubt he's even thought about having another set of grandparents. He'll be beside himself if they can come to dinner, too."

Rob dug around for his cell phone, which had fallen between the bucket seats. Flipping it open, he dialed his mother's number. "Hi, Mom," he said when she answered the phone. "Katie's family is getting together this evening for dinner, and then they're going to that country music concert in town. Katie's frying chicken and has invited me to stay. Don't you and Dad have tickets for that show? You do? Well, Katie wants to know if you all would like to come to dinner, too, and meet Bobby."

Kathleen could hear his mother's happy—and loud—reaction. Jerking the phone away from his ear, Rob held it a safe distance away until there was silence on the other end of the line. After a short pause, they heard Mary McKenzie again. "Rob? Rob? Are you there?"

Only then did he return the phone to his ear. "Yes, Mom, I'm here, but you almost broke my eardrum with your screeching. Now, don't you hold anything back...tell me exactly what you think. Do you and Dad want to join us for dinner or not?" He paused. "No...no...no! Absolutely not. No presents. Wait until you get to know Bobby first. I know you don't want to spoil him." Rob mimicked a hearty laugh at that statement while his mother continued to talk. Then he handed the phone to Kathleen. "She wants to speak to you."

"Katie?" Mary McKenzie said, "I'm really looking forward to seeing you again, but that's an awful lot of people to cook for. Are you sure it's okay for us to come?" She stopped talking only long enough to take a short breath. "But why did I ask that? We both know you couldn't keep Mike and me away now even if you tried. I hope Rob didn't coerce you into asking us."

Although Kathleen dreaded her first encounter in years with the McKenzies, she was gratified by Mary McKenzie's enthusiastic response to the invitation. Since Rob and his parents now knew about Bobby, there was no reason the two families couldn't get together and visit in a civilized manner. They certainly had before. Her own mother might feel ill-at-ease around Rob, but Kathleen knew she'd be on good behavior. She smiled, remembering that Brian would also be at dinner. Mr. Congeniality, her secret social weapon. Brian knew how to handle the most delicate, sensitive situations.

"No, Rob didn't talk me into it," she said. "I suggested it myself because I want you to come. Bobby will love it, Mrs. McKenzie, I know he will. Rob and I haven't had a chance to tell him much about you and Mr. McKenzie yet, but we will before you get to the cabin this evening."

"Oh, goodness, Katie, this is so exciting for us!"

"Then I'm glad you'll come. It's been a long time since we saw each other. We'd better eat early, though. Can you plan to be at the cabin at five? That'll give us plenty of time to eat and still get you all to Logan in time for the concert."

When Kathleen's words sank in, Rob questioned her with his eyes. She refused to acknowledge his unspoken query. But Rob McKenzie, *magna cum laude* graduate of WVU, wasn't slow. He knew it meant more time alone with Kathleen later, after everyone else had gone.

With a quick intake of breath, Rob realized again that Kathleen was still his wife, tied up nice and legal for now. He might not have her right away, but neither would anyone else. She was still married to him. And sooner or later...Rob cut that thought off abruptly, remembering the words that had become his mantra over the last couple of days. *Don't go there yet, McKenzie.*

He tuned back into the conversation between Kathleen and his mother. "Sure, I'd love for you to bring it. Carrot-raisin salad is Bobby's favorite, and I've been using your recipe for years."

Rob watched Kathleen closely, suspecting what was coming. He laughed as she jerked the phone from her ear, knowing she'd just been privy to one of his mother's howls of pleasure herself. That salad they were talking about was one of his favorites, too. He knew that any similarity Mary McKenzie found between Bobby and himself would bring joy to his own doting mom.

Taking the phone from Kathleen, he interrupted his mother's continuing exclamations. Placing his mouth close to the phone, he said, "Katie's got to go now, Mom. Bye." Hanging up the phone, he frowned. "I don't think Mom wants to come, do you?"

"No. She'll hate every minute of it."

Rob grinned. He'd always loved Kathleen's quirky sense of humor, and here he was, sharing it once more. He dialed his mother's number again. Busy signal. "Aha! Just as I thought," he said. "She's on the phone telling Dad."

Rob ended the call and put the phone away, this time in its cradle on the dash. "Sounds like you're not going to the concert. Right?."

"No, why do you ask?" Kathleen blinked her eyes, and Rob smiled. He knew that the innocent look on her face was a sham.

"Just wondering, that's all." Whistling under his breath, Rob sliced his eyes around at her. She looked back, and they both laughed.

"You're still pretty fresh, Rob McKenzie."

Rob tapped the end of her nose. "You bet I am. And don't you forget it."

# Chapter 16

By the time they stopped by Kroger's to pick up another chicken, Kathleen was late starting dinner. Rob was such good help she was glad she'd asked him to stay. After making a couple of calls from his cell phone, he discarded his jacket, tucked a dishtowel into the waistband of his pants as an apron, found a sharp paring knife, and began peeling potatoes. Kathleen dipped the chicken pieces into an egg and milk mixture, rolled them in flour seasoned with salt, pepper, and paprika, then set them aside to dry awhile before frying.

But the meal required more than just chicken and mashed potatoes. Checking the pantry, Kathleen found colorful jars of Mrs. Mitchell's pickled green beans and yellow corn which, added to the fried chicken, mashed potatoes, and Mrs. McKenzie's carrot-raisin salad, would round out their meal nicely. There was vanilla ice cream in the freezer, and her mother had laid in a supply of Bobby's favorite chocolate syrup. If any of her guests couldn't live without dessert, Kathleen would fix hot fudge sundaes for them. She didn't have the time or inclination to do anything more than that. It had been a long, busy day.

As the two of them worked together in the kitchen, Rob and Kathleen talked about her career as a writer, his experiences with the Reds' organization, and Bobby.

"Is what I heard true? You won the Newbery Medal a couple of years back? The Newbery Award for Children's Literature—that's sort of prestigious, right? Does that mean you're good?" Rob knew exactly how impressive the Newbery Award was. He had looked it up on the Internet after hearing she'd received it.

Rob was teasing her, and Kathleen knew it. "Oh, I'm sorry," she said. "Is that what you thought? Heck, you don't have to be good, or work hard, to win literary awards. They give them to mediocre writers that they feel sorry for."

Rob smiled. "Sure they do!"

Kathleen found her mother's cast-iron Dutch oven in the storage cabinet under the stove. She filled it with half an inch of canola oil so she could start frying chicken. As the oil heated, she kidded Rob in return. "Will fourteen years at what I hear is the easiest position in all of baseball qualify you for the Hall of Fame some day?"

Like a young swain out to impress his girl, Rob puffed out his chest and grinned. "When you factor in my hitting, it will."

He couldn't hear enough about Bobby. "Did it hurt when you gave birth?"

Kathleen rolled her eyes. "What do you think? He was twenty-one inches long and weighed seven pounds eight ounces!"

"Seven and a half pounds? And tall? I refuse to even consider how bad that must have felt. How long were you in labor?" He paused, holding up his hand. "Don't tell me if it'll make me feel worse."

Kathleen turned the chicken pieces and lowered the heat to keep them from burning. "Some of it was bad," she admitted, "but I was only in labor six hours. Ellen called that a miracle; she was in labor more than twelve hours with Janie. But you want to know something? When I saw Bobby for the first time, it more than made up for the pain."

Rob lightly touched her shoulder. "I do wish I'd been there," he said. "I'll never forgive myself for that."

Kathleen had known he'd respond that way as soon as he began asking questions about motherhood and babies. Angling away from the stove, she slanted her head around to look at him. Reaching up, she touched his hand. "Listen to me, Rob. I've already forgiven you for everything that happened, and I hope that you've forgiven me. Let's not talk about that anymore. It was more my fault than yours that you weren't there when Bobby was born. I could have gotten in touch with you—I had a pretty good idea where you were—but I didn't. So stop beating yourself up about it. We can't erase what happened, and we'll never totally forget it, but let's not let it get in our way anymore. Agreed?"

Rob nodded. With no more fanfare than that, they eliminated a major obstacle that could've hung around between them forever.

"Wow, thanks for being so generous," Rob said. "But let me ask you something else, not really changing the subject. Was my perfect son a good baby?"

They laughed briefly, then Kathleen stopped and made a face. "He wasn't perfect the first three months. He was colicky, which almost drove me and everyone else nuts. If it hadn't been for Brian and Ellen, I don't know how I would've managed. We lived with them until Bobby was six months old, and Ellen was always available to encourage me in my new role. She was the consummate pro, and I was just a needy novice who studied under her tutelage. But let me tell you something, Mr. McKenzie. I was a smart needy novice…smart enough to know I didn't know anything at all about raising my child. I listened to Ellen and absorbed every piece of advice she gave me."

Kathleen paused to check the chicken again. "Although it may surprise you, Brian helped a lot, too. Janie was sleeping through the night by the time our son came along, but when Brian would hear me up for Bobby's middle-of-the-night feeding, he'd often stumble in to keep me company. They never let me feel isolated or alone, and I truly believe Bobby sensed their love for him, even then.

"I'd gotten my own place long before Ellen died eight years ago, but I still miss her every day."

The potatoes Rob had placed in a pan of water on top the stove began to boil. He reached around Kathleen to adjust the heat. As he did, she leaned closer. As if it were a state secret, she whispered in his ear, "Let me tell you something very important, new daddy and first-time father. Disposable diapers are a mother's best friend!"

"Well, thank you, Ms. Mitchell, for sharing that fascinating piece of information with me." The manner in which she had passed that tidbit on amused Rob, as evidenced by the huge grin on his face. "I'll try to work that into conversation the next time we all meet on the pitcher's mound in the middle of a game."

Smiling, Kathleen punched him lightly on the arm. "You should. Really. It's guaranteed to enhance your reputation as an athlete."

Rob never tired of hearing what she'd done and how she had lived while they were apart, and he liked the name she called him, too—new daddy and first-time father. It was so on-target for their situation. "How was it, at first, being a mother?"

"A lot of work and scary, but after the colicky period was over, Bobby was a happy, beautiful, well-behaved…dare I say, perfect?…baby. Oh, Rob, it's true what people say. Newborn babies truly are a mixture of wonder and hope wrapped up in diapers and sleepers. I wish you could have smelled our baby after he'd had a bath, when he was oiled and powdered and changed. There's nothing quite like it. I wish I could bottle up that smell and sell it to people who aren't parents."

Kathleen's statement met with dead silence. Rob had braced his arms against the edge of the counter and bowed his head, but when he did look up, there were unshed tears in his eyes. He would never be able to regain those years he'd lost with Bobby, and even though she freely shared her memories of the things he had missed with their son, those experiences could never be repeated for his benefit and participation.

The cabin seemed to shrink, forming an isolating bubble around them, and they kept bumping into each other. Each time they touched, one of them would carefully move away, wondering if the other had noticed.

"Our families will be here soon," Rob finally said. "You know they'll be curious about the two of us. How much should we tell them about the divorce?"

Kathleen pondered the question shortly. "Let's tell them that the final decree was never entered, but nothing about Judge Johnston. The original fault lies with him, it's true. But it was compounded by poor record keeping in the Clerk's office at that time, and by the person who misfiled our divorce papers after Judge Johnston died. Everybody knows everybody else in Logan, so I don't want the details to get out. It's enough that you and I know what happened, right?"

"Yes," he said, a smile lifting the corners of his mouth. "Shall I tell our families that we're going steady?"

"I don't think so! I'm not ready to talk about you and me; we're too iffy. Besides, you don't know for sure how you'll feel about me next week, or next month, when you get to know me better."

"Get used to it, Katie. I already know for sure how I feel about you. Just accept it."

Not ready to address the issue of their relationship any further, Kathleen forged ahead without responding. But Rob could tell she'd heard what he said. "We need to give Bobby an explanation as soon as he gets home from the park," she said, still skirting the subject. "Would you like to discuss it with him?"

Rob didn't reply, and the silence lengthened. "You're awfully quiet. Is something wrong?"

"No, I'm sort of mentally rehearsing what I'll say. Father-son talks where I'm the father and not the son are something new. I want to make sure I get it right."

"Oh, Rob, you'll do great. Don't worry!" She squeezed his hand. "You don't have to rehearse to talk to Bobby...he's your son. You'll be fine."

*He's your son...you'll be fine.* Rob repeated Kathleen's words, imprinting them indelibly in his brain. Could she possibly know what a massive impact those six welcome words had on him? He closed his eyes and listened as they echoed through the chambers of his heart again: *He's your son...you'll be fine.*

They were enjoying their time together even more than expected. In a way they were sorry when Brian dropped Bobby off after their outing at the park. Kathleen rushed outside to catch Brian before he drove off. "Rob and his parents are having dinner with us," she hollered from the porch. "Can you all be back here by five-fifteen, ready to eat?" Brian nodded and gave Kathleen a thumbs-up sign before driving off.

"What did the lawyer say?" Bobby asked first thing when he rushed into the cabin.

Kathleen winked at Rob, turning the floor over to him. "Well," Rob said, "there was a lot of rigamarole leading up to it, but the gist of it is, our final divorce decree was never filed with the court."

Confused, Bobby wrinkled his forehead. "Does that mean you and Mom are still married, or what?"

"Still married. At least, still legally married."

Bobby threw his fists into the air, but when he realized what he was doing, he stopped, aborting his victory dance. He hadn't been all that happy early that morning, having Rob McKenzie for a father. Yeah, Rob had answered all his questions at lunch about why Rob and his mother divorced. And Rob had been awfully nice to his grandmother, when they stopped there on their way out of the hollow. But Bobby thought maybe he'd better wait a little while longer before giving this non-divorce thing his unqualified approval.

Not knowing Bobby well, Rob couldn't interpret the confusing mixture of hope and fear on the boy's features. Bobby had seemed excited about their news at first, but now he didn't seem nearly as pleased. Well, Rob might not know how to deal with a teenager's mood swings yet, but he did know he wanted to spend more time with his son on his own. He handed Bobby the keys to his Mustang. "Why don't you run out and get a couple of gloves and a ball from the trunk of my car? We can throw a few while your mom finishes dinner."

Bobby left, his feet barely touching the ground. "But, remember, I'm injured," Rob called after him. "Show me some mercy."

Rob walked up behind Kathleen at the sink and slowly rubbed his hands along her upper arms. He hadn't missed the fact that she had not pulled away from him when they'd unintentionally brushed against each other today. In fact, if he'd read the signs correctly, she had enjoyed those close encounters as much as he. And that encouraged him. He nuzzled his chin over the top of her head. "Cross your fingers, Katie-girl. I haven't been a father long, and I'm feeling mighty nervous."

Kathleen repeated, "You'll do fine." As she reached to place a dish in the drainer, she inadvertently leaned back against him.

"Mmmm...that feels good," he said, pulling her closer and boldly kissing the soft, sensitive side of her neck. "Maybe I should stay inside with you. He can bounce the ball off the side of the house and catch it by himself."

Kathleen looked up and arched her brows. Then she inched away with a smile. "Get out of the kitchen, Rob McKenzie. Your son is waiting for you."

As Kathleen watched him go, she couldn't keep from grinning. Last week, she would have never imagined anything like this: Bobby Mitchell and his father, playing baseball together...in Logan County, West Virginia, of all places!

\* \* \* \*

His uncles, Brian and David, had taught Bobby how to throw and catch a baseball when he was barely old enough to walk, and he had played on organized Parks and Recreation teams in Prince William County since turning six. He often played catch with his uncles, as well as with the fathers of his friends while visiting at their homes. But this was the first time he'd played baseball in any way, shape, or form with his own father, Rob McKenzie—first baseman for the Cincinnati Reds, #89. Bobby had been told many times that he was an excellent baseball player for his age, but he still felt a trifle nervous as he searched the trunk of the Mustang for gloves and a baseball that Rob and he could throw. He'd be tossing the ball with his own father this time.

Rob was mindful of his injury when they began throwing the ball back and forth to each other. He started out slow, being careful not to stretch any farther than his injury allowed. He and Bobby talked, but not about anything of importance. They were just getting to know each other better.

The muscles in Rob's leg throbbed, reminding him it had been a long time since his physical therapy session that morning. He hadn't rested at all since then, and if he wasn't careful, he would slow down his recovery. The Reds' trainer would have a fit if he could see what Rob was doing now, but Rob didn't want to stop to rest, not when he had a chance to spend his first-ever quality time alone with his son. *Quality time?* Where did that come from? Rob grinned. A father for one day, and he was already talking the talk.

The physical therapist had cautioned Rob over and over on what he could and could not do, and Rob intended to follow those precautions to the letter. He didn't extend his leg far enough to hurt it again, but he did vary his pitches so he could assess Bobby's skills. The kid was a natural athlete with an excellent arm, he discovered. Bobby could catch and throw almost as well as a major league rookie. He just needed more practice.

Taking a break from frying chicken, Kathleen sneaked a look at Rob and Bobby out the window and was struck by the similarity of their movements. So much for environment, she mused…genes must rule, after all.

As they tossed the ball back and forth, Rob told Bobby what it was like growing up in Logan County. He even described his first meeting with Kathleen. "You've seen old pictures of your mom, haven't you?"

Bobby nodded.

"Well, even though she was always the prettiest girl in school, I never paid much attention to her until I was about your age. We didn't attend the same school until she was in the seventh grade and I was in the eighth, but I had seen her around town a time or two. To tell the truth, I wasn't interested in girls back then, not even her—I just wanted to play ball. But one day—and I'll never forget it—I was standing in front of my locker, stuffing my books inside and talking to Billy Joe Taylor. I looked up, and there she was, walking down the hall with her friends, talking a mile a minute with a smile on her face." Rob caught a throw from Bobby, then held the ball in his glove for a few seconds while he stared into space, remembering. "It was like I'd never seen her before, you know what I mean? She really knocked me for a loop. And from then on, I knew. Kathleen Mitchell was the only girl for me."

"It must have been the same for Mom," Bobby admitted, catching the ball as Rob tossed it back. "She dates, but she's never gotten serious about any of the guys who've been serious about her."

The conversation turned to Rob's own mother and father. "I told my parents about you when I went home to take a shower this afternoon. They were some kind of happy to hear that good news. I'm telling you, Bobby, it's been embarrassing. For years, every time one of their friends had a grandchild, they called me up about it, like it was my fault someone else had become grandparents instead of them!"

Bobby questioned Rob in depth about his new grandparents. Finally, Rob said, "You sound curious about Mom and Dad. Want to meet them sometime?"

Bobby grinned. "Are you kidding? You bet your life I do. They're my new grandparents. You think I might get to see them while Mom and I are here?"

Rob couldn't resist kidding his son. "Gee, I don't know. When I was talking to Mom on the phone an hour or so ago, she didn't seem excited about meeting you."

Bobby's face dropped, and Rob roared. "I'm sorry, Bobby. I couldn't resist teasing you about Mom. If you'd heard all the squealing and screaming she did when we talked to her earlier, you'd know I'm only kidding. She didn't *seem* excited about meeting you, that part is true. She was *beside herself*. I had to hold the phone away from my ear until she quieted down. Honestly, your new grandmother almost deafened me today!" Bobby smiled, realizing his father had set him up for that story. "In fact," Rob said, cupping his ear and looking down the driveway, "you might find out for yourself how excited she is in just about a minute. That car coming up the driveway is probably theirs."

"You mean Mom invited them here for dinner tonight? And they're coming? Oh, wow, that's cool."

"Yeah, they're coming, but I don't see how they got here so quickly. It's not even five o'clock yet and that's when your mom told them to come. When we called this afternoon, Dad was still at work over in Charleston. I'd bet almost anything that, as soon as she hung up from talking to Katie, Mom called Dad and ordered him home right away."

Mike McKenzie had barely stopped his car in front of the cabin when his wife saw Rob and Bobby standing side-by-side and threw open her door. A smile split Mary McKenzie's face. She started walking their way, but then slowed and held out her hand for her husband so they could meet Bobby together. She knew Mike was excited about all of this, too. When she'd called earlier to tell him they were invited to Kathleen's for dinner and would get to meet their grandson, he said, "I'm leaving Charleston right now so we can get there early." Before she could respond, he'd hung up the phone without saying good-bye. When he arrived home forty-five minutes later, making mighty good time coming from Charleston, she told him what he'd done. Mike was embarrassed, but swore she'd get in big trouble if she even hinted to Rob that he'd hung up on her.

Mary McKenzie couldn't wait to tell her son.

As his parents approached them, Rob placed his hand on Bobby's shoulder. "Mom, Dad...this is my son, Robert Michael Mitchell."

Rob gestured toward his mother, a slim and pretty woman with short salt-and-pepper hair. "Bobby, this is your second grandmother, Mary Margaret McKenzie." Pointing toward his work-toned, gray-haired father, Rob explained, "Katie once said if we ever had a son, she would name him after both me and my dad, so I suspect she chose the Michael part of your name to honor your grandfather as much as me. I want you to meet the guy we both were named for—my father, Michael Joseph McKenzie."

Mike McKenzie's voice broke a little. "Rob, it's great that you remembered that story about Katie." He smiled at Bobby. "It's a pleasure to share a name with you, Bobby. I'll have to thank your mother myself for that honor."

During the introductions, Bobby's heart almost beat out of his chest. His Grammy Mitchell was just about the most important person in his life, next to God, his mom, and now, perhaps, his father. Bobby's life was full and sweet, but having two more grandparents was like getting buttercream frosting on his favorite chocolate cake—an extra-special treat. When he reached out to shake their hands, they opened their arms instead and hugged him.

The three of them didn't seem to want to let each other go, but the teenaged Bobby felt only slightly embarrassed by their unrestrained affection. "Bobby, this truly is a joyous day for us," his Grandmother McKenzie said. "We've been looking forward to being grandparents for years."

"Yeah, that's what Rob said."

Mary McKenzie, surprised somewhat that Bobby called his father Rob, sent a questioning look at her son. But when she frowned at him and spoke, it was not about that. "What have you been telling him?"

"Nothing but the truth, Mom. Nothing but the truth."

"She's right, Bobby," his grandfather confirmed, his arm still around Bobby. "We've been looking forward to this day for what seems like forever. Seeing you is like seeing Rob all over again at thirteen, except you're a lot better looking than your father. I think you must take after me."

Everyone laughed at Mike's quick wit. Rob leaned over to whisper to Bobby. "They're teasers and huggers. Didn't miss that, did you?"

Bobby had to chuckle. Everything he did seemed to please his new grandmother. She hadn't taken her eyes off him for more than a few seconds at a time. "You laugh like your father," she said.

From her position at the kitchen window, Kathleen had witnessed their arrival, and then had deliberately given Rob time to introduce his parents to Bobby on his own. When she walked down the steps to welcome the McKenzies, the hugs began again. Rob lifted an eyebrow at Bobby. "Told you, didn't I? Huggers, each and every one of them. Even your mother." A tenuous bond, but a bond nonetheless, was forming between father and son. They had discovered, among other things, that they both loved to tease and be teased.

But Bobby had discovered something else. That his father had always loved his mother, and probably still did.

Noting the baseball gloves Bobby and Rob were wearing, and that Rob was tossing a baseball up and down, catching it in his glove as they talked, Mike McKenzie asked Bobby if he liked to play baseball.

"Yes, sir. I love baseball. I was just playing some catch with #89."

Rob looked at his father, rolling his eyes, wondering if Bobby would ever call him dad. Bobby seemed to enjoy coming up with a different name for Rob each time he alluded to him.

While the guys talked baseball, Kathleen offered to help Mary McKenzie carry her things to the house. Overhearing, Mike McKenzie looked over at Rob and jerked his head toward the women. "Limp on over and help your mother with her stuff, son. Those bags aren't that heavy. I'll just throw awhile here with Bobby till the rest of Katie's company arrives."

As Rob ambled over to help unload what looked like more than just one bowl of carrot-raisin salad, his father confessed over his shoulder, "We went to Nu-Era Bakery to pick up a cake for dessert, then your mother started nagging me to stop somewhere else so she could pick up a few things for Bobby and Brian's girls. She'd already told me that you said not to spoil them yet, which made a lot of sense. But when I refused to turn around and take her back to Wal-Mart, she got ticked off with me. Can you believe it?"

Mary McKenzie stopped what she was doing and stared at her husband. "Well, I'll be! You said you wouldn't tell that Wal-Mart story, Mike. But now that you have, I'll just have to tell one on you…about you being so excited about coming here that you hung up on me today." Mike groaned as his wife told her story with graphic embellishments, jazzing it up for Bobby's amusement and keeping him enthralled with her storytelling skills.

When she finished, Mike had a look of bafflement on his face that any man who's ever lived with a woman would recognize instantly. "Can you believe women?" he asked Bobby.

"No, sir," Bobby said, aping his grandfather's puzzled look. "I've lived with one all of my life, and I don't understand her yet!"

\* \* \* \*

From the living room window, Rob watched his father and Bobby throw the ball to each other. His dad was doing okay for an older fellow, but when he complimented him about it later, he wouldn't phrase it quite that way. His father was doing the same thing he had done, challenging Bobby with some of his throws so he could see how good a player he was. The thought that went through both their minds, as they watched Bobby show them his stuff, was that Bobby's hands were impressive. They wondered if he could hit.

"Rob, you might as well go back out there. They know you're just standing in here watching from the window," his mother said. "Katie has everything under control, but if she does need any help, I'm perfectly capable of assisting her."

"Do you mind, Katie?" Rob asked. "I did promise to help."

"No, I don't mind. Dinner's almost ready, and it wouldn't be if you hadn't pitched in earlier, so go ahead." Kathleen grinned at her former mother-in-law—no, Mary McKenzie was *still* her mother-in-law, she reminded herself—as Rob rushed outside to rejoin his father and Bobby. He left so readily, they both knew he'd only been waiting for permission to bolt.

Mrs. McKenzie took Rob's place at the window. "I think Rob was torn. He couldn't decide whether he'd rather be in here with you or back outside with Bobby and Mike." For a moment, she watched her husband toss the ball back and forth to Bobby, as Rob searched for another glove. "Bobby's a handsome boy, Katie. I'm amazed how much he looks like Rob. Yet, at the same time, there's something about him that is so very much like you. I don't mean to pry, but if you ever need to talk about what happened between you and Rob, and why you divorced him, I'd be happy to listen. I talk a lot, as you know, but I'm not a gossip. I never pass anything on that I hear."

Kathleen knew that Mrs. McKenzie's words were true. Mary McKenzie had never been one to carry tales. Kathleen knew, too, that she would have to address the issue of her divorce from Rob with the McKenzies someday. After taking a few seconds to ready herself, she replied, "What happened is no secret, Mrs. McKenzie—"

Mary McKenzie interrupted firmly. "Sorry to stop you there, Katie, but please try to call us Mary and Mike."

"I'd like that, Mary," she said, smiling. "But as I was saying, Rob and I were too young, too immature, to handle the emotional trauma we faced at the beginning of our marriage. You know how it was at that time: I needed him when Dad had his accident and died, and he needed me while launching his career. The bottom line is, we couldn't be in two places at one time, so we weren't there for each other. Coming so soon after we eloped, that put a strain on our relationship that we weren't mature enough to handle."

Kathleen told Mary that she hadn't known she was pregnant with Bobby until after she had filed for divorce and returned to college, but she didn't tell her any more than that. If Rob wanted his parents to know that he was the one who'd asked for a divorce, and that he had refused, for no reason, to come home when her father died, he'd have to tell them that himself.

"I'm really sorry things didn't work out for you and Rob," Mary said. "Wasn't it awfully hard being divorced, then having a baby and raising him on your own all those years?"

Rob had not had time to tell his parents about their present marital status, or about their visit to Dan Hoffman's office that afternoon. Mary had no inkling that Kathleen and Rob weren't legally divorced. Kathleen felt, however, that it was up to Rob, not her, to explain their current situation to his parents. She took the easy way out—she answered Mary's direct question while letting lie the assumption of divorce she had raised.

"Bringing up Bobby was never a hardship, strange as it may seem. Though it looks like it's been just the two of us for thirteen years, I've had a lot of help from Mom, David, and Brian. And Brian's wife Ellen couldn't have been nicer to me before she died. She was my mainstay, my best friend."

Rob's parents would have eagerly joined her other relatives in supporting her during her pregnancy and after Bobby was born, Kathleen realized belatedly. But one of the reasons she had stayed away from Logan County was to keep them from finding out about Bobby and passing that knowledge on to Rob. That portentous decision, which had seemed so reasonable and right at the time it was made, had affected more lives than just hers and Rob's and Bobby's...including Rob's parents, who'd been ecstatic to learn of their grandson's existence today.

"Mary, tonight when you and Mike have your nightly prayers, will you pray for Bobby and Rob and me? That we can keep this upheaval in our lives a little one?"

"Oh, yes, Katie, you know we will. Mike and I have prayed for you often since you divorced Rob. Having you separated from our son didn't mean we stopped caring for you. You and Rob always seemed so perfect for each other. Naturally, we wondered what happened, but he never told us, and we didn't pry. Through the years, when the platonic friendships Rob had with other women never developed into anything even close to romantic, Mike and I assumed your separation wasn't because he stopped loving you. We knew you were still single, and we hoped that you still cared for him, too. But there was nothing we could do except pray that God would guide you back to each other, if that was His will—and that's what we've been doing." Mary stopped and sighed. "Life can sure get messed up when people stop talking and listening to each other, can't it?"

"You are so right. I wish I'd heard—and heeded—those precious words of wisdom years ago."

Kathleen wanted to lighten the somber mood and change the direction of the conversation. "I'll tell you what let's do," she said. "Let's put the platter of fried chicken in the oven to keep warm, then go outside to watch the guys. My family will be here shortly, and there's nothing else we need to do until then. Unless I miss my guess, you'd probably like to watch all three generations of McKenzie boys play ball, and so would I. I'll bet it's not often you see Rob in a front-yard game of catch when he's home, is it?"

Mary allowed that indeed it was a rare treat to see her son play ball anywhere outside of an official game in Cincinnati. The two women sat on the front steps and watched the guys toss the ball back and forth to each other. Rob and his father put Bobby through his paces until Brian arrived with his two girls and Lettie Mitchell.

Kathleen and Mary left the porch to join the group, and once again, pandemonium ensued. Everybody talked at once…and hugged. Kathleen spoke to Rob over everyone's heads. "This sure hasn't happened in a while, the Mitchell family and the McKenzie family en masse! What does the world's greatest first baseman think about large family gatherings now? Are they noisy enough for you?"

Strands of damp hair had stuck to Rob's forehead, making him look like a teenager again. Laughing, he pulled Kathleen away from the others, looping his arm around her neck. "Who do you think you're talking to?" he teased. "A wimp? This isn't the first time I've been stuck in the middle of a large, loud McKenzie/Mitchell gathering. If I remember correctly, and I do, I wasn't the one who always suggested sneaking away from the others so we could be alone. We both know who that was, now don't we, Katie-girl?"

Kathleen features took on a look of faux perplexity. "Gosh, Rob, this is terrible! I must have reached that age when the memory goes. Quick! Bring out the gingko biloba, the St. John's Wort, the ginseng. I can't remember a thing about that!"

Rob impulsively cupped her head, then ran his fingers through her hair before dropping a quick kiss on the end of her nose. Both of them were still chuckling when they turned back to the others, unaware until then that everyone's attention was focused on them. Other than their laughter and teasing words to each other, it was so quiet you could hear a mosquito fly by.

Rob looked at Kathleen and shrugged. They'd been caught in a moment of hilarity and fun that had apparently surprised everyone, given their past history.

Rob didn't quite know what to say, but Kathleen did.

"Dinner's ready, everyone. Come on inside. Let's eat."

# Chapter 17

Kathleen directed Brian to a chair at the opposite end of the long dining room table, then seated Rob to her right. Rob winked at her when Bobby slid into the chair on the other side of him. Once everyone was seated, she asked Rob to say grace.

Rob felt honored by Kathleen's request, but also surprised. She could have followed her family's traditional practice by asking her older brother to pray, but she had chosen instead to favor him. Their family members seated around the table weren't yet aware of what had transpired between them that day, or what they'd learned from Dan Hoffman, but later on when they were, they'd remember this meal and appreciate the significance of what Kathleen had done.

It was a meaningful moment for Rob, sharing a meal with his parents, his son, the Mitchell family, and his wife. His *wife*! Ah, the untold joy conjured up by that word, a word he'd never thought to hear again in relation to himself. Everyone joined hands, then Rob bowed his head to give thanks for the food. When he finished, he squeezed Kathleen's hand, then Bobby's, and smiled at each of them.

Waiting for the food to come his way, Brian spoke from his end of the table. "Now that the pleasantries are out of the way, tell us how your visit with the lawyer went today."

Kathleen yielded the floor to Rob with a nod. He leaned forward to peer down the table at Brian, who was helping himself to the mashed potatoes before passing them on. "It was all pretty wordy—you know how lawyers are—but what it boils down to is this: our final divorce decree was never entered. It looks like Katie and I aren't legally divorced after all."

Mrs. Mitchell dropped her hands to her lap, looking from Rob to her daughter. "You mean you're still married?"

Rob glanced at Kathleen, who indicated that he should continue. "Yes, that's exactly what it means, Mrs. Mitchell, and it's as much a surprise to Kathleen and me as anyone."

Mike McKenzie's eyes flew open, and he looked quickly at his wife. She didn't seem to know what Rob was talking about either. Their son hadn't said a word to them about his plan to visit an attorney today with Kathleen, but they wouldn't question him now about that. They'd wait and ask him later. "What in the world are you going to do, Rob?" Mary asked. "Does that mean Katie will have to file for divorce all over again?"

Rob's answer was slow in coming. "Well…she can if she wants to, Mom. But I'm hoping she won't."

"But what will the two of you do? What are your plans?" Mike inquired, plainly puzzled.

"My plan is to do what I should have done a long time ago, Dad. And I think you and Mom will approve." Rob paused. "I'm going to set about courting Katie again."

The unexpectedness of his blatant declaration caused Kathleen to blush and lose her composure. Rob grinned when he saw her flushed cheeks. "I'm devising the most romantic courtship you've ever heard of, because I want to win Katie's hand again. And this time I want to make sure I keep it forever. Come on," he said, looking from person to person, "what're my chances of pulling this off? It's true, I'm older than I was the first time around, but I'm wiser. That should count for something. You think I can get her to say yes again?"

The adults around the table sensed that Rob was using levity to mask his serious ambitions. Everyone smiled, getting into the spirit of things.

"What do you think, Aunt Katie?" Janie asked. "Are you willing to let him court you again?"

Kathleen's smile was almost as broad as Steven's Hollow. "I think I might just let him try." When everyone laughed, she followed up. "Okay, McKenzie, you've declared your intentions in front of God and everybody—embarrassing me in the process, I might add—so I'm giving you another chance. But only one. Give it your best shot!"

Bobby chimed in, too. "Well, since I'm your son, shouldn't I lay out some ground rules for this courtship? I could be tough to get around, Rob. I might just set an early curfew for Mom."

"You can try it, squirt, but don't get too tough too soon. I called a friend of mine this afternoon and reserved five tickets for a day game when the Reds play at home a week from Monday. You wouldn't want to get on the bad side of me before then, would you?"

Bobby sat straight up in his chair. "Are you serious? We get to see a game with you in Cincinnati? Who? You, me, Mom, that's three. Who else?"

"Janie and Sally, if it's okay with Brian."

The surprised girls bounced up and down in their seats and squealed. Rob didn't understand why everyone seemed so amused by his words until Brian explained. "Think about it, Rob. Two bonafide teenagers and one who's nipping at their heels? Cincinnati's around two-hundred-and-fifty miles away, more than a six-hour trip by car. You're kind of new at this parenting stuff. You sure you're ready to take on that much this early in the game?"

"Are teenagers that bad, Katie?" Rob asked. "These kids seem so nice!"

Shaking her head, Kathleen teased, "Why don't we let you find that out for yourself?" When he continued to look worried, she leaned over and confided in a whisper, "Teenagers aren't bad…they're just talkative and inquisitive. You've already experienced some of that with Bobby. It doesn't get any worse than what you've already seen."

"Whew." Rob pretended to wipe sweat from his brow. "Thanks for straightening that out." He, too, spoke in a whisper. "Man, I'm glad I chartered a plane!"

At seven o'clock, as soon as they'd finished the devil's food cake with white buttercream frosting and chocolate sprinkles Mary had purchased at the bakery—accidentally hitting on Bobby's favorite dessert when she did—the kids began pestering the adults to leave for the concert. Brian checked to see if Rob and Kathleen wanted to join them. "They may have extra tickets at the door," he said. "Shall I call to verify that?"

"Uh…no…thanks anyway, Brian. I need to stay and straighten up," Kathleen stammered.

Rob stumbled over his answer, too. "I'd…uh…better say no, too. I'll…well, uh…I think Katie needs my help in cleaning up."

Brian glanced from one to the other. Something was definitely up. Neither of them was making eye contact with him, and there wasn't that much straightening up to do. After trying in vain to read their expressions, he asked, "Would you like Bobby to spend the night with us again tonight?"

Without even looking at Rob, Kathleen said, "I don't think so, Brian. Thanks anyway, but not tonight." Brian quirked a brow at Rob, who shrugged his shoulders. Rob apparently felt that the decision was Kathleen's to make.

While the kids made last-minute trips to the bathroom, Rob followed his brother-in-law out to the porch. Brian, who'd sat down on the swing to await the arrival of his gang, looked up as Rob came outside. "What was behind Katie's negative answer in there? Didn't I hear you correctly, that the two of you are still married?"

"That's right. We are still *technically* married," Rob said. "But Katie's not ready to be *physically* married to me again, at least not yet. And I don't want to push her now and ruin this chance I have to finally make things right with her."

"So what's your plan? I tell you, Rob, whatever it is, courting again will be a strain on both of you."

"You're sure right about that. I'm already finding that out. If I hadn't loved Katie before, it'd be a lot easier now. When I found out today we were still married, my first inclination was to toss her over my shoulder, take her home, and lock the bedroom door forever. But she's not ready for that, and after thinking it over, I'm not too sure it would be the wisest thing to do myself.

"I'll be honest with you, though," Rob continued. "I've dated several women since Katie, but I've never been involved in a long-term serious relationship with anyone but her. And it wasn't like I swore off other women because I still felt married. I'd learned to live with the fact that Katie and I were divorced. I just never met another woman who appealed to me the way she does. When we found out today that our divorce decree was not entered, I decided I'd do almost anything to have her for my spouse again. All the things I hadn't felt for other women through the years, I felt for Katie as soon as I saw her yesterday." He paused, giving Brian a sheepish grin. "And those feelings are amazingly hot and deep and strong…well, I think you know what I mean."

Rob had never discussed the problems he and Kathleen suffered early in their marriage with anyone except Pete Sanders, but Brian put him on the spot about them. "What did happen between you and Katie? You seemed so right for each other. Were you aware that Katie never told any of us what caused your breakup?"

"No, I didn't know that before, Brian. But I don't mind telling you now. When Katie and I were first married I was a selfish son-of-a-gun who wanted my own way most of the time. I didn't solicit her input or consider her viewpoint in any decision I made about my career. I just expected her to drop everything that was important to her and do what I felt was right for me. But I'm different now, and she says she is, too. We both want to make a successful go of our marriage. This time the plan is to take things slow while we learn everything we can about each other. If we decide that being together again is the most important thing in the world for us, we want it to be a well-thought-out, mature decision on both our parts."

"How will your pursuit of Katie affect Bobby?" Brian sounded worried. "Bobby's future is important to all of us, you know."

"Katie's done a wonderful job with him—with your all's help, of course—and I won't interfere with that," Rob promised. "If she and I do reconcile, I want us to continue to raise him in a Christian home just like yours and Ellen's was, with Katie and me setting an example of how a man and woman can love each other totally, and live together forever, while teaching their child to be moral and caring."

Rob restated what he'd told Brian before. "If it makes our relationship stronger, I'm willing to wait as long as it takes for Katie to make a lifelong commitment to me."

"Well, my friend, I'm sure you realize that you've got a long row to hoe ahead of you. I watched the two of you at dinner, and if you don't both have it bad, I haven't seen anyone who does. When you love someone completely, and a huge dose of lust is thrown into the mix for good measure, it's hard to wait until you tie the knot to experience the ultimate closeness of married love. I can't imagine how tough it must be to abstain from loving someone you were married to before. Do yourself a favor, Rob. Make this a strong, intense, and very, very, very, short courtship!"

The two guys shared a carefree laugh at that. "Seriously, though," Brian said, "is there anything I can do to help you out?"

"Yes. Let the girls go to Cincinnati with us when I fly there to have my leg checked next week. When I called Pete Sanders to tell him what Katie and I heard today from Dan Hoffman, Pete said he'd pick up some game tickets for me. I went ahead and ordered five tickets, hoping you'd let the girls come along. Having them with us might make it easier for Katie and me to be alone, but not really alone. You know? I don't want to forget that our goal is getting to know each other better before jumping in with both feet. It'll help, I think, having Janie and Sally along."

"I'll talk to them tonight. If they want to go, it's okay with me. You saw their reaction at dinner—can you imagine them saying no? I'll run it by them again later and call you in the morning."

By then, everyone else was ready to leave, and Brian was the last one down the steps. He just shook his head and chuckled, thinking of Rob and Kathleen back together again…courting while abstaining.

# Chapter 18

Rob was quiet as he dried the last of the dishes, his mind miles away. Kathleen glanced at him a time or two as she puttered around making coffee. If he would only sit down and rest his leg for a while, she was convinced he'd feel better. But he wouldn't leave her there to straighten up on her own. It had been a satisfying day, but chaotic, Kathleen reflected, inhaling the scent of the rich Colombian brew that was just starting to gurgle. Rob must have worn himself out.

Kathleen hadn't complained, but Rob knew he wasn't good company right now. His leg throbbed and he felt weary all the way down to his bones. Ever since dinner, he'd been unable to decide what to do about the letters Mrs. Mitchell had returned to him that afternoon. He couldn't get a firm grip on how their reappearance might affect his relationship with Kathleen. Most of the emotional pain he had suffered through the years stemmed from Mrs. Mitchell's interception of those letters. Oh, he had forgiven Mrs. Mitchell totally; that was no longer an issue. As a follower of Christ he could not have done otherwise. He just could not comprehend why she had not given the letters to her daughter, upon receipt. Or why she hadn't mentioned them to Kathleen when Bobby was born. Wouldn't that have been the perfect time for her to confess what she'd done? Mrs. Mitchell had to have known that the first letter, at least, was an apology from him to Kathleen.

Lettie Mitchell's one horrendous act had changed the entire course of Rob's life, and he knew he'd be grappling with the ramifications of that for an extremely long time. It had also changed Kathleen's, Bobby's, and Mrs. Mitchell's lives, too. They also would be dealing with Lettie Mitchell's treachery—as best they could—in days to come.

Rob had poured out his heart in those impassioned epistles. He couldn't help thinking Kathleen might have had second thoughts about their divorce if Mrs. Mitchell had passed them on when they arrived. At the very least, Kathleen might have contacted him when she discovered she was pregnant, even if she did decide later to proceed with the divorce.

He didn't know what to do. Should he show Kathleen the letters, or not? If he did decide to share them with her, what real purpose would it serve? It wouldn't lessen the loneliness of the years they'd lived apart. It wouldn't give him back the thirteen years of Bobby's life he'd missed. And it couldn't erase the fact that Kathleen had kept their baby's birth a secret from him. That was something they'd have to live with forever.

It was the note Mrs. Mitchell wrote, the note warning him not to contact her daughter again, that had broken Rob's spirit and ravaged his soul for so long. If he'd only known that Kathleen hadn't seen his letters—that those hurtful words were Mrs. Mitchell's, not Kathleen's—nothing would have kept him from reclaiming her then. She might not believe it now, from the way he used to be, but he'd have forfeited his career in baseball for a chance to be with her.

Blowing out a lengthy breath, Rob reached a decision. He had to let Kathleen know he had not totally abandoned her, as she had believed. "I'd like to tell you what your mother and I talked about today, if you're still interested," he said. "We about finished in here?"

"Just about." Kathleen frowned at his somber expression.

"Come into the living room when you've finished," he said, without a trace of his usual smile. "I need to get something from my jacket."

Once they were sitting side-by-side on the sofa, Rob placed the packet of letters on the coffee table in front of them. "I don't know exactly how, or even what, to tell you about these letters, Katie. Anything I say will sound self-serving. It might be best if you just read them in order, then draw your own conclusions."

He pulled out the first letter he'd written and handed it to her. Before breaking the seal, Kathleen noted when it was mailed. How puzzling, she thought, glancing beside her at Rob. The letter was addressed to her in Rob's handwriting, but date stamped in late-September of the year they were married. She unfolded the letter and read: "Dear Katie: Please forgive me for treating you so badly the last time we were together. I've known since I was thirteen years old that you were the girl I'd someday fall in love with and marry. But when my dreams came true and you were finally my wife, I ruined it all by being stupid. I can't believe I said those awful things to you in Denver. And I regret not rushing home to be with you the night you called to say your father had died. Your dad was always nice to me, though I was the guy who was dating his only daughter, which makes my failure to be there even worse. I'd do anything in the world to make things right between us again.

"Please don't get a divorce. I know I said I wanted you to, but if you'll just give me another chance, I'll prove I'm not really a jerk. I'll always love you, Katie-girl." He'd signed the letter, "Your loving husband, Rob."

Tears slowly made their way down Kathleen's cheeks. She understood exactly what that letter meant. Just as he had declared in his sworn deposition, Rob hadn't wanted the divorce any more than she. When she hadn't answered his written plea, he must have assumed she didn't love him anymore.

Without another word, Rob handed her a second, thicker letter, one he'd written six weeks after mailing the first.

"Sweet Katie-girl," she read, "I can't blame you for not answering my letter. You must hate me, and I can see why. I don't like myself much either, if you want to know the truth. But something happened here in San Juan I need to tell you about.

"Last week, while I was spending the night with a teammate at his family's place outside town, some of the guys on the team got a key to my room and hired a local stripper who hangs around the stadium to go there and wait in my bed. They thought it would be funny, seeing me walk in on a near-naked woman, and they wondered what a straitlaced guy like me would do with a woman like that. So they bought a case of beer and drank it while they waited for me to return. Someone phoned a tabloid reporter who'd been sniffing around our team, looking for any kind of dirt he could dig up, and told him about the stripper they'd hired. He came to the motel and waited around outside with them, not knowing I wouldn't be coming back that night.

"In the middle of the night, the guys knocked on my door to check on the woman. The reporter took a picture of her as she opened the door. That photo shows her in a negligee and, in the background, my messed up bed where she slept. I swear, Katie, she slept there alone. I can prove I was somewhere else that night.

"Since you didn't answer my previous letter, I know you're through with me. But I still love you, Katie, and I'd never dishonor you that way. Every day I pray for another chance with you, and each night I dream that we're together again. Please let me know you got this letter, and that you understand. Love, Rob"

As Kathleen's tears continued to fall, she reached out to squeeze Rob's hand. He pulled a white handkerchief out of his pocket. "There's more," he said, blotting the tears from her eyes. "After Thanksgiving, I wrote again, but this time I sent my letter inside an envelope addressed to your mother."

He handed her the envelope, which had been carefully slit open by Mrs. Mitchell. Inside was a smaller, sealed envelope, addressed to Kathleen McKenzie, with his short note to her mother still attached: "Mrs. Mitchell, I desperately need to get in touch with Katie. Please give her this letter and ask her to contact me as soon as she can. Sincerely, Rob."

Kathleen opened the sealed envelope and began to read the one paragraph message: "I still love you, Katie, and always will, but I'm worried about you. You haven't responded to either of my letters, and I need to know you're okay. Please call me collect as soon as you can. I'll ask the clerk at the desk to accept the charges if I'm out. Should we miss each other, please leave a number where I can reach you." The telephone number to Rob's motel in Puerto Rico, and his room number, were added to the bottom of his note.

By now, Rob, too, was near tears. "In December, when I came back to the states for Christmas, I hadn't heard a word from you. I looked for you at your mother's house, to no avail. My parents and the friends I talked to here said they hadn't seen you in town since you went back to school. The next place I searched was Morgantown," Rob said, "but you weren't there. None of our friends at WVU had any idea where you were. I thought for sure the university would have a forwarding address, but they didn't. I couldn't get David on the phone, which didn't surprise me, given his schedule. Then I tried to call Brian. All I got there was a recorded message saying his number was no longer in service. I even drove to Virginia, but the house Brian and Ellen had rented in Stafford was empty. Their neighbors, who'd just moved in themselves, had no idea who Brian was or where he'd gone. I was so frantic that I drove back down here to your mother's house again, thinking I could force her into telling me where you were. But she was still gone. I did everything I could to find you, Katie. Even though I thought we were divorced, I couldn't let myself give up on us. After a while, I became a man obsessed."

Holding her gaze, Rob continued, "In January, I got a letter from your mother. She said you never wanted to see me again, to leave you alone and not try to contact you anymore. That's when the bottom dropped out of my world. If I hadn't met Pete Sanders then, I'm not sure I would have survived. Believing you'd read my letters and didn't want me anymore almost killed me."

Tears flowed from Kathleen's eyes down her cheeks. "But if I had seen those letters, it would've changed everything. Why would Mom do that to me? Yeah, after seeing that story in the paper, I did say I didn't want you to know I was pregnant, but answering or not answering your letters was my decision to make, not hers, no matter what I'd said before. How can I be civil to Mom, knowing what she did?"

All at once, Rob felt emotionally and physically exhausted. Combing his hands through his hair, he solemnly studied Kathleen. "Look, I feel exactly the same as you, but we have to be careful with your mother. You saw how remorseful she was after giving me the letters, didn't you? She's been living with a guilty conscience for a long time, and I think she has already punished herself enough. Can't you just imagine what your mom has gone through? This thing has been hanging over her head like a dark cloud for years. And every time she has looked at you and Bobby, she has remembered and regretted what she did. That's punishment, Katie, no matter how you look at it." Rob paused to ponder the situation for a moment, then turned his attention back to Kathleen. "Can't you at least try to forgive her?"

"All I can promise is, I'll try. But it's not just the letters that gnaw at me, Rob, although they are the worst of it. She told Bobby about the problem with our divorce, and even named you as his father, before I could do it myself. I didn't want to confront her tonight, not with everyone here, but I have to tell Mom how I feel. Now that I know about the letters, on top of the other, how can things ever be the same between my mother and me?"

Rob nestled Kathleen close to his side and tried to consider the problem from her point of view. Mrs. Mitchell was guilty of concealing things from Kathleen, that much was evident. She'd failed to pass on his letters to her daughter. And the things he'd said in those letters were things Kathleen needed to hear from him before Bobby was born. But Rob knew, deep down in his soul, that Kathleen needed to cool down a whole lot before confronting her mom. He also knew, more than anyone, that angry words can never be recalled. If Kathleen dealt with Lettie Mitchell in anger now, someday soon she'd be sorry. After all, they weren't talking about some casual acquaintance they may have run into at the grocery store. Lettie Mitchell was Kathleen's mother—and Bobby's grandmother.

Rob prayed for a happy resolution to the problem, one that would keep all the ties intact between Kathleen, Bobby, Mrs. Mitchell, and himself. He would have to tread a fine line between the two women. He loved Kathleen, but he had discovered, surprisingly, that he cared more than he'd thought for her mother. He didn't want to see Lettie Mitchell hurting any more than she already was.

Kathleen's attitude toward her mother was too harsh, in Rob's opinion, but he was careful not to say that out loud. Kathleen had always been so easy-going, he'd never seen her quite like this before.

He closed his eyes and exhaled quietly. The reality of the situation was, all the contrition in the world wouldn't erase what Mrs. Mitchell had done. Could he help the two women avoid a permanent falling out with each other? No quick, easy answer—no "aha!" revelation—came to mind.

Bottom line. As her in-name-only husband—for now—he'd stand beside Kathleen, whatever her approach to the problem might be. But he hoped she'd stop and think things through before rushing into them half-cocked. "Please give this a little more thought and prayer, Katie," he finally pleaded. "Show your mother the same compassion and consideration that we've shown each other over the past couple of days." He rubbed his chin against the top of her head where it rested on his chest. "Think you can do that, baby?"

Kathleen raised her head and scooted a short distance away. "Look, Rob, don't hassle me on this. I said I'd try with Mom, but that's all I'm willing to do at this point. Don't expect miracles from me."

It would require a ton of self-control on Kathleen's part to heal the breach between her mother and herself, and Kathleen wasn't sure she had what it took inside her to do it. She'd have to subdue her temper, totally stifle her feelings, before it would work. Why should she be the one to work things out with her mother? Her mother was the culprit here, not she.

Excusing herself, Kathleen carried Rob's letters with her when she went into the kitchen for coffee. A weary Rob, his leg aching again, wandered outside to sit in the swing.

\* \* \* \*

Rob watched the quarter moon slip over the top of the trees, and tried to count the flickering stars that littered the sky. But he couldn't get Kathleen's venomous, negative feelings toward her mother out of his mind. His thoughts kept wandering, and when he realized that he kept losing count, he abandoned the star-counting game he'd played night after night on his parents' back porch as a kid. Rob didn't think it was much of a pastime for an adult to be involved in, anyhow, but he needed some kind of a distraction. He'd felt slightly edgy earlier, seeing those old letters, and he still hadn't calmed down.

This day had been so filled with distractions that calling it eventful didn't do it justice. Every facet of Rob's life, even the projected course of his future, had shifted and would be influenced by what he had heard and experienced today. He should feel like a different man after those stunning revelations in Dan Hoffman's office, but right now, other than a slight twinge of apprehension about learning to be a father and a great deal of excitement over courting Kathleen, he felt about the same as before. Maybe the full force of it would hit him tomorrow, or as he lay in his bed, alone again, tonight.

Alone. How many nights had he slept alone through the years, his body and his mind aching for Kathleen? He would try to keep the bargain they'd made to take things slowly, but oh how he needed her now. Maybe he shouldn't stay here; being alone with Kathleen was too tempting. He should get up off the swing right now, tell her good-bye, and leave.

Yeah, right! Like that was really an option.

\* \* \* \*

In the kitchen, Kathleen's emotions ran the gamut, too, from extreme highs to impossible lows. Her strange, absurd new status as a woman hit her abruptly—she was not single, not divorced, and yet not really married. Weird! And the letters. She couldn't believe the love Rob had shared in those letters. If only her mother had delivered them as soon as they arrived! Why keep them a secret from her? Kathleen shook her head. She could ask herself that question a dozen times a day for the rest of her life and never find a satisfying answer.

She didn't need to wonder why she suddenly felt drained. Perhaps it would be best to send Rob on his way and make an early night of it, herself. No, that wouldn't work; it wasn't what she wanted. She'd spent too many nights alone already, crying herself to sleep, wondering where he was and what he was doing and, when she was feeling especially low and most honest with herself, who he might be with.

Reading those old letters had placed things in a different perspective for Kathleen. Like a kaleidoscope, her world was already being rearranged into a different, more colorful pattern. A frenetic, multi-faceted design that, strangely enough, was beginning to make sense. Kathleen sensed that if she could just make that final, slight adjustment, if she could toss aside her preconceptions and her past negativity toward Rob, something beautiful and lasting would emerge.

She picked up the serving tray, poured the coffee, turned off the pot, and walked to the porch. When Rob heard the screen door close, he glanced up, the stark longing and desire he felt for Kathleen blazing from his eyes. She was serving coffee; he was thirsty for her.

He spoke just above a whisper. "Through the years, did you ever miss the closeness we had with each other? The intimacy? Can you remember how it was with us back then?" He held his breath and waited.

Kathleen's heart seemed to skip a few beats. For a moment, she stood just outside the front door, frozen in place, as the kaleidoscope again came to mind. She forced herself to breathe naturally. "Of course I missed the closeness," she said. "That's the worst thing about being divorced or, in our case, thinking you are—the loss of that intimate connection with the person you love. You don't even have to ask if I remember. I could never forget something that intense, that sweet." She felt self-conscious, offering up her feelings to Rob again like this. "Bobby asked the other day why I never dated any man more than a couple of times, and I suppose that's why. I gave my heart to you, Rob. There's been no one else for me since then."

"And I spent all of my years dreaming of you. You were there with me in my imagination, in my fantasies, each and every night." Rob sent Kathleen a sweet, gentle smile. "We're quite a pair, aren't we? I could kick myself for not hiring a private investigator to locate you, but I never even thought of that until I was sitting here tonight. I just let your mother's scarring words convince me you didn't want to hear from me again. Running into you this week was a total surprise, Katie, but now that I've found you once more, I can't imagine never seeing you again."

A tender smile passed over Kathleen's mouth at his words, and that mixture of sweetness and innocence lit a flame of desire deep down in the core of Rob's being. How had he lived without her for so long? She moved at last, walking toward the swing with the tray. The slow, subtle, unintended sway of her hips was poetry in motion. Rob dug his nails into his palms, fighting his yearning for her.

"Don't come any closer, Katie! Unless you're willing to pay the piper, keep your distance. When you said there'd been no one else for you but me, you erased that imaginary line between taking-things-slowly and full-scale-attack that I promised not to cross. Even with my leg hurting like crazy, which it is, there's no way I could deny myself or you tonight. You'd better stay as far away from me as you can...and that's your final warning!"

Rob had propped his leg on the swing to ease his pain, so Kathleen knew he'd done too much today, and he looked tired. His ashen countenance was graphic confirmation of the punishment he'd forced upon his body. He had to be as psychologically drained as she, and she didn't have a physical injury to contend with on top of the emotional disturbance. She really should send him home. They'd said everything that could be said for now. He needed his rest more than being with her.

But he was so beguiling, she didn't want to send him away. She placed the tray on a table nearby, then picked up a small pillow and cushioned the arm of the swing. Pushing against his shoulders, she said, "You stop talking like that. I'll be levelheaded enough for us both. We can have coffee later, if you still want it. But for now, slide around and rest your head on the pillow. Stretch out your legs on the swing. You need rest more than you need me."

"That's the most erroneous, silly assumption I have ever heard in my life, Katie," Rob said, obeying her orders. "I don't need anything more than I need you. And someday—very soon, I hope—I'll show you just how wrong you are." Tilting his head back, he looked up. "Did you actually say that with a straight face?"

"Well, I tried to," Kathleen smiled, moving to stand at the end of the swing. "Shhhh," she said, hushing Rob. She slid her fingers through his hair, softly massaging his scalp and hoping to help him relax enough to ease the aching muscles in his leg. It wasn't wise, Rob knew, to give himself up to her tender ministrations, to lose himself in her sweet caresses. Not when he remembered all too well where those soothing strokes of hers could lead. He warned himself that what they were doing wasn't smart, yet he relished her gentle, loving touch.

Kathleen talked softly, saying nothing, really, as she slowly combed her fingers through his soft, thick, brown hair. Trailing them lightly along his temples, she traced his ears and his forehead, his face and his jaw, massaging away the stresses of the day.

Rob's eyes were half closed. "It's not working, Katie. Stop."

She leaned over, brushing his forehead so softly he couldn't tell whether it was her lips or her delicate fingertips that gently skimmed his brow. "Second chance, Rob—everybody gets one. You sure you want me to stop?"

He tilted his head to better see her. "Why, you little brat! You know I'm suffering here, yet you're deliberately tormenting me. That's mean, Katie."

He twisted around and slid carefully out of the swing. Standing up, he gave her a quick kiss—the first kiss they'd shared since he showed her the letters. "I'll call Pastor Harlow first thing in the morning," he said. "Early. Before I blow my good intentions." Kathleen smiled.

"It's not funny, Katie."

"Yes, it is, Rob. After years of wondering why you didn't want to stay married to me, it is delightfully amusing!" After spending almost half her lifetime hundreds of miles away from Rob, Kathleen finally felt she had the upper hand. And she loved it. In dulcet tones, she cooed, "Sweet dreams, my almost husband," as he started down the steps.

Halfway down the steps, Rob moaned. He didn't dare turn around and kiss her good-bye again. But as he walked away, she did hear him mutter, "That is *so* not funny, Katie."

Easing into his car, Rob said, "I'll phone you in the morning after my physical therapy appointment. But I hope you don't sleep a wink tonight. You're hard hearted, Katie!"

Kathleen smiled her final good-bye and laughed softly as she watched her *husband* drive away.

# Chapter 19

▼

Kathleen was sitting at the kitchen table with her second cup of coffee, proofreading a magazine article she'd written for *Mothers of Toddlers*, when Brian called the next morning. "Hey, Katie," he said, "you had your first cup of coffee yet this morning?"

"Ha-ha-ha, Brian, very funny," Kathleen responded. "Those rumors that I'm a bear before I get my caffeine fix each morning are vicious and untrue. You wouldn't know who started them, now, would you?"

Brian chuckled. If anyone knew his sister's early morning temperament, it was he. And those rumors were true, no matter how vigorous Kathleen tried to rebut them. "Well, if you're sure you're functioning at full capacity, I'd like to leave a message with you for Rob. When I called the McKenzie's house earlier, Mary was on her way out the door, headed for a Women's Guild meeting at church. She said Rob left around seven for physical therapy, and she doubts she'll see him again before you do. If he calls or comes by, will you tell him I reviewed 'Brian Mitchell's Official Rules for Ladylike Behavior at Baseball Games, 1st Edition' with the girls last night? And they still want to go to the game."

"Great! If I can remember what you said, I'll pass it on. What's the name of that rule book again?"

"I never repeat myself, you should know that. If you don't get it the first time, you don't get it at all." Brian knew exactly how to transmit a smile through the telephone line. "Ah, yes," he said, "Monday, Monday…estimated day of departure. Just a week or so away, but it can't come too soon." He paused. "Oh, excuse me for a minute. Swami Mitchell just walked into Mom's kitchen."

"Yeah, I'll bet. Let me clarify something, okay? You're still the only person Swami shares his predictions with, right?"

"Don't interrupt with silly questions, Katie. Swami doesn't like it." Brian's voice changed, became deeper, and Kathleen could have sworn he was talking to someone in the room with him…someone real. "You'll never believe what Swami just said."

"I'm sure."

"Well, you can either accept his forecasts or not, Katie, that's up to you. But I'd pay close attention; Swami's latest prediction is right on the mark. He said, and I quote—" Brian's voice became even deeper, "—'In the not-too-distant future, I see a time of peace and quiet for handsome, debonaire, loved-by-women-of-discernment, man-about-town Brian Mitchell. But I see a time of loud, constant chatter for those two other people…uh, what *are* their names?'

"Wow, Katie, did you get that? Swami must be talking about you and Rob and the trip to Cincinnati!"

"Right!" Kathleen rolled her eyes. Brian was brilliant…most of the time. The rest of the time he was a tease.

"Sorry, Katie…gotta cut this conversation short. Swami's ready for a cup of high-test coffee, himself. So you just give the novice parent my sympathy when you talk with him today, you hear? Tell him Swami has spoken and should not be ignored. Emphasize the part about loud, constant chatter."

Kathleen snickered out loud. "No way! I'm not telling Rob any of that. We promised to let him learn about teenagers on his own. Just between you…oops, Swami…and me, I think Rob will discover that ours are delightful!"

"Care to wager real money on that?" Brian sounded amused. "Put your money where your mouth is."

Kathleen just smiled. Her brother would be good for anyone's early morning mood. After a few more moments of idle chitchat—with Swami apparently sipping his coffee in silence—Kathleen made arrangements to pick up the girls a little later for a tour of downtown.

While she warmed up the unfinished cup of coffee she'd set aside while talking with Brian, Bobby bounded noisily down the stairs, playing an air guitar and doing a fairly good vocal rendition of Brad Paisley's hit "Me, Neither." Kathleen wondered again at the resilience of youth. Bobby had been totally exhausted when Brian brought him home late last night, but just look at him now. He was—as they like to say in West Virginia—bright-eyed and bushy-tailed, ready to take on the world. He raved about the concert while consuming an extremely large bowl of cereal and four slices of cinnamon-swirl toast, convincing Kathleen anew that his stomach was a bottomless pit!

When the phone rang, Bobby grabbed it first. "Hi, #89," he said, hearing Rob's voice. They talked about the concert for a while, then Rob asked to speak to Kathleen.

"Is he still in the room, Katie?"

"No, he's upstairs now, taking a shower."

Once assured the coast was clear, Rob lowered his voice to soft, slow, and suggestive. "Did you sleep as poorly as I did last night, Katie-girl?"

Kathleen laughed quietly, leaning into the phone. "Probably."

Rob's voice became huskier, tickling the nerve endings that connected Kathleen's ear to the sound from his lips. "Let me tell you how last night was for me, sweetheart. The air-conditioner was on full blast, but my room felt as warm as a Mississippi night in mid-summer. Way back, when I thought I'd never see you again, remembering us together was agony for me. But last night I let myself relive exactly how it was when I loved you. You remember how we'd love each other, then hold hands until we'd talked ourselves to sleep? And then, an hour later, or two, or even the next morning, how we'd wake up, snuggled tightly in each other's arms?"

Kathleen's mouth went dry. She didn't say a word. Rob continued speaking, his seductive, daring words meant only to be shared by a husband with his wife. "I tried to visualize you alone in that cabin, perhaps thinking of me, too, but I couldn't see just you or just me as separate individuals anymore. I could only see us together. Just a few short miles away, almost close enough to throw a kiss and have you catch it, what I wanted was to have you here beside me, Katie, kissing me to sleep."

By then, Kathleen wasn't sure she *could* speak, even if she tried. Those forgotten memories Rob invoked had been completely tamped down, or so she'd believed, but his sweet-talking words brought them back to the surface again. "I don't know how to respond," she said, leaning closer to the phone. "Don't say anything more, please. As it is, I won't be able to face you today without blushing."

Rob chuckled softly. His words were amazingly gentle. "All I can think about is you, Katie-girl. You know that, don't you? You brought this sweet misery on both of us by being a mean, cruel woman last night. I think Little Miss Innocent has turned into a tease!"

"Not with anyone else, though. Just you."

Rob growled deeply, then the line was filled with silence.

Kathleen enjoyed the unexpected, mildly suggestive repartee with her husband, but the cabin was small and sound carried. Bobby had gone upstairs to take a shower, but she hadn't heard the water running yet. "We'd better change the subject," she said. "I know warming up this cabin isn't the real reason you called."

"Not the primary reason, it's true. But a close secondary one." He sighed, almost under his breath, and became practical again. "I called Pastor Harlow after leaving my p/t session this morning. He can see us at four o'clock this afternoon. Is that okay?" Kathleen acknowledged that it was.

When Kathleen had awakened earlier to a beautiful West Virginia morning—low humidity and temperatures in the 70s—she had decided to take the kids to Logan for a walking tour as soon as they were dressed. They would quickly tire of shopping and be all out of sorts once the temperature rose into the 90s later that day, as predicted by local forecasters. She wanted to get going as soon as she could. She mentioned those plans to Rob, assuring him they'd be finished well before four, and invited him to join them.

"No, I shouldn't walk that much today. Yesterday was rough, but the therapist did say I'm still coming along well. I'd just slow y'all down, so I'll pass on the tour. How about meeting for lunch at Mabel's, instead?"

"Sure. One o'clock?"

"That's fine. I may get there early, though. I haven't seen Billy Joe and Carrie yet, and I'd like to check in with them. I'll meet you at our usual place…remember? And I'll treat."

"Of course I remember—the back corner on the side closest to town. We'll be there at one. But since I'm still in my nightgown, I'd better hang up and get dressed. The kids'll want some time to shop before lunch."

Rob groaned. "Come on, Katie, have mercy! Don't use words like nightgown in conversation with me…not before we talk to Pastor Harlow!"

"I'm just having fun, Rob, getting some of my own back. You're the one who mentioned old sleeping habits, not me." His low rumble of laughter reminded Kathleen how easy it always had been to talk and tease and flirt with him.

"If Bobby can stay with your mom this evening, how about us having dinner together after our meeting at the church? Is Charleston okay? I'll take you to your favorite kind of place, which Bobby says is anywhere that dinner isn't wrapped up in paper and served with plastic forks."

Rob's invitation delighted Kathleen. Charleston was only forty-five minutes away. While she'd been favorably impressed by the new eating establishments she'd seen while driving through Logan, it would be nice eating at an elegant restaurant in Charleston with him.

Stating that he, too, had better get going, Rob ended the conversation. "I'll miss you this morning, Katie-girl. Take care till I see you again."

Kathleen lowered her voice. "I'll miss you, too." With a chuckle, Rob hung up the phone, feeling mighty good about the progress he'd made that morning with his courtship of Ms. Kathleen Mitchell McKenzie.

Kathleen, for her part, wondered if things might not be heating up too quickly. She didn't want to fall back into old habits too soon, not until she knew where their relationship was headed. She really didn't know that much about the modern-day Rob McKenzie, and it was up to her to set the pace and slow things down.

She pivoted to go upstairs only to find Bobby standing near the stairway, his mouth stretched into a grin. "I think I got the gist of that conversation," he said. "Sounds like you and Rob are warming things up. Acting as your chaperone might turn out to be too challenging for an innocent teen like me."

There was no way Bobby could've heard Rob's end of their chat; he'd still been upstairs. Kathleen pretended to be indignant. She hit him on the head with a small pillow and tried to scurry past him up the stairs.

"Mom," Bobby teased, placing his hand on her arm, "you're blushing!"

Bobby had never seen his mother like this, not with any of the other men she'd dated off and on through the years. Her eyes sparkled, and for the last couple of days she'd seemed to always be happy. Not quite old enough yet to know exactly what was going on with his mother and father, he had seen enough to know that something was happening between the two of them.

"Talk to me," he said, pulling her down beside him on the step. "You think you and Rob are getting together again?"

Kathleen shied away from giving Bobby too much hope. She and Rob needed to spend a lot of time on their knees before making any decisions about the future. There were several major issues they needed to work on—parental visitation being just one.

Bobby was right, though. Her relationship with Rob did seem to be warming up. But Kathleen reminded herself that she'd vowed to never again go by feelings alone. "I don't know that we'll ever reconcile," she said. "How would you feel if we did?"

"Well, it's true I haven't known old #89 long, but he seems to be a pretty decent guy. I believe him when he says he's sorry about the way he treated you before. He would like to have known about me sooner, or so he said. But he admitted that it was just as much his fault as yours that he didn't. I really didn't want to like him at first, but I'm beginning to think he's okay. How about you?"

Kathleen carefully considered her answer. "I do like Rob. He's making an honest effort to make up with me, and I'm meeting him half way. But there's nothing more I can tell you than that. In a way, I'm afraid we're picking up where we left off years ago, and that might not be smart. He's still right much of a stranger to me."

"Well, you know what you want more than I do," Bobby agreed. "But Rob is my father. I would sort of like to see you get back together someday. You understand, don't you?"

"Sure," Kathleen said, reaching out to pull him into a hug. "You've wanted to be part of a real family for a long time, haven't you…for even longer than I realized, right?"

As he leaned against his mother, Bobby nodded, his lips tightly sealed.

Kathleen settled him closer, closing her eyes as they sat there together. Though she'd tried to be everything Bobby needed as a parent, she'd never been able to compensate for his lack of a father.

It surprised Kathleen that Bobby didn't immediately pull back. Holding a teenager close like this for more than a few seconds at a time was no mean feat, in her experience. Placing a soft kiss on top of his head, she said, "You know that Rob loves having you as his son, don't you?"

Bobby gave a small shake of his head, surprising Kathleen.

She reached down to cup his chin and tilt it up. "Where did that negative shake come from, Bobby Mitchell? You've got to be kidding! You listen to me right now, because I'm telling you the truth." She looked directly into his eyes. "It was love at first sight the other morning when Rob first saw you. And no matter what happens between Rob and me, he will always be your father and a real big part of your life." She paused, holding back tears. "Don't you fret for even one minute over what might or might not happen with the three of us as a family. We'll work everything out, Bobby, I promise. Just give it some time."

Bobby nodded. "I'm okay, Mom, really. Guess I just felt insecure for a minute."

"Well, don't spend too much time worrying. I want you to get to know the area where I grew up and have a good time with your cousins while we're here," Kathleen said, giving Bobby one last squeeze before he headed up the stairs for his shower.

\* \* \* \*

Walking the streets of Logan later with the kids reminded Kathleen why Logan was such a great place to live and call home. People greeted them with a smile and a hello whether they knew them or not.

They began their tour near Logan General Hospital, where Kathleen found a convenient parking place. Using a map of Logan they'd torn from a tourist booklet their grandmother had picked up last week, the kids plotted out the route they wanted to follow. They'd leisurely stroll up to the end of Main Street, passing the Coalfield Jamboree on the way, cut over one block to Stratton, check out the stores there, then end up back at the car before meeting Rob at Mabel's.

As they meandered by the *Logan County Sentinel*, Kathleen glanced in and saw Millie Samson, a reporter she'd met the summer she worked there. Poking her head inside the door, she called out a hello. It was Saturday and the paper had been put to bed, but Millie, now the managing editor, invited them in for a tour. Millie knew Rob McKenzie, of course, and that Kathleen had been dating him the summer they worked together. But she didn't let her curiosity show when Kathleen introduced her to the two girls and her son, Bobby Mitchell, who looked so very much like Rob.

Kathleen played the part of interested observer as Millie told the youngsters how a news item made it from a reporter's field notes through a networked computer onto the printed pages of the paper. Millie knew what she was talking about, and she knew how to make it interesting for the kids.

Kathleen's mind harked back to the summer she met Millie. Millie had just begun working as a reporter for the *Sentinel* when Kathleen served her college internship there. As she recalled, Millie had grown up in Madison, a small community mid-way between Logan and Charleston, and had been living at home while attending college part-time and working at the paper.

Using the paltry number of clues she had at her disposal, Kathleen calculated Millie's age as being somewhere between her own age and Brian's. But Millie didn't look a day older than she had the last time Kathleen saw her, and that was at least fifteen years ago. Millie was petite with big green eyes and lots of long, thick, curly red hair that bounced each time she moved. There was also, Kathleen noticed for the first time, a smattering of small freckles across the bridge of her nose.

As Millie answered a question about local sports coverage from Janie and Bobby, Sally sidled close to Kathleen. "Aunt Katie, this is so much fun. Thanks for stopping when you saw your friend. It's interesting, isn't it, what reporters do? I've never been in a newspaper office before today, but, you know what? I think it's what I'd like to do when I grow up."

Kathleen sensed that Sally's interest in journalism was no sudden whim on the part of her niece. "It's sure an engaging profession, I'll give you that. I loved working here as an intern, even though it was for only three months. When did you first become interested in newspaper work?"

"Gosh, I can't remember when I first thought about it. It seems like I've always wanted to write for a paper. I've seen TV programs and read a lot of books about reporting, and I even keep a journal that I write in almost every day."

"That's exactly how I started writing, and I was just about your age at the time. Isn't it fun to pour out your feelings on paper? Have you mentioned this to your dad?"

"No, but he knows I keep a journal. He says that someday I'll look back at what I've written and be really, really glad I was faithful about doing it." As she thought about her dad, a bright smile lit her face. "You know what Dad did when I told him about my journal?"

"No, but he's my brother. I'm almost afraid to ask."

"Don't worry, he was great. He said a person should be able to write their most secret, most personal thoughts in their journal, holding nothing back. So he bought me a box with a key to keep mine in. He promised he'd never read it unless I asked him to, and he warned Janie not to sneak around and try to read it either. He called that a betrayal of trust between sisters, and he said he'd punish her big time if she did." Sally placed her hand over her mouth when she laughed, her eyes sparkling. "I loved it when he told Janie that! But best of all, Dad promised not to bug me if I ever stopped keeping it up."

"Hey, Mom," Bobby interrupted from across the room, "come look. Ms. Samson found one of your articles. Did you know they kept ancient stuff like that?"

Millie snorted indignantly, then winked at Kathleen. "What do you think? Should we get rid of the good-looking kid with the smart-alecky mouth?"

"Ancient stuff, indeed!" Kathleen said. She mimicked a street fighter pushing up his sleeves. "The two of us can surely take him out. Let's do it!"

For a few seconds they pretended to go after Bobby. Then Millie asked, "Seriously, Katie, what do you think? We have any aspiring reporters in this bunch?"

"At least one, but I don't know about the others. Sally keeps a daily journal and has read several books on reporting. She says she's interested in journalism as a career, so who knows? Someday you may see the by-line of Sally Mitchell and say to yourself, I gave her the tour that started her on the road to journalistic success."

Millie glanced at the quiet, studious child. "You're seriously interested in journalism, Sally?"

"Yes, ma'am, I think so," Sally answered. "But this is really the first time I've seen how a paper is run."

"You're already off to a good start, keeping a journal. I started that way, too, and I still keep a daily log of my activities. Most of the reporters I know developed their love for words early in life, Sally. So you're not too young to start thinking about how to turn that passion into a career. Would you like to spend some time with me one day while you're here? It might give you a better idea of what real reporters do."

"I'd love to," Sally said, wide-eyed, "but I'll have to ask my dad."

Millie could see a problem looming on the horizon but didn't mention it to Sally. If the young Mitchell girl was even remotely interested in journalism as a career, a tour of the paper might help her decide definitely one way or the other. Millie figured she'd made a sincere offer to help; the acceptance would have to take care of itself.

"Ask him this afternoon and try to give me a call on Sunday. If he says yes, I'll juggle my schedule around and open up some time for you early next week."

Sally almost glowed as she waved good-bye to Millie and walked out the door with Bobby and Janie. Kathleen laughed, "I don't think her feet touched the ground as she left, do you?" Millie smiled and shook her head.

Kathleen moved to follow the youngsters, but turned when Millie touched her lightly on the arm. "I'm afraid your brother may not want Sally spending the day with me. Will you try to get him to agree that she can? What happened between Brian and me was years ago, and it has nothing to do with Sally. Brian and I won't even have to see each other." She paused and smiled. "Sally sure does seem to have the itch to be a reporter, doesn't she? I'd like to see if it's a real itch to write or just a minor case of the hives. Will you help?"

Kathleen didn't know Millie and Brian had met. Brian had never mentioned the editor of the *Sentinel* to her. And the shuttered look on Millie's face did not invite questions. "I'll do what I can," Kathleen promised. "I'll mention it to Brian."

\* \* \* \*

Kathleen spent half an hour helping the kids pick out new shorts and shirts to wear in Cincinnati. They were beginning to be hyped-up about the trip now that Brad Paisley's concert was behind them.

Near lunch time and the end of their shopping spree, Kathleen gave each of them five dollars to spend on anything personal they wanted to buy—no questions asked and no pre-approval required. "Don't do anything stupid," she admonished them, handing over the money.

Bobby hurried back to a sports card shop he'd seen on one of the side streets, his five-dollar bill tucked safely in the front pocket of his shorts.

Janie and Sally raced to the drug store. After a quick visit to the jewelry counter, they returned to Kathleen's side, excitement oozing from the pores of their bodies. "Can we get our ears pierced, Aunt Katie? It costs fifteen dollars, but that includes starter studs. With the five dollars you gave us and five dollars from Dad, plus some money we saved from our allowance, we can afford it."

Oops! Kathleen wouldn't dare make that decision, not for all the sassafras roots that could be found in the hills around Logan—and she was an avid drinker of sassafras tea. "Hold on," she said, pulling out her cell phone to call Brian.

"You'll never believe what the girls want to do," she said when he answered. "They want to get their ears pierced. Should I let them?"

"Are you kidding? They're babies, not women. Let me talk to Janie."

Kathleen could hear only Janie's end of the conversation, but her niece's facial expressions, which moved from dread to acceptance then bliss, were easily read. "Yes...yes...yes," Janie answered. "Thanks, Dad! I'll put Sally on now."

Sally's conversation followed the same pattern: three yeses, a thanks, and then, "You won't be sorry, Dad. We'll really be pretty!"

The two girls, slapping hands and hugging each other, finally remembered to return Kathleen's phone. "They seem awfully pleased, Brian. I could hear their answers. What did you ask?"

"I asked first, do you know it will hurt. Then, do you think the pain will be worth it. My last question was, will you love me more if I allow you to do it."

"Brian! You're a fraud. You were planning to say yes all along, weren't you?"

"You'll never know, baby sister, now will you?"

"Maybe not, but I can speculate, brother soft-touch!" As Kathleen started to hang up, she remembered Millie's request. "Oh, yeah, before I forget, Millie Samson, the managing editor of the *Sentinel*, asked if Sally could spend a day there next week learning what reporters do. Apparently Sally's interested in journalism. Were you aware of that?"

There was a long, uncomfortable pause. "Millie Sampson is in Logan?" Brian seemed to spit out each word. "Absolutely not. Sally can't do it."

"But Sally wants—"

"I said no, Katie. Didn't you hear? You can tell Millie Sampson there's no way my daughter will be spending a day with her. No, on further thought, don't you tell her anything. If I ever have the misfortune to run into that woman, I'll tell her myself. If Sally asks, tell her my answer is no."

He hung up on Kathleen.

Kathleen stared at the phone, wondering what *that* was about. But Bobby was jogging down the street in her direction, and she didn't have time to dwell on it then. She would certainly have a serious talk with Brian about it later, of that she was sure. What had gotten into Brian? He'd been in a jubilant mood until she mentioned Millie's offer. She couldn't imagine what his problem might be, but she planned to ream him out later for hanging up on her. She didn't tolerate rudeness like that from anyone else, and she wasn't about to take it from him.

She noticed that Bobby was clutching one of his father's baseball cards in his hand. He'd never been interested in card collecting before, but she didn't have to wonder what had brought it on now. "Did you tell the shop owner Rob McKenzie's your father?"

"I didn't need to. The dealer, Fred Horne, said he played baseball with Rob in high school. He said he could tell who I was just by looking at me, especially after I asked him about a Rob McKenzie card. When I told him you were showing me around town, he said to tell you that he was surprised and pleased to meet Rob and Katie's son."

By now, several other people in town had seen Bobby and the girls with Kathleen, and had casually passed the time of day with them. Kathleen figured that they would all draw the same conclusion as Fred. *C'est le vie,* she thought—what is, is, and there was nothing she could do about that. "Fred's a great guy," she said. "We were in the same class in school. Tell me, did you spend all your money on a Rob McKenzie card?"

Bobby hesitated, not sure how his mother would view his transaction. "Mr. Horne wouldn't let me pay for the card when he found out who I was."

"That was nice, but we can't let him do that. Fred's in the business of selling cards, not giving them away."

"I did try to pay him, Mom, honest. But he kept saying no. So I told him I'd accept Rob's card as a gift only if he'd sell me five dollars worth of cheaper cards.

He went into his safe and came out with two cards that he sold me for five dollars."

"What are they?"

"A Pete Rose and a Ken Griffey, Jr. Two cards—plus Rob's—for only five dollars! I didn't have to use any of my own money."

Kathleen knew less about baseball cards than Bobby, but even she knew Pete Rose and Ken Griffey, Jr. were superstars like Rob. Their cards had to be worth more than five dollars, and she told Bobby so. "But let's not worry about that, at least not until you've talked it over with your father. He'll know what's the best thing to do."

Having an "almost husband" is quite handy, Kathleen decided—especially in situations like this. She and Bobby walked toward the drug store to see how Janie and Sally were faring.

"Oh, gross." Bobby turned pale when he heard the piercing gun snap the first earring into Janie's ear. "Can I wait outside?"

The girls and Sarah, the young clerk who'd been piercing ears at the drug store for three years, kidded Bobby about being a typical male who couldn't stand the thought of minor pain. But Bobby didn't care how much they teased him. He refused to stand around and watch.

When Bobby acknowledged later that Janie and Sally did look good with pierced ears, he wondered aloud if their new look was worth the pain they'd endured to attain it. "There was no pain," Sally assured him. "Just a slight pinching sensation."

Janie looked down her nose at Bobby. "Men!" she said, rolling her eyes in a supercilious manner. "At least one good thing came out of this, Aunt Katie. You'll never have to worry about Bobby getting a tattoo or having body parts pierced!"

It was Kathleen's turn to laugh then. "Thank God for large favors," she said.

# Chapter 20

▼

When Kathleen pulled in beside Rob's car at Mabel's, the girls rolled the window down on the side nearest him. "Hey, Uncle Rob, notice our new look?"

Rob's smile grew; it felt mighty good being called Uncle Rob by such pretty little girls. It was the first time Brian's daughters had addressed him by any name at all. But, new look? He hadn't a clue. He checked them over again, this time more thoroughly, but saw nothing different…until he glanced at Kathleen. She was caressing an ear lobe between her index finger and thumb. "Aha!" Rob said, peering back at the girls. "You've had your ears pierced, I see. And diamonds—oh, baby, we're talking glamour! You sure you're not two young movie starlets who've flown all the way from Hollywood to Logan in a private jet just to call me Uncle Rob?"

The girls grinned at each other, then giggled. "Uncle Rob," Sally said, "stop talking so silly!"

"Yeah," Janie said, looking around to see who might be nearby. "You're embarrassing us."

Rob's glance clashed with Kathleen's, and they burst out laughing. It was refreshing, knowing someone felt embarrassed about being seen with a professional baseball player and a winner of the Newbery Medal.

The kids talked non-stop about their tour of town as they moved from the Explorer to Rob's convertible. Under cover of their movements and chatter, Rob lightly ran a finger down Kathleen's arm and squeezed her hand. The corners of his mouth tilted up. As green eyes held hazel ones, Kathleen knew he, too, was thinking about their conversation on the phone. A tell-tale blush tinted her cheeks. Rob grinned fully, lifting her hand to graze her knuckles with a kiss.

"I've been wondering," Kathleen said, leaning closer. "Where were you calling from this morning?"

"The cell phone in my car."

"Yeah, that's what I thought, you were so brave. I almost got caught," she said, emphasizing her words, "*by our son!*"

Rob laughed, imagining the scene at the cabin, but he didn't have time to ask how she nearly got caught. Carrie and Billy Joe came walking up to Rob's car to say hello. The Taylors declared it was exactly like old times, seeing Rob and Kathleen together. Rob had waved hello when he pulled into the lot, but now he took time to introduce Bobby and the girls to his friends. Bobby had met the Taylors on Thursday, or course, but this time Rob revealed the fact that Bobby was his son. Not wanting to say too much in front of the kids, Rob kept his explanation short and to the point.

Carrie elbowed Billy Joe in the ribs. "I knew it, I knew it," she crowed. "After almost worrying myself sick about it Thursday afternoon, didn't I say Katie's son looked just like Rob?" She elbowed her husband again.

"Ouch, woman!" Billy Joe yelped, pretending to be hurt. "Carrie loves being right," he said to the chuckling group in the car. "I like it better when she's wrong."

With the three youngsters chatting in the backseat, Rob and Kathleen quietly explained their divorce entanglement to their friends, knowing half the people in town would hear that the two of them were still legally married—and about Bobby—by nightfall. Food wasn't the only thing served at Mabel's. So was local news.

"That's unbelievable, Rob," Carrie said. "There'll be a lot of disappointed women in town when they find out you're not divorced."

Rob winced and turned to Kathleen. "She's only kidding. Honest."

"Oh, really?" Kathleen responded in a bland tone of voice. Rob's comical look of dismay broke all of them up.

Business was brisk, so the Taylors needed to rush back to work, but Billy Joe tarried long enough to playfully punch Rob on the shoulder. "Rob, buddy, you're just the same as always—way too easy! Toughen up or these two girls will get the best of you every time." Rob grinned, so euphoric being there with Kathleen, he cared not a whit if they did. Billy Joe walked away, shaking his head. Rob laughed when he heard Billy Joe say under his breath, "Wimp."

While they ate, Bobby told Rob about his baseball card transaction with Fred Horne. "Mom said you'd know what I should do," Bobby finished.

Rob pondered that for a moment. "Well, you don't need to feel bad about what happened. You didn't do anything wrong. Since you're not a collector, you wouldn't have known what those cards sell for. Those two players are legends, and even though the cards you bought aren't signed by the players, they'd still sell for more than what you paid. But it's a touchy situation, Bobby. Fred wanted you to have the cards or he wouldn't have quoted you a price of five dollars. I think he'd be insulted if we took them back or offered him more money, don't you? What do you suggest we do?"

"I've been thinking about that. Let's do something nice for Mr. Horne to pay him back. That's how Mom returns a favor. Will you help me think of something?"

"Sure. In fact, Bobby Mitchell, this is your lucky day; I already have something in mind. I just need to talk it over with Fred. Would the three of you like to go back there with me after lunch?" Rob included the girls in his invitation.

"That would be great," Bobby said, speaking for them all. "You know I didn't mean to take advantage of Mr. Horne, don't you, Rob? I just wanted to spend my money there as a thank-you after he gave me your card." Bobby seemed to be a mile away for a moment, thinking over what Rob had just said. He held out his Rob McKenzie card to his father. "Hey, McKenzie, if cards are worth more when they're signed, how about autographing this one for me?"

"Sure thing," Rob teased. "The only thing is, I should charge you for it like a lot of players do. Otherwise, you might sell it to the first person you meet on the street for more than the five dollars you were willing to pay." Rob winked at Kathleen as he surreptitiously signed Bobby's card.

"You think I'd really do that? Come on, I'm your son," Bobby teased back. "Where's the guy who needs to stay on my good side because he's courting my mom? Did he disappear?"

Rob had written "To my son, Bobby" on the front of the card, and had signed it "Rob McKenzie, #89." He'd dated it the day Kathleen told him that Bobby was his son. Reaching over to hand him the card, he mussed Bobby's hair. "The guy who's courting your mother, and I hope and pray that I'm the only one, just signed your baseball card for you!"

As Bobby thanked him for his autograph, Rob winked at Kathleen again. Bobby's card, signed and dated that way, would be quite valuable once the public learned of their relationship.

"I'd like to drop by the house to see Mom and Dad after we finish at Fred's, if that's all right with you, Katie," Rob said. "When I told them I was meeting you for lunch, they asked me to bring the kids by later. I can have them home before our appointment at the church, say three-fifteen, if that suits."

"Yeah, that's fine. They'll love the spoiling," Kathleen said with a chuckle…leaving it unclear whether her pronoun referred to Rob's parents or the kids.

Kathleen finally headed home alone, which was fine. She wanted to stop and talk things over with her mother before going to the cabin, and she figured she might as well clear the air with Brian, too, while she was there. Kathleen bit the inside of her lip. She was not looking forward to two unsavory showdowns in one afternoon.

\* \* \* \*

Kathleen had worried off and on all day about this confrontation with her mother, and she'd rather be almost anywhere else in the world right now than here. But the list of her mother's transgressions had continued to grow like Topsy, and there was no disregarding them now.

After Rob drove away from the cabin last night, and Bobby had returned home from the concert and things quieted down, she'd tossed and turned in her bed for hours. Once she cooled off and could see things more clearly, she'd conceded that Rob's words of caution were wise. She did need to face her mother with love, not just censure, in mind. But that didn't mean that Lettie Mitchell's egregious deception, and her latest indiscretions, could just be ignored. Kathleen didn't want to drive a permanent wedge between her mother and herself; Rob was right about that. But she did feel compelled to explain exactly how she felt—and why.

Face-to-face with her mother, Kathleen counted to ten. She thought maybe a few deep breaths would help keep her temper under control, so she tried that, too, before speaking.

"Mom, I can't tell you how angry I am by what you did yesterday. Why did you tell Bobby there was a problem with my divorce? And did you actually think it was your place to reveal the name of his father to him? Coming on top of the letters Rob showed me last night—you know, the ones you kept from me for years—that has really angered me. How could you justify intercepting mail that Rob meant only for me?"

Lettie Mitchell dipped her head, fighting tears. "I'm sorry I told Bobby, but I was so upset the words were out of my mouth before I knew it. Most of all, not passing Rob's letters on to you was wrong. I've felt dreadful watching you raise

Bobby without a father, not knowing exactly what was in Rob's letters to you. After telling him to leave you alone, I couldn't bring myself to read his letters. And I couldn't let you read them either. I hoped you'd never discover that I'd kept them from you.

"You're my only daughter, Katie. I guess I saw you more as my little girl than a married woman back then. When Rob's first letter came, all I could think about was the despicable way he acted when you stayed home to take care of your dad. Then, each time I thought about him not coming home for the funeral, something inside me snapped. I thought I knew what was best for you then, but I shouldn't have been playing God. I told myself the two of you had divorced, gone separate ways, and that you were better off not hearing from him anymore. It was only much later that I learned Rob never remarried and, from what people said, had turned into a very nice man. When I heard you tell Brian that Rob was back in town, I knew in my heart there was no way the two of you could stay away from each other. I figured I'd better give the letters back to Rob and get out of the way.

"I'm really sorry, Katie," Lettie said, her eyes and lips turned down in despair, "and there's nothing I can add to that. No one would condone what I did, but I'm asking you to forgive me if you can. If you can't, then I'll just have to live without your forgiveness. Even that won't be as bad as the guilt that's been eating me alive since I intercepted those letters."

Kathleen's temper had cooled off some, but not much. "I'm trying to forgive you, Mom, but I can't just disregard what you did. It wasn't your place to keep what Rob sent me, and I'm having a hard time dealing with that. But it also wasn't your place to tell Bobby about the divorce or who his father is."

"I know," Lettie said, placing an arm around her daughter's shoulder. After only a slight hesitation, Kathleen hugged her mother back. Someday soon, Kathleen hoped, she would feel true compassion again for her mom. It was enough for now, though, that everything was out in the open between them again.

As Kathleen left her mother's house, she recalled what she, herself, had done, and the weight of her guilt caused her to stumble as she walked down the steps to the yard. She'd had chance after chance to tell Bobby about his father and the divorce, even after she'd been summoned back to Logan by Dan Hoffman. If she had been honest and open about everything from the beginning, Bobby wouldn't have heard about his father and the divorce from his grandmother. He would have heard about it all from Kathleen.

\* \* \* \*

Kathleen decided she might as well chase Brian down, now that she was here. Facing her mother had left her with loads of excess energy to work off. She hiked up the mountain in the direction her mother said Brian had gone.

Walking among cool green trees and the rainbow-colored wildflowers that grew beside the path used to calm Kathleen when she was tense. But not today. Today she walked too briskly to notice they were there. Ten minutes into her hike, she located Brian. He was sitting on a rock perched precariously at the top of the hill, staring out over rolling valleys and the abandoned Steven's Hollow mine.

Brian's expression was relaxed, but guarded, as he watched her hike his way. Luckily for him, Kathleen had gotten over the worst of her annoyance by then.

"You weren't trying to hide from me, were you?"

Brian's response was a half-laugh, half-snort. "Not exactly. I just felt like getting away for a while, that's all. I should have gone back earlier so Mom wouldn't worry, but it's so peaceful up here I couldn't make myself get up and start back down the hill. I'm not even going to ask why you're here. Just tell me where the girls are, and Bobby."

"Rob had to run an errand, and the kids couldn't resist riding in the convertible with him. He's also taking them by his mom and dad's for a visit, but he'll be bringing them home before long. Mom knew I was hiking up here to find you, so we don't have to hurry back home right away. Give me permission to sit on your rock, and I'll join you."

Brian grinned at his single-minded sister. "You can sit and visit, Katie, but I'll pick the topics of conversation."

"No way! You know what I want to talk about, and I'm not leaving until I get what I came for." Kathleen stood on the rock beside him, taking her time as she turned in a three-hundred-sixty degree circle. With arms outstretched, she embraced the mountains and the cloud-speckled sky. "Makes me want to sing 'Oh, Those West Virginia Hills.' Want to sing along with me?"

Brian shook his head emphatically. "Not on your life! Sound carries in these hills. Besides, I haven't thought of that old song in years. I'm surprised you remember the words."

Grabbing Kathleen's jeans-clad legs, Brian pulled her down beside him, fearful she might lose her balance and fall. "You're welcome to sit for as long as you like, but there are two ironclad conditions: you can't sing and you have to sit still. You scare me, moving around so much. Mom always warned us to be careful on these rocks. Don't make me have to tell on you!"

"Like that would be new! You were *so* worse than David. You always tattled."

"David was an old man by the time you came along. He couldn't be bothered with trivial stuff like that," Brian said, referring to his two-years-older brother.

"You believe in living dangerously, don't you, big brother? Watch your mouth, or I'll call David and tell him what you said. I've already threatened Rob about a comment he made yesterday, badmouthing his father, so I'm a virtual repository for blackmail-type secrets right now. You don't want to mess with me."

They grinned at each other. Easy-going, self-confident Dr. David Mitchell wouldn't be bothered at all by taunting words, no matter who they came from. And neither would Mike McKenzie. Most likely, if Kathleen actually quoted those statements to them, those two guys would just laugh—at first. Then they'd dare the younger guys to just try to take them on. David and Mike ascribed to the belief that "sticks and stones may break my bones, but calling *me* names will end up hurting *you*."

For a few minutes, Kathleen and Brian sat in silence, thinking their own private thoughts. Brian decided that he'd not be the first to mention his anger over the phone. Kathleen decided that she'd not ignore his comments about Millie Samson.

"What's with you and Millie? Did you meet her in Logan on one of your visits?"

"No."

"Did you meet her here at church?"

"No."

"Come on, Brian. Short, terse, evasive answers won't deter me. If it takes all day, I'll just keep chipping away till you answer. You know how I am, so why not just tell me why you don't want Sally around 'that woman' and get it over with? What did Millie do to make you dislike her so much?"

Brian shrugged, not wanting to answer. "She didn't do anything," he finally said. "It's what I almost did to her that's the problem."

A second or two passed in silence. Kathleen raised both hands in supplication and verbally prodded her brother. "So? What did you *almost* do?"

A sigh of vexation escaped Brian's lips. "It's really none of your business, Katie. But, remember that undercover field assignment I had three years ago? The time you kept Sally and Janie for a month? Well, that job was in Charleston. That's where I met Millie."

When he didn't continue his explanation quickly enough for her, Kathleen raised her voice. "*What happened in Charleston with Millie?*"

The conversation was clearly uncomfortable for Brian. There were a few things he felt awkward talking to his sister about, and this was one of those things. "Just something that was all my fault, Katie. I don't want to go into detail, but I will tell you this. She'll never forgive me. No woman would."

"Brian, if you don't tell me exactly what you did, I'll be forced to draw my own conclusions. And I'm already upset enough with you as it is."

"It's none of your business, Katie," he said. "I don't want to talk anymore."

"Fine," Kathleen said, glaring at him. As she unfolded her legs to stand up, she moved too fast and the rock they were sitting on wobbled.

"Okay…okay," Brian said, pulling her down. "Initially, Millie and I were only friends in Charleston, more like casual acquaintances or part of a group. But we were becoming more interested in each other, and everyone we worked with knew it. Ellen had been dead for five years by then, and believe it or not, I hadn't been with any other woman I was attracted to in all that time. So that last evening, after I'd tied everything up, I asked Millie for a date. We were having dinner alone in a dark booth at the back of the restaurant where our group usually met. As I sat beside Millie, she moved in my direction, bumped into me, and my hand accidentally—I swear it was an accident—touched her silk-clad leg. Before I knew what hit me, I had her pushed up in the corner of the booth, kissing her like I'd never kissed a woman before. You couldn't have put a piece of onionskin paper between us, but I wanted closer. I finally came to my senses and got the heck out of there as quickly as I could." He glared at Kathleen, who'd been staring at him with a look of disgust on her face the entire time he was spilling his guts. "And that's it, Katie. I'm not telling you anything else. I've told you too much as it is."

"Do I have this right?" Kathleen asked, ticking off the pertinent facts. "You touched her inappropriately—by accident, you say. You kissed her passionately. Well, I doubt that was unintentional. And then you stalked out like an unthinking, ignorant oaf because you were frightened by the depth of your feelings? I can't believe you, Brian. You embarrassed her! Did you say anything at all when you left?"

"Yes, and I'm not proud of that either. That's the worst part of all. I blurted out something like, 'This is wrong. You're not Ellen.' I threw enough money on the table to more than pay for dinner and a tip and left." He wrapped his arms around his bent knees and lowered his head to rest it there. "I can't face her, Katie, I just can't. I ran off and left her there by herself, and you know that's not like me. I just want to erase that night from my memory." Raising his head a few inches, Brian scowled at his sister. "And I had almost forgotten until you mentioned her today. I can't possibly see her again. She must think I'm an idiot."

"You never got in touch with Millie after that? You made her think you cared for her, Brian, and then slammed her with unpardonable words. You owe her a big apology."

Brian had calmed down somewhat by then. "Maybe I do, but I'm not seeking her out to deliver one. I probably will give in and let Sally spend a day with her next week. If I don't, the girls—who're exactly like you—will just hound me till I do. I'm staying as far away from that red-headed bombshell as I can, though, Katie. But don't you tell her that."

Brian's vehemence and the defensive expression on his face when the words "red-headed bombshell" spewed out of his mouth tickled Kathleen. She laughed so hard that Brian feared she'd knock their rock off balance and send them plummeting down the hill. So he pushed her off the side of the rock instead—a preemptive strike.

"You're terrible, Brian," Kathleen said, still laughing when she landed lightly on her bottom. "Honestly, one day you're gonna get your proper comeuppance, and Millie Samson might be the one to give it to you."

With those parting words, Kathleen got up, brushed dried leaves off her slacks, and hurried away.

Brian's eyes were closed, so he didn't see her leave. All he saw was the look on Millie Samson's face when he threw his money on the table and said she wasn't Ellen.

* * * *

Rob followed Bobby up the steps to the cabin. They'd dropped the girls off at Mrs. Mitchell's, where Rob had received an awkward welcome from Kathleen's mother. It was about what he'd expected, seeing Mrs. Mitchell again, but he had deliberately chosen to walk the girls to the door so he could greet his mother-in-law in person. He was determined to win Kathleen back as his wife, and with Kathleen and Bobby came her mother—a package deal, in a manner of speaking. He figured a good relationship with Lettie Mitchell was worth some extra effort on his part. And strangely enough, even after all that had transpired, Rob found himself feeling sorry for Mrs. Mitchell.

Kathleen had showered and was ready for their meeting with Matt Harlow when she heard Rob's car turn into the driveway. She grabbed a chilled pitcher of fresh lemonade from the refrigerator, poured three frosted mugs full of the sweet, tangy brew, then met the two guys on the porch. She overheard Bobby telling Rob what a great time they'd all had at his Granddad and Grandmom's house that afternoon. Mmmm...interesting, Kathleen thought, hearing that. Bobby had come up with a special name for each new grandparent, ones she admitted to liking, herself. But he still hadn't decided on one for his dad.

"You spoiled yet?" she asked Bobby.

"Totally," Rob jumped in, answering for their son. "But not just Bobby. The girls came in for their share of spoiling, too. Bobby told Mom he'd been learning a lot of Logan County history from you, so she promised to take the three kids to see *The Aracoma Story* next week. I'm supposed to tell you not to worry about anything—she and your mother will buy tickets and pick up supper from Hardee's." Rob grinned. "From what Mom said, our two mothers warmed up the phone lines this morning. My ears were burning—how about yours?"

Not at all surprised, Kathleen laughed. She had known the two women would rehash yesterday's events as soon as they could do so privately.

"Anyhow," Rob continued, "I guess one of them will let you know when their plans are firmed up."

"I'm sure they will. From what I've heard, that play—the story of Princess Aracoma and Boling Baker—is not only historically accurate, which can sometimes be boring, it's a tense, dramatic tale that Mom believes the kids will love. With a picnic thrown in for good measure, it's something they won't want to miss."

As they drank their ice-cold lemonade sitting on the porch, Rob and Bobby—mostly Bobby—told Kathleen about their visit to Fred Horne's sporting goods shop. "We didn't mention the price of the cards, Mom. We just thanked Mr. Horne for such nice ones. Then Rob asked Mr. Horne if he'd like him to come in one Saturday to sign posters, pictures, and baseball cards for free."

Clearly, Bobby hadn't missed a word that was spoken between the two men. "Honestly, Mom, I wish you'd been there. Mr. Horne almost fainted when Rob volunteered to do that. Rob's doing it for his favorite charity, the CCA's Cancer Fund for Children."

Bobby's enthusiasm about their visit was contagious, and Kathleen soon became interested, too.

"Here's the deal," Bobby said. "The Cincinnati Reds are sending Rob a bunch of free pictures, some of him alone and some with the team. He'll sign one for any kid under twelve whose parent makes a donation to the Fund, or for any teenager who makes a contribution of his own. And it doesn't matter how small or large the contributions are. Nobody's checking."

Bobby, almost breathless, was talking pretty fast, but Rob noted that he'd related the details quite accurately to Kathleen. So far, he hadn't left anything out.

"Rob will sign posters and baseball cards, too—old ones people already have or ones they buy from Mr. Horne. Mr. Horne even phoned in a rush order for more posters and cards while we were there. He thinks he'll sell a lot of them that day. Don't you think that's a great way for us to thank Mr. Horne?"

Rob added a note of clarification. "I've never charged for my autograph, Katie, and I don't want you to think I'm charging now. Fred and I are soliciting donations for the Cancer Fund, and I'm just the draw to encourage people to come by and give. But if any parents can't afford to contribute, their child will still get a free autographed photo. I've never turned anyone away before, and I'm not starting now."

Rob cocked his head to the side as he studied Kathleen. "You know, I think you'd like the concept behind the Cancer Fund. It's an arm of the CCA that's run by some of the players' wives. Because they work for just a dollar a year, almost all the proceeds go to help sick children. I'm behind them one-hundred percent, as are all CCA members."

"Sounds like a good use of donated money to me," Kathleen stated. "It's discouraging to read about charitable organizations that're so poorly managed their high administrative costs leave hardly anything for the people who need it, especially when it's an organization you've given to yourself."

"I'm with you on that," Rob agreed.

Bobby certainly had enjoyed his first experience as the son of a celebrity ballplayer. Listening in on Rob's conversation with his old friend had given Bobby a glimpse of the respect his father had earned in his career. But Kathleen had to smile—Bobby seemed almost as impressed by Fred Horne.

"Where were the girls when all of this was going on?"

"Oohing and aahing over posters, most of the time," Bobby took time to say. Then he picked up right where he left off. "Listen to this, Mom," he said, his voice rising, "Mr. Horne called some guy he knows with a band, and they agreed to play that day in front of the vacant building across the street from his shop. You know why? So they won't get in the way of his customers! Oh, and did I tell you he also ordered a large sign to put over his door that says 'Rob McKenzie Day?'"

Kathleen nodded her head and grinned. Bobby never slowed down. "Well, this part is even better than that—he's lowering prices on everything in his store that week. Bats, gloves, everything. Since people will be coming in to see Rob, lower prices might make them buy more while they're there. Isn't that exciting?" A dreamy expression made its way across Bobby's features, then he sighed. "You know something? If I don't make it in baseball, I'd like to have my own business someday like Fred Horne."

Rob and Kathleen tried not to look at each other, but they couldn't help it. When their eyes met, they chuckled a little…then laughed slightly louder…and finally just roared.

"Honestly," Bobby said, laughing along in spite of himself. "I'm being serious here."

Rob and Kathleen tried, they really did, but they just couldn't seem to stop. Kathleen rummaged around in her pocket for a tissue. Laughing uncontrollably, she swiped at her eyes, wiping away tears.

And Rob was every bit as bad. Parenting was a brand-new experience for him, and Bobby's boundless enthusiasm over every little thing continued to fascinate and tickle him.

Bobby, still grinning, finally threw up his hands. "Why me?" he asked, with his nose pointed toward heaven. "What did I do to deserve parents like them?"

# Chapter 21

▼

Matt Harlow ran back, his glove in the air, but he took one step too many and missed the ball thrown by the smallest boy at the pick-up game of catch out in front of the church. The young minister seemed to have a knack for making himself appear clumsy while making the kids playing ball with him look good. Parking his Mustang, Rob watched as he did it again. A small boy, about six or seven, threw a hard one that hit the tip of the pastor's glove and bobbled around a time or two before falling in. Pastor Harlow held the ball up and did a victory dance before throwing it back. It hit right in the center of the boy's waiting glove. "Good catch, Timmy," Rob heard him yell. "You're looking like Ripken."

As Rob and Kathleen exited the car, Rob looked the pastor over, taking his measure. Seeing them arrive, one of the kids tossed the ball to Rob. "You try it, mister," he said. "You'll look good even if you're bad. Pastor Matt misses a lot of the balls we throw him."

Rob rolled the ball around in his hand, pretended to spit on it to amuse the kids standing by, and then winged it right into the disreputable-looking baseball glove the pastor wore. As the ball whacked against the well-worn leather and stayed, the kids' jaws dropped open. "Pastor Matt finally caught a good one," one of the disbelieving kids said to the other. Then he looked over at Rob. "Mister, you must really be bad!" Rob and Matt Harlow laughed as the kids walked away, still shaking their heads.

"I thought I recognized a man who was holding back," Rob said. "Any guy who wears a well-used glove as naturally as you do couldn't possibly be the slouch you have those kids thinking you are." He pretended to wipe sweat from his brow. "As soon as that ball left my hand, I regretted throwing it so hard. If you hadn't been what I thought you were—a good catcher as well as an encouraging coach—it might really have hurt."

Matt Harlow laughed. "The kids were sure surprised when I caught it, so I don't think that one good catch polished my *bad* reputation too much, do you? If they'd known that throw was from a major-league first baseman, now that might be different. So let's just keep that to ourselves." Still smiling, the minister extended his hand. "Let me introduce myself. I'm Matt Harlow, Mr. McKenzie."

"It's good to meet you, Pastor Harlow," Rob said, returning the minister's handshake. "This is my wife, Kathleen Mitchell, but call us Rob and Katie, please."

"Only if you'll call me Matt," the pastor replied, shaking hands with Kathleen. "I'm very pleased to meet you both. I'll admit I recognized your name when you called this morning, Rob. And, of course, I've heard of Kathleen Mitchell. You two are local celebrities, plus your parents have mentioned your names to me from time to time." Pastor Harlow waved in the direction of the church. "Come on inside where we can talk."

After ushering them into his air-conditioned office, Matt went into the adjacent rest room to wash the street dust from his hands. Rob chuckled again at the way Matt had bamboozled the kids into thinking he was at least partially inept. He and his teammates often used the same ploy when working with Cincinnati's inner-city kids. It was easier to coach a child, and be accepted by him, after meeting him first on his own level, Rob believed. He would bet that the teens in Matt's church saw a more intensely competitive ball-playing minister than the younger kids did.

"So what's this intriguing marital problem you folks have?" Matt asked, entering the room and taking a seat behind his desk. He had observed Rob's solicitous manner with Kathleen, and the warmth that seemed to flow between them, since they arrived. "I don't detect any overt animosity between you," he said. "In fact, you appear to be rather friendly with each other. What's the story?"

Taking turns, they explained their divorce/marriage dilemma in detail, starting with their long courtship and hasty elopement. They told Matt about their separation and the reasons behind it, laying things out in front of the pastor exactly as they had occurred.

Kathleen told Matt she'd discovered she was pregnant with Bobby only after filing for divorce *and* why she hadn't contacted Rob at the time. A shocked look flickered across Matt's face when she said Dan Hoffman had written almost fourteen years later saying there was a problem with that divorce. It seemed far-fetched, almost unbelievable, at first. Matt finally understood why their predicament was so strange and unique when they told him in confidence why their final divorce decree was never entered.

Matt's questions about the break-up of their marriage were insightful and, of necessity, rather pointed. Their individual answers convinced him that they had faced up to the hurtful things they'd done to each other and that those old issues were no longer a source of friction between them. In fact, as mature adults they appeared to have put that part of their relationship to rest. They seemed ready to go forward, not back, from where they were right now.

When they described their discussion at the mine about getting to know each other better before making any life-altering decisions for the future, Matt understood exactly why they'd come to that conclusion. Although it didn't look that way on the surface, they were almost strangers to each other now.

Matt's chair squeaked as he tilted it back. He steepled his fingers beneath his chin and considered their situation. After a moment, he said, "I've never counseled anyone in circumstances quite like yours before, so we'll be seeking God's guidance in this together. Let's make sure I understand this correctly, though, before we start. You want to work toward a marital reconciliation and, eventually, a renewal of your vows. Is that right?"

With a glance at Kathleen, Rob answered, "Yes, more than anything that's what I want, but I'm not speaking for Katie. That's where I went wrong before, trying to tell her what to do."

"How about you, Katie? What do you want?"

"At this point, a reconciliation is what I'm looking for, too."

Rob hadn't planned to mention the powerful physical attraction that still existed between him and Kathleen. But the pastor's advice would encompass every aspect of their relationship, so he confessed, "I want to court Katie again, but I don't want to make any mistakes this time. I feel the same intense desire for intimacy with her that I did during the short time we were married. And it's not just that I want and need a woman; that isn't it. I don't want just any woman, I want Katie. I guess what it boils down to is this: technically we're married, but emotionally and psychologically we're not. After all the years we spent apart, how do we—as practicing Christians—handle both the practical and the physical part of getting to know each other again?"

"Well, first off," Matt said, "there's certainly nothing wrong with what you feel. If those feelings weren't there between you, you wouldn't be here discussing reconciliation. Since you're still legally married, you could resume your marital relationship at any time. It wouldn't be sinful or unlawful. But I have to tell you, I feel very strongly that taking that step wouldn't be wise."

Rob had been afraid Matt would say that.

"Since you asked how you should handle both the practical and the physical part of becoming reacquainted, my advice actually comes in two parts," Matt continued. "First, let's take the practical issues. Vowing again, before God, to love each other forever is a serious step that is not to be taken lightly or entered into rashly merely because you still want each other physically. You obviously feel a need to learn more about each other as mature adults and co-parents before renewing your vows, and I agree. In fact, with your history, I'd go a little farther than just agreeing. I'd say that step is crucial.

"So don't hurry that part of the process. Take all the time you need to discuss what you want from your marriage and expect from each other. I'm a firm believer in non-confrontational communication, where both spouses have a say and neither one sits back and suffers in silence. I can't emphasize enough the benefits of just talking things out with each other, and it doesn't sound as if you did that before. In a committed relationship, an open, honest conversation is an amazingly powerful facilitating tool."

Matt paused, then said, "Sit down together and make a list of issues you know you'll have to compromise on in the future, such as where you'll live, how you'll handle a two-career household, and how you'll raise your teenage son—and then talk them to death. Any decisions you make now as partners and parents, and any problems you can solve before you're forced to face them head-on, will make the future easier for all of you. Whether or not you decide to stay together—and I pray that you will—the two of you will always share a child, and that's important to remember when you deal with each other."

At that point, Rob interrupted. "Matt, you know I haven't been involved in Bobby's life to this point, but I have to say this—Katie and I seem to be in perfect sync on how she has raised him thus far. He's lucky to have her for his mother, and I'm really proud of the job she's done. He's a great kid, and she gets all the credit for that. On the other things you mentioned, I think we're both willing to discuss and, if necessary, compromise on issues we haven't faced before."

"That's good, Rob," Matt grinned. "You might not agree with me quite as readily, though, when I give you my advice on the physical issue."

Rob threw back his head and laughed. "I probably will agree with you, but I won't like it coming from you any more than I did when it came from Katie."

Matt smiled at Rob, knowing exactly where he was coming from. He glanced over at Kathleen, and they all laughed together. Kathleen liked a minister with a sense of humor, and she was beginning to like the Reverend Matthew Harlow a lot.

"Then I might as well jump in with both feet," Matt said. "Based on my study of human nature, and the knowledge I've gained from couples I've worked with in the past, I strongly advise you to make a mutual pledge of celibacy right now. Abstaining from physical intimacy until you've made a mature—and joint—decision to commit your lives to each other again will remove a lot of stress from what's already a stressful situation."

Matt's words were more beneficial than he knew. Hearing them, Rob and Kathleen felt more comfortable with the strong feelings they had for each other. They could handle them better, knowing their decision to remain celibate while pondering their future would only be a temporary one. Each time they were together, sharing some aspect of their lives, they moved closer to an emotional marriage instead of just a legal one.

"I'm convinced that you'll sense when it's time to pledge yourselves to each other again and ask God's blessing on your union. But I'll touch just briefly on the mechanics of that.

"Given your circumstances, you may decide, as some folks do, to restate your vows formally in a full-fledged wedding ceremony in church, or semi-formally, still in a church setting. But I want to emphasize this—it doesn't have to be in church. You can renew your vows in a casual manner and setting, restating them in your own words at a place that's special to you both. How you do it is up to you; it's the actual process of doing it that's critical. A well thought out, formal pledge before God to love each other forever will mean a lot to you, and the people you share it with, for many years to come."

Matt's chair squeaked again as he leaned forward. "Rob, you mentioned on the phone that you and Kathleen just accidentally ran into each other the other day. Well, I don't believe it was happenstance that the two of you were on that same stretch of road at the same time. Or that it was just a fluke that the final decree in your divorce was never filed. Your commitment to each other seems strong, even though you have been apart for many years, and I don't think that's due to mere luck. When I add everything up, it seems like more than just coincidence to me. Logan is where you fell in love before. I think God chose this time and place to bring you back together."

Rob and Kathleen's eyes met and held; they hadn't considered that before. Matt chuckled when he saw two identical, happy facial expressions. "Just thought I'd give you something to think about while you're exploring what God's will might be in all of this."

With another smile, he said, "I feel confident about the two of you and the outcome of your marital problem, which I concede is unique. As a minister, I counsel people with broken relationships and discouraging, unhappy situations almost every week. When I meet a couple like the two of you, who really want to make things work, a happy ending is pretty much assured. Now, that's the kind of counseling session that makes a pastor feel good!"

Matt glanced at his watch. "I'm not in any hurry, but I suspect you may have other plans for this evening. Unless you have more questions, shall we pray together?"

Kathleen and Rob nodded their assent. "I'll start the prayer," Matt said. "If you'd like to pray along, feel free to join in." Bowing his head, he began, "Thank you, Heavenly Father, for setting up this institution called marriage, this covenant partnership between a man and woman who love each other that's sanctioned by you. Please bless Rob and Katie's relationship. In the next few weeks or months, help them build on the love they have for each other so that their marriage turns back into one that's sanctified by you."

After Matt finished, Rob prayed. "Thank you, God, for letting me find Katie again this week. Thank you, too, for Bobby." He prayed over a knot in his throat. "Teach me how to be a better husband to Katie and a father to our son. Show me how to keep you first in my life and in my relationships with them."

Kathleen took a deep breath. It was hard for her to pray aloud, much easier for her to write down what she felt. "God, please be with Rob and Bobby and me. If you feel it's right for all of us, transform us into a close-knit family of three. As we address the problems we had in the past and look toward the future, please turn the obstacles that once seemed like mountains into little mounds of dirt we can step over together."

Matt finished the prayer with a quiet, "Amen."

"Now," he said, looking up, "will I see you in church tomorrow and get to meet Bobby?"

"I'll be there," Kathleen replied. "So will Bobby."

"Me, too," Rob said. Matt stood and shook hands with them again.

Rob looked at Kathleen. "Ready for dinner, Katie-girl?"

"Yes, I'm ready," she said, smiling back.

Matt smiled, too. "You folks will be just fine. I can tell there's no lack of love between the two of you, and I also get the feeling that you're committed to each other. If I were still a betting man, which I'm not anymore, I'd lay odds that you'll choose to stay together as a family. And that you'll make that decision real soon."

*As a family.* After being categorized as single man and only parent for so long, the pastor's optimistic words sounded wonderful to Rob and Kathleen. They left the counseling session with open minds and lighter hearts, looking forward with excitement to the future.

Rob reached around Kathleen to open the outer door of the church. "How're you feeling about all this, sugar?" he asked quietly.

"Pretty good, Mr. McKenzie." She smiled. "Pretty doggone good."

# Chapter 22

▼

Brian Mitchell was in a blue and funky kind of mood.

While Kathleen and her still-legal husband enjoyed a candlelight dinner in Charleston, Brian sat on his mother's front porch feeling sorry for himself. And he didn't usually sit around and sulk over nothing. He wondered briefly what had caused his normally upbeat morale to plummet, but in truth he knew it wasn't a *what* that had his stomach tied in knots—it was a *who*.

He hoped his mother wouldn't notice that he'd deserted the television program he'd been watching and had moved to the porch. He'd left the TV on, which was a little sneaky, but he just could not face another rehash of the Kathleen/Rob/Bobby situation.

Brian didn't want to talk to anyone right now, not even his mother. If she came out and noticed the mood he was in, she would just tell him to get over it, and he wasn't ready to get over it yet. He wanted to wallow in his unaccustomed moodiness for a while in peace without having anyone advising him to buck up. Upon occasion, Lettie Mitchell still treated her grown-up children like…well, children.

For Brian, the quintessential extrovert who loved interacting with others, pity parties like the one he was celebrating there on the porch rarely ever occurred. It was worse this time because he recognized the root of his problem…at least, in part…but the knowing hadn't helped change his mood. Seeing his sister's eyes sparkle every time Rob walked into a room this week had caused Brian to feel envious of them at times, but he really didn't begrudge the new closeness his sister shared now with Rob. Brian was happy for Kathleen and Rob and wished them the best. Right now, though, he felt…lonely.

As he swayed back and forth, inhaling the faint scent of nearby roses and listening to the sound of noisy crickets, Brian closed his eyes and smiled, remembering how things used to be with Ellen. He could recall the good times now without feeling torn apart the way he had right after she died. That had been a rough time for Brian, the toughest blow he'd had to take in his lifetime. While he knew he'd never forget Ellen and the love they'd shared, he no longer fell to pieces when he saw the best of her manifested in their two precious daughters. Janie's pertness and Sally's beautiful eyes, so very much like Ellen's that it used to break his heart, were now sources of pride he could revel in without fearing he'd fall back into that old morass of hopelessness and despair.

No, it wasn't lingering grief that had Brian brooding and feeling sorry for himself tonight. And it wasn't really jealousy of Kathleen and Rob, although he would like to have blamed it on one of those two things. Instead, it was the tenacious, growing perception deep down in his soul that a red-headed, emerald-eyed, sassy little army of one had him solidly under siege that was laying him low. Just the possibility of seeing Millie again had eroded his usual foundation of sanity. *Three years! And I've never run into her here.* The fact of that truly was hard for Brian to believe. *How many times have we walked the same streets in three years? We could have passed each other by and never known it!*

What should he do about the situation? He'd thought of Millie with regret at least a hundred times since walking out of that restaurant and leaving her alone to cope with his desertion. A constant, under-the-skin awareness of his insensitivity had made it impossible for Brian to totally erase that experience from his mind. He'd actually begun to believe...no, hope...he'd never see Millie again. But now, just when he thought he'd learned to live with what he'd done, she'd popped up again, seemingly out of the blue here in Logan.

Brian ducked his head and drew a deep breath. Just thinking about Millie Samson reminded him that he—FBI's man among men—had been, at least once, a world class heel.

No, better make that twice. Because he didn't want Sally spending a day at the *Sentinel* with Millie, no matter how interested in journalism his daughter might be. If she did, he wouldn't be able to avoid seeing Millie, and he just wasn't ready to face Millie yet. He stopped the swing with his foot, dropped his head back, and sighed again. Who was he trying to fool? He knew he'd say yes if Sally asked him for permission to go. Though twelve years old, Sally still was his baby, and he kind of liked being perceived as a hero by his girls. A hero...hey, that's it, he thought, snapping his fingers and sitting up straight. He'd figure out a way to control the situation himself. A leader with a mind like a steel trap...wasn't that what the government paid him to be? "Heck, a man like me can't be twisted in knots by one gorgeous woman and two adorable girls," he muttered under his breath.

*One gorgeous woman and two adorable girls? Did I actually say that?* Brian moaned out loud and dropped his head into his hands. No doubt about it, the three of them would soon be making mincemeat of him.

Hearing movement in the house, he turned his head toward the sound. When Lettie Mitchell called his name from inside the screened door, he felt ashamed that he had been avoiding her. "I'm out here, Mom," he answered. "Come on out and join me in the swing."

By the time his mother walked out to the porch with a cheerful voice and two cups of steaming, rich, homemade hot chocolate, Brian welcomed her company.

He still hadn't decided what to do about Millie.

\* \* \* \*

Georgio's was a fashionable, exclusive, and expensive restaurant in Charleston. Its understated elegance reeked of sophistication, but Rob and Kathleen barely noticed the low array of candles on the linen-covered, artistically appointed table where they sat. They had eyes for only each other. As the tuxedo-clad waiters, who recognized the baseball superstar, hovered unnoticed around them, Rob and Kathleen touched souls and talked.

They discussed anything and everything that came to mind and were pleased to discover that on most things they agreed. At one point Rob mentioned he'd like to have more children someday, but Kathleen warned, "They cut down on your mobility and independence. You sure you'd want to go through that at this stage in your life?"

Rob squeezed her hand. "Of course I would, but only if you'd want it, too—I'm sure not planning to have a child with anyone else! I figure we're young enough that having another baby isn't a decision we'd have to make right away. That comment just slipped out, so don't pay any attention to it. Now that I see you as Bobby's mother as well as my wife, it's easy to imagine how satisfying it must have been raising him from day one. But I'm happy just being Bobby's father, Katie. I'm not trying to pressure you into doing something you don't want to do."

Kathleen forced herself to take a step back emotionally. She felt a twinge of uneasiness each time Rob assumed they'd be sharing a future together. She had told Pastor Harlow she wanted to work toward a reconciliation, but nothing had been settled yet. "Working toward" didn't necessarily mean "arriving at." She did have to smile, though, remembering the joys and challenges of raising Bobby. She'd loved every minute of it.

She knew it would only encourage Rob more, but she decided to be candid with him. "I guess, since I was single and assumed I'd never have another baby, I didn't let myself dwell on that possibility. But it might be nice to have another one someday."

Rob rewarded that comment with a quiet smile, but didn't speak.

Because of their previous problems, there was one issue they still felt reluctant to discuss. They'd each avoided bringing it up, even on those occasions when they could have gracefully segued into it from another angle. It would have to be addressed sometime soon, though, so Kathleen decided to embark on a discreet and subtle fact-finding mission, herself. "Exactly where do you live?" she asked...and almost groaned. Apparently, subtlety was not her forte.

Rob hid his smile. He'd been hoping she'd ask him that question. "I have an old house Dad helped me renovate in Wyoming, Ohio, a suburb that's a few minutes north of Cincinnati," he said. "Wyoming's an older community, small-ish, but near enough to downtown that it's convenient to everything. I think you and Bobby might like it up there."

Knowing he'd made mistakes before in not soliciting Kathleen's opinions in every aspect of their marriage, especially where they would live, Rob didn't want to fall into that old trap again. "I love my house there, but I can live anywhere," he added. "I have to be in Cincinnati at least part of the year, but that doesn't mean I must live there year-round. Wyoming's just a convenient home base, that's all." He smiled at Kathleen, thinking back to the early days of their marriage. "Wherever I live and wherever I go, you know I'll call on Sunday nights, right?"

Kathleen wagged her head from side to side. "Weekly phone calls weren't enough when we were separated before, and they won't cut it this time, Mr. McKenzie. And please don't mention e-mail to me. I spend too much time on the computer as it is."

"Not even daily e-mails?"

Kathleen shook her head again. "Too impersonal."

Rob smiled. He'd found those Sunday night calls at the beginning of their marriage to be pretty frustrating, too. Weekly phone calls and daily e-mails wouldn't be enough for him now either.

When they finally drank the last of their after-dinner coffee and glanced away from each other, they discovered that they were the last diners there. Georgio's patient manager and serving staff were waiting to close their doors for the night. Rob paid their bill, left a more than generous tip to make up for staying so late, and they left.

Driving back to Logan, traffic was sporadic on Rt. 119. Kathleen had fallen asleep shortly after they left Charleston, and her face was serene and beautiful at rest. Rob kept glancing over at her as flickers of on-coming headlights highlighted her face, bringing it back into focus each time. Knowing she was deep in sleep and wouldn't hear, he whispered softly, so as not to awaken her, "I dream of taking you and Bobby home to live with me forever, Katie-girl."

He reached out a shaky hand and feather-brushed her sleeping form with the tips of his fingers. Kathleen stirred, but he knew she hadn't heard his wistful words or felt his loving touch.

\* \* \* \*

The next morning, having arrived early on purpose, Rob waited for Kathleen and Bobby in front of the Bible Church his parents and the Mitchell family had attended since he and Kathleen were in their early teens. When Kathleen and Bobby arrived, he pretended to mess up Bobby's slicked-down, Sunday-combed hair, and then kissed Kathleen on the cheek. A crowd had gathered outside, waiting to go into church, but Rob ignored their curious looks as he leaned over to whisper in Kathleen's ear. "You're looking mighty sexy in that short red skirt, Miss Katie."

Kathleen glanced quickly at Bobby, hoping he'd not overheard. "Rob McKenzie!" she scolded in a whisper, "we're almost in church!" Rob grinned, surveying her slowly and wickedly, silently reminding her of the passionate goodnight kiss they'd shared the night before. She tried to keep up a pretense of disapproval, but the upward curve of her lips belied the stern tone of her voice. "You are *so* fresh!" she finally said, giving in to her smile.

A hush fell over the three of them when they stepped inside the church. Off-white walls, trimmed with antique pine woodwork that still carried the soft scent of a recent rub with lemon oil, drew them through the narthex and into the quiet sanctuary. The crackled glass of the side windows admitted light but filtered out external intrusions. But it was the baptistry, surrounded by an exquisite mural of John the Baptist immersing Jesus, that caught Bobby's eye. Kathleen whispered that the local artist who painted that mural had done others in churches all across the United States. "I think he did one in Nova Scotia," she said, "as well as Baja, Mexico."

"Wow!" Bobby, plainly impressed, whispered back.

They sat on a pew with Kathleen's family, where Bobby felt an immediate sense of closeness and belonging. When Mary and Mike McKenzie arrived, everyone scooted down the pew to make room for them. For the first time ever, Bobby felt he understood what the psalmist meant when he said his "cup runneth over."

Clearly, Carrie and Billy Joe had spread the news that Rob had shared with them the day before. Several heads turned to greet the family and check out Bobby, but with the insouciance of youth, Bobby ignored their interested stares.

* * * *

Sunday morning was, without question, Pastor Matt Harlow's favorite time of the week. Standing before the congregation, he spoke in a powerful, enthusiastic voice. "It's a glorious morning to gather with fellow Christians to worship and adore the Lord," he said with a smile. "Let's stand and praise God together as we sing '*When Morning Gilds the Skies, My Heart Awaking Cries, May Jesus Christ Be Praised.*'"

The gray-haired organist, Grace Adkins, who had been the children's choir director and youth leader there when Kathleen was a kid, played melodiously as Rob and Kathleen shared a hymnal for the first time in years. Their exuberant voices merged with those of their fellow Christians as the cream-and-green garbed choir entered the sanctuary through the middle aisle.

After the morning announcements by Elder Jacob Lodge, Pastor Harlow read from the first chapter of the Book of James. "Consider it pure joy, my brothers, whenever you face trials of many kinds, because you know that the testing of your faith develops perseverence.... Blessed is the man who perseveres under trial, because when he has stood the test, he will receive the crown of life that God has promised to those who love him."

Pastor Harlow glanced around the congregation before beginning his sermon. "Don't the words of that writer sound a little radical to you?" he asked in a conversational tone. "Facing hardships is bad enough, but isn't James implying that we're supposed to feel joyful when troubles come our way…and glad when we're faced with trials and tribulations?

"I can hear you saying to yourselves, I don't think so! Toughing it out goes against the grain of our modern-day culture, doesn't it? We're into overnight success, fast food, and—" he paused for effect "—short sermons!" As the congregation laughed, he added, "Well, at least I know you're listening!"

He raked the faces of his listeners with eyes that seemed to pierce into their souls. "Tell the truth, now," he said, "I'm not asking for a show of hands. Have you ever hit a snag and given up? Well, I have. Many times. Let's face it, as a rule most of us do give up too quickly—on jobs, relationships, church affiliations, and, sometimes, even on God."

Kathleen found herself paying rapt attention to the young pastor's words, most of which seemed directed at her.

"But James was a wise, courageous man as well as an insightful writer," Matt Harlow continued, "despite the facetious questions I asked when I started this sermon. The joy James speaks of is in the *outcome* of the trials we face, not the trials themselves, and that's a powerful incentive for us to stick with it. But is that what we usually do?" He slowly shook his head. "No, when something isn't easy, we act rashly and quit—now that's a human trait we're all familiar with, right?" He laughed as several people, who suddenly felt guilty, started to squirm. Singling out a tennis-playing friend he often teased from the pulpit, Matt grinned. "Don't feel bad, Ted, I'm not singling you out this time. We're all alike in that respect!"

All at once, sitting there, Rob felt as if God had tapped him on the shoulder and whispered in his ear, *Are you listening, son?* Without taking his eyes off the charismatic minister, he reached out to squeeze Kathleen's hand. He'd lost out on years of delight because he hadn't had the patience, or the willingness, to go the distance with her...or as Pastor Harlow said, to persevere through troubles instead of just quitting.

The sermon also hit home with Kathleen. Clasping Rob's hand, she searched her own conscience. Had she truly sought God's will in her life, or had she depended on her own wants and desires when making decisions? Ashamed, she closed her eyes and admitted silently that she'd left God out of the equation too many times.

Pastor Harlow paused to take a sip of water from a styrofoam cup on the lectern. "Knowing how to persevere is not an inborn trait, unfortunately. But our Bible, or what I like to call my user's manual, is full of helpful instructions. In his second letter to Timothy, Paul writes, 'I have fought the good fight, I have finished the race, I have kept the faith. Now there is in store for me the crown of righteousness, which the Lord, the righteous Judge, will award to me on that day....'"

"Fighting the good fight. Finishing the race. Keeping the faith. Three things only...A-B-C. Doesn't sound hard at all...or does it? Well, let me give you a personal illustration of how this thing works, then you can decide. As some of you know, I run to stay in shape. In fact, I've come close to knocking a few of you down a time or two as I've barreled down the sidewalks of Logan. Running's hard, and many people start. But not all of them continue." He took a quick look at several people in the congregation. "But I don't think God holds it against people who start to run and then quit…so that should reassure a lot of you!"

Several men, including the chairman of the Board of Elders, and a couple of women laughed. It was a close-knit congregation, and they all knew who their pastor meant.

"Here's the drill. You start to run, then after awhile you get an ache in your side, a dry mouth, heavy legs, and you're positive that at any minute you're going to die, right there on the sidewalk outside Peebles. At that point, all you want to do is quit. In fact, you feel you *have* to quit. But if you keep going, the pain goes away, your legs feel lighter, and you get what's called a 'second wind.' And then comes the runner's high, when you feel like you could run forever.

"Paul's words about perseverance—fighting the fight, finishing the race, and keeping the faith—are amazingly similar to the words we use to describe the sport of running. When we try without ceasing, work through our problems, and never give up, we get that second wind. And it's that second wind…the indwelling of the Holy Spirit in our lives…that ultimately enables us to win the race."

Pastor Harlow scanned the faces of the congregation. "I've challenged you this morning to persevere, which isn't easy. Let me end my sermon with a promise: Jesus said, 'Lo, I am with you always.' If you don't remember anything else I've said today, remember this: when we try, even when it seems to others that we've failed, God is right there beside us, helping us overcome the hardships we face. Not just sometimes, because that's not the way He operates, but always. That's His unbreakable promise!"

Pastor Harlow concluded the service with a prayer, "Father God, help us endure all things for your sake. And, someday, greet us with the words, 'Well done, my good and faithful servant. Welcome home.'"

\* \* \* \*

The usual delay as people exited the church and spoke to Pastor Harlow irritated Millie Samson. She was not a patient person under ordinary circumstances, and this was not an ordinary Sunday. Usually she was nimble enough to exit early and beat the crowd, but arriving late and finding an elderly gentleman sitting in her customary back row seat had put her right in the middle of the group that was mingling and socializing as if they had all day to stand there blocking the aisles. If she couldn't push her way out of the pew quickly, she'd run into the Mitchells. And she did not want to see Brian Mitchell today.

Why didn't the Bible Church have side exits near the back of the church like First Baptist down the street? If it did, she could get away quickly. As it was, she could either go with the slow flow of traffic down the middle aisle toward the back of the church where Matt stood, or she could buck the tide and try to sneak out through one of the emergency exits near the pulpit. Either way, since she was delayed by the crowd, she was sure to run into the Mitchells. If she remained trapped in her pew, they'd pass her; if she tried for an emergency exit, she'd pass them. She "hmmphed" a couple of times, then released a frustrated sigh. Hunkering down slightly to minimize her chances of being detected, she pushed her way into the crowd headed toward the back of the church.

She hadn't seen Matt Harlow in several days. As she straightened up and shook his hand, complimenting him on another insightful sermon, he invited her to lunch. Being single adults in a church full of senior citizens and young couples with children, Millie and Matt banded together for odd meals out every now and then. They rarely ate together on Sundays, though, because Matt was usually too busy putting out metaphorical fires among various members of his congregation that day. Many people considered Sunday to be their day of rest, but not their pastor's.

"Sure, I'll wait by my car under that tree near the street," she said, pointing to where she had parked. "We can decide later who's driving."

"I'll drive," Matt volunteered. "My car's parked in front of the church. It's not locked, why not just wait there for me?" Millie indicated that was fine and had turned to walk away, pleased that she'd eluded Brian Mitchell, when someone called her name.

Kathleen, a step or two behind, spoke warmly. "I looked for you before we went into church but didn't see you. I wanted to thank you again for the time you spent with us yesterday."

Caught by a person she liked, Millie turned and smiled at Kathleen. "Well, to be honest, I wasn't here when you went into church," she said. "That buzz of activity you heard after the first hymn was me trying to sneak in late without getting caught."

As the two women stepped aside to chat, Pastor Harlow continued shaking hands with other members of the congregation, including Rob—who introduced him to Bobby—and the rest of the Mitchell and McKenzie clans. The two Mitchell girls hurried through the line to join Kathleen and Millie, who'd become one of their favorite people during yesterday's tour.

Sally stood by quietly until Millie asked about one of their shared interests. "Hey, Sally, how's it going? When you wrote in your journal last night, I hope you mentioned my name."

Sally grinned, confessing that she had covered their visit at the *Sentinel* in her writings the evening before. "I wanted to get it all down while everything was fresh in my mind."

"That's what I do, too," Millie said. "If you miss a day, your memory becomes faulty and it's hard to remember exactly how things unfolded. Once you've written something down, you can return to it as many times as you like, and it comes alive each time you read it again."

Everyone, except Brian, took part in the lively conversation around Millie. Even Rob's parents and Lettie Mitchell were called over to join the animated group.

Millie admitted that she'd seen the elder members of their families before, usually from her vantage point at the back of the church. She laughed and said she doubted they'd seen her. She always sat so far back that they would've had to twist around one-hundred-eighty degrees and crane their necks to see where she was! As she acted out the contortions required on their part to get her in view, she had them in stitches.

Brian had to hand it to Millie. His girls were hanging onto every word she spoke, and his mother and the McKenzies seemed quite enchanted by her, too.

Rob, totally in the dark because Kathleen hadn't yet clued him in about Brian and Millie, invited her to go to lunch with them. "I don't know where we're going," he admitted, "but we'd love to have you join us." He raised his brows and grinned. "My treat."

"I'm sorry, Rob, I can't, although I do adore being treated. I've already made other plans." Switching gears, she said, "Fred Horne called me at home last night. I understand next Saturday's going to be Rob McKenzie Day at his shop, and that there'll be other big doings around town that day, too."

Rob just shook his head. "That Fred! I only talked to him for half an hour yesterday, but within a few hours of our meeting, he'd organized the entire event. I understand he bullied the downtown merchants into offering special sales for next Saturday, then broadened his shop-wide event into a town-wide celebration."

Millie chuckled. Fred's steamrolling tactics, new to Rob, were familiar to the downtown business community. "Fred really is a force to be reckoned with," she said. "The *Sentinel* will cover everything in detail, of course, but we're also giving Fred free advertising space to promote the charitable part of the day."

She reminded Rob he hadn't dropped by the newspaper yet to say hello to everyone there. "Why not come by one day this week," she suggested. "We'd like to take some photos to add to our coverage of Rob McKenzie Day."

Brian's eyes remained on Millie as she finished her conversation with the others, but she never looked in his direction. Not even once. As she turned toward Matt's car, he followed. Realizing he was behind her, she increased her pace. She had almost reached her destination when he touched her on the arm. "Millie, please...can we talk?"

"No. Just leave me alone." She eased into Matt's car and locked the door, which left Brian standing in the middle of the sidewalk alone. Knowing he'd gain nothing by forcing the issue, he turned to walk away. His girls and Bobby were waiting in his car. Brian was thankful that Kathleen and the others had already driven away, that they, at least, had missed his embarrassing snubbing.

"I was only trying to apologize," he sputtered angrily and walked back to his car. "*What is wrong with that woman?*"

# Chapter 23

From the time they met six months ago, shortly after he accepted the call from the Bible Church to serve as its pastor, Matt Harlow and Millie Samson, two of Logan County's most dynamic individuals, had made it a point to spend as much time together as their busy schedules would permit. People around town and in Matt's church speculated about the exact nature of their relationship, because a special affinity did seem to exist between Millie and Matt, but their interest in each other was purely platonic. Having lunch or dinner together, or going out for an occasional movie, was only a friendship thing with them, although they did enjoy each other's company immensely. Early on, they'd found they could talk to each other about anything, so when their workdays were over and they had no one at home with whom to share the things they'd done that day, they often called each other up, just to talk.

"I don't mean to pry, but I couldn't help seeing the brush-off you gave Brian Mitchell after church," Matt said, once they'd been seated in a booth at the Pizza Hut and had ordered their lunch. "Is he the guy from your past who hurt you so much? The one you refuse to discuss, even with me?"

Millie sighed. She didn't want to discuss Brian with Matt now either, but she'd hate to hurt his feelings. She'd already brushed off one man today; she couldn't afford to alienate another one, especially not Matt. He was a true friend, and true friends were few and far between. "Yeah, but let's not talk about him right now," she finally said. "I'd like to enjoy this beautiful day without thinking about Brian Mitchell or the past."

Matt glanced up as the door to the popular restaurant opened. "Uh-oh! I don't think that'll be possible. Don't look now, but the subject of our discussion and the other members of his party are being greeted by the hostess, as we speak."

As people always seem compelled to do, Millie turned to look. Her eyes latched onto Brian Mitchell's as he followed the hostess to their table. She averted her gaze, pretending she hadn't seen his puzzled look when he saw her in the booth with Pastor Harlow.

Before sitting down, Brian excused himself to wash his hands. He detoured past the booth where Matt sat with Millie, even though it was not on the way to the restroom.

As Matt stood to shake hands again with Brian, he was surprised by the look of outrage that came over Millie's face when the other man stopped by their table. He noted, too, that Brian's jaw clenched in response. Purely by chance, Matt had gotten caught in the center of the cross hairs between the two of them, not knowing that Millie had already asked Brian to leave her alone once today. Something seemed to sizzle in the air between Brian and Millie, and Matt didn't relish being stuck in the middle of whatever it was. "Brian, it was good seeing you and your girls in church today," he said, sizing up the situation. "I think you know Millie Samson, don't you? I was just about to abandon her for a moment to say hello to the Waltons. Why don't you keep her company until I return?" Matt's gaze was steady as he looked back at Millie. "I'll be close by," he promised. "Right over there."

Now Millie seemed to be upset with *him*, which Matt regretted, but he continued over to a large table occupied by a young family from their church. While they waited for their pizza and discussed church affairs, he kept an eye on Millie.

A mask of aloofness had settled over Millie's face, and she refused to look directly at Brian. He slid into the booth beside her. "Millie, don't act like this, not that I don't deserve it."

Millie finally turned her head in Brian's direction…and she should've known better. The flash of anger and hurt in her eyes contradicted her previous air of indifference.

Brian knew he wasn't the same man who'd treated Millie so cavalierly in Charleston, but Millie didn't know that. He was ready to move on with his life again now, unlike back then, so he wouldn't be making the same mistake again. But how could he get that point across to Millie without having to rehash *ad nausium* what had happened between them before? He wanted to avoid a scenario like that at all costs, if possible. And, who knows? Maybe Millie had already forgotten.

Right. Talk about the eternal optimist. From the way she'd treated Brian after church and since he had stopped by their booth, even he wasn't enough of a Pollyanna to believe that.

Brian almost smiled, his eyes still focused on Millie. He found her masquerade of nonchalance, which she intended as a put-down, more intriguing than if she had ignored him completely. He recognized the emotion behind her attitude and sympathized with it. No one liked being dissed, and unfortunately, that was the impression he'd left Millie with three years ago.

Glancing over at the handsome young minister, passing the time of day now with his friends, Brian felt an unfamiliar twinge in the region of his heart. "Are you dating Pastor Harlow?"

Following his gaze, Millie smiled slowly, but the coolness of her words negated her smile. "That's none of your business, Mr. FBI. Just go away so Matt can return. Your girls must be wondering what happened to you, they're looking in this direction."

Brian didn't care who was looking in their direction. He cupped her chin and forced her to look up at him. "Look, Red," he said softly, using the pet name he'd given Millie shortly after they met, "you can't imagine how sorry I am for the way I acted in Charleston. We don't have to discuss what happened there, if you'd rather not, but I would like to explain it if I can. Can I call you while I'm here?"

Millie narrowed her eyes as she jerked her face away and focused on a point to the left of Brian's shoulder. "Feel free. I have Caller ID." The implication was clear. She could monitor her calls and might choose not to answer one from him. Her eyes sparkled, and Brian's appreciation of her feistiness grew. She was a high-spirited Irish spitfire that only someone fearless and brave would dare try to tame. He laughed out loud, liking what he saw.

Millie's fingers curled into her palm, almost breaking the skin. How dare he make light of her! She itched to slap his laughing face, but didn't want to make a scene. The church crowd was rapidly filling up the spaces around them.

Matt began wending his way back to their booth, but he was stopped several times by people he knew. Ignoring Millie's sarcastic comment about Caller ID, Brian slid out of the booth and left to rejoin his family.

"Well, that seemed to go well," Matt said, sitting down and flicking his napkin onto his lap.

Millie waited until the waitress had placed their pizza on the table and served each of them a slice. Then, clipping off each word, she threatened, "If you ever desert me again, Matt Harlow...if you ever, even once, leave me alone with Brian Mitchell...you won't live to tell the tale."

Matt's booming laugh caused everyone in the restaurant to turn around and grin. Everyone, that is, except Brian Mitchell, who scowled. His sister took in his glowering look and hissed, "What is wrong with you now?" Brian threw up his hands in disgust when everyone at his table laughed aloud. Most of the diners nearby knew the Mitchell and McKenzie families well and smiled along with them. But not Millie Samson. She frowned.

*       *       *       *

While Matt waited in line to pay for their meal, Millie stopped by the Mitchell/McKenzie table. In a voice as cold as the iced tea she'd had with lunch, she asked Brian, "Well, can she or can't she?"

Not everyone at the table knew what she was talking about, but Brian did. With a cynical smile on his face, he spoke with a drawl. "Is this about Sally spending a day at the *Sentinel* next week? Gee, I'm sorry, Ms. Samson. I wasn't aware I could speak with you about this." He leaned around Janie to say something to Sally. "Did you know I could answer her directly, sweetie? I thought I had to use the same circular route Ms. Samson used…you know, from me to you to Katie and then on to her." He winked at Sally.

Missing the wink, Millie demanded, "You know perfectly well what I'm talking about. Can she or can't she? Make up your mind and tell her or tell me."

"Okay," Brian shrugged. "If she wants to, she can."

Millie wanted to stomp her foot…on Brian's toes! Instead, she turned to Sally and spoke in a softer, friendlier voice. "Hey, that's great, Sally. How about me picking you up tomorrow morning at nine?"

Sally glanced at her father, who mimed the word no. "Tomorrow's okay, Ms. Samson. Dad said so last night. But he'll drop me off, then pick me up at lunch time. Is that okay?"

"Sure, that's fine. I'll meet you at the receptionist's desk. Just give her your name when you get there; she'll know who you are. But if your father can pick you up at two instead of noon, I'd like to take you to lunch."

"I'll take both of you to lunch around twelve-thirty," Brian interjected.

"Your father doesn't have to do that," Millie said, still looking at Sally. By then it was apparent to everyone at the table that Millie was avoiding eye contact with Brian, and except to communicate with Sally, he hadn't taken his eyes off her even once. Brian hadn't looked at a woman like that, to his family's knowledge, since Ellen died eight years ago.

"He wants to, Ms. Samson," Sally said, ad-libbing a little. "He is *really* looking forward to it."

Brian bit his lower lip to keep from grinning. That devious little mischief-maker, he thought. I must be doing something right as a father!

Clenching her teeth, Millie turned a half-look on Brian. "Thank you, Brian," she said, syrupy sweet. When she turned her attention back to Sally, she was cordial again. "Tomorrow will be fun for me, Sally. I hope you'll enjoy it, too. See you in the morning."

Kathleen noticed Brian's look of satisfaction as Millie walked away. "Brian...Brian! I have a bad feeling about this. I predict you've finally met your match in Millie Samson."

The brilliance of Brian's grin surprised everyone. "Good. Let's pray your prediction turns out to be true."

Rob reached over to lightly tap the underside of Kathleen's chin. "Close your mouth, Katie. Brian's a big boy. He can handle this on his own."

Looking past Kathleen, Rob gave Brian a stern look and some cautionary words of warning himself. "Look, Brian, everyone in town likes and respects Millie. If you don't treat her right, you'll have people all over your case, including me." Rob sputtered. "You should have seen the way you looked at her!"

That broke Brian up. "Back off, Rob, and just listen to yourself. You sound worse than any pesky brother I've ever seen, and that includes David, who's the peskiest one of all! Not that I'm complaining, mind you, having another brother's kind of nice. Bear in mind, though, that unlike you, I grew up with two siblings. I know what to do when one sticks his nose in my business!"

Rob's look of shock was ludicrous. He'd been back in the good graces of the Mitchell family for less than a week. Criticizing one of their own was idiotic. Anyone with half a brain could see that Kathleen was warming up to him, and a sweet warming up it was, too. He'd better apologize now. "Brian—"

Brian held up his hand. "Don't say another word, *Brother Rob*. I wouldn't treat Millie badly for the world, I assure you. It's nice that you took up for her, though. Not that she needed it."

For some reason, seeing the famous first baseman for the Cincinnati Reds looking anxious over nothing continued to tickle Brian. Plucking the lunch tab from Rob's hand, he cuffed him gently on the chin the way he often did Bobby or David. "Welcome back to the Mitchell family, brother. Lunch is on me."

As they left the restaurant, an exhilarated Brian threw an arm around his sister. "Tell the truth now, Katie. Have you ever, in all your life, seen a day more glorious than this?"

Kathleen laughed, shaking her head. "Brian, I have to be honest. Sometimes I worry about you!"

# Chapter 24

Rob's physical therapy session seemed unusually long and exhausting Monday morning. By the time he arrived at the cabin shortly after nine, however, he'd begun to recover. Bobby would be working with the volunteers at the Habitat house that day, but he wasn't quite ready to leave when Rob arrived. While Bobby raced up to his room for the work gloves his mother had bought the day before, Rob sat down to share a cup of coffee with Kathleen.

"I'm baking a ham this evening," she said. "Want to join us for dinner?"

Rob nodded, studying her face. He couldn't seem to get enough of her, and it showed. "Are my parents invited?"

"No, do you mind? I thought this time it could be just us—you and Bobby and me."

Rob smiled over the top of his mug. "Sounds mighty good," he said with a wink.

Bobby came clattering down the stairs, his backpack slung over his shoulder. "What are you doing today, Mom?"

Kathleen wondered how to answer that question; she'd been so involved with Bobby and Rob, her family and his, that her to-do list kept growing longer by the day. Bobby was in a hurry to leave, but Rob stopped half-way out the door to look back. "Dad's having lunch delivered to the site around noon, so Bobby will be eating pizza with the rest of the volunteers. Why not take the day off?"

Kathleen smiled as the guys drove away. Good-bye, to-do list, she thought, as she fired up her computer to check her e-mail messages. She answered a couple of new ones, then decided to place everything else on the back burner until tomorrow...except dinner, of course, which was hours away.

She replenished her coffee and grabbed Sue Grafton's latest mystery—the one she'd picked up on Saturday in Logan. Kicking off her shoes, she headed for the sofa. "A tip of the hat to you, Rob McKenzie," she said out loud as she started to read. "Great suggestion!"

* * * *

At precisely 9:13 a.m., Brian parked his car across the street, two parking spaces down from the newspaper building. Sally jumped out of the car and would've run up the street by herself had her father not restrained her so firmly. "Didn't I say I'd walk you in? Hold on."

Millie had only partially cleared her calendar for the day in order to give Sally a realistic picture of what reporters and editors do during a regular workday. Sally would be working alongside Millie and the other *Sentinel* employees, so Millie had factored in enough time for all of them to consider Sally's comments and answer any questions she might have.

But there was one thing Millie hadn't factored in. She hadn't expected Brian to escort Sally all the way to the door. As father and daughter neared the *Sentinel* building, Millie set her jaw and vowed to rein in her temper. How hard could it be, getting along with Brian for the small amount of time they'd be together today?

Easy as pie, she answered herself.

She gazed out the window, watching Brian and Sally as they walked up the street, but her thoughts were focused mainly on Brian. He could be a fractious cuss if he chose to be, but he sure was a looker. His hair was shorter now than when she'd first met him in Charleston, but he'd been working undercover then and had outfitted himself with a different persona. Brian was a perfect example of what the rigorous physical conditioning his job required for survival could do for a man. *Mmmm...mmmm.*

Millie blushed, remembering the last time she'd been alone with Brian. He had made it painfully clear that being with her caused him to feel disloyal to the memory of his wife, even though, up until that fateful night, she and Brian had only been friends. She'd felt sorry for Brian when she learned later of his young wife's terminal illness and tragic death, which had occurred several years before Millie met Brian in Charleston. Millie knew more than anyone that Brian had still been grieving the loss of his wife when she met him, no matter how much time had passed since Ellen's death. After that experience, she never even considered trying to reach him again.

To her shame, she hadn't resisted Brian that night in Charleston, even though his kiss was more aggressive than she liked and had made her feel uneasy. But that was a moot point. The fact that he had not been interested in her, when he'd been the one to initiate the date *and* the kiss, still mortified Millie. She had responded to Brian in a wanton way that was quite unlike her, and he had no way of knowing she wasn't always like that.

Brian was probably still convinced she was easy, and that wasn't true.

On a practical level, Millie knew that she should have forgotten, and gotten over, that unpleasant encounter long ago. And that maybe, just maybe, she'd feel more in control of the current situation with Brian—and he would have a kinder, more realistic, impression of her—if she had reacted differently then.

She stepped back from the window. Her co-workers were watching. The last thing she needed was to start a new rumor; folks around town already wondered about her friendship with Matt.

But Brian saw Millie at the window and stopped abruptly to look up. With the light from the office behind her, she resembled a modern-day Medusa with snakes of fire swirling around her head. The quick pep talk he gave himself then was combined with a prayer: *I'm an experienced FBI agent, for Pete's sake. I'm trained to stay calm. But please, Lord, give me a miracle. Help me keep my cool today.* For a man who had briefly turned his back on faith and God after the death of his wife, Brian certainly was experiencing a complete about-face today. Resuming his walk, he digested what he'd just done. Not only had he prayed again for the first time in months, he fully expecting his prayer to be answered! That was something he'd have to think about later.

Obeying her new Rule for the Day, Millie greeted Brian in a semi-friendly manner, then smiled at Sally. "Ready to roll, Ms. Reporter?"

"More than ready," Sally smiled back, looking around the newsroom with stars in her eyes.

Watching Sally, Brian knew exactly how excess baggage must feel. He turned his gaze to Millie. "So I'll pick you all up at, what? Twelve-thirty?"

Millie didn't want to go to lunch with Brian, not even with Sally along. Their showdown at Pizza Hut the day before had not gone well at all. But, she had taken a vow of peace for the day, so she'd abide by it. "Twelve-thirty's fine," she agreed.

Before leaving, Brian gave Millie his cell phone number in case something came up.

\* \* \* \*

Millie was answering a question from the paper's receptionist when Brian and Janie walked through the door at twelve-thirty. Glancing up, she greeted them cordially. Brian wondered what had changed Millie's personality so much in the past twenty-four hours. She'd actually smiled at him again. He chalked that up as a miracle, another answer to his prayers.

Brian could hear Sally's voice as she spoke to someone at the back of the building. Even from that distance, he could tell she was enjoying herself. His "quiet" daughter was talking a mile a minute with two *Sentinel* employees who stood by her desk, apparently instructing and encouraging her. Sally gestured for Janie to come check out the monitor where she sat.

Millie and Brian continued to talk as Janie headed across the room to join her sister. "Those two guys are graphic designers who taught Sally how to set up some box ads for tomorrow," Millie explained. "Because you were so reluctant to let her spend time here today, I'd glad you can see how much she has blossomed in this atmosphere this morning."

"She sure seems to be having a good time," Brian admitted, watching his youngest child scoot over to make room for Janie at the computer.

"Having a young person in the office has given everyone an extra spurt of enthusiasm," Millie said. "They're showing off for her, as you see. I won't get a lick of work out of any of them as long as she's here!"

Millie's grin implied that having the advertising department at a temporary standstill wasn't all that disturbing. "Let's go to lunch so things can get back to normal for the staff," she said. "I'd better warn you, though—Sally probably won't be eating much lunch. She had donuts with everyone around ten-thirty while they shared old war stories with her."

As Millie led Brian around several desks, Janie shared a conspiratorial look with Sally. "Let's see what Dad can do with this program, okay, Sal?"

Sally rolled her eyes at the group around them. "Our father says he's never met a computer yet that was friendly enough. You guys will *not* believe him!"

That statement was true—as far as that particular software was concerned. To Brian, the complicated grid-type graph on the monitor looked exactly like gobbledygook. The girls covered their mouths and laughed, imagining their dad being able to master the advertising department's graphic design program.

Brian glanced at Millie, the corners of his eyes crinkled by a smile. "As you can see, a man with two *perfect* daughters has no room for ego. They're constantly looking for ways to trip me up. When they find something promising like this, it's Katie-bar-the-door." When Millie asked, he explained that each girl had her own computer and combination printer/scanner/copier in her room. "That's put an end to their daily arguments about who gets to use the computer, and when. Sally tried inputting her journal entries each evening, when we first bought her computer, but she decided she'd rather write it by hand so she could lock it away."

Out of earshot of the girls, Millie tilted her head to the side. "Don't they know you're a computer expert for the FBI, among other things? As I recall, you broke that money laundering investigation in Charleston by comparing the restaurant's handwritten reports with what the bookkeeper and owner thought were hidden computer records on multiple off-shore accounts. Aren't they aware that you're skilled in electronics and computer programming?"

Brian quickly placed a finger vertically over her mouth. "Don't mention that," he implored. "They get so much pleasure out of teasing their 'computerly nerdless' dad that I go along with it. They'll catch on sooner or later," he teased, "but in the meantime, only you and I will know the truth!"

Millie laughed at that before interrupting the group. "All right, guys and girls, here comes the meanie. I hate to break this up, but it's back-to-work time for everybody. If I allowed you all to have playmates every day, we'd never get a thing done around here." Her employees pretended to protest, begging Sally and Janie to stay and save them from the ogre. Brian was impressed. The *Sentinel* employees obviously felt comfortable enough with the boss to tease her back.

Sally and Janie said their good-byes and thanked everyone as Brian herded them out the front door. Millie appreciated the softer side of Brian that he'd revealed that day. Narrowing her eyes, she assessed him again. *Not bad. Not bad at all.*

An hour later, walking back to Brian's car after lunch at Shaw's Dairy, Millie threw an arm around Sally. "Did you like what you saw at the *Sentinel* today? Or did we turn you off on journalism forever?"

Sally's terminal case of reporteritis had been obvious to everyone that morning. "I wasn't turned off at all," she said, returning Millie's hug. "It was fantastic. Thanks again." Millie had to blink her eyes a time or two as the girls grinned at her. She realized then how much she envied Brian Mitchell. He was a lucky man, having parented two daughters like Sally and Janie. For years Millie had accepted her unmarried, childless state as being part of God's plan for her life. But at times like this, she realized how much she had missed, not being a mother.

Brian left the girls beside the car while he walked on with Millie. Glancing sideways at her, he confessed, "What you said earlier is true. I was reluctant to let Sally come here today. It was nice of you to encourage her, though, and I appreciate it. I'm sorry I was such a bear yesterday. I'll call you later so you can ream me out about it privately, okay?"

A nimbus of fiery curls blew across Millie's face as she pivoted to face Brian, her hands on her hips. She could not resist this man, no matter how hard she tried. Her lips turned up at the corners. "Good heavens, you're persistent. Don't you ever give up?

"Not on something this important. What do you say?"

"Well...I guess a woman doesn't have to pay attention to Caller ID, just because she has it."

Brian was still grinning as he walked back to his car. As the girls buckled their seatbelts, he told them what Millie had said.

What a difference a day makes, he marveled. Maybe having Caller ID in Logan wasn't as bad as he'd thought.

"Dad, can we get Caller ID when we get home?" Janie asked.

"Nope. Like most everyone else, you'll just have to take your chances, answering the phone."

"You're mean," Janie said, grinning.

"Yeah." Sally tried to frown. "Real mean."

Brian grinned again, recognizing a tease-fest when he saw one. "Learn to live with it," he said. "When you're thirty years old and independent, you can order your own Caller ID."

\* \* \* \*

Rob helped himself to a slice of ham before passing the platter at dinner, raving all the while about Bobby's carpentry skills. "No one could believe Bobby learned that much from the guys you all worked with last summer. They think he inherited his flair for construction from his two grandfathers." Rob grinned at Bobby. "You made me proud today, son. Real proud."

Pleased, Kathleen gave Bobby a two-thumbs-up sign. He had been nervous about working with his father, he'd wanted to please Rob so much. It was clear from the conversation around the dinner table that he had.

"Want to walk over the mountain with me?" Bobby asked Rob after dinner. "Uncle Brian can drive me home later." Having dinner with his parents had been fun, but now Bobby couldn't wait to get to his grandmother's to tell his cousins about the day he'd spent at the construction site with his dad.

Rob groaned and grabbed Kathleen's hand. "If I have to hobble all that way on a full stomach, so do you. I'll help you with the dishes later."

Rob's leg had improved so much that Kathleen could barely keep up with him and Bobby on the path. Each time she lagged behind a step or two, she sighed. Her feelings about Rob's quick recovery were mixed. She wanted him to feel better; she just hated seeing these idyllic moments out of time come to an end. Everything that happened between them—the things Rob said, the things they did together—she tucked away as memories to relive later. Only two more weeks, she told herself sadly. Two short weeks, then he'll be gone.

At one point they had to walk single file. Rob was slightly in front of Kathleen, near Bobby. "Tell me about school," she heard him say. "Have you gone to the same school since kindergarten?"

"No. I went to Woodbridge Elementary through fourth grade, then to middle school a few blocks down the street from our house. I finished seventh grade a couple weeks ago."

"Is that where you'll go in September?"

"No, I'll go to a private Christian school in Woodbridge. They teach eighth grade through senior year there. It's new, but Mom and Uncle Brian checked it out and liked it, so they enrolled Janie and me for the term starting this fall."

"Will some of your other friends be going there, too?"

"No, just Janie, but she's a year older and in a different class. Sally can't go till next year. She's a grade behind me."

Rob stopped and held his right hand over his heart, his eyes beginning to sparkle. "Are you telling me it's possible for some poor unsuspecting teacher to have a Mitchell in her class, three years running?"

Bobby threw his head back and laughed. "Yeah, it's not a very big school; I guess it could happen that way. Janie and Sally will love hearing that."

With a calculating look, Rob glanced back at Kathleen. She could almost read his mind. Bobby had said good-bye to his public school classmates before they left Woodbridge for Logan. Although a few of them would continue to pal around with each other this summer, Bobby would be attending a different school than most of them in the fall. If it came right down to it, Bobby could change to any school and the end result would be the same: new school, new friends.

They could hear everyone outside pitching horseshoes as they neared Mrs. Mitchell's back yard. Kathleen and Rob stayed long enough to say a brief hello but turned down Lettie Mitchell's offer of dessert. Kathleen had told Rob about her conversation on Saturday with her mother, so he knew that each of them was making an effort to mend the rift between them. But he'd still continue to tread a fine line between the two women. The truth was, in different ways and to different degrees, he loved them both.

Rob was determined not to settle for a lukewarm relationship with his mother-in-law. "Mrs. Mitchell," he said, throwing an arm over her shoulder, "you did a great job teaching this girl of yours how to cook. If I eat many more meals at her table, the trainer will be putting me on a diet when I get back to Cincinnati."

Lettie Mitchell, still ill at ease around Rob after what she had done, was flustered but pleased by his attention. She patted his washboard stomach. "That'll be the day! If anything, you need a little more meat on your bones."

"That's all muscle, Mrs. Mitchell," Rob teased, "but Katie's trying to turn it to fat."

Kathleen grabbed his arm and tugged him back toward the path. "Come on. Mom knows I'm not trying to fatten you up. Let's go home."

She realized immediately what she'd said in front of her family, but Rob didn't mind that everyone heard. He snagged an elbow around Kathleen's neck and pulled her close. "Home sounds mighty good, Katie-girl. Let's go."

Walking back, they held hands. "You had something in mind when you asked Bobby about his schooling, didn't you?" said Kathleen.

Sheepishly, Rob admitted that the subject had crossed his mind a time or two since their counseling session with Pastor Harlow. "I wanted to see how Bobby felt about schools before it came up between us," he said. He twined their fingers together. "I shouldn't fret about his education or anything else, knowing full well you're a wonderful mother. But I couldn't help it this time. Chalk it up to inexperience, okay?"

Rob tried to tug Kathleen closer as they ambled along the path. Her hand stayed snugly wrapped in his, and yet she still seemed awfully far away. "I am glad we talked about Bobby's schooling," he said, as she gave in and moved closer. "Apparently, it's not a problem, after all."

"I understand your concerns completely," Kathleen said after a moment. "I'd be disappointed if you weren't interested in your son's education. But let me make my position crystal clear: I'm not opposed to having Bobby change schools, per se. I just want the values I teach him at home to be reinforced by the school he attends. That's why I enrolled him in a Christian high school for this fall."

Rob finally pulled her close enough that they could walk arm in arm. "Listen, I heartily endorse that decision, but there are good Christian schools in other places, too. In fact, the public school district in Wyoming—suburb, not state—ranks among the top school districts in Ohio. I was worried about uprooting Bobby from a close, supportive group of friends, but he'll be making new friends in the fall, anyway. That was my main concern."

Rob gave Kathleen a quick squeeze, hoping she hadn't caught his inference that they might be living together in Ohio by fall. "We seem to be on the same wave length here," was all that he said.

Rob left the cabin shortly after helping Kathleen wash and dry and put away the dishes. Being together was too dangerous, too tempting, with Bobby not there. As the pain in his leg lessened, his longing for her grew. After a prim and proper kiss, not much more than a peck on the cheek, he left. Kathleen gazed wistfully down the drive till she no longer heard the humming of his car.

Shortly after reentering the cabin, she thought she heard the rumble of another vehicle. Brian wouldn't be bringing Bobby home this early, she knew; the girls and Bobby wouldn't allow it. Looking out the kitchen window, she was amazed to see Rob's Mustang again. She rushed to the bottom of the steps to meet him. If the animals in the woods around the cabin had been watching, the glow in Kathleen's eyes and the smile on her face would've convinced them she hadn't seen Rob in hours, not minutes.

Rob got out of his car and walked slowly to where she stood in surprised stillness, like a beautiful doe caught in the headlights of a car. He slipped his arms around her waist. "I can't leave with a washed-out kiss like that, Katie-girl. Come here."

Wrapped in each other's arms, they swayed from side to side. "I'm tired of fighting this need for you, Katie. I need a kiss that'll hold me till morning, one we can think about when we're in our separate beds again later tonight."

That new kiss, the one they both sought, turned serious all too soon as Rob unleashed the passion he'd been stockpiling for days. When they almost reached the point of giving in, he remembered the promise they'd made to take things slowly. He accepted full responsibility for seeing that they did.

"Ah, Katie," he said, his breathing rapid, irregular, "leaving you is tough to do." He backed slowly toward his car. As he went, he slid his hands from her shoulders to the tips of her fingers, not breaking their powerful physical connection until the last possible moment.

Once they were no longer touching, he turned and threw Kathleen final kiss.

Kathleen pretended she had to stretch to catch it, then she tucked it in her pocket.

*     *     *     *

Kathleen was not agreeable at first when Brian called to suggest that she co-host a dinner party with him the next evening. "You all were just up here a few days ago," she groused. "Why not just go out for dinner one evening, dutch-treat?" In the background, she could hear the muted sounds of Brad Paisley. Her mother had bought two of his CDs at the concert, according to Bobby.

Brian's pause lasted a second too long.

"Why propose a dinner party now?" she asked, suddenly suspicious.

"Isn't being with good friends reason enough for a party? I thought we might eat early and then swim in the pool above the dam after dinner. If the water's too cold—"

"Wait just a cotton-pickin' minute! You're suggesting a *swimming* party? If so, you're completely nuts. Rob and I still remember you enticing us into freezing water the last time we swam here with you. We vowed we'd never go near the pool again when you were around, and as you well know, Brian, we haven't."

Brian tossed her misgivings aside as being unimportant. "That's sort of stupid, you know? No one bears a grudge that long. Let me finish before you get all out of sorts, okay? If the water's too cold, as I was trying to say, we can use the hot tub."

Even after he promised to finance it all, thinking that might move Kathleen closer to full enthusiasm, she still wasn't gung-ho about having a party. As further inducement, Brian agreed to shop for the food and help with meal preparation. When he mentioned buying four porterhouse steaks—because they were "such impressive entrees"—and promised that he and Rob would grill them on the deck, Kathleen finally saw the light. "Four steaks, Brian? *Four*?" she teased.

"Come on, Katie, don't be dense. You know exactly where I'm coming from. You just want to make me spell it out, so here it is in a nutshell. Four steaks. Adults-only party. You, Rob, Millie, me. And since I need to tell Rob that he and I grilling the steaks, I'll invite him. You invite Millie."

Apparently, Brian had planned everything before phoning his sister. As he ticked items off one by one, Kathleen knew he was reading from a list. "Mom says Bobby can stay here tomorrow evening. She'll feed the kids and let them play board games or dance in the basement. I'll shop in the morning and then stop by there to fix a large salad and get some baking potatoes ready to throw in the oven.

Rob and I will grill the steaks after everyone's there. All you have to do is invite Millie, make sure the house looks festive—I'd suggest lots of candles, have the hot tub ready to go, be charming, and treat me with respect. You should be able to handle all that." Brian tried to make his voice sound tough, which wasn't easy, his sister could read him well. "I especially mean that part about treating me with respect. We're grown ups now, Katie. You're a successful writer, and I'm an esteemed, high-ranking, federal employee. Cut back on the teasing."

Kathleen laughed. Famed in the family for thinking ahead, her big brother had broken his own record for efficiency this time. He hadn't even mentioned a party when she saw him at her mother's house a couple of hours ago, yet he'd already organized this one. The names on his guest list were no surprise either. But when he mentioned again that he expected her to call Millie, she declined. "After what you did in Charleston and the way you acted at the Pizza Hut Sunday? Huh-uh. No way. If you want to make a date with Millie, ask her yourself. I'm not getting caught in the middle of that. Count me out."

Brian ignored Kathleen. Living as near to each other as they did, and depending on each other as much as they had through the years, they rarely said no to each other. "Look, we're not talking about a real date here. If that was the case, I could've asked her in person when we had lunch together today. Or I'd call her myself. This is just good friends getting together for dinner. Don't make more out of it than that."

"Oh, really?" Kathleen said, tongue in cheek. "Then let's invite our children. And Mom. And Rob's parents."

Brian laughed. "Well, maybe it is a little more than just good friends getting together for dinner," he admitted, "so let's leave our kids and the parents out of it. And for Pete's sake, stop kidding around. I'm doing everything I can to help with the party. Didn't I say I'd call Rob, pick up the food, and help you cook? Gosh, I'm even paying for it." He sighed dramatically, but he was such a poor actor his efforts were totally ineffective. "All right, I'll do one more thing, and that's it—I'm already doing more than my share. I'll get the hot tub ready. I'm better at that than you, anyhow. Now go on, be a good sister and do your piddling little part. Call Millie right now. Then call me back and let me know if she'll come. It's not part of my plan to treat just you and Rob and me to porterhouse steaks—it's all four of us, or nothing."

Kathleen continued to gripe, but half-heartedly. Brian said a quick good-bye and hung up. She dialed Rob's cell phone first to talk it over with him.

"You told me he never dates anyone," Rob said. "Without making a big deal out of it, just help the guy out. He's right, you know—how much trouble can one small dinner party be? We both like Millie. It'll be a lot of fun for all of us to get together." Before hanging up, he added, "You can count on me. I'll come early to help set everything up."

"Yeah, yeah, yeah," Kathleen mumbled. She dialed Millie at home.

Millie accepted the dinner invitation with pleasure. Kathleen didn't mention that the party was Brian's brainchild, which bothered her at first. She just couldn't bring herself to reveal that fact after Millie's positive response.

Brian was exultant when Kathleen called back. "Thanks. I knew she'd come if you invited her."

"Well, don't pat yourself on the back. I didn't tell her that the idea for the party was yours."

Brian let out a long, relieved sigh, grateful that Kathleen had helped pull it off. In truth, the air of confidence he usually exuded was sometimes just that—an *air* of confidence. Though he suspected he was way too old for developing crushes, he recognized his feelings for Millie as the late-30s, adolescent-like infatuation it was. But it had mystified him, having descended upon him so quickly.

"Katie?"

"Yeah?"

"You're great to do this, you know. I appreciate having you for a sister."

"Brian, you have a knack for saying the nicest things just when I'm gearing up to blast you good," Kathleen said, a hint of a laughter in her voice. "How do you know exactly what it takes to calm me down?"

"Well, you've been my little sister for thirty-five years. You think that might be it?" He paused momentarily. "Thanks again for your help, sis. I love you a lot. See you tomorrow."

"Yeah, I love you, too, Brian," Kathleen said softly. But her brother had hung up and didn't hear.

## Chapter 25

Millie dressed carefully for dinner. Kathleen hadn't mentioned Brian, but she suspected he would be there to greet her when she arrived at the cabin. She tossed aside the bikini she wore only at the beach in favor of a tank-styled swimsuit in emerald green that made her eyes appear bigger and brighter. Around her waist she tied a sarong splashed with leaves of the same emerald green and tropical flowers in shades of vivid orange, yellow, and red. She slid her feet into yellow high-heeled sandals and threw a large towel and her make-up bag into an oversized straw purse. Glancing in the mirror that stood in the corner of her bedroom, she made a last minute check of her appearance. The dangling gold hoops she inserted into her earlobes were the perfect finishing touch.

As she was searching for her car keys in the bottom of her purse, the doorbell rang. She hoped it wasn't someone just stopping by to chat. She was cutting it close and didn't want to be late.

Brian was leaning against the door frame when she opened the door. As Millie asked herself why he was there, she noticed how kind the years had been to him. He still had the athletic physique of a high-school quarterback—broad shoulders, narrow waist and hips, strong thighs. Why wasn't there a warning label glued to his forehead? In casual clothes he sure didn't look like the staid church-going father of two adolescent girls that she knew him to be.

Their gazes locked for a second or two before Brian's eyes swept over Millie from her head to her toes. He'd never seen her in party clothes before, and he liked the way she looked all gussied up. He visibly gulped, then swallowed again, before he could speak. Millie laughed so hard she had to root around in the bottom of her bag for a tissue to wipe tears from her eyes. Red-faced, Brian grinned, his eyes never moving from her. How long had it been since he'd seen a woman laugh until she cried?

Now, every woman, whether she admits it or not, likes receiving compliments, verbal and non-verbal, and Millie was no exception. "If you could only see yourself, Brian. Stuff those baby blues back inside your head. It's only me, the woman you tossed aside three years ago."

Brian chuckled, finally finding his voice. He deserved Millie's teasing comeuppance. "Well, you know I'm sorry about that, because I've said so more than once. I've seen you several times since that unfortunate episode in Charleston, but you've never looked like this before. You're the image of a model advertising a tropical cruise. Turn around, let me see the rest of you."

"Not on your life! That look was recognition enough, Mr. Mitchell. Thanks."

"No thanks needed. You deserve it...I think." He crooked his head to look past Millie, sweeping his gaze around her living room. "Is there a fairy godmother somewhere in this house that I should thank, instead?"

As their laughter faded, Millie tilted her head to the side. She had firmed up her schedule with Kathleen early that morning, so Kathleen knew she planned to arrive at the cabin on her own around five. "This isn't what Katie and I planned."

"So? I wanted to pick you up. You ready to go?"

Millie shook her head slowly. "This doesn't make sense. You'll have to drive all the way back to Logan to bring me home later."

Stubborn to the core, Brian rarely changed his mind once making it up. He took Millie by the hand and tugged. "It will if you think about it, so don't be dense. Grab your bag, lock your door, and let's go."

\*     \*     \*     \*

Kathleen waited on pins and needles for Brian and Millie to arrive. She wanted this party to be a success, and she and the guys had worked hard all day to make sure it was. Brian's favorite dessert, Key Lime Pie, was in the refrigerator chilling. She and Rob had set the table, and the hot tub was ready to go—thanks to Brian. The potatoes were in the oven, almost ready to serve, and Brian's caesar salad waited in the refrigerator to be dished up later. All systems were go.

*Where were Brian and Millie?*

Rob wondered why Kathleen was suddenly so tense. She was acting as nervous as a hen on hot eggs, brooding over Brian's last minute decision to pick up Millie. She maintained it wasn't like her brother to do something that rash. But Rob didn't believe driving into town for Millie had been a spontaneous act on Brian's part. He figured Brian had planned to pick Millie up all along…he just hadn't run his plan by his sister.

He sighed. Why worry over things they couldn't control? "Let it go, Katie," he said. "Millie's a mature adult, she can take care of herself. You're making me nervous with your pacing." He beckoned her closer. "We're alone now, in case you hadn't noticed, but that won't last long. Brian will be back any minute with Millie."

He'd been watching Kathleen closely since Brian left to shanghai Millie, and he was rapidly running out of patience. He wanted her sitting beside him on the sofa, not pacing a rut in the hardwood floor. "If you aren't careful, you'll trip on a scatter rug," he cautioned, patting the cushion beside him. "Come, sit down before you fall." He smiled a wicked smile and widened his eyes. "You know my main concern is your safety."

"Yeah, right!" Kathleen replied, still distracted.

As he watched her continue to pace, Rob secretly gave thanks for the aerobic classes Bobby said Kathleen attended thrice weekly at their YMCA. Her familiar curves seemed to go on forever, and here he and Kathleen were—alone. He could admire her appearance as much as he liked, even compare her to a Grecian goddess if he chose to, without anyone knowing. Wearing a white bathing suit and a pair of those gauzy, wide-legged white cotton pants he'd fallen for so quickly, she was his genie from the magic lamp.

Rob didn't have to ponder what his three wishes would be: Katie…Katie…Katie.

She finally sat, throwing him a look he couldn't read. "You think I'm worried about Millie? Well, I'm not. I'm worried about Brian! He hasn't dated in years, and I'm sure dating rules and etiquette have changed a lot in that time. When he left abruptly at four-thirty, saying he was on his way to Millie's, he turned this friendly little dinner party for four friends into a double date. I feel responsible for both of them. Sparks fly when they're together. I just hope he's nicer to Millie tonight than he was on Sunday."

"Look, they've seen each other since then, and I'm sure they've ironed out whatever it was that was hovering between them on Sunday. Move closer and stop talking about them. You're wasting too much of the time I'd planned to spend alone with you."

Kathleen complied, sitting stiffly beside him. Rob closed his eyes and sighed. Things were not going the way he had expected them to.

\* \* \* \*

"I may never eat again," Brian moaned as he lay back in his lounge chair after dinner. "The food was great, as always, Katie, and you've been the perfect hostess."

Kathleen smiled, pleased with the way things had gone. Her uneasiness over Brian and Millie as a twosome had been totally misplaced. There had been no fireworks between them at all, unless you counted the blue sparks in Brian's eyes now as Millie slipped off her skirt and stepped into the pool. Millie quickly dunked herself, and as she came up out of the water, she flipped her dripping hair back over her head and yelled to Brian. "Come on in. The water's warm—"

Brian didn't hesitate. Slicing into the water with a shallow dive, he came up sputtering. "This water is icy, Red! I've never felt it this cold. Enticing a person into water this frigid is downright cruel. You should be ashamed of yourself."

"Oh, come on. You missed the last part of my sentence, that's all. Why didn't you wait? As you jumped in, I finished what I was saying."

"Oh, yeah? What?"

"I said *after you get used to it*, but I guess you missed that part—you know, 'the water's warm after you get used to it.' What's wrong, big g-man?" she taunted. "Are we feeling a mite cold?"

Brian disappeared underwater. The next thing they knew, he'd flipped Millie into the air. As she landed, splashing chilly water on Rob and Kathleen, Brian reappeared at her side. "That'll teach you to kid a kidder. Ask Katie and Rob. Lying about the temperature of this water is my right…mine alone. No one takes it from me, not without being punished!"

Millie looked over his shoulder, her features suddenly softening. "Oh, my goodness, would you look at that baby fawn. That's so cute!" She slowly batted her lush, dark-fringed eyelashes a time or two at Brian. He couldn't look away. Her voice lowered and she smiled. "Oh, look, Bri…she's drinking from the pool."

As Brian swung around to look for the invisible deer, she grabbed him by the neck, kicked his legs out from under him, and dunked him in the pool, administering her own brand of retaliation. When he surfaced, ready for an all-out water fight, she laughed. "Sorry. You didn't say I could only kid the kidder once, did you? Your fault."

They looked at each other for a moment, communicating silently, and then their mouths curved into two identical, diabolical smiles. Turning in unison, they floated innocently toward Kathleen and Rob, sitting by the pool. "You know, you're right," Brian said, loud enough for Rob and Kathleen to overhear. "It is getting warmer."

"Absolutely," Millie agreed, floating closer to the edge. "It seems quite pleasant now."

Nearing Rob and Kathleen, Brian urged, "Why don't you guys join us? The water's really nice."

But Kathleen and Rob had heard those words before. Several years ago, in fact. From Brian. As fleet as deer, they dodged a water bombardment and escaped to the hot tub, giggling like kids all the way.

\* \* \* \*

As Brian turned right onto the road into Logan, Millie sighed and rested her head against the back of the seat. "Your car smells new…is it?"

"Yeah, we've only had it a month. Not long enough for the three of us to mess it up yet."

She snuggled further into the buttery-soft leather. "Dinner was incredible…I had a lovely time. It seemed almost as if Katie and Rob had never separated, didn't it?"

Brian's response sounded like "Mmm hmm," which she took to mean yes. Later, he used her key to unlock her front door.

"You want to come in for a minute? I can fix coffee."

Brian shook his head. "Not a good idea."

Millie smiled, not even pretending to misunderstand. "Yeah, you're right."

"Then I'd better say good night here, lovely lady, hadn't I?"

She leaned back against the door and gazed up at her good-looking date. "Mmm hmm," she replied.

Brian laughed quietly. "What's 'Mmm hmm' supposed to mean?"

"You used it in the car to mean yes," she said, smiling, "so I guess it means we'd better say good night out here."

Brian placed an arm on either side of Millie, loosely bracketing her between them. She could have escaped easily by dropping under his arms, but she didn't. She raised her face instead and repeated, "I had a lovely time," as his lips descended on hers.

They'd been flirting toward something like this since she'd opened the door earlier and found him on her doorstep.

Her mouth was warm, with just a hint of Key Lime Pie and coffee on her breath. Brian pressed forward with caution. He didn't want to scare her off this time.

It was time to cast aside the embarrassing self-image she'd been carting around in the back of her mind since the infamous incident with Brian in Charleston, Millie decided. She moved back slightly, her hooded eyes still on him. Watching him interact with Rob and Kathleen at the cabin earlier, and listening with amusement while he described some of the funny things his girls had said and done, had shown her a different, softer side of Brian Mitchell. He had treated her with nothing less than warm affection and respect since coming by to pick her up, showing her time after time over the course of the evening that she was every bit as precious to him as his sister Kathleen.

With a flash of insight, Millie concluded that Brian, too, might like to put that awkward scene behind him. But before that could happen, they would have to discuss it again. Stretching up, she kissed his cheek and spoke softly. "It wasn't one-sided in Charleston, Brian, though it may have seemed that way at the time. I wanted to kiss you, too. But if you hadn't ended the kiss when you did, I would have stopped it myself. Responding to each other as passionately and as quickly as we did that night left me feeling stunned for a moment, or I would've ended it sooner. I had never experienced anything as potent as that before then, and to be totally honest, Brian, it hasn't happened since."

Her innocent confession stole the breath from his lungs. Didn't she know to be careful, telling him something like that? He closed his eyes and breathed deeply, afraid he'd lose his self-control again. Millie reached up to kiss him on the lips once more…a very proper kiss this time…then moved away. "I think we'd better say good night."

"I guess you know I don't want to."

"Yeah, but if you say good night nicely, I'll still respect you in the morning," Millie teased.

After a long hug and a quicker kiss, Brian turned to walk away. At the top step, he looked back over his shoulder. "Can I call you tomorrow?"

Millie paused on her way through the door, then angled back toward him. "Only if you think it over with a clear head later tonight and decide it's what you truly want." They both knew she wasn't talking about just tomorrow's phone call. She was thinking about their friendship and where it might lead in the future.

And so was he.

Brian's eyes held hers as they communicated silently again. He had loved Ellen completely, and he'd been totally devoted to her. The two of them and their girls had stored up years of beautiful, lasting, loving memories together, memories that would be passed on from their daughters to their children, and then on to *their* children's children through the years. Suddenly Brian has hit by a thought that made a lot of sense to him: new memories would only enhance old memories, not erase them.

Millie respected Brian more than any man she'd ever met. He was a responsible, caring father to Janie and Sally; the girls couldn't have asked for a better role model. But Brian had also been a loving, faithful husband to his wife, and she admired that, too, about him. As sad as it was, Ellen had been gone for eight years. Eight long years. Millie wondered whether Brian was ready for a relationship with someone else…with her…even now. She didn't want any part of him if it meant she'd be competing for the rest of her life with those memories from his past…those memories of Ellen he couldn't get over.

The intensity of their feelings for each other three years ago had apparently taken Brian by surprise, just as it had Millie. She wouldn't chance another rejection like that without first knowing that Brian was ready to go forward…that he was emotionally ready to place the past in the past.

Brian started to smile, and that dazzling, sexy smile of his took a long time to complete. "When I call you tomorrow, *and I will*, I'll know exactly who I'm calling, Ms. Millie Samson—also known to me as Red. And I promise you this: there will be no shadows between us then or in the future, and no repeats of that regrettable Charleston experience either. Not ever again." He bent his head to give Millie a kiss on the cheek. Then, thinking better of it, he straightened and gave her another soft kiss…on the lips.

Still smiling, he waved good-bye and walked to his car, whistling a jaunty, unrecognizable tune under his breath.

✳ ✳ ✳ ✳

"Matt," Millie said later, over the phone, her voice a little quivery. "I had dinner with Brian Mitchell tonight. Can I talk to you about something that happened?"

Matt smiled. He'd had a strong premonition about Brian and Millie on Sunday.

"You can talk to me about anything," he responded, with genuine warmth in his voice. "Isn't that what a best friend…and your favorite pastor…is for?"

# Chapter 26

On Wednesday evening the cabin seemed almost too peaceful and quiet for Kathleen. The solitude had been tolerable—even enjoyable—at first, but waiting for the proverbial pin to drop so she could hear a little noise had gotten old pretty fast. She liked having that noisy, rambunctious son of hers around—he kept her poised on her toes. But Mary and Mike and Kathleen's mother had picked the kids up an hour ago with plans to stop by Hardees for dinner on their way to see *The Aracoma Story* at the park. And that left Kathleen alone.

She sat at the kitchen table in well-worn baggy jeans and an ancient red t-shirt, her bare feet propped up on the chair opposite her. Having already read the newspaper and brewed a cup of Lady Gray tea, which she continued to sip although it was barely lukewarm, she wondered what to fix herself for dinner. There was still some ham from Monday night, but leftovers didn't sound appealing right then. She could open a can of tomato soup if nothing else, but that wasn't what she wanted either.

Rob had called after lunch, and they'd talked for five minutes or so, but other than sitting at her computer working out a few kinks in her latest short story, she'd accomplished nothing of substance all day. She could fire up her computer again, she guessed, but her neck was stiff and writing sounded kind of boring now, too, to be honest.

She'd tried calling Brian, thinking he might come over and have a bite to eat with her. The phone rang at least ten times with no answer, which was as good an excuse as any to forego offering him dinner.

She had just started working the crossword puzzle in the *Sentinel* when she heard the sound of a car in the driveway. Suspecting who it was, her breath caught in her throat. Would she ever stop feeling this way each time she thought about Rob? Just knowing it might be his car put a bounce in her step. By the time he'd stopped in front of the cabin, she was on the bottom step, bare feet and all, elated to see him again.

"Jump in," he invited, motioning her over to the car. "We finally finished the electrical inspection down at the house. C'mon, I'll take you to dinner."

Kathleen laughed, pointing to her feet. "I'm barefoot, or hadn't you noticed? And my outfit could only be called sub-casual. I can't go to dinner looking like this."

Since he was wearing work clothes himself, Rob refused to listen. "No excuses, Katie. This is a come-as-you-are party."

Kathleen laughed again. A come-as-you-are party? That phrase hadn't been in use since her parents' generation!

Exiting the car, Rob advanced toward Kathleen, clearly feeling frisky and up to no good. She tried to elude him by running into the house, but he overtook her before she made it to the porch. Scooping her into his arms, he kissed the tender skin on the side of her neck and carried her back to his car. He swung her over the door, into his seat.

That maneuver caused a pain to shoot down his leg, but he figured she was the only woman he knew worth the effort. "Move over, baby. Where we're going, you won't need shoes."

"Out in the real world, we call this an abduction," Kathleen said, but they both knew she hadn't resisted. She scooted over to make room for Rob to get into the car. "At least lock up the cabin for me, will you? The key's hanging inside the back door."

When he returned, Rob was carrying a pair of scruffy slippers. "Found these under the table. Yours?"

"Yes, thank you," Kathleen said primly, reaching for them. Although the rest of her attire was definitely scroungy, Kathleen felt better, after having slipped on some shoes. Those slippers had seen better days, but what did she care? They were comfortable, and she usually only wore them around the house.

Before Rob started the car, Kathleen scooted up on her knees and reached across the seat to kiss his cheek. "Thanks for locking the door and getting my shoes," she said. Taking advantage of her off-balance position, Rob caught her around the waist and tipped her onto his lap.

"Huge mistake, Katie, giving me that advantage," he said, lightly nuzzling her neck. "That's one point to me. Now you'll have to pay a toll for the trip."

"Oh, well," she drawled, sounding bored, "what is it this time?" In direct contrast to the sound of her voice, there was a bright glow of interest in her eyes.

"A big kiss," Rob said, full of mischief. He dropped a wet kiss on her neck that was so loud and sloppy she started to giggle. Then, with reluctance, he lifted her off his lap and back to her side of the car.

"So," she asked with an exaggerated sigh, still faking disinterest, "what could you possibly offer for dinner that could top such an ultra-romantic kiss like that?"

"We'll see, won't we, Katie-girl?" he said, slanting a sexy half-smile in her direction.

\* \* \* \*

After demolishing the carry-out pizza they'd picked up in town, Kathleen and Rob sat on the bank of Dewey's Lake, their arms draped over bent knees as they watched the moon rise over the fifty-acre span of water that was really more pond than lake.

The only sounds to break the nighttime quiet were muffled voices from across the lake as a mother finished feeding her children their dinner—and the fluttering wings of evening bats as they began to search for theirs. The placid surface of the small lake was motionless, reflecting the moon and stars like artistic etchings from some long-ago medieval master. As they watched, two airplanes crisscrossed high above the earth, leaving their silvery, illuminated vapor trails mirrored on the water.

Kathleen was reluctant to leave, but she needed to get back to the cabin before Bobby returned. As she moved to gather up their pizza box and used napkins, Rob touched her on the arm. "Don't go yet," he said. "Move closer. We haven't snuggled yet today."

She turned back, a wide grin bisecting her face. "Your short-term memory has started to go, Mr. McKenzie. I distinctly remember some…well, what I'd call major snuggling…shortly after you kidnapped me."

Still smiling, Kathleen settled back down to rest her head on Rob's shoulder. Rob's a powerful man…all man, she thought. Years of sports conditioning, weight training, and countless hours spent hitting and catching baseballs had turned his already sleek body into rock hard muscle. Being held by this mature, masculine male should have felt different from being held by the young man she had married, and in a minor way it did. But being close to Rob was still where she wanted to be, even though the intervening years of painful experiences should have negated the strength of his magnetic appeal.

Rob's arm tightened, and Kathleen moved nearer, her breath warming his skin. Pressing her nose into the triangular indentation where his neck met his chest, she snuggled into place. "This is my favorite spot in all the world," she said.

"Yeah," Rob replied, moving his lips across her peach-scented hair to kiss her forehead. He knew she didn't mean that geographical spot in West Virginia that they called Dewey's Lake.

Being that close to Kathleen, Rob felt lightheaded and dizzy...and what a powerful sensation that was, too. He realized all at once that he had hungered for the same desirable woman, the one he now held firmly to his side, for more than half of his lifetime. This past week, while lying in his bed at night—the time of night when he used to feel so lonely—he'd marveled over this miraculous chance he'd been granted to get to know her again. And to get to know their son.

He leaned closer. "How shall we celebrate our anniversary tomorrow?"

"Our anniversary?" Kathleen sat up so abruptly she bumped into his chin.

"Ouch!" Rob teased, rubbing his hand over the spot. "I didn't deserve that attack."

"It's your fault...you shouldn't have made me move so quickly," she said, placing the blame where it lay. "Tomorrow's not our anniversary, Rob."

"Yes, it is. Exactly one week ago tomorrow, I looked up and saw you checking out the guys at the Habitat house."

Kathleen snorted. "I was not *checking out the guys*. I was checking out *you*. But only because you looked like someone I knew long ago." She shook her head and laughed. "You're nuts, McKenzie, you know that?"

Rob grinned. "You're just trying to change the subject, and I'm not gonna let you. We can take Bobby to that Arnold Schwarzenegger movie that's playing in town, if you can't come up with anything better. You think he'd like that?"

Kathleen laughed again. "Honestly, Rob, your heightened sense of romance leaves me breathless." Action movies were not high on her list of things to see, but she figured Rob must like them now, as did Bobby. "Okay," she added, giving the plan her nod of approval. "Bobby will love that. Would you like to come by for ham and cheese sandwiches and chips before the movie?"

"Of course. Why do you think I hang around you all the time?"

Kathleen rested her forefinger against her chin. "Well, it can't be my cooking, no matter what you say. I didn't cook tonight, and you still came around. What else could it be?"

Rob reached over to push her hair aside and cup the back of her head. "It's you, Katie. Just you."

Kathleen could hear the speedy cadence of his heart when she leaned against his chest. And even though she whispered, there was no mistaking what she said. "It's you, too, Rob...for me there's only you." She raised her head to look at him. "But everything's happened so quickly this week, I still feel a little scared by it all. Can you hold me close and hug me for a couple more minutes before taking me home?"

"Sure can, sweetheart," he answered, hitching her closer.

And then he proved that Rob McKenzie was a man of his word.

# Chapter 27

When everyone met at Lettie Mitchell's after dinner Friday night to play cards, it became increasingly apparent that Rob, a cutthroat competitor, played only to win—and that he had inherited that particular trait from his father.

Rob and Mike McKenzie, ordinarily perceived as easygoing and nice, were overpowering, obnoxious, and aggravatingly gleeful as they vanquished every other player in each game that was played. Poor Bobby, Kathleen shuddered. What have I unwittingly done to my son? She could only hope he'd inherited enough positive genes from her side of the family to negate that one unattractive McKenzie characteristic.

Too bad Brian and his girls had gone off somewhere by themselves. Kathleen needed someone else who was sane—like her—to even the odds. "What do you mean, one-eyed jacks, jokers, and fours are wild? Surely you're kidding, Mike," she complained as her father-in-law dealt the hand and laid down his rules. "Who in the world can remember all that?"

A smiling Mike McKenzie, peering out from under bushy brows, took delight in badgering his daughter-in-law, all in fun. "If you can't stand the heat, Katie, get out of the kitchen. You're playing with the big boys now."

Bobby enjoyed the camaraderie of the McKenzie men. He sorted through the so-so cards he'd been dealt and talked nonstop about the movie he'd seen with his parents the night before.

"Granddad, you should have seen Mom during the exciting parts," he tattled. "Not only did she close her eyes, she covered them with her hands. Like she needed to do both? She slid so far down in her seat her knees poked her chin. It was embarrassing to find out that the mother I'd always respected so much was…well…sort of a wimp."

Throwing down his discards, Rob defended Kathleen. "Your mom just needed a little comforting, Bobby. Some of those action scenes *were* overly graphic."

"Yeah, I saw the comforting. I tell you, Granddad, it got downright awkward. There we were, in a theater full of people like me who love action-packed adventures, when all of a sudden, during the most exciting part of the movie, my father had to calm down my mother. Tell the truth, Dad, did you see any of the movie? Or did you spend most of your time comforting Mom?"

When Bobby called him Dad, Rob tried to catch Kathleen's eye, but she had turned away to respond to something her mother had said. Thinking Bobby might have spoken the word inadvertently, Rob decided to ignore it.

"It wasn't mere comforting, Bobby," he said, continuing his thoughtful perusal of the cards in his hand. Rob was close to scoring five hundred points, and he needed to win this hand to tromp his father. Bobby's constant chattering, and the fact that he had called him Dad, was beginning to break his concentration. He wanted to get on with the game so he could win.

"What *do* you call it, *Dad*?" Bobby persisted, arching his brows in perfect imitation of Rob.

When Bobby called him that a second time with emphasis, Rob knew Bobby thought he hadn't heard him before. He smiled broadly and gave Bobby a two-thumbs-up sign, which Bobby responded to with a grin. It was a meaningful moment for father and son, but not one other soul even noticed. They were all too intrigued by Bobby's description of what had gone on at the movie—except for Kathleen. She felt the little blabbermouth had strayed too far over the line this time. Where was that muzzle when she needed it?

Rob threw down his cards with relish. "Rummy!" he said, grinning at Bobby. "And just so you'll know, son, I call it courting, not comforting!"

"Deliver me!" Bobby said, rolling his eyes. Rob cut his eyes around at Kathleen and winked.

"Hey, everyone," Brian called, entering the house with his two girls and Millie. "Pull out the welcome mat, company's here." He placed two boxes of assorted donuts from City Bakery in the middle of the table, where everyone could help themselves, and handed a large bag of Slurpees to Bobby.

Kathleen welcomed the arrival of Brian and his gang. She didn't want to hear another word about the movie from Bobby, not unless it pertained to something he had seen on the screen.

Lettie welcomed Millie warmly to her home before heading for the kitchen. She remarked over her shoulder, "Those donuts smell so good, this might be a good time to take a break and make a fresh pot of coffee." Mary gathered up the used mugs and took them to the kitchen to wash while she and Lettie waited for the fresh pot of coffee to brew.

Mary sidled close to her friend. "What's with Brian and Millie, Lettie? Is he dating her, do you think?"

"I don't know that for a fact. But if he is, it'd be a real good thing for him and his girls. When the three of them came home Monday afternoon, Brian mentioned they'd had lunch downtown with Millie. I really got tickled at the girls—you know by now how they are—because all they could talk about for the rest of the day was Millie this and Millie that. After spending the morning with Millie at the newspaper office, Sally wants to be a reporter some kind of bad when she grows up." As Lettie spoke, she moved around the kitchen, refilling the cream pitcher and sugar bowl. "Brian's been alone for too long," she said, "and Millie's a nice woman from all I hear. Robin told me at the beauty shop yesterday that she once suspected that Millie and Pastor Harlow were dating, but from something Millie let drop the last time she got a hair cut, Robin thinks the two of them are just friends. You know what we ought to do for Brian, Mary? Keep our fingers crossed and pray hard."

"Count me in," Mary said with a grin. "Looks like our prayers are being answered for our other children, doesn't it?"

"I hope!" Lettie said.

In the dining room, Millie stood talking with Bobby and Rob for a moment. Kathleen sauntered over to Brian. "Tell me something," she asked in a low voice, "is this a real date or just good friends getting together?"

Brian whispered back. "I didn't talk you into asking her to go out with me this time, did I? I was even able to take her to a movie night before last—sans children—without any help. What do you think?"

Kathleen continued to speak quietly. "It means you owe me big time for paving the way with that 'piddling' dinner party at the cabin. That's what I think."

Brian tossed his head back and laughed. "Don't taunt me, Katie. I'll make you say 'uncle' again. Don't forget I'm trained in martial arts!"

Kathleen smiled. "Well, for what it's worth, I approve. And I'm not referring to your expertise in martial arts."

Brian threw an arm around her shoulder. "Your opinion's worth a lot to me, as you know. Just don't get sappy about it, okay?"

Returning from a quick trip to the powder room, Mike McKenzie took his previous seat at the table and sized up the new arrivals. "Where've you been, Brian?" he asked.

"We picked Millie up after work for dinner at Steak 'n Ribs, then decided it might be fun to join you all for cards and dessert."

Ignoring the last game of Rummy that Rob won, Mike said, "Good, good…glad you're here. We need some new blood. I've won just about all the games I can from these amateurs. Pull up a chair and join us." Mike's attention homed in on Millie, who was still talking to Bobby and Rob. "Come sit by me, little missy," he teased. "Let me show you how a real man plays this game."

Millie detested being called honey, sweetie, or little missy. Some men just didn't seem to get it—what had sounded okay coming from John Wayne's lips didn't sound the same coming from any other man's. Besides, John Wayne had ridden off into his final Western sunset a lifetime of Saturday matinees ago. He should have taken his sweet little names for women along with him when he left. She gave a disapproving sniff and turned up her nose. She'd ignore Mike this time, but only because he seemed like such a nice man. She wouldn't let his chauvinistic words turn her off now, but he'd better not try it again.

From behind Mike's back, Brian looked at Millie and grinned. The two of them had passed some of their free time together in Charleston teaching each other card tricks. Over a period of several weeks, Brian had gotten pretty good at it. But Millie was a pro. He caught Rob and Kathleen's attention, pointed at Millie, and mimicked the actions of a professional card sharp shuffling the deck. "Go ahead, Millie," he said. "Show Mike how 'little missy' deals the cards."

The girls and Brian took the chairs vacated by Rob, Kathleen, and Mary McKenzie. Millie sat in the only other vacant chair, which just happened to be beside Mike. She pushed her hair behind her ears and slid her reading glasses on. "I'll use my own deck, Mr. McKenzie," she said, to Mike's surprise, and pulled a well-worn deck from her purse. She shuffled the cards, flipping them from hand to hand too fast for him to follow, then dealt them like a pro, turning the last one up on the table for everyone to see.

She patiently explained the game to Rob's father. "You can take this one, pick a card from the deck, or take a card from the hand of the person to the left of you, Mr. McKenzie. Then discard one of your own, face up on this stack. Your discard can be the one you just chose or one you were already holding in your hand. The object is to make pairs of as many of the cards in your hand as you can. The person left with the gray-haired woman is the loser and, thus, the Old Maid."

Mike looked at his cards and grimaced. A game for kids, and he didn't have one matching pair to start off with. His luck had surely changed for the worse; he'd swept almost every game they'd played since coming to the table, except the ones he had lost to the guy he'd taught everything he knew—his son Rob.

As the game progressed, everyone seemed to be making pairs on every play, but Mike was left with nothing good in his hand. He wrinkled his brow and wondered…had he forgotten how to play these children's games…or was something sinister and crooked going on? Tilting one unruly eyebrow and squinting his eyes, he looked at the dealer—the woman who'd insisted on using her own personal deck. Nah, he thought, she wouldn't do that to me…or would she?

When all the cards were played and everyone had made pairs from the ones they held, the only card left was the gray-haired woman in Mike McKenzie's hand. Mike looked over at Millie, still wondering about her. When he saw her poker face and sparkling green eyes that were as wide open as the mouth on that shark in *Jaws*, he realized that Brian and this Irish lass had set him up. Why, he'd just been hustled by a couple of pros!

"Okay, okay, everybody, go ahead and laugh," he said as everyone roared. "But when you're done, deal again, little missy. And this time, don't stack the deck and I'll let you call me Mike."

\* \* \* \*

"Granddad," Bobby asked as they started their second hand of Old Maid, "how do you feel about me changing my name?"

Silence. Dead silence. Everyone stopped what they were doing to listen. For days they'd wondered when the issue of Bobby's surname would surface. Well, now it had.

The Mitchells well understood why Kathleen had called Bobby a Mitchell. She'd been divorced—or so she thought—and using her maiden name when he was born.

Mary and Mike McKenzies didn't understand the situation *in toto*, but they were determined not to say or do anything that might rock the boat. It didn't matter what he was called; Bobby Mitchell was just as much their delightful grandson as Bobby McKenzie would be.

"Change your name?" His grandfather asked, then shrugged. "Why?"

Oblivious to the attention his conversation had drawn, Bobby continued to ponder the cards in his hand. "Well, you know Mom thought she and Dad were divorced when I was born. That's why my birth certificate shows my last name as

Mitchell. Boy, Dad must have been some kind of peeved when he learned about that—"

"You've never heard even a hint of that from me, Bobby," Rob said. "You're projecting."

"Okay, Dad, I guess I was. Sorry."

Rob quickly looked at Kathleen, wondering if she'd heard Bobby call him Dad this time. From the smile on her face, she had.

Without missing a beat, Bobby returned to the conversation with his grandfather, unmindful of the fact that eight other people were standing around, wondering what in the world he might say next. "Well, okay, Dad didn't *say* he was peeved, but he must have been pretty upset, don't you think?"

Not wanting his words to be misconstrued, Mike McKenzie wisely said nothing. He gave a noncommital grunt, which could be taken either way.

"Mom and I went by and talked to the lawyer today—you know Dan Hoffman, don't you, Granddad? He told Mom and Dad last week he'd help them out if they needed any legal advice, so when I talked to Mom about this name change thing this morning, she said maybe Mr. Hoffman would help us with it. And he did. He called a lawyer friend of his in Virginia...what's that lawyer's name, Mom?"

"Cynthia Douglas."

"He called Cynthia Douglas while we were in his office, and she said she'd file the form to have my name legally changed on my birth certificate. Instead of being Robert Michael Mitchell, I'll be Robert Michael McKenzie, Jr."

No one in the room would have interrupted Bobby at that point for anything, not even a trip to this year's World Series...and the Reds were in the running.

"Mom said she picked the Michael part of my name because it's your name, too, Granddad. That means I'm named after both you and my Dad. Pretty neat, huh?"

"I sure think so," Mike McKenzie said. He twisted around in his seat until he located Kathleen, standing behind him. He reached out until he touched her hand, then squeezed.

"But since Dad's full name is Robert Michael McKenzie," Bobby was saying, "and that'll be my full name, too, Mom said I can be a 'junior,' if I want. So that's what I asked them to put on my birth certificate: Robert Michael McKenzie, Jr."

Bobby realized that he'd passed on a lot of information in a short period of time. "Do you understand this so far, Granddad?"

Mike McKenzie solemnly nodded his head. "Yes, Bobby, I think I do. You did a good job, explaining everything."

"Anyhow, the Virginia lawyer, Cynthia Douglas, faxed the papers to Mr. Hoffman's office while Mom and I were there. Mom signed them this afternoon. She says she's gonna have Dad sign them tonight as soon as they can get away from here and be alone. What do you think about that?"

Bobby's final comment was met with stunned silence from everyone in the room except his mother. Kathleen groaned softly and covered her face with her hands. There were no inaccuracies in what Bobby had said, but she wanted to wring his neck for the way he had said it. He made it sound as if she could hardly wait to escape the scene at her mother's and get Rob to herself.

For the first time since beginning the conversation with his grandfather about changing his name, Bobby looked up from arranging the cards in his hand. Everyone, including his grandfather, was staring at him with eyes wide-open and mouths agape. Bobby laughed out loud at the expressions of amazement he saw. He'd surprised his father most of all.

Mike looked first at his son, then back at his grandson, before his face, too, broke into a grin. A thread of amusement ran through his voice. "You're something else, you know that, Bobby? Let me be the first to call you Robert Michael McKenzie, Jr." He reached across the table to shake the hand of his grandson and namesake.

Conversation buzzed around Bobby as everyone discussed what they'd heard. He glanced over at his mother to see if she'd minded his spilling the beans about what they had done. She must not have cared too much; she and his dad were looking at each other as if they were already alone.

Bobby had never seen his parents quite like this before, and he couldn't bring himself to look away. When the corners of his mother's mouth began to quiver, he couldn't tell whether she was getting ready to grin or to cry. He shifted his gaze to his father for help, but his dad wasn't looking at him. His dad had eyes for only his mom. And the look on his dad's face was one that Bobby had never seen before, except, perhaps, in mushy movies.

His parents never looked away from each other. It was as if they were absorbing each other's unuttered words, their unspoken thoughts. Indeed, anything audible between them would have been superfluous then; they were communicating things to each other that could not be put into words.

He watched as his father reached out to welcome his mother to his side. His dad held his mom tight for just a moment before kissing her gently on her cheek and whispering something in her ear. His mom just smiled and leaned her head against his father's shoulder.

At one time it would have embarrassed Bobby to witness feelings that intensely private between his parents. But not now. Somehow, at that moment, he knew he had seen something rare and precious, something he would never forget for as long as he lived. He'd seen love vibrating in the air between his mother and father.

As Bobby turned back to the table, his grandfather caught his eye. Bobby had not been aware until then that his grandfather had seen him watching his parents, and that his grandfather had seen what happened, too. Bobby was glad that someone else, someone he trusted, had witnessed that unique and silent conversation between his parents.

His grandfather held Bobby's solemn gaze for a moment, then winked at him and smiled. Feeling an easy mantle of maturity settle on his thirteen-year-old shoulders, Bobby winked back. "Your deal, Granddad," he said, as they resumed their game.

# Chapter 28

▼

By the time Rob and Kathleen left her mother's house, it was midnight. Bobby, who'd been running on a full tank all day, finally ran out of gas halfway home. He was draped across the back seat of Rob's car, sound asleep, when they arrived at the cabin. As Rob leaned in to rouse his sleeping son, he discovered that Bobby'd had to bend his knees in order to fit across the seat. "Just look at this, will you?" He glanced over his shoulder at Kathleen. "Our boy's legs are poking even farther out of his jeans than they were a week ago. You'll have to forego feeding him quick-acting growth hormones for a while."

Kathleen chuckled quietly. "He's growing into those size eleven sneakers he wears."

Kathleen knew that, most days, Bobby was a live wire, energetic and operating at full speed ahead. When he finally did conk out—as now—he was dead to the world, and moving him for Rob was like trying to shift a ton of coal. Bobby did wake up, but only marginally. As Rob guided him up the stairs and into bed, Bobby was almost catatonic, rousing only long enough to say, "G'night, Mom. G'night, Dad," before sinking into oblivion again. Sitting on the edge of the bed, Rob removed Bobby's shoes and peeled off his son's jeans before throwing a light blanket over him.

"You think he'll be okay like this?"

Kathleen nodded, then turned out the light as they left Bobby's room.

Walking down the stairs in perfect step with one another, Rob laid an arm across Kathleen's shoulder. It was the first time they'd been alone since Bobby dropped his bombshell about his name change at Mrs. Mitchell's. Rob chuckled, picturing Bobby as he told everyone that Kathleen would have him sign the paperwork as soon as she finally got him alone.

And here they were…finally alone.

If Millie hadn't changed the game from Five Hundred Rummy to Old Maid, a game his father never did get the hang of, Rob would have left Mrs. Mitchell's with his father's earlier gloating ringing in his ears. He'd played well initially, giving his dad every bit as much dog-eat-dog competition as he got, but his concentration fell apart after Bobby described his legal dealings with Dan Hoffman. From that point on, Rob couldn't recall half the hands they played. After re-entering the game, he and his father had ended up the Old Maid an equal number of times, much to everyone's amusement, but he didn't care. Like Kathleen, he simply wanted to get away from Mrs. Mitchell's as soon as he could. He wanted to hear more about the legalities involved in Bobby's name change without their families listening in. And their families would have listened, no question about it. They hadn't been that entertained in years. Anything that happened between Rob, Kathleen, and Bobby was part and parcel of them all, and they gobbled up each tidbit of information like chickens in the barnyard do corn.

They reached the bottom of the stairs before Rob spoke again. "Katie, I can't find adequate words to describe how I felt when Bobby said he'd changed his name. I had no inkling you were considering that."

"Then don't say anything. It was Bobby's idea entirely. He asked at breakfast if I'd mind if he changed his name now instead of waiting, and I said he should've been a McKenzie all along. Strangely enough, he didn't think changing his name was that big a deal. When I mentioned Dan Hoffman's offer of legal advice, Bobby asked if he could call him right away. All I did was give Bobby the telephone number. From that point on, he handled everything. After he and Dan discussed it briefly over the phone, Bobby made an appointment to set things in motion."

Kathleen paused, looking up at Rob. "Bobby plans to start using his new name right away, even though it isn't legal until we get notification of the change." She smiled. "You don't mind, do you?"

"Are you kidding?"

Rob seemed so pleased, Kathleen's smile grew even wider. "You should have seen him in Dan's office, Rob. Next thing we know, he'll be telling us he wants to be a lawyer like Dan Hoffman when he grows up…along with owning his own business like Fred Horne and playing baseball like you."

Rob laughed. He could imagine Bobby saying those words. "Well, it may not have seemed like a big deal to Bobby, but it's a real big deal for me." Rob pulled her closer. "It's important to me that my son have my name—heck, it would be important to any man. I would never have pressured you to do it, honestly. But the joy I felt when he said his name would be Robert Michael McKenzie, Jr. was, and still is, beyond expressing. The two of you sure made me a happy man today."

Cupping her face with his hands, Rob kissed Kathleen slowly, running his fingers through her silky brown hair. When he felt and heard her quick intake of breath, he moaned softly, pulling her close as they exchanged shuddering breath for shuddering breath. Kathleen was warm and soft, and nothing had ever felt as right as she did in his arms. He lowered his hands slowly, feeling the soft, thin fabric of her blouse as he crossed his arms behind her back to urge her closer.

Kathleen began to tremble, and he knew it wasn't because the night was cold. It wasn't. She didn't have to say she wanted him; he felt it through the pores in his body, through her breath in his mouth. Feeling her smooth, warm back beneath his rough, calloused hands merely made him want her more.

Rob turned Kathleen's head and breathed his words into her ear. "Oh, baby, it's never easy to leave you and go home…I want you so much, my Katie-girl." He closed his eyes, and as he held her, he sighed her name again and again. "Katie…Katie…kick me out now."

Overwhelmed by emotions that she hadn't felt in years, Kathleen longed to tell Rob how she felt…how deep her feelings for him had grown over the past several days. She opened her mouth to speak the words she knew he was yearning to hear, but nothing came out. She hid her face against his chest and wondered why she—a professional writer!—was unable to verbalize her deep-seated feelings, her innermost thoughts.

Rob sighed. The look on Kathleen's face and in her bright, expressive eyes revealed her love for him each time they were together like this, but something always kept her from saying the words aloud. He tucked a finger beneath her chin and tilted back her head to see her face. He placed the tips of his fingers gently over her mouth as he inhaled deeply and fought for control.

Kathleen couldn't say she loved him yet in words, but that was all right. Rob wasn't interested in a declaration of love that had to be pried out of her. He wasn't interested in merely a physical relationship either, not even with Kathleen. He could have hundreds of physical relationships if that was what he wanted. No, he wanted it all, and he wanted it all with Kathleen—the deep recesses of her heart and her mind, as well as her body.

He stared into Kathleen's slumberous eyes and vowed, "I'm warning you, baby. Once you say those three special words I'm longing to hear, you're mine. Nothing, absolutely nothing, could ever make me let you go again."

His hand slid from her lips to wrap around the side of her neck. "I want you, Katie. But not until you're ready to give me everything…all of you…all the way…nothing held back." He placed his thumbs against her lips again, sculpting her mouth with a soft, gentle touch.

Kathleen seemed poised on the edge of complete physical surrender, but she wasn't quite ready, Rob feared, for the total, all-encompassing mind, soul, and body kind of love he wanted them to share. The rekindled feelings between them were too important, too strong, to settle for anything less than a lifetime of passion and commitment together.

He felt compelled to ask, though he sensed she wasn't yet there, "Are you ready tonight to go the distance with me, Katie? To live with me forever as my wife, no matter where we go…or what we do…or in what circumstances we find ourselves?"

She hesitated for only a moment, a moment too lengthy for Rob. "I do want to," she finally said on a sigh, "but there are still a lot of decisions you and I need to make, important issues we haven't even talked about yet, other things—"

Rob interrupted, speaking firmly. "If there are any reservations lurking in your mind, no matter how small, you're not ready enough for me. I don't want you half-ready or even three-quarters ready. I want your faith in me and our future to be so strong that you come to me with no misgivings at all."

Large, shiny tears pooled in the corners of Kathleen's eyes. "I'm sorry," she said, her voice ragged. "I know you're disappointed, but please don't give up on me. It's such a big step, I need a little more time, that's all."

Reluctantly, Rob's fingers trailed away. He believed himself to be a fairly patient man, but sometimes he wondered if Kathleen would ever trust him completely again…if she would ever stop looking back over her shoulders at the past.

"I'll never give up on you, sweetheart," he said, reassuring Kathleen. Holding her tenderly, he planted a kiss full of love on her brow, then left to go home.

# Chapter 29

Saturday morning, humidity was low and the temperature was a moderate sixty-five degrees with a high predicted only in the eighties—perfect weather for Rob McKenzie Day in Logan. Each of the participants and planners of the day-long event breathed a sigh of relief, especially Fred Horne, who'd been sweating it out.

Earlier in the week, signs had been posted on telephone poles in the county and all over town proclaiming this to be a special day. A hastily-prepared brochure containing a list of planned events and discount coupons had been published in the *Sentinel* on Friday, and extra copies were available at participating businesses around town.

The parking slots inside the city limits filled to capacity first, followed quickly by the ones over on Midelburg Island near the schools. Following previously enacted procedures for handling large crowds, the city and county police departments were allowing vehicles to park along the shoulders of the roads leading into Logan, and a special temporary police force had been tasked with keeping traffic flowing around those parked cars.

Fred Horne had spent the past week rearranging his stock so people would have room to mill around as they selected and paid for their merchandise. The fluid traffic pattern began at his front door and wound back through the store to a table where Rob sat talking to kids and their parents, signing whatever they'd brought in—or purchased from Fred—to be autographed. Fred walked around with a satisfied smile on his face; sales at his shop had been brisk all week.

Bobby and Fred's son Rick, about the same age, talked baseball and card collecting as they presided over a table they'd placed beside the exit. It was angled so everybody had to pass it on their way out of the shop. The "donation station," as the boys called it, consisted of a card table, two metal chairs, and a large fish bowl they'd found at the back of a shelf in the storeroom. How that dusty bowl came to be stuck behind a box of baseballs, they couldn't fathom. Rick swore he'd never seen it before, and a fish bowl did seem a little out of place in a sporting goods shop, even to two imaginative teens like Bobby and Fred.

Earlier, before the store opened and customers began to arrive, the boys had embellished their work station with posters and homemade signs. They had even salted the fish bowl with dollar bills they'd conned from their fathers after promising to return the money once real donations were added to the bowl.

That bowl was almost full, and Rob had yet to develop writer's cramp, when Kathleen arrived to scope things out. After giving her a few minutes to look around the shop and check in with Bobby, Rob beckoned her over to keep him company as he interacted with the crowd.

He smiled as she walked in his direction. It made the day and his mood even brighter, having her nearby. When she was close enough for him to see and hear and touch, it was easier to believe they'd be a real couple again someday—hopefully, soon. He didn't like giving in to despair, but when he was alone the way he'd been last night after leaving her at the cabin, he sometimes feared his dream of a permanent reconciliation might never come true.

Rob sloughed off that pessimistic thought when Kathleen arrived at his side and touched his hand to say hello. He decided not to let anything negative affect his enjoyment of this moment…this woman…or this day.

To the few people who didn't already know Kathleen—mostly newcomers to town—Rob introduced her as his wife and explained that she'd grown up at Steven's Hollow and now wrote imaginative, educational stories for children.

Kathleen talked with the crowd around Rob for a few minutes, then observed the autographing process for a while. She noticed a bottleneck near Rob's table, where people awaited their turns, and realized it could be alleviated with a little reorganization of the process. When she mentioned it, Rob happily relinquished that duty to her. With her greeting the people in line, finding out the names of their children, and getting the photos and other items ready for him to sign, Rob could spend more of his time talking with his fans.

Fred ultimately ran out of individual cards despite his meticulous planning, but the parents there with their children did not seem to mind. They switched to sealed sets of this year's cards so their child could pull out Rob's most recent one for him to inscribe.

But it wasn't only Rob McKenzie who drew crowds to Logan on that balmy, beautiful day. Music could be heard on every corner, mostly country or gospel, and a magical air of celebration permeated the area downtown. Up the street in front of the County Courthouse, where the American flag, the West Virginia flag, and the Logan County flag unfurled in the gentle morning breeze, a combination bake sale and yard sale was doing a land-office business. People crowded into stores where local merchants offered sale prices on summer items, and most of them exited with shopping bags full.

Near the outside corner of Fred's store, where a large number of people congregated, the Jaycees were raffling off a bat signed by every member of Cincinnati's squad. The money raised from that raffle would go into a special camp fund to benefit local handicapped children. The Jaycees were pleased with the response they'd gotten from the crowd; the day had barely begun, but they were almost out of tickets. Rob and Kathleen smiled at each other each time they looked out and saw people waiting in that line. The Jaycees didn't know it yet, but Rob had signed and set aside one of his specially-designed first-baseman's mitts for them to auction off later. He'd hidden it beneath the table and would keep it out of sight until they'd sold all their raffle tickets on the bat.

The crowd was large, in part, because the day's activities had been promoted heavily in the *Sentinel*. As Millie strolled down the congested streets toward Fred's shop with one of the *Sentinel*'s reporters and the photographer who covered local affairs, she couldn't keep from grinning. It wasn't the *Sentinel* that had rallied the town together; the major sparkplug behind today's events was Fred Horne. He had reason to be proud of the interest generated by his efforts, and Millie was on her way to his store to compliment him again.

All the lines around town were long, of course, but the longest line of all was outside Fred's sporting goods shop. Quite a few reporters and photographers had gathered near the group of people waiting patiently to talk to Rob and get his autograph. Millie frowned when she saw a couple of out-of-town tabloid sharks mixed in with the crowd of mostly-familiar reporters; she hated having those scumbags invading her bailiwick. She didn't pay them any heed, though, once she homed in on the line of individuals extending out onto the sidewalk in front of Fred's store.

Noting the genial comradery shared by the people in line, the reporter and photographer left Millie's side to mingle with the crowd. Sure, they sold more newspapers when photographs and quotes from local citizens were included in an issue, but the *Sentinel*'s bottom line wasn't Millie's sole reason for giving Rob McKenzie Day such extensive coverage. Knowing readers love seeing their own likeness, or that of their friends, in the paper, she had already planned a special pictorial feature for tomorrow's *Sentinel*. That should pique the interest of everyone visiting Logan today, especially those who were photographed with Rob McKenzie. She'd make sure Rob didn't mind having her staff photographer sit in on his autographing process for a while before proceeding, but she knew Rob would cooperate. He'd never failed to yet.

Almost everyone in town knew, or knew of, Millie, but she still flashed her credentials as she made her way into the store. The *Sentinel*'s reporter had interviewed Rob previously about this event, plus they had taken several candid photos of Rob when he stopped by the paper for a friendly visit on Friday. She didn't want anyone thinking she was trying to pull rank, so out came her press pass.

Without warning, flashbulbs began to pop and a ruckus broke out near the donations table at the front of the store. As soon as the first bulb flashed, Rob and Kathleen were out of their seats, rushing to their son. Although he'd prayed fervently that nothing would mar the pleasure of this day, in his heart Rob had feared something like this. He'd adapted to having the press surround him, but he didn't want them bothering Bobby or Kathleen.

Millie's first instinct was to pull out her cell phone to alert Brian; she knew he was somewhere in town by now. When he answered on the third ring, she sighed with relief and told him briefly what had occurred. Brian warned his girls to stay right where they were, then continued to talk to Millie as he ran toward the store. "I'll be there within minutes. Stay out of it. Don't make me have to worry about you as well as everything else."

By the time Rob got to the front of the store, he was furious. He grabbed the arm of a tabloid reporter, whom he recognized, standing too close to Bobby. "What are you doing here, Hawkins?" he demanded. "Didn't you learn anything from that fiasco down in Puerto Rico?" Rob jerked the reporter away from Bobby as the tabloid's photographer took Bobby's picture again.

"It's a free world, McKenzie," the guy named Hawkins snarled, making sure his photographer continued to record the confrontation. "When a Goody Two Shoes like you fouls up, it's up to guys like me to make sure people know about it. I'd heard about this young boy you've been spending so much of your time with down here." He jeered, "How about getting a picture of you with your *little boyfriend*, McKenzie?"

As Rob moved to confront the reporter, Brian reached out to pull the out-of-shape guy away from Bobby and Rob. Unfortunately for the guy named Hawkins, though, Kathleen got there first. And there was fire in her eyes. The tabloid photographer didn't have a chance to get off another picture before his camera was knocked out of his hands by the staff photographer from the *Sentinel*, who promptly tore it open and exposed the film. There was no photographic evidence for the tabloid of Kathleen McKenzie's assault on the reporter called Hawkins.

Kathleen didn't know she could fight until then. Without being totally aware of what she was doing, she mimicked the actions she'd seen her son take the day he first met his father. Now that she knew who the reporter was, she advanced on him. With her hands thrust out in front of her, she pushed hard, knocking him off balance.

Rob reached out to stop Kathleen, but Brian held him back. "Let her be. She's more than due a round with this guy."

Hawkins sputtered as Kathleen pushed him in the chest. "How dare you?" she demanded. "You almost ruined our lives forever once before. I'm not letting you mess things up for us again." Hawkins tried to speak, but Kathleen pushed him repeatedly as they moved closer to the door that led to the street. "That boy is Rob McKenzie's son, you big goon, and I'm Rob McKenzie's wife. Don't you dare report anything in your paper except those two facts."

By the time Kathleen had pushed him one final time, they were on the sidewalk and she was bellowing. "Did you hear what I said, Mr. Hawkins? If you dare publish anything other than those two things, I, personally, will sue you and your quote newspaper unquote so fast that you'll never be able to find a job as a reporter again. You'll be pushing pencils on street corners, if you're lucky. Did you get that, or do I have to tell you again?"

Kathleen nudged him so hard that final time, he lost his balance again and stumbled over the curb. "You owe Rob a big apology, Mr. Hawkins," she yelled, "for this time and for what you did in Puerto Rico." Kathleen glared down at him with her hands on her hips and naked fury in her eyes.

Hawkins would like to have bluffed his way out of the tense situation. But even if he'd been able to wiggle away from Kathleen, it would not have been wise. Rob McKenzie wasn't finished with him yet; he was standing off to the side flexing his fists, just waiting for an excuse to justify going at him again. Rob McKenzie's wife was a powerful force to be reckoned with; that fury-filled woman wasn't going to stop pounding on him till she got her apology. And the big blond guy? In warm weather like this, he could only be wearing that lightweight jacket of his for one reason, and one reason only. It was exactly like the ones worn by the Feds to hide a shoulder holster. He wasn't about to be making that guy mad. So he took the only way out available to him. He looked at Rob and said quickly, "Sorry, McKenzie. Didn't know you were married and had a son." Rolling over onto his hands and knees, he slowly pushed against the curb until he was upright again. He motioned for his photographer to pick up his empty camera and hightail it after him to where they'd parked their rental car. Moving away, he spoke over his shoulder, "Sorry, Mrs. McKenzie. Didn't mean to set you off. It won't happen again."

Kathleen sagged with relief as the tabloid reporter and his photographer fled, certain she'd ruined Rob McKenzie Day for everyone and that Fred would never forgive her for the fight she'd started inside his store. She turned around to dead silence. With the small amount of adrenaline left in her system, she glared at Bobby, Brian, and Rob. "What are you all looking at?"

Rob and Bobby broke into identical grins. Easing out of his smile, Rob placed a calming hand on her arm. "I didn't know you had it in you, Katie-girl. You handled the situation far better than I would have. I wanted to punch his lights out, but then I'd have been sued for everything we've got. You might've just gotten that guy off our backs forever."

Bobby continued to grin at his mom. "He'll be sorry he took you on, Rocky. You're quite the fighter. Wow! I'm sure lucky you didn't believe in…what's it called?" He looked at his father.

"You know, where parents spank their kids?"

"Corporal punishment," said Rob.

"Yeah, Mom. I'm sure glad you didn't believe in corporal punishment when I was a kid."

The crowd outside the store, who'd been watching the fracas with interest, joined in with their laughter.

Throwing his arm around Kathleen, Brian led her back inside the store. "You okay, Katie?" Her nod assured him she was fine. "You did great, sis, but don't you ever do anything like that again. I'm older than you. My heart couldn't take much of that."

"You don't have to worry, Brian. My knees are so wobbly they won't hold me up, my heart's racing like crazy, and I'm very, very embarrassed."

Her worries about ruining the day were soon put to rest. The father of one of the autograph seekers, standing with his child at the head of the line, grabbed Kathleen's hand as she walked by. Holding it high over her head, he announced, "All right, folks, the fight is over, and the pretty lady won." When he grinned at Kathleen and said, "Take your well-deserved bow, Mrs. McKenzie," everyone cheered.

Kathleen looked around to assure herself that Bobby was okay. He was surrounded by several teenage boys whose cards had already been signed. Apparently, from what she could hear, they had just dropped their contributions in the bowl when the excitement began, and were hanging around now, still talking about it. She knew he'd be okay when she heard one of the boys say, "Hey, man, I didn't know Rob McKenzie was your dad. You play baseball, too?"

When Bobby replied that he did, one of the other boys added, "We have a pick-up game over on the Island every evening after dinner. You want to play sometime?"

"Sure," Bobby responded, sticking his thumbs in the back pockets of his jeans, which Kathleen knew was his most nonchalant look.

"Cool! Come around seven o'clock any evening," the boy said. "That's when we choose sides."

The boys were leaning against the donation station, laughing about something else, when Kathleen finally turned around and saw Rob looking at her...still smiling.

\* \* \* \*

When Brian located Millie, she was instructing the *Sentinel* employees to destroy any undeveloped photographs they may have taken of the incident. There would be no evidence anywhere of Kathleen Mitchell's bout with the low-life reporter if Millie had her way.

Relieved that she'd stayed out of the fray, Brian assumed she'd been unaffected by the scuffle, until he caught the slightly dazed look in her eye. "Everything all right?" he asked, bending his knees to better see her.

Now that it was finally over, Millie could breathe. "Yeah, I'm okay. Honest."

Okay? Sure you are, Brian thought. She was holding on by a thread.

*She is one gutsy broad.* Brian darted a look in Millie's direction, hoping he hadn't spoken that thought aloud. A woman who hated being called honey, sweetie, and little missy would cut out the tongue of a man who called her a broad, even if he did consider it a compliment.

Walking close, Brian escorted Millie onto the sidewalk. "Let's walk around awhile and let everything settle. That encounter had to have scared you. Heck, I'm still psyched up, myself. I didn't know what would happen next." Concerned, though she insisted she was fine, he touched her on the arm. "You sure you're okay?"

Millie raised her eyes, and the look on her face sucked the air from Brian's lungs. "I didn't even think of myself, once you ran through the door. I figured you were armed, and I was scared something might happen to you." She lowered her head, fearful that the sudden tenderness she felt for him might be telegraphed through her facial expressions.

Hooking his forefinger under her chin, Brian tilted Millie's head to meet his gaze. "You're something else, you know that, Red? It's been a long time since someone special worried about me."

With a satisfied look on his face, he cupped her elbow and steered her up the street toward the newspaper office. "Come on, baby. Before I walk you back to work, let's go pick up the girls. I warned them to stay put near the Courthouse, and I'm sure they're wondering why I ran off in such a hurry."

\* \* \* \*

Rob kept looking around at Kathleen and smiling as they worked the crowd. Almost everyone had kind words to say about what had happened earlier, and complaints to air about reporters not respecting the privacy of public figures. But by then, because of his wife's somewhat kooky, brave, and unanticipated actions, Rob McKenzie was just another hometown boy again. Those public figures they referred to were people they didn't know personally, not him.

# Chapter 30

Brian was as cranky as a bee-stung bear on Monday morning, and he blamed his nasty mood on his daughters. They had procrastinated over every little thing getting ready, which wasted his time as well as theirs. If his mother hadn't been there to help keep them on track, the two of them would've driven him insane. He'd volunteered to drive the five travelers to Charleston to meet the Lear jet Rob chartered, and that was the only thing that kept the girls' hopes of seeing that baseball game in Cincinnati alive. Why did each girl need her own separate suitcase for a night away from home, anyhow? What had happened to the days when he could throw shorts, a t-shirt, a pair of socks, and an extra set of underwear for each of them in a paper bag and take off for a night at his mom's?

By the time they finally arrived in Charleston, Brian felt like he'd been herding sheep. But the looks on the girls' faces when they saw the small jet was worth the hassle of forcing them out of bed before dawn and hustling to get then ready on time.

Once he'd chatted for a while with Jim Hager, the pilot, about planes, and had assured himself that Jim was knowledgeable and experienced enough to be trusted with his girls, Brian kissed his daughters good-bye, left the group on its own, and headed back to Steven's Hollow.

Jim Hager had known Rob for almost as many years as Rob had played professional ball. He'd flown Rob around numerous times before, the latest being two weeks before when he'd transported the injured first baseman to Logan on a smaller plane after that crazy play at home plate. Little had they known then what Rob's time in Logan would bring!

After piloting around baseball players and team executives, Jim looked forward to ferrying the kids to Cincinnati. He'd loaded the small on-board refrigerator with enough bagels, pastries, coffee, and juice for twice the number of people he'd be taking on the one-hour flight. It would be a different experience for Jim, and fun, watching the three youngsters on their maiden voyage in a small jet like his.

Jim couldn't help noticing that Rob's wife was a beauty. He chuckled, imagining how Rob must have felt when he learned they were still married. That would have been a shocker for certain. In Jim's opinion, after meeting Kathleen Mitchell, it was surefire evidence that the good Lord was still looking out for Rob.

Even with the newness of today's experience, and what appeared to Jim to be an abundance of hyperactivity over flying in a chartered plane, all three kids were polite and respectful. The smallest girl seemed quiet, like she was absorbing everything she saw. Her older sister must have said "Oh, wow" a dozen times since their dad dropped everyone off. And Rob's boy...Jim couldn't get over him. Not just his looks, but his mannerisms, too, were Rob McKenzie all over again.

Jim smiled as he thought about the reception the group would get in Cincinnati. Rob's good friend Pete Sanders, now retired, had been rushing around in a tizzy, organizing things and people, ever since Rob had explained the situation when he called him for tickets to the game. Jim was happy to be in the middle of it all. He hoped someone thought to bring along a camera; it would surely be an awesome sight to see.

Arriving at the Cincinnati/Northern Kentucky International Airport, just across the Ohio border in Kentucky, was always as intoxicating for Jim as it was for his passengers. He'd loved the idea of flying since he was a kid in the coalfields of Kentucky and had barely known what a real plane looked like. Though mindful of the landing instructions he'd been given by the air traffic controller, out of the corner of his eye Jim could see the crowd that had gathered at their landing spot, which was set off from the area designated for larger planes of major airlines.

Once Jim had landed the plane and cut the engines, Rob came forward and tapped him on the shoulder to tell him good-bye. As always, Rob's handshake included a generous tip and a sincere thank you for the extra care and attention Jim had shown them on this flight. Before Rob turned to go back to his family, Jim shared a few friendly words of congratulations with him. Rob smiled, agreeing that Kathleen was "every bit as nice as she was pretty."

Most of the time after a flight Jim was in a hurry to get home to his own young family, and once he'd escorted his passengers off the plane, he usually left. But not today. Today he wanted to hang around and watch what was happening before he taxied over to the hanger where he stored his three planes. He figured Rob would be too busy helping his wife and the young ones gather up their carry-on items to notice that he'd hurried off the plane without them.

Rob took Kathleen's elbow to assist her down the short flight of steps. As soon as they appeared in the door, flash bulbs started popping. Standing off to the side, Jim laughed; obviously more than one "someone" had thought to bring a camera! The waiting crowd, including Jim, cheered as Rob and Kathleen, and then the children, moved through the plane's open door and started down the steps. One look at the crowd had the youngsters almost jumping with excitement. Rob looked around for Jim and grinned. "You sneaky dog! You knew this was about to happen, didn't you?" Jim just smiled and tipped his hat to Rob.

Pete Sanders had assembled quite a crowd: fellow ballplayers and their families, some of the Cincinnati Reds' front office people, members of the CCA, and Pete's own vivacious wife, Angie. Most carried large homemade signs or placards that said GREETINGS TO #89'S FAMILY, WELCOME HOME, ROB, and HURRY BACK TO WORK, BUDDY. From his teammates came the largest banner of all, one that took four of them to hold: HEAL QUICKLY, MCKENZIE. The team had played well in Rob's absence, but it was more of a struggle to win without him, so Rob knew the sentiment expressed on that large banner was heartfelt and true.

Rob had missed his teammates and playing baseball the last couple of weeks, but so much had occurred in his personal life that he thought maybe they had missed him more than he'd missed them. At any rate, he hoped so.

When Pete blew the whistle he wore on a chain around his neck, everyone turned their signs over so each would read, WELCOME TO CINCINNATI. Several individuals pushed forward to thump Rob on the back and ask for an introduction to the family they'd never heard about, much less met. Pete fussed good-heartedly into the wireless microphone he carried. "Come on, people! Let's have some order and decorum. You want Rob's Katie to think we aren't civilized in Cincinnati?"

"You all *aren't* civilized in Cincinnati," Rob yelled back at Pete, causing his other friends to applaud. Everyone on the team loved teasing the easy-going former shortstop. Pete had certainly teased all of them unmercifully over the years.

By sheer force of personality and his skill with that piercing whistle, Pete finally quelled Rob's unruly colleagues. With his wife Angie by his side, Pete handed Rob the microphone, then shook his best friend's hand. "I've waited a long time for this day, Rob. Introduce us."

Rob fiddled around with the mike until he finally turned off. "Katie, this is the guy I told you about, the one who saved my life years ago: my best friend Pete Sanders." Rob then urged Angie closer. "And this beautiful lady, Pete's wife Angie, is every bit as great a friend of mine as Pete. Only she's prettier and nicer."

Once Kathleen had acknowledged Rob's introduction and had been hugged by Angie and Pete, Rob was ready to present her to the rest of the crowd. He turned the mike back on and brought it to his lips. "This brown-haired beauty beside me is my wife, Kathleen Mitchell, who's known to almost everyone as Katie. And yeah, you're right," he grinned, "there is a story here, but I'll pass it on later." He shifted the microphone so he could hold his steepled hands beneath his chin. "In the meantime, please don't say or do anything to make Katie not like Cincinnati."

As the laughter died down, Rob continued, "And this is my son, Robert Michael McKenzie, Jr., who's part of that story I'll be telling you later. I think he'll agree that you can call him Bobby. Right, son?"

Rob held out the mike to his son, who smiled and said, "Sure thing, Dad." That impish smile convinced Rob's teammates that in addition to hair color and the color of their eyes, at least one other part of Rob McKenzie—his devilish grin—had been passed down to his son.

Rob turned to the girls. "These are my nieces, Janie and Sally Mitchell." He shaded his eyes with his hand and scanned the crowd, looking for the rookie first baseman who had been called up to substitute for him during his period of disability. Locating him, he pointed his finger. "No flirting now, Austin! I know they're pretty but remember they're my nieces...they're too young for you!"

Austin Phillips was such a hard-working, serious young man, Rob couldn't resist clowning around with him in front of the others. Pete had told him over the phone that Austin had become a poster boy for the teens in Cincinnati, but he was still too young and shy to enjoy being in the spotlight. Knowing that, Rob was surprised to hear the bashful rookie yell back in his slow Texas drawl, "You sure got that'n right, McKenzie. They're both some kind of purty!" Janie and Sally blushed, but their eyes glittered as they smiled shyly back at Austin. It was such an exciting experience, one the girls would be describing to their friends in days to come, that Janie forgot to practice her flirting.

Rob walked into the crowd with the microphone. "Katie, Bobby, Janie, and Sally, now I want you to meet my crazy friends, employers, and teammates." Moving from person to person, he told them who each individual was and said something unique about each of them, most of the time something funny and personal which, from the sound of the laughter that greeted his portrayals, were right on the mark.

By the time Rob had finished thanking everyone for rolling out of bed in the wee hours of the morning to welcome them, he looked tired. Kathleen was beginning to worry about him when Pete took the microphone back. "Let me get these people out of here, guys," he said to the crowd. "We'll see all of you later at the park. Try to win one today for our guests."

Walking beside Pete to the waiting limo, Rob missed Kathleen and looked around for her. She was walking slightly behind them, chatting with Angie. He and Pete cut their eyes at each other and grinned.

"Rob, it seems like just yesterday when we first met in that bar," Pete said. "There was no doubt in my mind that night that God would answer our prayers about your marriage...no doubt at all. But I don't think either of us foresaw it happening fourteen years later like this!"

The two men silently marveled at the majesty of a God who could use the long-ago schemes of Judge Benjamin Johnston, and a freakish injury at home plate, to place Rob and Kathleen on that road in Steven's Hollow at exactly the same time.

Rob lightly squeezed his friend's shoulder. "That was one of the most meaningful nights of my life, Pete. Thanks for always being such a good friend. And for the exuberant welcome you organized today. Hopefully, the next time Katie comes to Cincinnati it'll be as my real, not just legal, wife." Pete roared when Rob added, "Gosh, I hope that doesn't take another fourteen years!"

As the limo driver seated the women and children, Pete asked if Rob thought the kids had enjoyed their welcome by the team. Rob laughed so hard, he had to brace his hands against the top of the limo. "Pete, I've been with these kids for a couple of weeks now. I assure you that before the limo driver delivers us to my house, you'll have your answer to that question in spades."

\* \* \* \*

Rob watched as Kathleen peered intently out the window, picking out sites he'd told her about the night before, starting with the bustling activity of the riverfront developments on both the Kentucky and Ohio sides of the river. She seemed surprised that there were so many high-rise buildings in the inner city, but he assured her that Cincinnati still retained its small town feel. There was also more green space than Kathleen expected. She particularly liked the Mt. Adams area, which they drove through slowly so she could see the restaurants and funky houses there.

As Kathleen took in everything outside her window, Bobby, Janie, and even Sally never stopped talking. When one would pause, one of the others would interject a comment about another aspect of their trip. By the time they got to Rob's, Pete knew everything Jim Hager had told Bobby about the plane, which of the welcoming signs the kids liked best, and how cute Janie thought Austin was, among other things.

"Rob, my ears are still ringing," Pete said as he and the driver helped Rob carry their luggage into the house. "Now I understand what you meant as we were getting in the limo. Our kids are inquisitive and talkative, too, but they can't hold a candle to these three."

Before leaving, Pete arranged to come by later to drive Rob and Bobby to the stadium for Rob's examination by the team's physician and trainer. He'd give Bobby a tour of the stadium while they waited, he advised. The limousine driver was scheduled to pick Angie up at eleven o'clock for the trip to the ballfield; they'd stop by for Kathleen and the girls on their way. The plan was for all of them to meet at their seats to eat hotdogs during batting practice.

\* \* \* \*

While the youngsters were getting settled upstairs, Rob found Kathleen looking out the French doors from the kitchen into his fenced-in backyard garden. He linked his arms around her waist to hug her from behind. She angled her head around and up. "I started to unpack," he said, "but when I heard the kids talking in one of their rooms, I knew you were down here alone. It seemed like a good idea to stop what I was doing and come give you a kiss."

Kathleen turned and raised her face to his. After he had kissed her thoroughly, she confessed, "I'm glad you did that; I needed a kiss. Your house is wonderful, Rob. It's even more beautiful than what we dreamed of having years ago. This must be an easy place for you to call home."

Once again, Rob found himself straddling the fence. He was tempted to ask Kathleen if she'd live with him there, but he feared she'd say no if he pushed too hard now. He'd stick to his original plan, he decided, and let things work out in God's time, not his.

The kids finished unpacking and rushed back downstairs. By the time Rob had given everyone the grand tour of his house and garden, Pete was back to whisk him and Bobby away. Kathleen walked with them to the door, and Pete saw his friend give her a quick hug and a kiss as he told her good-bye.

As the three of them got into his car, Pete said, "Mmm, mmm, good buddy!"

"Yeah, you're absolutely right," Rob said in return. And they laughed.

Old friends...best friends...can use a verbal kind of shorthand and know exactly what the other one means.

\* \* \* \*

While Rob was behind closed doors with the team's physician and trainer, Pete took Bobby on an insider's tour of the stadium. There were only a few players in evidence when they entered the locker room; the rest would come trickling in as it got closer to time for pre-game practice. Wally Mason, Cincinnati's ace pitcher, was one of the players already there. "Sorry I missed Rob's welcome home this morning," he said, walking over. "Our baby is teething and on the verge of getting a cold, so I didn't dare desert my wife until her mother got there."

Pete described the scene at the airport, then Wally glanced at Bobby. "Is this Rob's son? The one the guys were telling me about? Gosh, he looks just like his dad!"

Everyone knew Rob's exam was scheduled for that morning, so Pete introduced Bobby and explained that the two of them were just killing time, checking out the stadium before fans began arriving for the game.

"You play baseball, Bobby?" Wally asked.

"Yes, sir. Baseball's my favorite sport, but I also play soccer."

"Have you had a chance to play ball with your dad?"

"Not really. All we've done is play some catch this week. No hitting or running bases."

Wally started to smile. "Hey, Pete, we've got a few minutes. Let's see if the kid's a chip off the old block. Grab Rob's helmet over there for Bobby and some of the catching equipment for yourself. While the stadium's empty, let's see what he can do."

Bobby's eyes grew huge as he looked from one man to the other. "Can we do that? Is it legal?"

Both men grinned. "It's legal if Pete and I say it is," Wally declared. "Come on, let's do it before we get caught."

Wally winked at Pete over Bobby's head. As long as there were no fans in the stadium to be hit by stray balls, and if neither team was officially on the field at the time, no one would object to their giving Rob McKenzie's son a chance to see how it felt to play ball in a major league park. Wally peered at Bobby again and arched his brows. "You want to?"

Did he want to? Nothing could have thrilled Bobby more. He threw on the batting helmet and gloves they'd borrowed from Rob's locker and headed out the door behind Wally. They were followed by Pete and a few other players who'd overheard their conversation and wanted to see if Rob's kid had inherited his father's hitting prowess.

With Pete catching, umpiring, and coaching from behind the plate, Bobby was able to connect with most of the easy balls Wally threw his way. When he hit a long ball into center field, an excited Pete yelled, "Run the bases, Bobby."

Bobby ran as fast as he could. He wasn't playing under official game conditions, he knew, but it was still exciting to be on a major league field, hitting major league balls with a major league bat, while wearing his father's batting helmet and gloves. When he crossed home plate, the first one there to give him a high five was his dad. Rob had spied them on the field after finishing his exam and had hurried down to join them.

"Way to go, Bobby," Rob said. "You looked good out there!"

Wally gestured toward first base. "Get on over to first, Rob, and take your usual spot. See how he looks from there." Rob jogged over to first base and watched Wally wind up for a pitch. Three other players had taken up positions in the outfield: one at left, one at center, and the other at right. They were playing in some to shorten the distance they'd have to run to snag the ball if Bobby got lucky enough to hit another one.

Although Wally wasn't throwing his fastest balls to Bobby, he did vary his speed and his pitches the way he did while warming up for an official game. Nervous, Bobby missed the first pitch Wally threw. "Don't make it easy for him, Bobby," Pete teased. "Make him throw you one in the strike zone."

Bobby settled down. Standing back from the plate, he spread his legs slightly and dug in his toes. He reached out and touched the bat to the opposite side of the plate, positioning himself for the pitch. He tapped the plate and slowly raised the bat to his right shoulder. As Wally moved into position on the mound, Bobby swung the bat straight out in line with his shoulders a couple of times to get his timing right. When Wally wound up to pitch, Bobby bent his knees and eyed the ball. When the ball left Wally's hand, Bobby watched it all the way to the plate. And as he watched, his body did all the things it had been trained to do since he'd started playing T-ball. When the bat hit the ball, he knew it was a good one.

"Run it out, Bobby," Pete yelled. "Run!"

Pete, Wally, and Rob could tell by the trajectory of the ball that it was a good hit, just to the right of center and barely over the head of center fielder Allen Thompson, who had turned to yell something to Antoine Jones in left field.

By the time Allen could turn, dash back, and retrieve the ball, Bobby had thrown down his bat and was on his way around the bases for the second time that day. Only this time his dad was standing just outside the first base line, windmilling his arms and urging him on.

Allen scooped up the ball with his glove and turned with the ball in his hand. Seeing Bobby on his way around the bases heading toward home, Allen sized up the situation. He hesitated for a fraction of a second; for this to work, he had to get his timing right. At just the proper instant, he barreled the ball toward home plate where it landed in Pete Sanders' catching mitt a fraction of a second after Bobby slid into home. Just as Allan had planned. He started running in as soon as the ball left his hand and almost beat his throw to home.

This time, when Bobby crossed home plate, his dad caught him in a bear hug and swung him around. Pete, Wally, and the other guys slapped hands with Bobby, declaring this was his first ever major league home run.

"You did great, kid. When the old man retires, you might be the next McKenzie to play ball for the Reds," Allen Thompson told Bobby as they walked away from home plate.

Bobby shook hands with Allen and the other players. "Thanks a lot for letting me play ball with you guys," he said, his face split in two by a major league grin.

Bobby and Pete walked a short distance ahead of the others, talking to Wally Mason about the pitch Bobby hit. Behind them, Rob stopped for a moment and gripped Allen Thompson's shoulder. "Good timing, buddy," he said. "Thanks. He'll never forget it, and neither will I."

None of them noticed the film crew from ESPN loitering along the sidelines of the field as they left. That crew had set up their cameras earlier and were trying to decide where to eat lunch when they saw Wally and Pete and the other three players enter the field with Bobby.

The head cameraman had turned to the others and asked, "Didn't the producer say Rob McKenzie was hosting some special guests today? That we should try to get them on camera? I'll bet anything that kid with Pete Sanders is one of those guests." On the off chance he was right and that they might luck into something good enough for the pre-game show, they decided to postpone lunch and film a little of whatever was going on.

    They got every bit of it on camera.

# Chapter 31

Angie steered Kathleen and the girls to seats directly behind home plate where they'd have a batter's eye view of batting practice and the game. Janie and Sally had been to Camden Yards in Baltimore with Kathleen and Brian to see the Orioles play several times, but they'd never been this close to the action before.

The usher had just dusted off their seats when the three guys arrived, loaded down with trays of hotdogs, nachos, fries, pretzels, and soft drinks for lunch. Bobby tripped blindly over Sally's feet on the way to his seat and almost spilled his drink in Janie's lap. Though he offered a hasty, half-hearted apology to the girls, his focus was clearly on the field. Right then, the batting stances and individual hitting styles of the players were more important to Bobby than his cousins' goodwill.

When Rob had called Pete about picking up their tickets, Pete had suggested they get passes for the plush, well-appointed owner's box, where visiting dignitaries usually sat, but Rob turned him down. Watching Bobby now as he concentrated so intensely on the field, Rob was glad he'd refused Pete's generous offer.

ESPN's announcers were setting up a shoot in their section of the park, but as Rob's group ate lunch and talked about batting practice, none of them noticed the TV crew nearby. In the lull between finishing his first hot dog and beginning his second, Bobby leaned across his father to tell his mom about getting to hit off Wally Mason's pitching. But before he got into his story, they were interrupted by one of the cameramen who'd walked over to hand Rob a battery-operated portable TV. "Our producer thought you might like to watch the pre-game show on this."

Rob twiddled with the TV controls for several minutes before he finally got an acceptable picture. As the pre-game show began, all seven of them, children and adults alike, clustered in front of the small TV that Rob held out in front of him. With the noise of the crowd behind him, the announcer had to raise his voice and hold his microphone close to his lips to be heard. "We're coming to you live from Cincinnati, Ohio, where the Reds will play the New York Mets this afternoon. In the stands today is veteran first baseman Rob McKenzie, who is on the disabled list for a strained thigh injury he sustained in a freakish play at home plate two weeks ago."

As the videotape of Rob's injury was shown on ESPN, and on the large screen inside the stadium, the on-site camera veered in their direction. The announcer continued, "Earlier today, before the park opened, one of Cincinnati's retired players Pete Sanders, ace pitcher Wally Mason, and three other members of Cincinnati's starting line-up hosted a special guest down on the field. Our crew doesn't usually find much of interest to record before game time, but when they saw what was going on this morning, they started their cameras rolling and caught it all on tape. We're bringing it to you without voice over. Watch closely. You'll understand why."

As the film ran, the viewers saw Bobby at the plate. They saw him digging in his toes, measuring the plate, standing back, settling into his stance, staring at the ball, then connecting. The first sounds they heard were Pete Sanders' words, "Run it out, Bobby! Run!"

The camera caught the ball sliding over Allen Thompson's head. It followed Bobby down to first base, where a grinning Rob was circling his arms, urging Bobby on around first. It covered Allen Thompson's throw to Pete Sanders at home plate, then cut to Pete as he barely missed the tag at home.

The clip ended with pandemonium: Wally Mason jumping up and down as he ran to home plate, Bobby sliding straight into his father's arms, and Pete and the other players high-fiving it with Bobby and each other.

Hank Aaron breaking Babe Ruth's record couldn't have generated any more excitement among those six baseball professionals than Bobby's home run.

Kathleen couldn't stop smiling as she watched the small TV and saw what Bobby had done. She was still bouncing in her seat when Rob grabbed her, held her tight, and kissed her. They hugged each other and laughed, caught up in the joy of the moment and each other. The pride they felt in their son was pasted across their faces for all the world to see.

As a still photo of that quick kiss again filled both screens, the announcer, who'd learned by then who Bobby was, stated in somber tones, "Sorry, girls. I think the guy you voted one of major league baseball's most eligible bachelors for five years in a row just moved his name to the ineligible list!" His voice quickened as the camera focused on Bobby. "But if I were you, I'd keep an eye on this young man. He appears to be a lot like Rob McKenzie in looks—and ability."

Bobby prayed that his friends in Woodbridge were watching the game.

When the stadium announcer mentioned again later that Rob was in the stands, the fans gave Rob a standing ovation and craned their necks to get a better view of him. Kathleen and Bobby came in for more than their share of attention, too. But being used to celebrities in their midst, the fans left Rob alone to enjoy the rest of the game with his guests. Several times during game delays, reporters dropped by to talk with Rob about his injury and the progress of his recovery. Rob shared everything he knew: that he'd been examined by the team physician that morning but didn't yet know the results of the tests they had run. When the more aggressive ones questioned him about Kathleen and Bobby, trying to learn exactly who they were and what was going on there, Rob just grinned. "As my good friend, Jim Hager, told me this morning, having Katie and Bobby here beside me today is proof positive that the good Lord's been looking out for me through the years. Let's just leave it at that for now."

When they left the stadium later, every one of them was exhausted, but happy. The Reds had won their game, and each of the kids carried a ball that'd been autographed by Rob and his teammates. It was a day that would go down in their personal histories as a thrilling once-in-a-lifetime experience.

\* \* \* \*

Back in Steven's Hollow, Brian felt at loose ends. He liked vacations, really, although his know-it-all sister might not believe it. She was always hounding him to take more time off work to, in her words, "just lay back and enjoy himself." So he made it a policy to set aside a few days here and there to go hiking, mountain biking, and camping with his girls and, sometimes, Bobby and Kathleen. They'd gone to Disney World a couple of years back and almost walked their legs off. They'd cruised the Caribbean, and even spent a weekend in Annapolis, Maryland, learning to sail. But no matter where they went, it never failed: after several days, Brian got antsy.

He'd done all the chores that needed to be done around his mother's house and yard, and he'd lost interest in the baseball game shortly after the pre-game show was over. He thought he'd mosey down to Logan; something was always happening there.

That film clip on TV of Bobby's "home run" was quite amazing, Brian thought. And seeing Kathleen and Rob's kiss on nationwide TV was interesting, too. He had to chuckle, thinking about it. Rob might as well start counting down—his days as a legally-married bachelor were nearing an end.

Hoping to sneak Millie away from work long enough to get a cup of coffee at the bakery, Brian dropped by the *Sentinel*. "Your timing's perfect," she said, flashing him a smile. "I'm overdue for a break."

They were shocked to discover later that they'd talked over coffee and a pastry for more than an hour. "Oh, Brian!" Millie said, jumping to her feet. "I should have checked the time before now. I've got to get back to work."

"I'll walk you back, but only with reluctance. I hate having this end—the time seemed to fly. You've sure had a variety of entertaining experiences, working at the paper."

Before he paid the cashier, Brian picked up two peppermint patties, handing one to Millie and popping the other in his mouth. As Millie took the wrapper off hers, she said, "Come on! We both know your work's more interesting. But I'll stick with mine, thank you very much. I sleep lots better without all that excitement."

At the door of the *Sentinel*, she couldn't keep from teasing Brian. "Thanks for the coffee, Bri. I've enjoyed the break from work. Isn't it great that we've become such close, platonic friends this week?"

The dirty dog, Millie thought, stifling a smile. He needs a little shaking up! He hadn't made a romantic overture toward her in over forty-eight hours, and it was about time he did. She knew Brian well enough by now to know he'd never be able to resist the challenge she'd just tossed at his feet.

But he sure did take his good old easy time responding. Reaching out, he wound his fingers through Millie's flame-red curls and drew her close…slowly. After a flagrant, very public kiss, he moved back…again, slowly. "Platonic friends? You think?" Millie could feel his quiet chuckle all the way to her toes. "We've progressed way beyond platonic," he said. Brian wouldn't let her look away. "Substitute passionate or loving for platonic, and I guarantee I'd buy that."

Brian let her go with a light tap on the nose. "Think it over," he advised, "and let me know what you decide. The choice is between passionate and loving."

Millie returned to work, laughing under her breath. Her strategy had worked just fine…this time. She'd keep it in mind. She might need to use it again someday.

\* \* \* \*

Leaving the stadium, Rob overheard part of Angie's conversation with Kathleen. "Things are quiet at our house this week, with the kids out of town visiting Pete's parents. May we take your three home with us for the evening? They can swim in the pool while Pete fixes hamburgers."

When Angie's kind offer was firmly declined, Rob gave Kathleen a questioning look. He would've enjoyed showing her the city at night.

"The kids are worn out, Rob, and your kitchen's awfully inviting. If you don't mind, I'd like to pick something up at a market and cook dinner there."

"If I don't mind?" Rob asked, grinning. "You're kidding, right? There's never been a meal cooked in my kitchen to rival one of yours. We don't even have to stop at a store; the pantry and freezer are full of food. Let's just do it!"

"But only if Angie and Pete eat with us." Kathleen looked to the kids and Rob for back-up in case Pete and Angie felt inclined to refuse. As the Mitchells and McKenzies turned toward them as one, Angie elbowed Pete in the ribs. "We're staying," she said.

\* \* \* \*

Rob's kitchen, with off-white cabinets, loads of storage space, center island with cook top and grill, and a double oven almost large enough to bake an entire pig, was clearly the center of his home. Underfoot, antique-pine hardwood floors and multi-colored rag rugs gave the efficient, ultra-modern appliances a feeling of warmth. Kathleen and Angie, once they'd stopped drooling over the kitchen's special features, felt at home working there.

Angie placed the last of the dirty china in the dishwasher later, while Kathleen assembled an easy dessert. They laughed as they ranked the comments they'd heard about the spaghetti with marinara sauce they'd fixed for dinner.

"The kids raved about our spaghetti, but let's face it—those three are easy to please. On a scale of one to ten, let's give them only a five. I'm a sucker for foreign-sounding words though, myself, so I liked Rob's comment best. 'Deliciomoso,'" Kathleen said, the corners of her mouth turning up. "You think that's really a word?"

"I seriously doubt it; I've never heard it before. Rob was trying to impress you, so I'll give him extra credit for that, which brings him up to a seven in my eyes...no, maybe an eight." Angie smiled. "Admit it, Katie. You have to admire

Pete's panache. We both knew the grand prize was his the minute he brought his plate to his face and licked it clean. That's definitely worth an eleven on our scale of one to ten."

They looked at each other and smiled. "We're two lucky women," Angie said, "and don't we know it! Shall we confess it to them?"

"Heck, no. Not yet," Kathleen said, as they left to rejoin the others. "We're just coming into our own. Let's sit back and enjoy their praise and adoration for a while."

After dessert, Bobby, Janie, and Sally, unused to early morning wake-ups and days packed with new adventures, excused themselves to get ready for bed. The adults lingered over a second cup of coffee before Angie and Pete insisted they had to go home.

At the door, Pete said, "Katie, when Rob called and said he'd run into you again, Angie and I couldn't wait to check you out for ourselves. Ask Angie…it's all we've talked about around our house for days, wondering what you'd be like. Wouldn't you think we'd know that already, as much as Rob has said about you through the years?" Pete laughed and placed his arm around Kathleen's shoulder. "Anyhow, we've loved spending time with your family today, and I speak for both Angie and me when I say Rob was right…you *are* a special lady."

Kathleen didn't blush often, but then she did. She hugged Pete and said, "Thanks for those kind words, Pete. And for taking such good care of Rob when he needed a friend."

As Kathleen and Angie said goodbye to each other, their after-dinner conversation about their husbands came to mind and they started to giggle. They hadn't known each other long, but understood each other perfectly. They hugged, confident they would see each other again soon. Rob looked at Pete. Pete looked at Rob. Simultaneously, they leaned forward, wiggled their eyebrows at each other, and flicked imaginary cigars.

"Don't make me have to yank you out of here by your ears," Angie teased, pulling Pete along behind her to the car. "I've seen Groucho Marx, and you are not him."

Kathleen laughed, too, shaking her head as they left. "You and Pete are full of mischief, Rob. How have you stayed out of trouble through the years?"

Rob chuckled. "Well, things have been quieter in the locker room since Pete retired. Honestly, that man is the classic example of a bad influence…a trouble maker *extraordinaire*, if you will." He raised a brow at Kathleen. "You have to feel sorry for Pete…he can't help not being a paragon of virtue like me."

"Yeah, right!" Kathleen sniffed.

Still smiling, Rob threw an arm over her shoulder. "It's late, but can we sit on the patio for a while? It's too early for bed."

"I'd like to, but first let me check on the kids."

The girls were sound asleep, but Bobby had decided to read in bed for a while. "Is Dad coming up?"

"You want him to?"

"Yeah. Should I invite him?"

Kathleen nodded. "I bet he'd like that. I'll wait here till you get back."

Peering over the second floor railing, Bobby saw Rob turning out the lights in the kitchen. "Dad?" he called quietly, not wanting to wake Sally and Janie.

"Hey," Rob said, looking up. "I thought you'd be dead to the world by now."

"No, I was waiting to say goodnight to you and Mom. She's waiting in my room. Can you come up, too?"

"Sure," Rob said, heading upstairs.

Bobby jumped under the top sheet and patted the side of the bed for his parents to sit. "This has been the most amazing day of my life," he said, hugging his mother. "Thanks for going along with Dad's plan to fly here for the game. Meeting Jim Hager—a real pilot—was awesome!"

He hugged Rob next. "I'll never forget today, Dad. And not just because Wally Mason and Allen Thompson let me hit a home run."

Rob started to laugh, then placed his hand across his mouth to muffle the sound. "They didn't *let* you hit it, Bobby, you did that on your own. They just helped you turn a triple into a home run you'd always remember."

Bobby grinned. "Well, don't tell those guys I said this, Dad, but I'd never forget a triple, either!"

It was rare for a boy Bobby's age to still enjoy having his parents come into his room at the end of the day to say goodnight. With another quick hug, Kathleen told Bobby she'd see him in the morning and left so he and his dad could say their goodnights alone.

Before Rob left the room, Bobby hugged him again and said, "I love you, Dad. Thanks again for everything."

Rob could barely speak above a whisper. "Love you, too, Bobby. Goodnight."

Rob came out to the patio where Kathleen, deep in thought, was firmly ensconced in a wooden glider. He must have made a sound when he sat down nearby, because she turned to him and smiled. "I thank you, too, for making this such a perfect trip. The girls had almost as good a time as Bobby, and you can tell that I was very impressed by your friends. I've thoroughly enjoyed myself today."

Rob held Kathleen's gaze as he leaned back in the chair and stretched out his legs. "I'm a lot like Bobby, Katie. I'll always remember today. For one thing, it's the first time my wife and my son have spent a night under my roof. And tonight was the first time, ever, that Bobby has said he loved me."

Kathleen wiped away a tear from the corner of her eye. "Come sit with me," Rob said, inviting her over.

They were alone with three children sound asleep upstairs. And Rob's chair wasn't all that large. "Might not be a good idea, under the circumstances."

"Just for a minute?" he coaxed, his mouth tipped up at one corner.

"Okay, but just for a minute." Kathleen walked over to stand in front of Rob's chair. He pulled her onto his lap, and held her close to his chest while he rested his chin on top of her head.

She should have insisted again that this was not a good idea. But when she raised her face and met his eyes, she ignored her misgivings. They kissed lightly at first. But as they savored each other, it was if a dam had burst. "You taste like strawberries and coffee," he said, nibbling her lips. "Two of my favorite flavors."

"This is so incredibly un-smart, Rob," Kathleen warned, tracing kisses along his whisker-bristled jaw and up his temple. "I don't think Pastor Matt Harlow would approve of what we're thinking…and doing…right now."

"Sit still, Katie…please," Rob entreated, his voice sounding hoarse. "No more wiggling or squirming."

Rob sighed as Kathleen snuggled closer. He could hear far off rumbles of thunder and the night had grown cool, but the heat from her body warmed his. Holding Kathleen on his lap again like this felt almost too perfect to Rob…too married. The urge to sweep her off her feet and up the stairs was strong…almost overpowering…but above the growl of distant thunder her words filtered through. *This is so incredibly un-smart.*

He had vowed to not rush her like this, to not ask for more than she wanted to give. He closed his eyes and held Kathleen to his chest. Rob had never known until now that he possessed such self-control. He kissed Kathleen again, holding her still, then moved her from his lap.

Kathleen stood for a moment and considered Rob in silence. Numerous fleeting, mystifying changes of expression crossed her face, but Rob could not interpret what they meant. And then she smiled—a megawatt smile that dazzled him all the way to his toes.

"Rob, will you hold me close again?" she asked. She slipped onto his lap, loosely straddling his thighs, and curled her arms around his neck. Rob groaned and wrapped his arms around her back to steady her.

Kathleen bent forward, resting her brow on his chest. "Remember saying you'd wait till I was ready?"

He tightened his hold, not giving her a chance to leave his lap. "Yes. And I will. But this hasn't gotten out of hand yet. Everything's under control."

"Remember what you said would happen if I said those three words?"

Rob moaned. "Yes," he repeated, "I remember exactly what I said. You'd better remember it, too. When you say you love me, you're mine. Nothing will keep me away from you then."

She held his gaze, then spoke clearly. "I love you, Rob."

Rob's breath caught in his throat. He tightened his arms around her again.

"And I'm ready to renew our vows."

Rob gasped, seriously short of breath. "Are you sure? Really sure? I've loved you for so long, I can't believe you've finally admitted that you love me, too."

"Yes, I'm sure. Sure that I love you more than life itself. Sure that I trust God to take care of us and our future. And sure that I want us to renew our vows."

Rob closed his eyes and breathed in and out slowly…once…then twice…as he strove for composure. Half-calm, half-sane was about all he could manage. Kathleen cocked her head to the side, waiting for feedback from him.

"Sorry," he said, laughing slightly. "I'm still in a state of shock." He shifted until they were more comfortable. "Where do we go from here, Katie? Shall we renew our vows in a private celebration once we return to West Virginia? Or would you rather have me contact Matt about a second wedding ceremony in church? If this means what I think it means…that you'll accept me again as your husband…I'll do anything you want."

Kathleen pressed against the strong, muscular arms laced behind her. "Don't contact Matt Harlow. Even he knows we don't need him anymore. I want to do it now—right now—with just you and me."

"Wait a minute…wait a minute." Rob started to stand, but knew if he did, he'd drop Kathleen to the floor. "You mean tonight?" His voice rose as he squeaked out, "Here? Now?"

He had fantasized about exactly this for two long weeks—if you didn't count the times he had dreamed about Kathleen before they met again in Logan—but her unexpected capitulation had caught him by surprise.

"Yes, tonight. Here. Now. Let's wing it. Say whatever we want to each other. It's just the two of us."

"Hold that thought," he said, dropping a kiss on her brow and moving her off his lap again. "You've overlooked something important." As he rushed into the house to round up two sleeping girls and his son, he glanced over his shoulder at a befuddled Kathleen. "Did you forget we have three witnesses?"

"Yes." Kathleen laughed and followed him into the house, very glad Rob had remembered to wake the kids.

"Aunt Katie?" Janie asked. The three sleepy youngsters tromped down the stairs behind Rob. "Uncle Rob says you're getting married again tonight. Is that true?"

"He says we can be witnesses," Sally chimed in.

Bobby, grinning from ear to ear, set about gathering up all the candles he could find, including the ones they'd burned during dinner. He and Sally lit them in the living room, giving that room a soft, romantic glow. Meanwhile, Rob taught Janie—a quick study—how to use his digital camcorder. "We'll need pictures and sound when we get back home," Janie said as she passed Kathleen at the bottom of the stairs. "You know how the people in our family are. They'll want to know exactly what happened, and we might not remember it all."

Kathleen stood in awe as she watched the preparations. She hadn't realized those three kids were that organized or that romantically inclined. Then her glance bounced off Rob and she started to giggle. That handsome guy with the slightly goofy, off-center grin was not the calm, cool, collected baseball legend Rob McKenzie that no pitcher ever fazed. Rob looked as astonished as she.

It was kind of funny, Rob supposed, the way the kids had entered into the spirit of the occasion. Maybe he shouldn't have awakened them, but he'd been afraid it might turn out to be just another one of his dreams if no one else saw it happening for real.

When they'd done all they could to get things ready, the clueless kids turned to Rob and Kathleen, as if to ask, What happens next? They'd been to formal weddings before, but had never witnessed an informal restatement of vows.

Rob looked at Kathleen, took a deep breath, and his jitters disappeared. He felt again the solemnity—the permanency—of what they were doing. This time, forever would mean exactly that: forever. There would be no turning back after this night.

Rob raised Kathleen's hand to his lips and smiled. "Kathleen Mitchell McKenzie, the greatest day of my life—up to this moment, of course—was when God first chose you for my bride. Tonight, when you said you'd be my wife again, you made me the happiest man alive. I loved you with the love of a boy when we were kids. Now that we're grown, I love you with the mature love of a man. All I have or ever will have, and all I am or ever will be, are yours, Katie-girl. In front of

God, Janie, Sally, and our son Bobby, I promise to love and cherish, take care of you and protect you for as long as we live."

Kathleen spoke though lashes wet with happy tears. "When God chose you for my husband, Robert Michael McKenzie, he surely blessed me, too. You are the joy of my life…you and our son. I promise to honor and cherish you for the rest of my life. I'll love you and live with you and take care of you forever, no matter what our circumstances are. I give myself to you again as your wife, and I will love you as my husband for as long as we live."

Rob kissed Kathleen as the youngsters clapped and cheered and whistled. After they had all hugged each other several times, passing the camcorder from person to person so everyone appeared on disk, Janie laid the camcorder down. "I got it all, Aunt Katie. Can we go back to bed? I can't keep my eyes open much longer."

Kathleen and Rob continued to gaze at each other. Bewitched by the happiness that glowed in her eyes, Rob muttered, "Sure, thanks for standing up with us."

"Standing up? What's that mean?"

With eyes only for his wife, Rob shooed Bobby off to bed. "Get a good night's sleep, son…by now you must really be sleepy. Your mom will tell you what it means in the morning."

\* \* \* \*

The children were once again settled in their beds, more than likely fast asleep, and it was getting late. Restating their vows tonight had been Kathleen's decision, but now, all of a sudden, she felt worried and shy. Rob probably thinks I'm overly aggressive, she rebuked herself, nervously catching her lower lip between her teeth. She felt as if she had to fill the silence with something. "Do you want to sit outside for a while, Rob…or get ready for bed?"

Laughing quietly, Rob grabbed her hand and led her up the stairs. "Which do you think I'd prefer?"

He tugged her into his room and leaned back against the door with a determined look in his eyes. He reached around to lock the door behind him, then moved in her direction. Whispering over and over again how much he loved and wanted her, he lifted Kathleen into his arms. "Rob, I'm too heavy," she laughed, "you'll hurt yourself again."

"I don't think so," he said, carrying her farther into the room. "My leg…my arms…my head…my heart…every part of me feels new and healthy tonight."

Carrying her close to his heart, Rob walked toward the king-sized bed that dominated the room. It seemed overly large to Kathleen at first glance. He slowly eased her down till she was sitting on the side of the bed. Kneeling, he unbuckled the sandals she'd worn that day with her jeans. "I'm so crazy in love with you, I feel like a teenager again. It's been a long time, and I'm a little shaky…just look at my hands." He held out trembling hands for her to see. Tilting his head to the side, he grinned. "I'm not only feeling shaky, though, I also feel blessed. Excited! And astonished that you're mine."

"I'm scared and excited, too," she said, draping her arms around his neck. "But happy. Very happy."

He framed her face between his hands. "We'll take things nice and slow tonight, baby. If you change your mind and want to stop, tell me and I will. God knows how much I want to love and please you, Katie-girl, but it has been a long, long time for both of us. I don't want to do anything that might displease or hurt you."

Looking deeply into his eyes, Kathleen could see the love for her that occupied Rob's heart. She whispered, "You won't hurt me, and I won't be asking you to stop. I've waited a long time for you…for tonight. Love me like you used to."

\*       \*       \*       \*

Being the first to awaken in the morning, Rob propped himself up by his elbow and watched Kathleen sleep. He smiled slowly…a satisfied smile…remembering how it had felt waking up in the middle of the night and finding her snuggled beside him, fast asleep. The past two weeks, not knowing exactly how Kathleen felt about him, had seemed endless. But their waiting had served a purpose. Loving each other when the timing was right had been more erotic…and special…than they had remembered or could even imagine.

Rob closed his eyes, overwhelmed again by the love he felt for this incredible woman. *God, please let me live a nice long time so I can love, protect, and cherish Katie…and our son…forever.*

Reaching out, he softly caressed her hand that rested on the pillow. She opened her eyes and slowly smiled as she emerged from sleep. "What time is it?" she asked, pulling herself up to a sitting position. "Have I stayed in bed too long this morning?"

Sliding back under the covers, Rob gently tugged Kathleen down to his side. Burying his face in the sweet morning smell of her hair, he nuzzled her ear. "Not for me, sweet Katie…not for me."

# Chapter 32

As Kathleen served Rob and the children second helpings of maple syrup and homemade waffles, the telephone rang in the kitchen. Her hands began to shake and she felt chilled to the bone when the substance of Rob's words sank in. "Today? Does it have to be today?"

It was clear from his tone of voice that Rob didn't like what he'd heard.

"Well, I wanted to take Katie and the kids back to Logan myself, not send them with someone else…Of course I will…I've never let you down before, have I?" Rob never took his eyes off Kathleen as he listened to the speaker on the other end of the line. "If you say it has to be now, it has to be now…No, I'll drive myself to the airport." By the end of the call, he seemed resigned, as if he'd accepted the inevitability of whatever it was that upset him so much. "Yeah, it'll work out…I guess. If Jim can change his flight plan and make the trip later in the day, that'll still give us most of the afternoon together."

When Rob placed the phone back in its cradle, the grim look on his face nearly broke Kathleen's heart. Even the three youngsters had divined what the call was about.

Kathleen pulled her lower lip between her teeth, then steadied herself. She'd give anything she owned for just a few more days like this with Rob. Tears threatened to fall over the dam of her lower lids, but she blinked several times, holding them back. Rob closed his eyes as the shaky breath he'd been holding passed through his clinched teeth. Those gorgeous hazel eyes of Kathleen's, filled now to overflowing, would haunt his dreams forever.

"Katie—" he began, but Kathleen interrupted. She lifted her chin a notch and held tight to her composure. Only the soft, stilted pitch of her voice revealed the depth of her dismay. "I know what you're thinking, Rob, but you're wrong. This will not be a repeat of fourteen years ago, you have my promise on that. So tell me exactly what they said and when you have to leave."

"The team leaves here at six o'clock. Dr. Brandt and the trainer decided this morning that, based on my progress, they'd like me to work out with the team on the road this week. They think I'll be ready to play in a few days."

They both understood right away what the phrase "flying blind" really meant. They hadn't even had time to discuss their living arrangements with each other. Kathleen wasn't sure what was expected of her, and Rob felt every bit as confused as she.

"Let's start with this," Kathleen said, her emotions now under control. "Where are you going this evening? And do you have a schedule for the rest of the season?"

A copy of the schedule was tacked to the bulletin board near the phone. Rob pulled it off so Kathleen could look it over. She noted that the team would be playing in Kansas City on Wednesday, Thursday, and Friday; in Cleveland on Saturday and Sunday; then come back to Cincinnati briefly the next week for games on Monday and Tuesday. They would head down to Houston on Wednesday and Thursday before flying up to New York for an off day on Friday, then games on Saturday and Sunday.

The schedule for the next couple of weeks was a killer, she decided. Rob didn't need her to fall apart now. There was no time for that, besides. Even if she had been so inclined.

Rob felt heartsick. "All I ask is, please don't cry. I'll never be able to go if you do."

"I'm not planning to cry, but let me tell you what I *am* going to do." Kathleen stiffened her spine as she glanced again at the schedule. It showed where the team would play each game plus where they'd be staying. "I'll fly back to West Virginia tonight with the kids. Tomorrow, when Brian leaves for Woodbridge, Bobby and I will leave, too. We'll work things out from there."

When she mentioned heading home to Woodbridge, Rob's first inclination was to lodge a loud and angry protest. He wanted her in Cincinnati or Logan, places where he could close his eyes and picture her, not somewhere he had never been that was more her turf than theirs. But when push came to shove, what grounds did he have to complain? They hadn't had time to determine what rights they actually had with each other. And after the unforgettable night—and early morning—he'd just spent with Kathleen, he did not want to mess things up now.

"You call me every night, Rob. You hear?" Kathleen held herself together by the thinnest of threads. She must be brave for Rob, of course, but also for Bobby, who was noticeably upset, being separated from his father again. "And then," she went on, "we'll do the best we can. Whatever you do, don't worry about us. Everything will be okay, I promise."

\* \* \* \*

Jim Hager was almost as upset as Kathleen and Bobby McKenzie when the plane lifted off that evening. The farewell scene between the McKenzies was one Jim never wanted to witness again. Mrs. McKenzie was upset, no doubt about that. But she held back her tears like the real lady he judged her to be.

Jim had never seen a man more devastated than Rob, knowing he had to leave his family behind to go back on the road. Rob was just getting to know his wife—and son—again. To be faced with such a long separation…well, Jim thought that was more than a nice man like Rob should have to bear.

Somebody ought to do something about it.

Once he reached his cruising altitude and things leveled off, Jim called back to the cabin. "Mrs. McKenzie, can you come up here to the cockpit for a minute? I think maybe I can help y'all out."

\* \* \* \*

Over the next ten days, Rob's leg healed to almost one-hundred percent, and he'd never played better. His emotional health, however, was a different thing. It wasn't nearly up to that lofty level; it was only about twenty percent.

When he returned to the hotel after a grueling practice on Friday, it was a minor annoyance being told at the desk that his room had been changed. But he was feeling so blue, one more irritant didn't really matter that much.

He was just glad there'd be an early game tomorrow; more young families usually attended day games together. Closing his eyes, Rob leaned back against the elevator wall and cleared his mind of the minor irritations that had gotten to him that day. With only the hum of the elevator mechanism for company as it lifted him from one floor to another, he tried to erase the sad image of Kathleen and Bobby that was never far from his mind…that haunted look he'd seen in their eyes as he'd put them on the plane to fly back to Charleston without him. He forced himself instead to imagine the cheers of the youngsters he'd play for tomorrow, to see in his mind's eye the ones who'd line up near the dugout asking for autographs before and after the game. Those kids were what made playing baseball so rewarding for him, even when he felt down like today. They never failed to raise the morale of everyone on the team.

Rob knew that what it all boiled down to was this: he missed his family. The nightly phone calls to Kathleen and Bobby, and the e-mail messages and jokes he and Bobby sent back and forth to each other each day, weren't nearly enough. Not for any of them. He wanted to hug his son at the end of each day and sleep beside his wife at night. He'd decided just last night that he'd move to Woodbridge if that was where Kathleen and Bobby wanted to be. He just wanted to go home, and wherever they were was home enough for him.

Opening the door to his new room, Rob thought for a moment he smelled food. The aroma was so enticing, he realized he was hungry, really hungry, for the first time since saying good-bye to Kathleen in Cincinnati. He dropped his duffle bag inside the door, and as he followed the path of those delicious smells, he could have sworn he heard someone humming. *Please, God, don't let this be a dream*! He'd been thinking of her, missing her so much, he couldn't believe she might actually be here.

But she was. "Oh, Katie!" he cried, rushing into the kitchenette to lift his wife off her feet. He covered her face with kisses as they whirled around the room. Dancing over to the sofa, he dropped down and held Kathleen on his lap.

They couldn't stop laughing. "What are you doing here?" he asked, smiling as he kissed her again. "I was feeling sorry for myself, thinking I wasn't proper company for anyone. Suddenly, there you were, cooking dinner!"

The next kiss Rob gave Kathleen was long and slow and thorough. He allowed his lips to drift only far enough away to speak. "I sure have missed you, baby, and I'm delighted you're here. But how did you get to New York without me knowing?"

Kathleen's arms, still draped around Rob's neck, were as close and soft as a warm mink stole. "On our trip from Cincinnati to Charleston, Jim Hager and I decided we could surprise you. After I got back to Logan and told Mom you'd been activated again, she suggested that I follow Jim's advice to the letter and have him fly me up here to be with you. All of us swore each other to secrecy so you wouldn't get wind of our plans." She leaned back against the arms that enfolded her and grinned. "We almost had to muzzle Bobby!"

She snuggled into a comfortable position. "When Mom said she'd be happy to keep Bobby company so we could spend some time together, everything seemed to fall into place. There were a few things I needed to straighten out in Virginia, but I did all that as quickly as I could, and—" she spread her arms wide "—here I am!"

"And I can't describe how glad I am that you are," Rob said. "Did Bobby mind being left with your Mom?"

"Well," she began, "he wasn't left with Mom. That's why I had them move you from your single room to this suite. He and Mom flew here with me. They both wanted to see you, and after they went on and on about how great it would be to attend one of your games in New York, I just couldn't leave them behind. But they're not exactly here *right now*, if you get my drift. Mom took Bobby on a guided tour suggested by the hotel's doorman so we could have this time alone."

Kathleen pulled far enough back to see Rob's expression as she explained. "When we were checking in this afternoon, Mom asked the concierge about a special restaurant she and Dad discovered on the last trip they made up here together before Dad died. And can you believe this? The concierge not only knew the restaurant well, he indicated it's still a very popular eatery. According to him, it's located only a block or two east of our hotel. So, after lining up an escort and limo for Bobby and Mom's sightseeing tour—which you're treating them to—he also made a post-tour dinner reservation for them at the restaurant Mom recalled with such fondness.

"By the way," she added, "I heard what you said before. Don't expect home cooking. I'm warming up chicken chow mein and egg rolls I picked up down the street."

Slowly but surely Rob started to smile. He quirked an eyebrow at Kathleen. "Okay, let's make sure I have this right. You can correct me if I'm wrong, Katie, but I sure hope I'm not." Laugh lines marked the corners of his eyes as he rattled things off. "Your mother and Bobby won't be back until after they finish a guided tour that includes a visit to the Statue of Liberty, Ground Zero, and numerous other places of interest to tourists. Right? Then they'll have dinner at some unnamed, popular, fabulous restaurant not too far down the street where, I would imagine, service is probably slow?"

"Yep," Kathleen said, lightly nibbling his neck. "Plus, it's Friday night and they haven't been gone very long." Rob could feel her smile forming underneath his chin. "So I guess it'll be quite awhile before you get to see them. In the meantime, are you hungry?"

Laughing out loud, Rob stood. He wrapped her in his arms and kissed her quickly. "Yeah, now that you mention it, I am," he said. "In fact, I'm starved…which room did you say was ours?"

# Epilogue

▼

Kathleen McKenzie paused in the doorway of the Grand Hall and looked around. She could almost reconstruct the past six years of her life by scanning the crowd of family and friends who had gathered there to honor her husband.

Pete and Angie Sanders, good friends and neighbors now in Albemarle County, Virginia, sat near the front of the room with several of Rob's CCA brothers and a good-sized contingent of former teammates she and Rob hadn't seen in a while. Rob had made a lot of friends over the course of his major league career; he'd be delighted that so many of them had shown up here today. Friendships meant a lot to Rob and to her. Most of those in attendance had visited their farm outside Charlottesville on one occasion or another to ride horses or go swimming with their family in the pool.

The main offices for the Cincinnati Reds must have shut down for the day, Kathleen decided. She'd never seen that many corporate officers at any one time and place before. Those guys were the salt of the earth—they'd supported Rob in his career and they continued to support him in his retirement. It was only fitting that they be present when he received this newest accolade today. It was as much their award as his, Rob had insisted when he was notified about it. But Kathleen knew they would never agree with Rob on that. True, they had hired him and trained him and led him along in his career, but they argued that Rob's natural talent was God-given, that they'd had nothing at all to do with that.

Out of the corner of her eye, Kathleen watched as one of her greatest joys, her first born son, walked toward his front row center seat. Bobby, now nineteen and attending James Madison University on a full baseball scholarship, was listening intently as his five-year-old brother Jamie performed his own version of "Twenty Questions." She had to laugh. That was poetic justice if ever she'd seen it!

Jamie, named David James McKenzie after her father, was a faithful replica of Bobby at five. Both of them, in her opinion, were every bit as charming and dashing as their good-looking father.

Kathleen wasn't surprised by Bobby's unlimited patience with his brother. Jamie looked up to Bobby and attempted to emulate his every action…and why not? Bobby had helped them raise Jamie from the day his brother was born. When they'd brought Jamie home from the hospital, the teenaged Bobby had carried his newborn brother into the house for the first time, himself. It was obvious that Bobby adored Jamie, too; he never tired of having him tag along behind him, as now, dogging his footsteps and imitating his smooth, athletic walk.

Kathleen smiled broadly and waved to her sons when they looked around the hall and caught her eye. She would join them shortly when the ceremony began.

Leaning against the far wall, Rob McKenzie's gaze raked over his wife as she observed their children. He remembered calling her from Texas six years ago to tell her he wanted to retire when the season was over. It was near the end of that special year when they had found each other again.

Knowing he could easily play for a few more seasons, Rob had mulled over the pros and cons of his decision for a couple of weeks before mentioning it to her. With fourteen years in the majors under his belt, he'd loved baseball then with the same fervor he'd brought to the sport as a professional player at age twenty-two. His health was excellent. His energy level still high. His batting average was even better than the year before, to everyone's delight and his surprise. And the Reds wanted him to sign a longer, more lucrative contract. He could have listed those considerations and more for continuing to play. There was only one good reason for giving it up and retiring: he loved his wife and his son more than he'd ever loved the game, and he didn't want to live half his life away from them and home anymore. He made his final decision near the end of an unusually long road trip when he hadn't seen Kathleen and Bobby for almost two weeks.

The two of them, mother and son, had followed him from one end of the country to the other that summer, going from town to town with insufficient time back home in Cincinnati in between trips to recover. He still didn't know how Kathleen had managed it all. She'd packed each day full of activities for Bobby, calling the road trips "learning opportunities" they might not otherwise have taken the time to explore.

He remembered going with them to so many different hotels, in so many different cities, that he couldn't even recall their names anymore. But Kathleen and Bobby still remembered the historic and fun-filled places they saw and the kind, friendly people they met in the towns where he played. What a fabulous season that season had turned out to be—the best of his career, bar none. It couldn't have been easy for Kathleen and Bobby, packing and unpacking and living out of suitcases that summer, but after being separated from him for so long, they were reluctant to spend even one more night away from him. And he sure didn't relish leaving home without the two of them.

The night he called to talk over his decision to retire, they had been apart for way too long and he was worried about Kathleen. She'd seemed run-down to him for several weeks, and he hadn't been home often enough or long enough to assess her health for himself. She kept assuring him that everything was okay, but for some inexplicable reason he still felt scared. It was bad enough that Bobby was back in school and they weren't able to travel with him anymore, he sure didn't want to lose the love of his life now that he'd found her again.

He'd never prayed as hard before as he did then.

The back of Kathleen's neck began to tingle. Sensing someone watching her, she turned and looked directly into those gorgeous sea-green eyes she would never grow tired of. A few more gray hairs may have intermingled with his sun-kissed streaks of brown, but Rob still was devastatingly handsome. There had never been, and never would be, any other man for her but Rob McKenzie.

She, too, recalled the night he called to discuss his retirement from baseball. "The time seems right for this, Katie," he said. "I've been approached by the University of Central Virginia this week. They're expanding an already excellent baseball program and need a high-profile head coach. This seems to be the opportunity we've been praying for...do you want to raise our child in Charlottesville?"

Rob pushed away from the wall and approached his wife. As they met near the back of the crowded auditorium, they were the only two people in their world. As their eyes locked, Rob caressed the soft skin at the side of her neck. His low-pitched voice rumbled over her senses. "I was just thinking about the night I told you I wanted to retire. Seems like only yesterday, doesn't it?"

Kathleen's smile came slow and sweet. "Are you sure it wasn't yesterday? I was just remembering that, too. Do you recall my response when you asked if I wanted to raise our child in Charlottesville?"

Rob leaned forward to rest his head against her brow. "I remember it well, Katie. That's the closest I ever came to fainting. I meant Bobby, of course. But you said, 'I want to raise *both* of our children in Charlottesville, Rob—I'm pregnant again.'"

Their soft laughter was interrupted when Kathleen felt an impatient tugging on her dress.

"Mommy, Mommy." The voice of a small child carried up to Kathleen as tiny hands plucked at the hem of her skirt. "Pick me up, please. I wanna be carried."

"You're a big girl now, Mary Letitia, and don't need to be carried," Kathleen patiently explained. "You start preschool this year, remember? That's big-girl school."

Kathleen bent toward their baby daughter—the one they called their bonus child—to give her a hug. She asked firmly, "Didn't you promise to stay with Uncle Brian?"

Tisha cast her eyes to the floor. "Yes, Mommy."

"Did you ask Uncle Brian if it was okay to leave your seat, sweetheart?"

Tisha smiled impishly. "He knows I'll be back. Uncle Brian knows I'm a big girl now." She held up three fingers to emphasize again her mature age. Then she lifted her hands to Rob. "You hold me, Daddy."

As Rob leaned down to pick up his daughter, who wrapped him around her finger as easily as she wrapped her small arms around his neck, Brian worked his way through the crowd. "Sorry, Rob. We saw you and Katie standing here, so I knew where she was headed. She's just so quick, she was gone before I knew it."

Reaching for his charming niece, Brian said, "Come on, baby waterbug, you're going to miss the awards if you don't come with me now. You don't want to miss seeing Daddy get his award, do you?"

"No, Uncle Brian," Tisha said, reaching out to be transferred from father to uncle. "I wanna see the 'wards. Carry me...okay?" She smiled her most beguiling smile and widened her eyes as she flirted with her uncle.

"Okay, sweetie, come here." Brian scooped his niece, no bigger than a peanut, into his arms. He carried her to his seat, where a large group of family and friends awaited him: his daughters—Janie, a college sophomore, and Sally, a high school senior; his mother, Lettie Mitchell; his brother, David; Rob's parents, Mary and Mike McKenzie; Rob and Katie's two boys, Bobby and Jamie; and the world's most beautiful redhead, the former Millie Samson, who was now, thank God, his wife.

He passed Tisha off to her seat beside Millie. "She's all yours, Red, you watch her. It's your turn to keep up with the whirling dervish."

Tisha batted her eyes at Millie. "Can I sit on your lap to see the 'wards, my Millie?"

"Yes, sweetie, come on over," Millie said, putty in the little charmer's hands.

Brian arched his brows at the woman sitting to his right. "Where's your spunk, Red? Can't you ever tell her no? You always do exactly what she wants you to."

Millie slanted a grin in his direction and hugged Tisha close. "Yeah, that's right, isn't it, Tisha. Like I'm the only one!" She tickled Tisha on her side and snuggled closer. "Who do you love best, sweetheart? Me or Uncle Brian?"

Tisha sliced her eyes around at her uncle, then wrapped her arms around Millie's neck. Smacking her lips on Millie's smooth cheek, she said, "I love you best of all, my Millie...this time."

Brian moaned at the triumphant look he got from his wife, a look that said quite eloquently, *So there*!

"You'll pay for that later, Red," he growled. "As soon as we get home."

Even as Millie blushed, she took umbrage at his words. "Why do you persist in calling me Red? You even do it in public. You might as well be like Mike, who still calls me little missy."

"Okay, little missy, from now on, I will!" He gave her a quick kiss over Tisha's head and both of them laughed.

As Kathleen watched the by-play between Brian and Millie, her dearest friend as well as her sister-in-law, she felt Rob's arms snake around her waist, urging her back against his long, muscular frame. He dropped a kiss on the top of her head, and she turned into the familiar arms of her husband.

"God sure has blessed me, Katie, and not just with this honor today. Our UCV Warriors won over thirty games this season, we've had two players drafted by major league teams, and all the stars I'll ever need in my crown are here with me today. You're the brightest star of them all, Katie-girl," he said, hugging her tightly.

Kathleen smiled into his clear, wise eyes. "Thanks for those fine thoughts and pretty words, Coach McKenzie, but this is your day, not mine."

They turned toward the stage when the emcee said with a flourish, "Welcome to Cooperstown, New York. Without further ado, I'd like to introduce this year's first inductee into the Baseball Hall of Fame...the only man I know with a one-hundred percent approval rating from the fans...former Cincinnati Reds first baseman, Robert Michael McKenzie."

As Rob strode toward the podium, Kathleen rejoined her family in time to see their two youngest children stand up and yell "Daddy, Daddy!" as the crowd around them went wild. Hearing those words above everything else, Rob laughed and threw a playful kiss in their direction.

When things quieted down, Rob thanked the people who had believed in him early in his career—the management and coaches of the Cincinnati Reds, his former teammates, and his close friends in the CCA. He singled out Pete Sanders, who'd been elected to the Hall of Fame three years before. "You once saved my life and sanity, good buddy. Thanks again for that, and for all your many other acts of friendship through the years."

Pete left his aisle seat in the second row to embrace his best friend and shake his hand.

Rob thanked his mother. "You were always an example of Christ in action, Mom, by what you did as well as what you said. That's an unbeatable combination." To his father, he said, "Thanks, Dad, for showing me how to play baseball. Without your early coaching and encouragement, this award would be going to some other lucky guy today."

Mentioning Brian and the other members of the Mitchell family by name, he laughed. "I never really knew how much good, clean Christian fun large families could have together until the McKenzie family merged with the crazy Mitchell clan!"

Singling out his mother-in-law, Rob sent a special message with his eyes to Lettie Mitchell. "Thanks, Mom Number Two, for all those small and large things you've done for my family through the years. You're one of God's greatest blessings to Katie, our children, and me." Lettie smiled her thanks to Rob…and wiped a solitary, happy tear from her eye.

Rob paused and looked around the room until he'd found and saluted Jim Hager. "To paraphrase something Jim Hager once told me," he said, nodding again at his friend and frequent pilot, "having Katie, Bobby, Jamie, and Tisha here today is proof positive that the good Lord's been looking out for me through the years." He caught Kathleen's eye. "We couldn't have asked for better kids, could we, sweetheart?" Rob grinned, then said to the crowd, "I tell you, each and every day's an exciting adventure with Katie and the kids. I'm having to get up earlier and earlier each morning just to keep up with what's new!"

There was a rumble of laughter from the gathering of family and friends, many of whom had young, active families of their own.

Rob's final words were spoken so softly not everyone heard…but Kathleen did. "I'll always love you, Katie-girl…you are the best thing that ever happened to me."

### \<The End\>

0-595-29457-X